POISONED JUSTICE

ISBN: 978-1-68313-010-9

First Edition
Printed and bound in the USA

Cover design by Conor Mullen and Kelsey Rice
Interior design by Kelsey Rice

A RILEY THE EXTERMINATOR MYSTERY: ORIGINS

POISONED JUSTICE

JEFFREY ALAN LOCKWOOD

P
Pen-L Publishing
Fayetteville, Arkansas
Pen-L.com

CHAPTER ONE

The threesome of Victorians would've made a matched set, except that even in the moonlight you could see the middle one had a garden that put its neighbors to shame. I turned the wheels of my pickup against the curb and set the parking brake. Connecticut Street was a fine example of San Francisco having been draped over the hills like an urban blanket. A few cases of dynamite in the 1800s would've made the place much easier to navigate. But there's something to be said for the sheer cussedness of building a road straight up a thirty percent grade.

Walking up the stairs flanked by the exquisitely tended plantings, I could see that the lights were still on in the living room. My mother often stayed up late to have some quiet time for herself; her reading lamp glowing through the lacey curtains. I slipped off my shoes to muffle my footsteps and climbed the stairs. The music from the stereo would've covered the sound of my rust bucket, but I didn't want to disturb Tommy by clomping up to the porch if he was already asleep. Inside I could hear the opening to Mozart's Requiem in D Minor.

I savored the Introitus for a few moments, thinking how the one thing my mother had given me was a passion for classical music—and the one thing my father had given me was an interest in insects. A strange pair of gifts by any estimation. The one luxury that my mother had allowed herself when I was growing up was a top-of-the-line hi-fi system and a new record each month. She wore mended clothes and cooked simple foods. We always bought used cars, and vacations were two-dollars-a-night camping cabins along a state beach or in the mountains. Music was her only indulgence. I suspect that if the great composers had not written their assorted versions of the Mass and thereby received the blessing of the Church, she might've considered a record collection to be a sinful extravagance.

In my rebellious years, I tried listening to Elvis Presley, Chuck Berry, and Jerry Lee Lewis. I knew rock 'n' roll would annoy my parents, but I had no stomach for it. The hours of classical music in the evenings of my childhood had worked their way into my thick skull. My parents' aggravation just wasn't worth my own distaste. So I decided the best way to declare my adolescent independence was to reject the religion of my Irish Catholic parents and the music of my peers—that way, nobody would be telling me what was what.

I tapped softly on the door and heard the shuffle of my mother coming into the entryway. She pulled back the gauzy curtain to peek out, and her eyes lit up as if I'd just returned from brokering world peace. Even when I had been dragged through the internal affairs investigation, pilloried by the press, and had to resign from the force, she never doubted me. According to her, nobody could say for certain what happened in that alley, but she knew that her son had done what principle and duty required.

The door opened and she gave me a smothering hug. "Riley, you're back!" she announced in an exuberant whisper. Over the lingering aroma of dinner, which had evidently included colcannon given the hints of garlic and cabbage in the air, I could detect lavender soap. She was as soft and plump as a mother from the old country ought to be.

"That's right, your prodigal son returns from the decadence of southern California," I said. She scowled, believing that hedonism and the risk of mortal sin increased as one headed down the coast until the point at which women wore nothing more than "colored bras and panties" on the beaches. It might be 1976 for everyone else, but my mother was not about to concede ground to the new norms of dress—or undress. "How's Tommy been?" I asked.

"Come in, come in," she said, pulling me by the arm into the entry. "He's had a rough few days. You know how he misses you. And he was upset that you weren't here to collect insects with him, or whatever the two of you do at the park on weekends."

2

"Sorry Mom, but the convention was important. You know, new products, business connections, and all that."

"Oh, I didn't mean to make you feel guilty, Riley. You're a good man, providing for Tommy and me like you do. I know that means having to be away sometimes." Her voice had become serious but then brightened. "Now, come into the kitchen and I'll warm up a plate for you."

"That's all right, it's getting late. I just wanted to check on you two before I went home."

"But you're getting so skinny." She pinched my gut and didn't find any flab, then sighed as if she'd somehow failed in her responsibilities, and nodded toward the stairs. "Go on up. I put him to bed at half nine, but I suspect he's still awake hoping you might stop in tonight."

I slipped into Tommy's bedroom. The light from the hall illuminated his San Francisco Giants bedspread and the posters on either wall featuring Willie McCovey and the butterflies of California. He was propped up in bed with the tired and happy look of a little kid who'd stayed up past his bedtime. Tommy had the mind of a child inside the body of a thirty-two-year-old man. He'd been as normal as you or me until his version of rebellion took its toll. While I was getting into fights, Tommy was doing drugs. Mostly pot, but I know he tried other stuff as well.

He'd probably have turned out okay, but one night he smoked a few joints rolled from Mexican sinsemilla that nobody knew was laced with paraquat. The U.S. government had sprayed marijuana fields with this herbicide, and the result was poisoned plants and people. Tommy had gone into respiratory arrest at his friend's house, and the other kid had been so scared of getting busted that he cleaned up the evidence before he called an ambulance. By the time they got Tommy to San Francisco General, brain damage had turned him into a permanent child.

"I heard you and Mom whispering," he said with a big grin, as if he'd caught us in some secret activity. Then he rolled onto his stomach and declared, "Back rub!" Along with his mental limitations, Tommy wasn't able to walk normally. He'd thrust out his left leg and then swing his right leg in a wide arc, nearly falling over just before catching himself. This lurching gait put a strain on his lower back, so he was constantly seeking relief from the pain.

"Okay, buddy. But not too long. You're supposed to be asleep." I began to knead gently, then more firmly. Tommy groaned quietly, his knotted muscles slowly relaxing.

"I didn't get to go to the park. How come we didn't pin insects together like we always do?" he asked.

"I told you I had to go away to Los Angeles for a few days. Remember? Now that I'm back we can go to the park. And you can come to my house and work on our collection."

"When, Riley?"

"Let me talk to Mom about that. But I promise it will be this week."

"Tell me a story," he sighed. The kid loved to hear about my time on the force. He never complained about listening to the same tales over and over, so I picked one of his favorites.

"Back in '67," I began, "my best informant was an insect peeled off the grille of a Lincoln Continental."

"What color?" Tommy asked.

"Black."

"And shiny?"

"Yes, and shiny. Now then, it turned out that an FBI agent working the case figured that a hit man for the Grassi syndicate had dumped the corpse of an uncooperative building inspector somewhere in the San Francisco area. The city Board of Supervisors, along with the feds, was determined to find the body, track down the assassin, and send a message to the Grassi family."

"The Grassis must've been awfully mean people," Tommy said, shifting to put his left side under the press of my fingers.

"They were, but the FBI agent was sharper than they were mean. He'd thought to scrape a smashed butterfly from the killer's car a couple days after the building inspector went missing. Having heard about my interests, he dropped the mangled thing on my desk."

"You knew more about butterflies than anyone else in the police department, didn't you?"

"That's right. Dad taught me all about insects when you and I were kids." My father and I hadn't seen eye to eye on much. In fact, collecting insects was about all we'd had in common. It had taken us outside the city, while back home his Old World values and ways had been a source of embarrassment. But I created the illusion of a happy childhood for Tommy's sake.

"Keep going," Tommy insisted, as I'd fallen into a bittersweet reverie.

"Okay, sorry. Well, there was only one wing intact, and what was left looked like a run-of-the-mill metalmark butterfly."

"All silvery speckled. Isn't that right, Riley?"

"That's right buddy." The kid knew his butterflies but he also knew my stories. "But you just be quiet and listen or you're not going to fall asleep," I scolded softly. "So then, I also realized that the metallic flecks on the brown background of the wings didn't quite match anything I had in my collection. It took a couple days, but I figured out that the hit man had also managed to hit a specimen that our dad and I had been after for years. This butterfly was found only in the sand dunes out by the Fulton Shipyard."

"How'd you know that, Riley?"

I shushed him and continued. "Well, we knew from Dad's books that the Lange's metalmark laid its eggs on naked buckwheat." Tommy snickered, as usual. "It's called that because there aren't any leaves on the stem," I explained, as always. "And what with all the sand mining happening in the dunes, there was only one area near the shipyard that still had lots of buckwheat. I drew a map of the area for the FBI. It took them the better part of a week, but they managed to find the shallow grave with the inspector's body. I didn't get any credit in the report, but I got something even better. What with the Lange's metalmark butterfly being listed as an endangered species this year, I figure I'm one of the few private collectors in the world with a specimen. It's not in perfect shape, but it's special."

"Like me," Tommy whispered, finishing with the line that had come to be our traditional ending for the story. I pulled the covers over him. He began to breathe deeply and rhythmically, and I went back downstairs.

🌢

My mother was sitting beside her reading lamp. The Tiffany-style shade cast a garish light into the room, which was filled with lacework, doilies, and flowered upholstery. A gilded mirror over the fireplace reflected the colored light, making it seem as if a cathedral with stained glass had been shrunk into a Victorian sitting room. The effect was enhanced by the discordant "Confutatis," a movement that is both enchanting and disturbing. She sighed, her eyes focused far into the distance.

I sat on the velveteen sofa across from her. "You look like you're troubled by more than just a few rough days with Tommy. What's up?" She turned down the music so we could talk quietly without disturbing my brother.

"It's not good, Riley. Mrs. Polanski told me that Tommy's Fund will be depleted at the end of this month." The fund had been set up using money from my father's life insurance policy, and it had provided a daycare center for retarded adults at St. Teresa's. But as my mother explained, the recession meant declining returns on the investments. In order to keep the facility open, the director had spent down the principal. My mother depended on the center to give her some relief. Caring for a child in a grown man's body was exhausting—as I knew full well from the weekends that Tommy spent with me.

"It's not right that the center gets short shrift. Maybe the church can have a fund drive or something." I was grasping at straws, but I could sense her confusion and desperation. A few days or weeks alone with Tommy would be doable, but eventually she'd wear out. My help would only delay the inevitable, and she couldn't contemplate institutionalizing her son. "Jesus, it's always the weak who lose out these days," I grumbled.

"Don't take the Lord's name in vain, Riley." She'd sustained her faith through the difficulty of coming to America, setting up a household, Tommy's accident, and my father's death. She'd nearly bled to death after Tommy's birth, and the emergency surgery meant she couldn't have another child. I remember her lying in bed at home, her body weakened and her hopes for a houseful of children dashed. I suspect that her music, more than the visits of the doctor or the priest, brought her back to us. But afterward she'd always refer to her faith as having saved her. Even this procreative disaster—just two kids in an Irish Catholic family—was "the Lord's will." It was more than a person should have to bear, and more than I could understand.

"I'm sorry."

"That's okay, dear," she smiled weakly. "The Lord will provide. He always has."

I tried to reassure her that we'd figure out something, and then said I had to leave. She smiled at me, but I knew her mind was elsewhere. I turned the music back up a notch. Instead of walking me to the door as usual, she stayed in her chair.

I drove down to the shop and locked the truck in the compound. I wasn't fond of the razor wire that I'd strung on top of the chain link fence, but being squeezed between the Southern Freeway and the projects up the hill meant taking certain precautions. I headed back up Texas, the hum of traffic fading away, and stopped at 20th Street. This was the best place on Potrero Hill. My hill. Where people put down roots and then figured out how to live together—the Polish baker next to the Irish dockworker, the Chinese launderer across from the Czech bartender.

As a kid, I imagined traveling to each of the states after which the streets in the neighborhood were named: Arkansas, Connecticut, Missouri, Texas, Mississippi. Most of the people in the neighborhood would never leave California. I wondered why the states were so jumbled—the order didn't follow alphabet, geography, or statehood. None of my teachers seemed to know, but Mr. Shalinsky, a retired chief petty officer who coached boxing at the Mission Bay gym, explained it to me. The streets were named for naval ships in honor of our military and the San Francisco shipyards. I figured that was much better than being named after a haphazard assortment of states.

In the distance ahead lay the glitter of downtown, its buzz and vitality there for the taking. The Hill was a sanctuary above the city's crush. Not a mile to the east, the floodlights of the Central Basin docks silhouetted a cargo ship, while further out a tanker plied toward the mouth of the Bay, its portside red running lights telling me it was heading out to sea. And a block away, the warm glow from the window of Hill Top Grocery felt like a beacon from my boyhood, this being where my mother had sent me for milk and bread—and where I'd hung out with friends after school. I'd attended parochial school at St. Teresa's, but most of the kids on my block had gone to Daniel Webster Elementary just down the hill. They were taught that Webster had believed fervently in America and modern industry. I later learned that he was a three-time loser for the presidency. A fitting icon for the Potrero neighborhood.

I headed west to Missouri and then down to my house, a tiny two-story sliver sandwiched between a couple of nice bay-windowed Italianates. My place had a living room and kitchen on the main floor and a bedroom and bathroom upstairs. It wasn't much but it was all mine. While the other cops had bought fast cars and slick boats, I had managed to squirrel away enough for my own place. I went in, dropped my suitcase, poured a nightcap, and idly looked through the mail. Mostly bills and junk mail, including an announcement of a Billy Graham Crusade coming to Candlestick Park. Desperate people needing a reason to hope, not unlike my mother—although she considered evangelists to be shysters.

I did what I could for her and Tommy, but I knew that her faith was all she had in hard times. She used to tell me that God acted in mysterious ways. "His plan is not ours to understand," she'd say when life dumped on us. But if there was a God, He sure had a convoluted and perverse scheme for my corner of the world. The Master Plan for a distraught mother and a retarded man-child had started with my encounter with a stinking corpse in a Los Angeles hotel room earlier that day.

CHAPTER TWO

I hadn't figured there'd be maggots. Not enough time had passed. But then, I'd never checked out a corpse in the City of Angels. I'd seen enough bodies in my days with the San Francisco Police to know that no two places, times, and causes of death attract the same six-legged undertakers. So a stiff in a Los Angeles hotel room could prove interesting.

"What're the chances of my taking a look before your people mop up the mess?" I asked Sergio.

His firm had landed the cleanup contracts for most of the major hotel chains in the city. Sergio had leaned over and shared this insider tidbit about the corpse with undisguised pride while the conference speaker droned on. Neither of us had been much interested in the pompous professor from UCLA who was giving the closing speech at the California Pest Control Operators Convention. The over-educated, under-experienced scientist declared that we had to anticipate a future in which pesticides would no longer be used. The guy had obviously never had his house overrun with cockroaches, let alone seen a baby covered in rat bites. At that point, Sergio and I had headed to the hotel lounge.

"Let you into the room, eh? Depends," he replied, shifting his eyes up to the ballgame on the television above the bar. Sergio scowled. The play-by-play guy didn't hide his disappointment that Bobby Murcer had just launched an upper-deck shot off of Don Sutton, putting the Giants up by two over the hometown Dodgers. I knew Sergio was devoted to the LA ball club. Italians stick together, and with one of their own managing the team,

9

I figured that Tommy Lasorda would be nominated for sainthood if he won a pennant. I hoped my San Francisco roots wouldn't put Sergio in an ornery mood.

"Depends on what?"

"On the odds of you buying me a bottle of that eighteen-year-old Jameson you're drinking." He grinned as I rolled a mouthful of whiskey over my tongue. I obviously failed to hide my intense pleasure. The liquid velvet matched the blood-red drapes framing the dark paneling of the Hyatt Regency lounge.

"Why Jameson?"

"Because, Riley, you're my favorite mick. And while you don't know shit from Shinola when it comes to baseball, I figure you know Irish whiskey." He was right. I kept track of the Giants, but that was about it for baseball. It didn't help that they hadn't won a pennant since '62, and this season was more of the same. Football was more to my liking, and I followed Notre Dame out of ethnic loyalty. The Fighting Irish excelled at cracking skulls—a more watchable endeavor than swinging at curve balls. I love this country, but America's pastime is too tedious for me. The bartender at the hotel lounge, who I'd become pals with on the first night of the convention, stopped polishing the glass he was holding. He threw me a sideways smile.

For the past two days, I'd settled for the cheap American stuff. But this being the end of the convention, I had splurged. After sitting down next to Sergio, I'd asked the burly redheaded barkeep if he had any Bushmills or Tullamore. He didn't. But he reached under the bar and pulled out a bottle of Jameson Limited Reserve and gave me a conspiratorial wink. Whiskey drinkers can sense their own kind, and the hint of a brogue let me know that we came from the same stock. A shot was one thing, but a whole bottle was going to set me back nearly forty bucks. I figured it might be worth it.

"You drive a hard bargain for a dago," I replied. I wasn't much for ethnic slurs, but Sergio was the sort who used insults as expressions of endearment. I'd been around enough tough guys to play my part. A large part of succeeding as a cop or businessman was being able to meet people on their own terms. And growing up in the ethnic hodgepodge of Potrero Hill, you had to figure out to say "Doamna"—not "Missus"—Cosmescu and "Pani" Kowalski and "Frau" Müller, or get smacked for being disrespectful.

"That's why we own the East Coast. Give us a couple years and every neighborhood in California will have a place serving decent cannelloni. The Spaniards dropped the ball when they arrived. You can't bring culture to the wilderness by building a bunch of goddamn missions." He paused to quickly bless himself with a condensed sign of the cross to avoid God's wrath. "Any *paesano* knows it takes food and wine. We'll civilize this place."

Even though we're 350 miles apart, I'd gotten to know Sergio through these annual gatherings of exterminators. Like me, he refused to call himself a "pest control operator." Sergio lacked social graces, but he wasn't a phony—and that's worth something in today's world. They might call the guy who throws the switch a "State electrician" but he's an executioner in my book. A janitor isn't a custodian and a strip joint isn't a gentleman's club. I hate it when people try to hide behind fancy labels. If you're not proud of your work, do something else.

Sergio DiMaggio had a thriving extermination agency in LA. But he probably would've traded the whole thing for evidence that he was related to the Yankee Clipper. Joe DiMaggio was born and raised in California, but despite Sergio's best efforts he hadn't been able to link the two families. And he's never forgiven the San Francisco Seals—DiMaggio's minor league club—for selling the young centerfielder to the Yankees.

At last year's convention on my turf, we'd ducked out for a Giants game. After a day of listening to chemical salesmen lying about their products in air-conditioned meeting rooms with fake crystal chandeliers, I was getting bored and testy at the same time. I figured the ocean winds blowing into Candlestick Park would revitalize me. Besides, Sergio had nearly converted to being a Giants fan since the team had two Italian pitchers, Pete Falcone and John D'Acquisto.

While Sergio knocked back a beer per inning, he told me about his adding a crime-scene cleanup service to his business. His story was more interesting than the game, which was a pitchers' duel, meaning that even less was happening than usual. Even in our business, it takes a hard-case fellow to eat a bratwurst with sauerkraut and gobs of mustard while explaining that employees who are used to wallowing in roaches can be readily convinced

11

to scrub brains off walls and tear up blood-soaked carpets. "They'll roll up their sleeves if there's good money to be had," Sergio explained. He knew that clients paid well to get rid of their vermin, so he figured a grieving widow would "pay just about anything to get rid of the splattered leftovers of her suicidal husband." And he was right, which worked out well for his employees and customers—but mostly for Sergio.

"Okay Sergio, you know I'm good for the Jameson. When can your people let me into the room and where is it?"

"Let's see. The coroner should have the body bagged and out of there by one o'clock, and my crew is supposed to get here around one thirty. It'll be an easy job for them, as the hotel management tells me it was a nonviolent death. No blood or guts to wipe up."

"That's fine. I'll just cool my heels for an hour. So, what's the room number?" I asked, grabbing a cocktail napkin to jot down the information.

"You get that when I get my lunch."

"Now I'm buying your lunch?" I crumpled the napkin and tossed it into the wastebasket behind the bar.

"Think of it as a down payment on the whiskey."

"You're a slimy bastard, Sergio." And he was, but I liked the big-hearted slob.

"Yeah, but in our business a guy encounters all kinds of unpleasantness. You shouldn't be offended."

"But I'm used to eliminating pests, not feeding them meals."

"Riley, my friend, I hardly deserve such an insult." He put his hand on his chest. "After all, your whole life has depended on vermin. Even before entering the noble field of extermination, eh?"

"You win," I said and waved at the waitress, who sidled over to take our order.

Sergio was referring to my earlier days as a beat cop working my way up to detective on the San Francisco Police Department. I'd told him about my former life yesterday over breakfast at a diner. Between mouthfuls of greasy eggs, crispy bacon, and crunchy hash browns—a perfect breakfast compared to the prissy omelets filled with asparagus and mushrooms they served at the Hyatt—I told him that the transition from police work to running my father's company wasn't such a big deal. I'd just switched from one kind of pest to another.

Something about the brooding clouds, Sergio's sympathetic eyes, and both of us being second-generation immigrants put me at ease. Our lingering was further encouraged by Sergio's obvious admiration for the waitress, who kept bending over to fill our coffee cups while nearly falling out of her D-cups. Sergio left a dollar tip to show his appreciation. At least she gave us a reason to settle into the vinyl booth, our elbows propped on the gold-flecked Formica. I didn't usually talk about my past, although if people cared to, they could piece together the not-so-pretty details of my being run off the force, working as a private dick for a couple years, and then taking over the family business when my father died.

We got drenched on the five-block walk back to the hotel. I knew winter rains were common, but a September soaking was something of an oddity in this part of the state. At least it gave me the chance to rag him about "sunny California." He asked me if I was any happier when the sun broke out later in the day and turned LA into a sauna. I told him it just furthered my belief that southern California was overrated.

CHAPTER THREE

When our lunch arrived, Sergio and I moved from the bar to the table furthest from the door. Even the sunlight in LA felt fake, reflecting off the marble floors in the lobby after pouring through the floor-to-ceiling windows that framed gaudy pink bougainvilleas and a turquoise pool. The lounge's darkness fit my mood and hid the unappetizing aspects of lunch. The club sandwiches were slathered in mayonnaise and the fries were soggy, but that's what you get at a hotel. You might get a real drink or a decent steak, but breakfast and lunch were afterthoughts. And unlike the bartender, who evidently cared about his craft, the girl who brought our food was a gum-chewing blonde whose slouch and eye-rolling showed obvious disdain for us or her work. Probably both.

Sergio pressed me for more about why I was interested in the corpse, wanting to know if it had to do with my time on the force. I was reluctant, but he'd become a friend of sorts. A fellow something-American working his ass off because he took his obligations seriously. He loved and lived deeply. Sergio had told me all about his family, his beautiful but volatile wife, his plans to one day turn DiMaggio Pest Services over to his son if only the little shit would acquire a sense of responsibility, and his dreams of opening a café in the heart of the San Pedro neighborhood. So I figured it wouldn't hurt to reveal a bit more about myself, keeping the ugliest parts for some other day. Or never. If he really wanted to know, he could check out the *San Francisco Chronicle* headlines from the summer of '69.

"By the time I quit the force, I'd made detective. I was the department expert on postmortem insects. You know, like using flies and beetles to figure out how, where, and when a victim bought it. I didn't crack many cases this way, but we got some important leads."

"Like what?" Sergio was stuffing a triangle of club sandwich into his mouth. For a guy hoping to open a restaurant, he sure didn't seem picky about what he ate. I kept the butterfly-and-mafioso story for Tommy, but there were plenty of others.

"I remember the time a suspect's alibi collapsed when the maggots feasting on the victim's brains were three days behind those setting up house in his mouth and nose. Turns out his business partner poisoned him at his house in the middle of the week and stuffed the body into his car trunk for a couple of days, where the flies found easy pickings. Then he hauled the corpse up to their office on the weekend when nobody was around. That was the hard part. The easy part was propping him in a chair, putting his hand around a .38, and blowing out the guy's brains. The staged suicide might've worked, but a few enterprising flies found their way into the office through an open window. So, when I looked at the mess on Monday morning, the ages of the maggots on the splattered brains didn't match those who'd set up house in his face."

"That's a damn good story." Sergio nodded approvingly. "But I thought the universities had experts who picked up a few bucks with that sort of stuff."

"They do. But the cops and faculty at UC Berkeley don't play nicely. Hell, even the entomologists over there were peaceniks. For the most part the professors hated cops, and we didn't have a whole lot of interest in asking for their help. So I learned everything I could about maggots."

"Okay, but why you?" He was working his way through the soggy fries, although with less enthusiasm than he'd had for the sandwich. At least the man had some sense of taste.

"It's kind of convoluted."

He looked at his watch, a gaudy gold-plated number, and shrugged. "We got time. Go ahead."

"I wasn't what you'd call a 'good kid' in high school. In fact, I was hell on wheels. If there hadn't been that thing about welcoming sinners, the nuns would've kicked me out of St. Teresa's."

"I know what you mean. My kid is like that." Sergio nodded, hoping to salvage the fries by adding ketchup.

"In my freshman year, Father Fortier thought Golden Gloves would provide an 'outlet for my anger.' But it mostly taught me how to take a punch and the satisfaction of beating up people." Sergio smiled knowingly. I'd given up on my sandwich and fries, only to find that even the pickle was limp.

"How's that add up to an interest in insects?"

"During my renegade years, my father did what he could to stay connected with me. I rejected what I called his Catholic mumbo jumbo and old-fashioned ideas about character and virtue. But for some reason I shared his interest in collecting insects. Maybe it was something that didn't require us to argue. In any case, after beating the Japs in the Pacific, he came back with two things."

"Which were?" Sergio was evidently enjoying my story, because he caught the bartender's eye, ordered us a couple of beers—and put them on his own tab.

"About twenty cigar boxes filled with the most incredible insects you can imagine. He had Goliath beetles the size of my fist, walking sticks a foot long and as thick as your thumb, and butterflies with wings that looked like some acid-trip junkie had painted them."

"What was the other thing he brought back?"

"Experience with insecticides. He'd run mosquito-control programs in New Guinea, the Marianas, and Guam." The beer was ice cold, served in a frosted mug with a perfect head. Almost good enough to make up for the lunch.

"So he opened his own extermination business, eh?" Sergio paused and dropped his voice to a lower pitch, giving his best imitation of a newsreel announcer: "Uncle Sam trains American men for productive work at home."

"Yeah, something like that. I wasn't so keen on having to work for the family business, but collecting was entirely different. While he was making money killing cockroaches and fleas, he kept building his collection with insects from all over the Bay Area. He got me hooked. There's something about finding that perfect specimen. It's another world, and I needed someplace to escape."

"Crappy neighborhood?"

"Not really. At least Potrero Hill wasn't any worse than lots of the city. Better in some ways. And my parents tried hard. But being first-generation immigrants, they embarrassed me with their accents, foods, and stories from the old country."

"You should've tried being Italian. My family still believes they're in Assisi."

"That's a sweet irony, Sergio. You make your living poisoning insects, rats, and mice, while the blessed Francis is the patron saint of animals."

"Yeah, life does that sometimes. So, if you were a rebel without a cause, how'd you end up as a cop?" He took a deep swig of beer and muttered that whoever was in charge of the food needed some lessons from whoever was running the lounge. Maybe there was hope for his culinary aspirations after all.

"The courts had seen enough of me by the time I finished high school. I got nailed for stealing a car the summer after I graduated, and the judge told me I could enlist in the army, apply to the police academy, or spend six months in juvenile hall. If I'd been a month older, I'd have done real time. I picked the force and worked my way up to detective."

"And kept collecting bugs, eh?" Having drained his beer, Sergio held up his hand to stop my reply, got up to nab a toothpick from the dispenser on the bar, and settled back into his chair to attend to his dental hygiene.

"Yeah. Even when I was being a real jerk as a teen, I still went out with my father on weekends to look for new stuff. I started my own collection when I got on the force, and he'd go out with me when he wasn't working. In the evenings, mounting and labeling the specimens was my way to unwind. I could just sip whiskey, concentrate on this other world, and forget about the streets. Those were good times." I took a deep drink and stared into my past. The room was dark and quiet, and I savored my daydream for a while until Sergio broke the spell.

"A badass cop armed with a butterfly net. If your buddies only knew." He chuckled and punctuated his cleverness by shifting the toothpick to the other side of his mouth.

"They did. Sort of. In my rookie year, my partner came by my house and saw the display cases with insects. He ragged on me and told the other guys. At first they made fun of the 'bug guy,' but over time they brought me all sorts of interesting specimens in pickle jars and pill bottles, wanting to know about them. Mostly it was great."

"Mostly?" His eyebrow arched, as if he were a reporter catching a politician hedging on a campaign promise. I indulged him.

"Well, there was the sergeant who brought in what he thought was a tick that he'd found in his son's beard. The kid had been out the night before at a prayer meeting. It was one of those churches where the teens sing hymns around a campfire while some youth minister strums a guitar. The old man was a holy roller and figured his son must've picked it up walking through the beach grass. A good theory, except."

"Except?"

"It was a crab louse looking for a new home. He didn't pick it up going down to the beach. The kid picked it up going down on some girl. Pubic hair, beard—any port in a storm when you're a louse."

Sergio gave a belly laugh, leaned back in his chair, and resumed scraping his teeth. "Did you tell the sergeant?"

"Nah. Once the kid moved on to real sex, I figured he'd pick up the clap and learn his lesson."

"So that's why you're interested in seeing the body this afternoon. An ex-cop checking out a corpse for old times' sake?" Sergio started working the toothpick around his upper molars, like he was trying to flush a rat from a drainpipe with a broomstick.

"Yep. I still like trying to make sense of the insects at crime scenes. My old buddies call me to help out sometimes, off the record. So I like to keep up, learn new stuff. And I'd like to see which of my little friends answer the dinner bell in LA."

"You know, even the maggots down here dress in leisure suits." Like me, Sergio was not a slave to fashion and had little love for popular culture. He dropped the toothpick into his shirt pocket, having either succeeded or given up on the molar project.

"Sounds great. I could use a rhinestone-studded blow fly in my collection." I was tempted to tell him that I had stopped to check out a road-killed rabbit outside San Luis Obispo on the way down, and nabbed a gorgeous burying beetle. I doubt he would've been as disgusted as I was with his tableside hygiene.

18

For the rest of lunch we talked about some of the new equipment that had been featured in the exhibit hall, where each morning the conventioneers were welcomed with a banner saying, "Refreshments courtesy of Spray-Tech"—or whichever manufacturer had overpaid for gallons of weak coffee and trays of flattened pastries topped with gobs of jelly and striped with frosting. Sergio could afford the newest rigs, but I was too small-time for the fancy stuff. My company was growing, but with just three technicians and Carol managing the office, I wasn't going to be dropping a couple grand on shiny new sprayers.

My mind wandered as Sergio shared his analysis of motorized backpack sprayers. I was ready to get back home. I hadn't seen Tommy since I left on Sunday. And my crew would be disappointed that I missed today's after-work beers. Or more precisely, that I wasn't around to pay for drinks, although I guessed that Brian—the proprietor of our watering hole—had let them put the evening on my tab. I took them out every Wednesday to hear what was going right and wrong at Goat Hill Extermination (my father loved the nickname for Potrero Hill since it reminded him of the pastoral landscape of his childhood). I interrupted Sergio's monologue on the pros and cons of brass versus stainless-steel nozzles.

"I'd go with brass," I said, not knowing if they were superior but understanding that they were a helluva lot less expensive.

"You get what you pay for," he noted sagely, giving the impression that he'd just come up with the idea on his own.

"Speaking of which, you've had your lunch. Now what's the room number?"

"Oh yes," he murmured, as if he'd completely forgotten that he'd squeezed a free meal and a bottle of Jameson out of me. "It's 162. East wing, ground floor."

We shook hands, and I promised him the rest of his payment. I respect a man who drives a hard bargain. I don't need charity from friends, just integrity and companionship. Sergio had these in spades. I would've preferred to head back up the coast, but I couldn't miss the chance to see which of my insect pals were still milling around after the meat course had been removed from their dining room.

Chapter Four

A hotel security guard was standing in the hallway. His slouch suggested the poor sap had been manning his post since the body was reported sometime in the morning. The way his suit coat hung on him, he'd either lost a lot of weight while standing there or he'd gotten bad advice from a salesman. I told him I was with DiMaggio Pest Services. He grunted and lifted his chin toward the room as if I couldn't figure out which one it was.

I opened the door. The stench stopped me in my tracks. From what Sergio had told me, the guy had probably died last night. So the reek wasn't from decomposition. There might've been a sweet-musty hint of death, but there was none of the thick, sickly odor of rotting flesh. Instead, it was like the depths of a cesspool. A lot of people piss when they die, and in my experience a fair number shit themselves. We come into the world screaming and we leave crapping. It's always struck me that our two most rebellious moments are birth and death. But this was taking the last act of defiance to another level.

Hoping to keep my lunch down, I clenched my teeth and drew short breaths through my mouth, slowly exhaling through my nose, a technique I'd learned working on ripe corpses while a detective. I didn't need to turn on the lights, as the heavy curtain had been drawn back at the far end of the room. The afternoon light poured through the sheer drapes that hung over the sliding glass door. Past the short entryway, I found a pair of queen-size beds. The one nearest the doorway had the covers thrown back, as if somebody had just gotten up. A tan blanket, one of those cheap foam things that hotels favor, was piled at the foot of the bed, and the spread lay crumpled on the carpet. The floral print against the blue shag made it look like an overgrown island rising from the sea. The other half of the room was less artistically composed.

The bed was soaked in watery shit, as if the poor bastard had died of a diarrhea attack. The pillows were slathered in what I presumed had been his dinner. The sheets were pulled out from the mattress and twisted in clumps. And the blanket and spread lay off to the far side. He must have thrashed around for a while before surrendering to a most unpleasant end.

My gut was getting used to the reek. It's funny how you adapt to the environment. People can get used to most anything, which explains a lot about ghettos, dictators, and factories. The room, like the rest of the hotel, was overly air-conditioned, and the coolness made the place more bearable. I wasn't enjoying the odor, but at least it faded into the background. And this allowed me to concentrate on the flies.

A dozen or so metallic-green flies were buzzing around in circles, evidently frustrated by having the object of their devotion zipped into a plastic bag and hauled off. The blow flies were looking to lay their eggs on a corpse that they could smell but couldn't find. From what I've seen, they favor bullet holes and knife wounds. A shotgun blast is a virtual nursery. But they'll settle for most any orifice, including the openings that nature provides. I remember the naked corpse of a hooker that washed up on Hunters Point. Somebody had smothered her by tying a plastic bag over her head, and the flies had played the hand they'd been dealt. After working that crime scene I wasn't interested in sex for a month. Which was fine, given my luck with women at the time.

There was also a cluster of flesh flies, grayish insects with black stripes. They too were hoping to find a home for their little maggots. Several were resting on the landscape painting over the bed, making it look like a mountain valley invaded by giant flies. I thought the insects improved the unimaginative original. When I was on the force, I called these "sergeant flies," which pleased the guys on the beat to no end. I told them that three stripes meant you're dealing with a sergeant, so the same holds for flies. If only the two-legged sergeants could find bodies as quickly as their six-legged counterparts. The insects home in on the first whiff of death, before we can detect the faintest odor. I've seen 'em coming in for a landing ten minutes after a victim's last gasp, especially on a hot day. And LA had started delivering its renowned heat yesterday afternoon, once the rain quit.

Having accounted for the usual visitors, I turned to the unexpected arrivals. I was not used to so many house flies and other filth flies at a death scene. Dozens of them were having a feast on the soiled mattress. And that seemed to explain their numbers—they'd been attracted by the stench of the guy's final act. I waved my arm over the bed and a cloud of aggravated flies lifted off. Nothing remarkable there, but what caught my eye was what was left behind—a couple dozen dead flies. If somebody had sprayed the room, there should've been dead flies everywhere. These were all on the bed. A few were trapped in the smear of filth where the coroner had dragged the body to the edge of the bed. But I didn't see any on the floor. Which isn't to say that my search of the carpet was futile.

Along the track of the sliding glass door I found a frantic mob of winged ants. I pulled the door open a few inches to let in a breath of fresh air, or what passes as fresh in LA. The ants had evidently worked their way into the room through a tear along the bottom of the screen door. I figured the flies had availed themselves of the same opening. The little bastards are crazed when it comes to getting at a corpse, and they'll work their way through the smallest gaps. So a torn screen is like the Bay Bridge on a Friday afternoon. The sliding glass door opened to a slab of concrete which boasted a couple of cheap plastic chairs. You'd think that at seventy-five dollars a night, the Hyatt could do better. Beyond the low, neatly trimmed bushes edging the patio was an expanse of gardens overflowing with daylilies, begonias, and zinnias. Beyond those, the hotel swimming pool shimmered in the afternoon sun.

I coaxed a few of the ants into a medicine bottle. I'd already put a couple of the dead flies in another bottle, along with a few of their dumber living comrades, which I managed to catch because they were hell-bent on banging themselves against the glass door. I've carried a couple empty bottles in my pocket ever since I missed collecting a gorgeous spider wasp. She was perched on a bench in McKinley Square—a dinky park in Potrero that barely holds a dozen trees and should be the last place to find interesting insects—and I had nothing to contain what would've been a prized specimen. Neither the flies nor the ants looked anything special at first glance, but it's hard to know.

Having worked my way from one end of the room to the other, I put my face to the screen and took a few deep breaths of outside air. Then I headed back through the room, where a quick inventory gave me a good sense of the stiff and his roommate. The beds were a mess, but the rest of the place was neat as a pin. Aside from his last miserable moments, it seemed the guy had been anal retentive. There were no personal items left by the occupants on the low dressers, just a hulking color television, a coffee maker, a couple of paper-wrapped water glasses on a tray, and a glossy copy of *100 Things to do in LA*. The cover featured photos of Mickey Mouse wading through a sea of tourists, kids thrilled with riding a fake log down a water-filled trough, an enraptured couple sipping wine with palm trees in the background, some ditz emerging from a clothing store toting a jumble of shopping bags, and a gorgeous young couple emerging from the surf holding hands. There was something for everybody here.

Two suitcases were lying closed on folding stands. I looked inside one and found a few days' worth of rumpled clothes, presumably to be brought home and laundered. The other held carefully segregated clothing, including a section of neatly folded socks and briefs—who folds socks and underwear? A couple of dress shirts and pants hung in the closet. The occupants had evidently been running low on clean clothes, so I guessed they'd been close to leaving when one of them checked out early.

The bathroom had the usual toothbrushes, toothpaste, razors, and shaving cream beside the porcelain sink. The stuff on one side was arranged as if a butler had been included with the room. Or more like a pharmacist who moonlighted as a butler. On the neatnik's side was an impressive array of vitamins, herbal elixirs, lotions, and "homeopathic tinctures"—whatever the hell those were—lined up like medicinal troops. I glanced at the ingredient lists and figured whoever bought this stuff had to be from the Land of Fruits and Nuts. Only Californians are flaky enough to buy into medicines made out of seaweed and dandelion extract.

One of the bath towels was slightly damp, presumably from a shower last night. The dead guy hadn't bathed this morning, and I doubted his roommate had done so in light of the circumstances. The other towel was almost dry, but it might've been used sometime the previous day after the maid had provided clean linens. None of this was terribly informative, although a person's hygiene can sometimes make a difference in terms of the insects that show up to the funeral. In this case, however clean the guy might've been when he went to bed, it sure hadn't done him any good by morning.

I figured if I stayed any longer, I'd absorb enough of the room's odors that I'd need a shower of my own. And I'd already checked out, so I decided to get out of there with my meager collection of postmortem visitors. I had planned to just head back up to San Francisco, but something wasn't quite right.

At every death scene, the stiff and the insects are the only ones that know the truth. In this case, everything seemed pretty typical for the most part. Flies show up at deaths and ants crawl into buildings. But I'd never seen dead flies around a fresh corpse and the ants seemed somehow out of place. It wasn't a big deal, but I thought maybe I'd swing by the front desk. Hotel staff have a way of knowing things, and I wanted a little more information about the guests in room 162.

CHAPTER FIVE

On the way out of the room, I asked the security guy whether he'd been the first one on the scene.

"Yup," he said, "but can't say that I stayed long. Place smelled like a sewer. I told management they needed somebody to come clean up the mess. No way the maids are going in there. Not at what they get paid."

"Anybody else go into the room?"

"Just a couple of cops, but they didn't hang around. Some guys from the coroner's office picked up the body around noon."

"Doesn't sound like they were in a big hurry to collect the stiff."

"There's plenty of work for them in this city. We got bodies in dumpsters, dead bums in the parks, niggers shootin' each other in Watts, wetbacks dying under overpasses. It's a fuckin' smorgasbord of corpses." He smiled at his turn of phrase.

"I don't suppose the hotel is anxious to have bodies carted down the hall and through the lobby in front of guests during the morning bustle."

"You're telling me." He shook his head. "The Hyatt executives are pretty connected, so I'm sure they can have the meat wagon show up whenever they say. Late morning is a good time to bring the body snatchers in through the back. Minimizes the chances of having little Jimmy ask his daddy what's in the bag as the family heads out to Disneyland."

"So the room's just like it was when you saw it this morning?"

"Nobody moved anything around, if that's what you're asking. What's it to you anyway? You guys hafta clean it up in any case."

I'd nearly forgotten that I was supposed to be affiliated with DiMaggio's people. "Just trying to figure out the best way to get the smell out of there. It helps to know if the room's been aired out when we're selecting a deodorizer." It was a pretty good dodge, if you ask me. "Were the sliding glass door and screen closed when you got there?"

"You guys are real pros, eh? I'm sure the door was closed cuz I remember thinking some fresh air would help. I thought about opening it up, but I figured this was potentially a crime scene. So I knew not to do nothin' to disturb stuff. That's what they taught us. But what I couldn't figure was how all the flies got in the room."

"They're pretty wily. Maybe they found a crack or something." I hadn't seen any openings to the outside, so I shared his uncertainty. The hole in the screen wouldn't matter if the glass door was closed tight.

"Why's it matter to you how they got in?"

"After we're done, we want to make sure the flies don't come back. They're attracted to traces of odor that we can't smell. And the last thing we want is to leave a job and have a customer complain that there are flies."

I was getting good at this ruse. But Sergio's crew was coming down the hallway, and I didn't want them to blow my story. Besides, I had all the information I needed from my new pal. I thanked the guy and met up with the cleaners before they got too close to the room. I stopped them, said that I was turned around, and asked for directions to the lobby. This gave the impression that I was exchanging some professional advice, although the security guard seemed to have lapsed back into his bored slouch. As they headed down the hall, I headed to the lobby.

At the front desk I caught the eye of a petite woman who was talking on the phone. She was wearing the none-too-flattering uniform that some corporate genius had chosen to give the appearance of professionalism and dissuade guests from hitting on the staff. The straight skirt didn't do much for her, but it did draw my eye to a nice pair of gams. The navy-blue jacket and starched white blouse hid whatever upper assets she might've had, but her build suggested there wasn't a whole lot to showcase in that regard. I pushed aside further evaluations, having been warned about a women's liberation thing that makes it wrong for a guy to appreciate well-shaped bodies—as if my own shortcomings were not fair game.

I'm no great shakes myself. Between an unruly shock of sandy-blond hair and a nose that looks like it's trying to avoid my left cheek, nobody would describe me as tall, dark, and handsome. But I've kept myself in shape, and at five foot nine, what I lack in height I make up for in the width of my shoulders.

She gave me a quick wink and gestured at the phone with a roll of her eyes to let me know she was not avoiding me. I smiled back and shrugged sympathetically. I enjoyed watching her while she nodded patiently toward whoever was calling. I guessed she was in her mid-thirties, an age that I still had a chance of charming. She had a healthy look about her, not sexy but genuinely pretty without all the makeup and silicone that's been slathered onto and injected into the women of southern California. After three days of blue-eyed blondes, a brown-eyed brunette was refreshing.

Hanging up the phone, she stepped to the counter. "Now then, how can I help you?"

"Well, Linda," I began, reading her name from the tag on her lapel that indicated she was a "Customer Service Agent," which used to be a desk clerk before everyone needed their self-esteem massaged. "I need a favor."

"I see." She hesitated, with the slightest hint of a smile. "And you are?" I put my arms on the counter and leaned forward to suggest that we might need to get to know one another a bit better—at least if she was to trust me with a bit of inside information.

"I'm C. V. Riley. Everyone calls me Riley."

To my delight she edged closer. She smelled clean. Not the flowery cover-up of perfume but the scent of soap. "And so, Riley, what can I do for you?"

"It seems that one of your guests checked out last night, without paying his bill."

"Oh? And, assuming this happened, why is it any concern of yours?" she asked, cocking her head in a way that suggested more curiosity than suspicion.

"You see, Linda, that's the favor. I can't really go into why it matters to me. I'm just hoping you might be able to tell me something about the fellow."

She flipped through a ledger on the shelf below the counter. "I don't see any notes about a customer not paying his bill."

"I'm betting that management isn't going to insist on getting the money. He didn't actually leave your fine establishment until this morning, and nobody was too anxious to hand him a bill."

"What are you talking about?" she demanded. My coy approach had initially interested her but now she was getting impatient.

"The guest in room 162. I gather he checked out from this world sometime last night and the coroner's office picked up his remains a few hours ago."

"Oh, you mean that poor Mr. Odum." She winced, and I could tell she was the sort of woman who had sympathy for everyone. The warmhearted sort who give quarters to bums hoping that this time they'd buy shoes rather than booze. Not really naïve, just too kind for this world. I softened my tone.

"It's a tough thing to die away from home," I commiserated.

"Oh yes. And it couldn't have been easy for his student."

"His student?"

"Yes, we've learned that Paul Odum was a professor at Berkeley. He was attending a conference on forests, along with one of his students. The poor boy woke up to find his teacher dead."

"Helluva wakeup call." I caught myself and added, "Must've really rattled the kid. I suppose he headed back to school, eh?

"As a matter of fact, he's in the lounge. Probably trying to steady his nerves until the cleanup people can give him his belongings from the room."

"What's his name?"

"You sure ask a lot of questions. I shouldn't be giving out details if there's something suspicious. I thought he'd just died in his sleep. Are you a private investigator?"

"Nothing like that. I'm not looking to make things messy for your hotel." She scowled, and I immediately regretted my choice of words. "Sorry, that didn't come out right. I gather you heard about the room."

"Yes, it sounds terrible to die that way. He was a sickly man, so I suppose it won't be too surprising for his family."

"He had a family?"

"His wife lives in Berkeley. The manager was able to track her down from Mr. Odum's registration form. Of course, we let the police inform her of the death, but we needed an address to send his personal items."

"Did she tell you that he'd been ill?"

"No, but he looked frail. You know, too thin. Even a bit gaunt. I think a man should be sturdy." She looked approvingly at me, or so I imagined. "But the real tip-off was how he dealt with our housekeeping staff."

"Needed everything spotless, eh?"

"Even more demanding in his own way. Mr. Odum made it clear that he was very sensitive to chemicals. He insisted that there could be absolutely no room deodorizer, that we remove all of our scented soaps, and that the maids could only use a cleaning solution that he brought with him."

"Sounds like a challenging guest. He provided his own cleanser?"

"In fact, he gave housekeeping a bottle of it, and I know they did their best to comply. I heard that he left a five-dollar tip on the dresser every morning, which ensured that the maid provided custom service."

"At least he was a generous crackpot."

"Oh, don't be cruel," she said with a tone that reminded me of a Catholic school nun. "I'm sure he wasn't well, and he was just trying to keep whatever health he had."

"Sorry. I'm just a bit defensive given my line of work."

"Well, there're good reasons that exterminators aren't the most popular people."

"Until somebody finds cockroaches in the kitchen or termites in the walls. But how'd you know what I do?"

"Simple, silly. When I looked over the guest registry for the unpaid bill, I saw that you were paying the discounted rate we provided to the pest control convention." Pretty and smart. I was really starting to enjoy Linda. "So what's an exterminator care about one of our guests passing away in the night?" she continued.

"It's a long story."

"I'd like to hear it. But I'm working until six, and I see that you're checking out today."

"I'd love to take you to dinner, but I have to head back to San Francisco."

"I understand. I'm sure I'd enjoy your company, though I'm certain I wouldn't get your real story."

"So, you're okay with deception?"

"If I restricted my interests to truthful men, I might as well be a nun." It was like she could read my mind. Interesting but a little unnerving. "Your type I can handle."

"My type?"

"The mysterious sort. I prefer a man who won't answer my questions to one who lies. Evasion is fair game."

"You'd be seen in public with an exterminator with a mug like mine? Hardly a classy date."

"Give me a real man with a real face, who does actual work, over the fakes in this city. I can't tell you how many stars of tomorrow with hair plugs from last month there are around here. Their only roles have been pretending to be actors." Linda was my kind of woman. Not a bimbo you'd display like a Rolex, but one that'd drink a beer with you on the back deck while you flipped burgers. The sort I'd never managed to find.

"I don't make it down here often, but now I have a reason to come back sooner than usual."

She smiled and jotted her phone number inside a matchbook from the hotel. Her fingers brushed my palm when she handed it to me.

I was disappointed to be missing dinner with Linda, but there was also a sense of relief. She probably would've managed to get my real story between her wistful brown eyes, some tender touches stolen during the meal, and a few drinks. I'd learned that while women don't find exterminators to be sexy, we're a notch above ex-cops. And being both was a losing formula.

I felt like I needed to get back to Goat Hill Extermination, although I knew that Carol and the guys could have kept things running for a month without my help. In fact, they were probably more productive without my meddling—except for the new technician, who needed either a kick in the butt or a pat on the back, and I'd not figured out which. But there was one last piece of business in LA. I needed to have a chat with Professor Odum's student—and perhaps one last visit with the velvety Mr. Jameson.

CHAPTER SIX

I headed across the sunlit lobby and into the lounge. After the plunge into relative darkness, it took me a minute to make out the people in the room well enough to search for my mark. I quickly dismissed the customers at the tables, as they were all in some greater or lesser stage of graying. There were a couple of younger men at the near end of the bar, but they were dressed too snappily to be university students. As my eyes continued to adjust, down the way I could see a buxom blonde in a tight skirt being pawed by a middle-aged fellow with a bad comb-over. I could tell she had what he wanted, and I presumed he had something she desired. Most likely money or an audition. I took a few steps into the room and saw a fellow hunched over his beer at the far end of the bar. He had unruly, curly hair and a pair of wire-rimmed glasses perched on his prominent nose. Skinny arms that had never lifted much more than a college textbook poked out from a polyester shirt that looked like a collision between a truckload of bamboo and a busload of pandas. He didn't look to be much older than a good whiskey. This had to be my boy.

I took the barstool next to him and caught the barkeep's eye. He reached under the bar and gestured toward me with the bottle of Jameson. Carol was going to give me hell when she saw the bar tab on my travel account, but I nodded and said, "Pour me a short one, and pull another pint for my pal here." The kid looked sideways like he'd just woken up, confused and suspicious. "Don't worry, kid, I'm just buying a beer for somebody who looks like he's hit bottom."

"Uh, thanks," he muttered and drained the beer he'd been working on. The bartender brought our fresh drinks, and I raised my glass.

"As we Irish say, 'To live in the hearts we leave behind is not to die.'" He started to raise his glass and then stopped as if suddenly realizing where he was.

"How do you know about Professor Odum?"

"First, we honor your friend." I lifted my glass to eye level and he followed suit. When we'd both had a good drink, I set mine on the bar and turned to look at him. He looked scared and lost, and I felt sorry for him. I knew his kind, the sort who got beaten up in school for being smart. He sure didn't look like anyone who'd had much experience with death. "Kid," I explained, "in a hotel, two things are sure to spread: cockroaches and rumors. Now being an exterminator, I'm something of an expert when it comes to roaches. As for rumors, I suppose that's more your department at the moment."

"Christ, I didn't think everyone would find out," he sighed. "But I suppose with so many people, it's hard to keep things private."

"That it is," I commiserated and took another sip. "Maybe it's true what they say: God made whiskey to keep the Irish from conquering the world. If you ask me, we got the better end of that deal. The world's a mess."

"So, what's your interest in Professor Odum? Just morbid curiosity?" The kid wasn't softening up much, but at least he was talking.

"Worse than that."

"How so? You some sort of investigator? I already told the cops all I know."

"Relax, kid. We're sort of in the same line of work."

"How do you figure?"

"Well, I'm an exterminator from San Francisco and I hear you're a student here for that conference on forests. So we're both into the whole nature thing, eh?"

"I'm working on a master's in ecology. You make a living poisoning the world." He'd gone from impassive to testy, which at least meant he was coming out of his funk. "My research involves protecting species, not killing them. We're hardly in the same field." He took a long pull on his beer and stared at the rows of bottles behind the bar.

"Fair enough. But a good killer knows his mark. The Orkin boys are nozzle heads, but we small operators have to know what's going on with the insects. We can't afford to spray and pray. Gotta be a smart ecologist to stay in business."

He was quiet for a few seconds and then half-turned back toward me. "What's any of this have to do with Professor Odum?"

"Let's start over, and then I'll explain. I'm Riley," I said, extending my hand.

"Howard," he replied. "Howard Clements." We shook hands. His grip was strong for a kid with such skinny arms, but the softness of his skin suggested he'd spent most of his life working with his head rather than his hands. "Is Riley your first or last name?"

"Long story. It's the only name I use, except on legal papers."

"The cleanup crew isn't supposed to bring my things to the front desk until three o'clock. I could use a good story to distract me."

"Can't say it's a good story. It's just mine. My parents emigrated from Ireland. County Sligo, if that means anything." It didn't. "My father had been a peat cutter back home, and there wasn't much demand for that skill in America. So he joined the army. Before I was born, he and my mother moved all the time. Fort Hood, Fort Dix, and even Fort Riley in Kansas, where he met Joe Louis." The kid looked perplexed. "The boxer," I explained.

"Ah, right." Howard nodded as if he understood. Anything earlier than 1960 was ancient history these days.

"They settled in San Francisco when I was born. The Potrero neighborhood had lots of immigrant families, although my folks didn't know a soul when they arrived. But when you're in the military, your fellow soldiers are like family. One of my father's closest friends was a Russian immigrant named Vladimir. Turns out the Russians and Irish have one thing in common."

"And that would be?" Howard asked. I lifted my glass in a mock toast, drained it, set it on the bar, and gestured for a refill. Howard nodded again. This time he understood.

"Both people are fighters—more with fists than guns, but the two of them fought on Guadalcanal. Vlad took a bullet to the throat and drowned in his own blood while my father held him. So to honor his friend, he gave me the middle name of Vladimir."

"What about your first name?"

"Not much better. My grandfather's name was Cedric. A fine name in the old country, but not much of a name to avoid fights at school. Can you imagine telling kids that your name is Cedric Vladimir Riley?"

Howard laughed softly and shook his head. "Just like the Johnny Cash song."

"How's that?" Now it was my turn to be confused, being studiously un-interested in pop music.

"You know, 'A Boy Named Sue.' The song about the boy whose father gave him a girl's name to make sure he grew up tough."

"Yeah, well I got into plenty of fights without being named Cedric or Sue. For a while I went by C. V., but people kept asking what the letters stood for. So I started going with just plain 'Riley.' Keeps things simple."

"How'd you end up as an exterminator in San Francisco?"

I wasn't about to tell him about my days on the force. So I gave my father's side of the story. After catching some shrapnel in his knee on Guadalcanal, he was transferred from fighting the Japs to battling mosquitoes. He loved to tell the story about Douglas MacArthur declaring that for every division fighting the enemy, there were two divisions in the hospital with malaria. So the guys who sprayed DDT across the tropical islands probably saved as many soldiers as the enemy killed.

After the war, he'd been stationed at the Presidio for advanced training. The Army's 406th Medical Unit was responsible for sanitation and hygiene in the Korean War. He learned everything there was to know about getting rid of vermin—rats, mice, flies, fleas, mosquitoes. The whole lot.

I finished my autobiography by telling Howard, "With all that training, when my father decided not to re-enlist it just seemed natural to start an ex-termination business. He always said that you had to go with your strengths, and he knew how to kill pests. And when he died, I took over the company." The kid was now looking comfortable, so it was time to change settings and topics.

Chapter Seven

The sun was painfully bright, with the haze turning the afternoon into glaring whiteness. Howard and I took our drinks to the patio that extended out from the lobby into the manicured lawn. The air was hot, with a sticky wetness lingering from yesterday's rain. The lounge had been getting too crowded for the conversation I was hoping to have with the kid. We'd almost had the place to ourselves when the retirees headed off for their naps, and after the comb-over stud put a twenty on the bar with one hand while caressing the dame's curvaceous rear with the other, heading off to their tryst. But within minutes, they'd been replaced by a group of conventioneers wearing "Hi, I'm _____" name tags, so I suggested we catch some of LA's acclaimed sunshine.

I'm not one for slow roasting, so we sat in the shade provided by a hedge running along one side of the patio. The other chairs and tables were in the sun, and apparently none of the hotel guests were willing to risk second-degree burns from the scalding wrought iron. With some space around us, Howard seemed to relax. It probably didn't hurt that I'd ordered him another beer. I could've solved cases a lot easier if there'd been beer on tap in the interrogation room.

Howard was evidently no longer worried that I was a private eye, but not only that, I got the sense that the trauma had him looking for some sort of parental figure. I'm thirty-three, but most people add some years to account for the cocked nose I'd gotten from a rookie mistake on the streets, the crow's feet I'd inherited from my mother, and the premature gray around my temples that I'd received from my father. I had to be careful not to move too fast with our little chat, but I didn't have all day.

"So kid, that's the life and times of C. V. Riley, but it doesn't explain why I'm interested in what happened to your professor."

"Yeah, I was wondering when we'd get back to that." He sounded resigned but not terribly suspicious.

"Turns out I'm thinking about expanding my business. Extermination is profitable, but there's good money in cleaning up after a death. Sounds pretty awful, but it's a real public service."

"So the hotel has you cleaning up the room where Professor Odum and I were staying?"

"Not quite. I was here for a convention of pest control operators." As much as I hated that euphemism, I thought the term might be more acceptable to Howard. "But I have a pal who provides cleanup services in LA. I was just checking out the scene to get a sense of the challenges, if you know what I mean."

"I wish I didn't."

"Death isn't a pretty thing." We both took a long drink. When the silence became a strain I figured it was time to press. As a detective, I'd learned when to push and when to back off with a witness. In retrospect, the whole "cleanup services" gimmick wasn't a great lie, but Howard had that sort of look about him that suggested he'd really like to tell his story to a pal—or at least somebody other than an authority figure. There's a good reason we say a guy "spills his guts" during an interrogation. It's just like puking—unpleasant if you focus on the moment, but deeply relieving once it's over.

"So Howard," I began, "I can see that you'd rather not recount the last few hours. But I need to know what's in store if I get into this side of the business. You know, the big picture. And maybe it'd do you some good to lay it all out there for a fellow biologist." I winked, letting him know that I didn't really think we were both scientists.

"Okay," he said, taking a long pull on his beer. "What the hell. The whole thing might as well help somebody." He explained that he was one of the professor's graduate students. They were working on some project involving regrowing forests after they'd been chopped down. It was all much more complicated, but that seemed to be the upshot. The two of them were attending an international conference of scientists who studied agricultural and forestry practices of indigenous people. He was hoping to gain some ideas that he might apply to his own project, which involved restoring native forests in northern California. I managed to nod at appropriate times throughout his rambling story while gently moving things along to the professor's death.

"We didn't leave the hotel yesterday with so much happening at the conference. Everything was going great. I was so excited with all the talks, and meeting people from around the world. Everybody seemed to know Professor Odum."

"You didn't have any clue that he was ill?"

"Of course I knew he was hypersensitive to environmental toxins. But he'd made sure our room was free of all synthetic chemicals that could trigger a reaction."

"So, what happened last night after your conference was over?"

"We went back to the room around six, watched the news, and rested for a bit. Then we got dressed for the banquet. It was a decent dinner, nothing too special. I met up with some students from Mexico, Brazil, and Thailand. We went out for some drinks. And I'll admit that I had too many, but I didn't want to look like a wimp in front of the others."

"I know how it goes, kid. I can't keep up like I used to." I took a sip of my Jameson. These days quality trumped quantity.

"Yeah, well, I was lucky to find my way back to the room around midnight. Professor Odum was sound asleep. I'd seen him leave the banquet around eight, and I guessed he was headed back to our room."

"One of those early-to-bed, early-to-rise types, eh?"

"That was him. He was always watching his health, and he said that sleep was the best detoxifier. I suspect that he'd worn himself out during the day, given how amped he can get about science. He'd chaired a major symposium all afternoon with Mr. Srisai, a colleague from Thailand's Ministry of Forests and Wildlife. They were collaborating on a project, and Professor Odum seemed totally hyped about this new study."

I needed to nudge him back on track. "Okay, so what did the room look like when you got in? At least what you can remember."

"Everything seemed normal. Normal for Professor Odum, that is. He was a very systematic man. Everything in its place, you know."

"How about the door out to the garden and pool?"

Howard paused, as he suddenly realized he was giving a deposition instead of just telling a new pal what had happened. "Why does that matter to your new line of business?"

Damn. After having put him at ease initially, my questioning had broken the spell. I needed to lull him back into that reverie. "Sorry about that, it's just that I'm trying to get the whole picture. I've been told that one of the big things to worry about at a death scene cleanup is the insects. You can imagine what it's like if a client comes back into the house and there're flies everywhere. So I'm just trying to figure out that side of the job."

"Yeah, I can see that." I hid my relief. He took a draw on his beer and settled back into his story. "As usual, he'd left the sliding glass door open and the screen was closed. He thought the indoor air of the hotel built up harmful vapors."

"Not too worried about intruders, eh?"

"Only guests can access the courtyard, so I guess he didn't figure there was much to worry about. We kept the room closed up during the day, but we both liked some fresh air at night. I just didn't want the room filled with moths, given that the professor insists on having a nightlight in the bathroom. He has to get up to use the facilities pretty often."

I cringed at having missed the nightlight. In the old days, I'd have made a mental note of this detail. "And so you figure he just got back to the room and went to bed?"

"Not quite so simple. I'm sure he followed his routine."

"Which was?"

"Let's see. Every night he'd take a shower, even though he took one in the morning. He said it was important to wash off the airborne toxins, especially in Los Angeles. Then he'd brush his teeth for like twenty minutes, take a set of assorted medicines in a careful sequence, squirt some fluid up his nose to wash out his sinuses, put drops in his eyes, and apply a bluish lotion to his hands and feet and a yellow one to his face and neck."

"When I was in the room earlier, I saw the bathroom counter. Looked like somebody had opened a drugstore." There's nothing like injecting a bit of empathy to keep a fellow talking.

"It was like rooming with a pharmacist. After all of his treatments, he put on fresh underwear and used a roller covered in sticky tape to clean any toxic fallout from his sheets and pillow. Then, he'd sit bolt upright in a meditative position on his bed with his hands on his knees and his fingers in some contorted position. After about a half hour, he'd finally turn off the light and lie down. I'd learned not to be around when he was going through his ritual."

"Sounds like a good idea. So he was just laying peacefully on his bed when you arrived last night?"

"Best as I can remember. Nothing struck me as unusual. At least until morning."

"That's when you found that he'd died?"

"Yeah. Given that I was pretty smashed from the night before, I didn't wake up until a little after nine. I might've slept even longer except for the smell."

"Pretty bad, eh?"

"If you were in the room you know what I mean. Professor Odum had what might be politely called 'intestinal problems.' He was a strict vegetarian, and took all sorts of supplements. In any case, you wanted to give the bathroom a good half hour after he'd used it." Howard took a swig of his beer.

Even in the shade I had sweat running down my neck, but I suspected that the heat worked along with the ordeal to put Howard into something like a trance. I'd seen it plenty of times with witnesses recounting a traumatic event. Now, having paused, it was like he could hear what he'd been saying. So the kid tried to backtrack so as not to sound callous. "Geez, I hate to say this stuff about him. He was really a great adviser."

"It's all right. You've been a big help to me. Anything else I should know before I decide to get into the cleanup business?"

"Well, being an exterminator you're probably used to the flies. But the damn things freaked me out. Buzzing around his body and all. I figured they squeezed past the screen somehow, so I closed the glass door before I left to keep any more from getting in." That explained a roomful of flies without an open door.

"I'd have done the same thing," I commiserated. The kid's story was plausible enough. If anything it felt a little too neat. But I figured he'd given it at least a couple of times to the hotel management and the police. I didn't have any good reason to doubt his account. "I guess that covers it. Thanks again, Howard. Do you need a ride back up the coast?"

"No, I'm going to drive Professor Odum's car and drop it off at his house. My stuff should be at the front desk soon, if it's not there already." He drained his glass and we shook hands. As he headed back into the lobby, I savored the last few drops of my whiskey, knowing I'd have to settle for less extravagant refreshments back home.

🝆

The trip back to San Francisco gave me time to mull over Howard's story and what I'd found in the hotel room. I had taken the Ford pickup that I preferred over the Chevy vans the guys used for the business. The vans were pretty flashy, featuring our logo painted on the sides. One of Carol's artsy friends had drawn it for us—a goat standing on its hind legs, holding a pump sprayer in one hoof, a dead roach dangling from the other. I thought the image looked demonic, but everyone else liked it. The rusting F-100 had nearly 200,000 miles to its credit and the corrosion had eaten away chunks of the door and side panels, but it has been my truck since I took over the business. As I headed out of Los Angeles, the thrumming of the engine, the sun pouring into the cab, and the Bach cantata on KUSC put me into a mood for mulling over what I'd learned about Paul Odum.

There was no obvious reason to treat Odum's death as suspicious. At least, I couldn't imagine that the LAPD would. Given his health problems, the plausibility of Howard's account, and the inevitable backlog at the coroner's, I was sure the medical examiner would rule it a death by natural causes and store the body until a funeral home brought it back to San Francisco. The cop on the scene wouldn't have noticed them, but those dead flies had me wondering. And I had a nagging sense that something in the room didn't fit the kid's story, but I was damned if I could figure what.

If there had been foul play, then Howard was the obvious suspect. Always start with whoever knew and was last seen with the victim. Most often, people are killed by their lovers, friends, spouses, and presumably students, rather than strangers. But unless I could come up with a hole, the kid had a watertight story. And it's a lot harder to fabricate a coherent lie than most people imagine. What's more, Howard gave every indication of lacking what it takes to commit murder, although I'd learned not to underestimate the quiet, awkward types.

Even with all this in his favor, I couldn't shake the sense that something wasn't quite right. I hoped it would come to me, like when you can't remember the name of a movie or a person and you work and struggle until it's hopeless—and then a few hours or days later it just pops into your head. At least, it works that way sometimes. I didn't see how this case had any upside for me other than satisfying my own curiosity. And that doesn't pay the bills. On the drive home, I didn't yet know about the bill that was coming due at St. Teresa's. And even if I had, there's no way I'd have figured that Paul Odum's gruesome death would soon provide an answer to my mother's prayers.

Chapter Eight

It was good to sleep in my own bed, although the situation with Tommy made for a restless night. I woke up late, grabbed a quick shower and shave, and headed down the hill to Gustaw's Bakery. I looked forward to a raspberry-filled paczki and a cup of his coffee, which was nearly as strong as the old Pole himself. The morning was as clear as a glass of the finest Polish vodka, which Gustaw swore by—but never before noon. He was a grizzled character with a perpetual squint, who'd grown up working the docks in Gdańsk before immigrating to San Francisco, where the waterfront reminded him of home. His wife looked like she'd been a knockout thirty years ago but had put away enough pierogis over the years that she'd come to resemble the Polish dumplings. Ludwika drew the line for her hardworking, hard-drinking husband. I couldn't blame him for avoiding Ludwika's wrath after watching her deal with a kid who tried to steal a babka from the counter. He'd evidently heard about the rum sauce, and when you're an adolescent, alcohol in any form is a serious temptation. However, I suspect that being lifted off your feet by your ear courtesy of a babushka who's threatening to carry you down to the precinct, so that "the police mens will lock you away in jail for good," might be just the sort of experience to turn a boy into a teetotaler.

Between the caffeine and the walk back up the hill, and then down the other side to Goat Hill Extermination, I was wide awake when I pushed through the front door of the office.

"Our fearless leader returns," Carol mocked. She was as cute as ever. A pageboy haircut framed her smiling face, and a pair of utterly distracting half-erect nipples pushed against her silvery blouse. I'd never seen a woman who seemed so constantly stimulated and perpetually off-limits.

"Back to save the city from ravaging pests, and the business from marauding competitors," I replied, trying not to stare but finding it as difficult as usual. She noticed my struggle and took the opportunity to continue my education.

"Riley, what have I said about objectifying women?" That was the term I couldn't remember when trying not to admire Linda back at the hotel.

"Uh, it's bad," I tried. She rolled her eyes.

"And why?"

"C'mon, Carol, gimme a break." She just glared, although I knew she wasn't really mad at me. "Okay, women aren't just objects for the sexual gratification of men," I answered, like a kid having memorized a catechism lesson.

"My prize pupil!" she announced with mock pride. I should've left well enough alone.

"But I'll be damned as to why this means I can't appreciate a beautiful woman," I added. After all, a cantata can be sensuous—and it can also be technically complex, historically profound, and intellectually engaging.

"At least you're trying," she sighed. I shrugged. "And I am flattered by your schoolboy crush," she said, leaning over her desk to give me a kiss on the cheek and hand me a stack of papers. "You can't have what you'd really like, so you'll have to settle for the accounting report and work log." On her radio, some moron was singing "Don't go breaking my heart," as if to taunt me.

"Great. A cold shower of numbers." Carol knew how much I hated this stuff and how little attention I paid to such details. I trusted her completely with the finances. She was the most honest and competent office manager imaginable. As least she fulfilled one dream, because the other fantasy wasn't going to happen.

"Sweetie," she murmured in a sultry voice, "I've told you before, if I ever decide to convert you'll be the first to know." The radio had switched to another would-be crooner declaring that he'd "really love to see you tonight." It was like being in the world's most idiotic musical.

"You'd become a Catholic just to please my mother?"

"I'd be more likely to get on my knees in a pew than for a man," she laughed. Unlike most of the businessmen I knew and generally admired,

I had no problems with her being a lesbian. Hell, I liked women, so I can hardly complain that she had similar tastes. I wouldn't have given a damn if she'd been a one-legged Indian if she could keep the place humming. And her lack of interest in men as romantic partners actually made the whole place run smoothly. With none of the guys hitting on the babe in the front office, there was no drama to screw up the place.

Carol's only serious flaw was her devotion to pop music, which she played endlessly thanks to some tinny AM station with inane disc jockeys punctuating the musical atrocities with their pointless yammering. I swear, if I ever see another busker down by Fisherman's Wharf—a place I generally avoid, although cioppino at Alioto's makes the world right on a blustery January day when the tourists have headed down to San Diego and Tijuana—doing that stupid robotic "dance," I'm gonna deck the guy. A jury of my peers would not only acquit me but nominate me for a public service citation.

I poured myself a cup of coffee from the bottomless pot that Carol maintains, along with answering phones, setting schedules, billing customers, figuring payroll, keeping inventory, and whatever else keeps this place running. The coffee's nothing like Gustaw's, but Carol's too frugal to buy the good stuff. Anyway, not much business comes through the front door, so impressing potential customers isn't the point of the coffee pot.

In fact, the front office isn't much: Carol's gray metal desk, a wall of mismatched filing cabinets, a couple of wooden chairs next to a low table to serve as a waiting area, and a water cooler with those conical paper cups. (I'd like to meet the guy who thought it was a good idea to put water into a paper cone, but the idiot's probably dancing like a robot on the Wharf.) All this opulence is surrounded by dark wood paneling with a few posters from various chemical companies ("Raid Kills Bugs Dead"—as if there's some other result of killing). The room's illuminated by whatever light leaks through the metal grate covering the glass door and pulses down from the fluorescent fixtures.

I've offered to let Carol spiff up the place and even tried talking her into a new desk. But she insists that it's "comfortable." I bought her a new chair last Christmas, but it didn't turn out like I expected. She cried when she found the thing with a red bow behind her desk. It was just a damn chair. I can't figure out dames of any sort.

After thumbing through a couple of the trade journals on the table, I poured myself another cup of coffee and headed to the back of the shop. I stopped at my office to toss the papers onto my desk and went down the hallway out to the warehouse. I was met by a sulfurous odor emanating from the insecticide drums, and a familiar greeting.

"What's up, boss?" Larry called as I came through the door. He and Dennis were sitting in a couple of overstuffed chairs with the foam spilling out from the cushions.

"Not you two, or profits, from what I can tell."

"We's sorry, boss man. You be back from vacation and ready to crack the whip." Dennis loved to play the role. "My people been getting it from you honkies ever since you hauled our black asses over here." I smiled and gave him what he was looking for.

"If I didn't have Larry overseeing your lazy black ass, the hardest work you'd do would be filling out a time card."

"Shiiiit." He drew out the word in a thoughtful way, stretching out his lanky frame and putting his feet on the wobbly coffee table. "If you think I can't outsmart and outwork some crazy Vietnam vet, then you're dumber than the cockroaches we're spraying this morning at Luigi's Grill."

Larry smiled in his deeply ironic way. "Dennis, my boy," he replied, looking at the arching girders above and lacing his hands behind his nearly square head atop his truly square shoulders, "anytime you want to try fragging an officer in this unit, just know that we're harder to kill than cockroaches—and they've been around for a million years."

The two of them had been working together for almost ten years. And the only thing they loved more than busting each other's nuts was busting mine. My father hired them because he'd give anyone a chance to prove he could pull his weight. Along with Carol, the guys were the most valuable assets of the business. The whole place could burn down and I'd be better off than if I lost these people. Dennis could push my buttons with his righteousness at times and Larry was prone to the thousand-yard stare some days, but they knew and gave an honest day's work. And I tried to return their loyalty with genuine respect, decent wages, and time off when they needed to unwind—at least if it wasn't during the busiest months.

"Somebody has to worry about this place while you two are primping and pumping," I said, waving my arm toward their interior decorations. Dennis had mounted a mirror on the wall of the warehouse, while Larry had brought a weight-lifting bench to occupy himself when business lagged, which wasn't often these days. They made an odd couple with an Afro and a crew cut, but maybe that's why things worked so well.

"Do either of you know where Isaac might be?" The new guy had me a bit worried. I'd checked him out pretty carefully. His previous employers—the kid had bussed tables at Salvadore's and stocked shelves at Rainbow Grocery—said he was reliable. My guys were willing to teach novices, but people had to bring their own work ethic. The last three hires hadn't panned out, and we really needed a third technician the way things were going.

"We got him doing inventory." Larry nodded toward the far end of the warehouse.

I dropped my voice a bit. "That's fine, but he needs to get out with one of you on some jobs. He's book smart, so I figure he's teachable." Isaac had brains, but he was built like the artist he dreamed of becoming—a tidbit he'd confided to Carol. Not that what we did took lots of muscle, but it took a kind of mechanical and physical aptitude.

"Yeah, the kid's awfully green for a whitey." Dennis smiled at his own cleverness. "Larry had to explain about reverse-threaded gas cylinders or Isaac would've broken his skinny wrist trying to get the regulator off the propane tank."

I told the guys to work with Isaac, that he'd come along. Even with the recession, which was supposedly ending despite high unemployment in the city, I didn't have a backlog of promising applicants in my files. I headed to my office, a cramped eight-by-ten room across the hall from the restroom. This arrangement delighted Dennis and Larry, who had put a sign on my door saying "Riley's Stall." In a way they were right—some of my best ideas had come to me both in that office and on the crapper. And between wondering what to do about Tommy's care and Isaac's training, I was in need of good ideas.

CHAPTER NINE

My office, such as it was, had been straightened up in my absence. The odd-ball collection of coffee-stained mugs was cleaned and arranged on top of the filing cabinet, Chinese takeout boxes had disappeared, and the equipment catalogues that I'd left scattered across my desk were neatly arranged on a shelf. Carol couldn't stand my messiness. But I found the clutter comforting at work, just as the neat precision of my insect collection had a way of soothing me at home.

I looked over the papers Carol had given me and started composing a list of visits and calls I needed to make. Aside from being the owner of Goat Hill Extermination, my major job was to cultivate new clients and ensure that existing customers were happy. I wasn't all that good with homeowners, who wanted every insect annihilated but without using any chemicals. Just like wanting the streets cleared of criminals without the cops resorting to nightsticks, handcuffs, or guns. But I really liked doing business with restaurant owners, hotel managers, and landlords—folks who worked hard for a living and knew the importance of honest labor and attention to quality. The four of us were good at what we did, so the business was doing well. Well enough to support Tommy and my mom, to give me everything I needed and a few things I wanted, and to provide a decent living for Carol and the guys.

&

Looking through the phone messages on my desk, I saw that Carol had jotted a note to visit the manager of Bay View Terrace, a public housing complex in the Mission. I remembered talking with Tony a couple months ago when he took over as manager and was looking for an exterminator to clean up the property. He seemed like a nice guy, a little young and idealistic, but he cared about the tenants. I told him that the national companies would give him a low bid, but he'd get what he paid for. He ended up signing a contract with Orkin.

The big boys were good at muscling in with their shiny vans and nozzle heads, dressed up like paramilitary troops. If some grinning moron wearing a starched white shirt with red epaulets showed up at my door with a sprayer, I'd figure the Salvation Army had branched out into pest control. But I know from my days as a cop that people trust uniforms.

Now it seemed that Tony was having some problems. I was headed for the door and looking forward to catching up with Tony when Carol's phone rang. She covered the mouthpiece and said, "Riley, it's some woman asking for you."

"Ask her what it's about." Carol did so and listened for a long minute.

"She says you don't know her but it's a very serious matter. She indicated that it has to do with Los Angeles. The lady sounds hysterical, Riley. What the hell happened down there?" The only woman who might have my number was Linda from the hotel. Maybe she'd come across something.

"Nothing big, Carol. Just a dead guy in the hotel."

She pursed her lips and frowned. "Riley, don't you go getting involved in one of your 'projects' until you've cleaned up the phone messages and visits stacked on your desk. I'm serious, damn it." I'd occasionally used my detective experience to help out people in a jam, and sometimes these little ventures took on a life of their own.

"Okay, okay. Transfer the call to my phone." I headed back to my office, closed the door, and picked up.

"Riley here." I expected to hear Linda, but it was another woman with a much less melodious voice.

"Mr. Riley, this is Laurie Odum." She paused and inhaled sharply, her voice on the edge of breaking. "Paul's wife. I believe that you know about my husband."

"Yes I do, Mrs. Odum. I'm sorry about your loss. I'm sure it's a very difficult time for you."

"Yes, thank you. Mr. Riley, I need your help."

"I really don't know how you got my name or what I might be able to do for you. I run an extermination business."

"When Howard brought Paul's car back last night, he told me about you." Her voice became steadier now that we were past the dead-husband part of the conversation.

"There's not much to tell."

"He thought you might be a good person to contact about what happened to Paul."

"I don't see why. I don't know anything more than what you can find in the police report." I couldn't tell what she was up to, and I've learned to move cautiously in these matters.

"Because, Mr. Riley, I don't think his death was natural."

"And?"

"And from what Howard said, you might be the right person to figure out what happened."

"I don't know what Howard told you, but I just spray pests these days." The kid probably figured my questions were overreaching once he had time to think about our little chat.

"Let's just say that I think you might have the skills I need. And I'm willing to pay very well for your services." Between worrying about the depletion of Tommy's Fund and the backlog of calls at work, I'd pretty much put Odum's death out of mind. Now the dead flies and the nagging doubt about Howard's story flooded back. If Laurie Odum was offering substantial cash, maybe there was a windfall that could get the daycare center through the next couple of months until the church could put together a fund drive or something.

"Look, I'm absolutely flooded with work this morning, but I could meet with you late this afternoon. Say, five o'clock."

"That would be fine, Mr. Riley. And until then, please keep this conversation between us."

I promised her I was discreet, and she gave me her address in Berkeley. A pretty nice neighborhood, if memory served. I'd once taken up the slack for a one-man extermination company over there while the guy was laid up with gallbladder surgery. I started to slip past Carol's desk, relieved that she was on the phone.

She put her hand over the mouthpiece and said, "Hold it there, buster." After apologizing to whoever was on the other end and promising to call them back in just a minute, she glared at me. "Riley, you're onto another one of your projects, aren't you?"

"Carol, look. I'll make a big dent in the list of contacts today, and then there's somebody who needs my help. By the end of the week, I'll be all caught up. Promise."

She sighed. "Face it, Riley. You can't stop being a cop."

"That's not it. Well, not this time. At least entirely. You see—"

"Stop already. You're digging yourself a hole. But then if your brain was half the size of your heart, you wouldn't be an Irishman, eh?"

"Carol, this one could pay." I thought about how much I should say and decided she deserved to understand my motive. "Tommy's Fund is in a bit of trouble." Having worked for my father, she knew all about Tommy and my mother.

Her face softened momentarily. "Go, go," she commanded and waved her hand to dismiss me. A hint of a smile undermined her cross expression as she shook her head in dismay.

The drive out to Bay View Terrace was tedious in the morning traffic. As I climbed out of my decrepit truck, Tony came around from the side of the building, wearing a tie-dyed T-shirt and bell-bottom jeans and hauling a couple of overstuffed garbage bags. As the new manager of the apartment complex, he had some big plans for landscaping, a community garden, and a playground, all of which would be trashed within a year. But his heart was in the right place, and maybe someday a guitar-strumming idealist will pull it off in one of the projects. Until then, I was just hoping to wipe out the vermin.

We walked to his office, where he settled behind a military surplus desk and I pulled up a folding chair on the other side.

"I sure appreciate your time," he began.

"So what's up? Things not working out with Orkin?" I was a little curt with him, but he was the one who'd decided to take his business elsewhere.

"Hey, I hope there's no hard feelings, but their bid undercut you by a third."

"Business is business, Tony. That's the past and I gather you've got a problem in the present."

"Yeah, Orkin's regional manager called and said they wouldn't send out another technician unless I paid a five-grand damage deposit."

"The cockroaches been chewing up their uniforms?" I pretty much knew what the problem was, but wanted Tony to lay it out.

"No, it's their service vans. The last three times they parked in the complex, my residents helped themselves to tires, radios, and engine parts."

"And the small print on their contract says that if they experience repeated loss or damage of equipment at a worksite, they can impose a payment of up to ten times their losses to be held as a deposit against future losses." I'd seen plenty of the corporate contracts.

"You got it. And I can't afford that with my budget."

"So let's figure out how you can pay me to make this place livable."

We talked for a while and agreed on a rate ten percent higher than my original bid. I told him that Carol would mail a contract and I'd have Dennis come out early next week. He'd take my truck and the residents wouldn't pay any attention to a black guy driving an old junker, unlike the fancy vans being driven by the white guys in white shirts.

CHAPTER TEN

My metamorphosis from cop to exterminator—and from homeboy to pariah—began with a tip that Jamal Watson was a member of the African Liberation Front: a group of angry blacks who didn't seem to know what they wanted other than power. And it wasn't clear what they meant by that, except it involved inflicting pain and extracting money. The ALF had snatched a Chinese kid from a bus stop and demanded a ransom to finance their "War on White Privilege." Not that the Chinese are white, but I guess being not-black was good enough. I knew the girl's family from my youth. Mr. Wang had a dry cleaning store on Van Ness, and every November my mother had me take our wool coats and sweaters to him after San Francisco's Indian summer had passed. The Wangs—and I don't think anyone ever figured out how many of them there were—operated at least a dozen dry cleaners and laundromats from Chinatown south to Bernal Heights. According to my father, nobody in San Francisco worked harder than Mr. Wang. If the ALF wanted to get even with rich whites, they picked the wrong target. Rather than kidnapping some rich kid from Pacific Heights, they grabbed Mei Wang from the street in front of Commodore Stockton Elementary.

The case would've been hot enough without little Mei having a seizure disorder that required daily medicine. After Mr. Wang got the call from the kidnappers, he called the police. I was on the margin of the case, helping with grunt work as needed. But I stopped by to visit the family because Mr. Wang and my father had become pals through an organization that promoted immigrant enterprise.

Years later, Mr. Wang took me aside at my father's funeral. Frustrated by his limited English, Mr. Wang struggled to express himself, falling silent while grasping my shoulder. Then he smiled at having found the right words and declared that my father was "trustworthy and honorable." To Mr. Wang there was no higher praise.

When I got to the house, Mr. Wang was beside himself. While he paced, Mrs. Wang sat catatonically on a floral sofa, staring at a row of photos on the mantel across the room. I told them that I wasn't running the investigation, but that I'd squeeze every snitch in my book for a lead. Mr. Wang said the police didn't want him to pay the ransom, but if Mei didn't have her medicine soon she could die. I said he was right to trust the police with his daughter's life because they knew what was best.

The ALF was a diffuse and disorganized group, and the federal boys didn't have a good bead on who were members, let alone ringleaders. Hard work is essential in these cases, but oftentimes it isn't enough. The investigators needed some luck, and I had the luck of the Irish. At the time, I was working a case involving a dead junkie—a once-pretty, nineteen-year-old runaway found in a dumpster near Market and 6th. I didn't figure to solve the case, but I had to give it a go for the dead kid. My mother would have said that St. Jude, the patron saint of lost causes, was with me as I headed to an interview with the deceased's last known boyfriend. Whatever the explanation, as I turned the corner at Turk and Franklin I nearly collided with Li'l Sly, one of the Tenderloin's busiest dealers. He was moving fast enough that the ridiculously large collar flaps on his overcoat might've allowed him to take off like an inner-city version of the Flying Nun. I figured he might be good for some information on the girl, so I asked him a few questions while giving him the customary pat-down.

Li'l Sly seemed unusually nervous, so I thought maybe he had some connection to the dead girl. But he had a better reason for being anxious. He'd been on his way to a major sale at Jefferson Square Park and his coat pockets were stuffed with smack. Hoping that I might overlook the size of his inventory, which was more than sufficient to boost the charge from possession to intent to distribute, Li'l Sly became highly cooperative as I asked about happenings on the street. He didn't have anything to offer about bodies in dumpsters, so I took a shot to see what he knew about the ALF. He gave me the name of an ALF "lieutenant" living in the North Beach projects and looked hopeful that this would help me forget the contents of his pockets. If he was telling the truth, tracking a hot lead on a kidnapper trumped booking a lowlife dealer. So I kept his junk and cut him loose with a promise that I'd be back to nail his skinny, leather-clad black ass if Jamal Watson wasn't my man. I was betting that his information was good, given the stakes and the fact that a year earlier he'd saved his own skin by ratting out Big Sly, his own brother, during a homicide investigation.

The day was getting late, so I drove straight to the projects before darkness ushered in the nightly insanity. To find Jamal's hangout, I shelled out a five-spot to a couple of kids who were throwing rocks at one of the last surviving streetlights on Taylor Street. It seems that Jamal hadn't cultivated much fidelity among his friends, because when the red light on the unmarked police car announced my arrival at Jamal's favorite alley, it looked like cockroaches scrambling for the baseboards when the kitchen light comes on. But Jamal wasn't going anywhere fast between his Jesus boots and the purple dashiki that hung down to his knees, just in case his footwear wasn't enough of a hindrance. Catching him was mostly a matter of letting the rest of them escape.

Jamal was more defiant than smart, a common shortcoming in amateur militants. All it took was for me to mock the ALF by calling it "a bunch of chump revolutionaries" and Jamal came on like I'd called his mother a hooker, which wouldn't have been a bad guess. Knowing he was connected, I got down to business. There was a damp chill in the air, and I could sense that the fog was rolling in. That was fine for the most part, as it would muffle my interrogation. I half-worried that the fog might make some of the hoods a bit braver when their pal needed help, although they hadn't shown any loyalty when I arrived. His Afro made him nearly a foot taller than me, but I took care of that with a solid shot to his scrawny gut. When he finished puking up his dinner, I dragged him to his feet. The stench of his vomit mixed with the smell of rotting garbage. The moisture in the air trapped these odors in the alley, providing our own vile fogbank.

"What was that for, man?" he asked between gasps.

"For lying to me."

"I've been straight with you. I was just hanging with some brothers, minding my own business."

"Tell me Jamal, does your business include ALF?"

"Not sayin."

I delivered a sharp right to his ribs and a left jab to his mouth—just enough to split his lip and keep my finger from popping out of joint, a legacy from my Golden Gloves days. I did most of my hard hitting outside of the ring with my right.

"Shit, man," he mumbled, grabbing his side with one hand and using the other to wipe the blood from his mouth. "I won't jive you. I know some brothers with connections."

"Very good, Jamal. But I think you know more than that."

"Like what, man?"

"Like where a little Chinese girl is stashed."

"I don't know nuthin' about no chink."

A hook to Jamal's ear made him squeal in pain. The stakes were high and the light was fading, so I followed up by smashing his nose. He started to reach up to his face, then stepped back with rage in his eyes and took a wild swing at me. I ducked and his punch glanced off my head. I put an end to that nonsense with a shot to his solar plexus. As he writhed on the ground trying to take a breath, I knelt beside him.

"Jamal," I whispered into his intact ear, "I'm tired of you jacking me around. There's a kid who's going to die without her medicine. Your pissant pals have her and you know where."

"Fuck you, pig," he wheezed.

"You want to do this the hard way, eh?" I grabbed him by the front of his dashiki, which was now splattered with blood from his nose, lifted him to his feet, and slammed him into the brick wall. I was faring much better than Jamal, but I wasn't enjoying myself. It wasn't a fair fight given my training. And I had no doubt that Jamal had been dealt a crummy hand by life, but how he played his cards was his call. There was a black kid from the Potrero projects who my father hired to clean up the warehouse in the afternoons. Willy worked hard and had a shot at making something of himself, a long shot maybe, but there're no guarantees. Jamal had made his own decisions and now he had to account for them.

&

A car drove by the end of the alley, and I turned to see if it meant trouble. I figured Jamal's friends might have screwed up their courage in the form of a zip gun. In the fading light, I was relieved to see that the car was a newer-model Caddie. Probably just a lost tourist, but the passing car reminded me that I needed to get the information out of Jamal, and my ass out of the alley, before my luck ran out.

"Jamal, I don't have all night. And I think you know where she is." My shot to his midriff would've put him back on the ground, but I held him up.

"You can't do this," he moaned. "I have my rights." Another blow to the same spot made it clear that his rights were not at issue. He moaned and I let him crumple.

"Tell me where she is, Jamal. Or so help me, you'll be ALF's first martyr." His gaze seemed to lock on a pile of empty liquor bottles across the alley. I guessed he was thinking about his chances of making it to one of them and converting it into a weapon, versus dying in this filthy place. Death won out. Gritting his teeth against the pain and rage, he spat, "Hunters Point. Fitch Street warehouse."

I told him he'd done the right thing, maybe the only one in his pitiful life. In any case, it was the last right thing, because Jamal Watson was found dead in the alley the next morning. By then, a little girl was back with her family. An hour after I radioed in the location, federal agents along with San Francisco's finest had surrounded the warehouse. The ALF soldiers had less guts than Jamal and surrendered without a shot being fired. My regret about how I'd extracted the information from Jamal was balanced by knowing that the police had not betrayed Mr. Wang's trust. But my luck had come to an end.

At first, nobody asked too much about how I came by the information. However, the car that had driven by during my interrogation had been occupied not by a lost tourist but by one of the city's Board of Supervisors inspecting the projects with a professional do-gooder from one of the bleeding-heart organizations who feel a need to save the poor, redwoods, seals, and other victims of "the system." They'd seen me working over Jamal and written down my license plate. When IAD interrogated me, I tried the "resisting arrest" ploy. But since I hadn't gotten around to arresting him, my story didn't hold water. I suggested that maybe somebody else had killed Jamal for cooperating with me, but the coroner concluded he'd bled to death from a ruptured spleen. And the witnesses recounted my punching him in the abdomen.

When the commissioner came to see me, I knew the jig was up. I told him I hadn't meant to kill Jamal, but I could live with trading the life of a street punk for that of an innocent kid. Besides, kidnapping is a capital offense, so I had just moved along justice a bit faster than the courts might have. We both knew that Jamal would probably never have seen the inside of a gas chamber, but I thought it was a valid point anyway. I'd traded my career for a little girl's life, and I told him I'd do it again. He said that just between us, he'd make the same deal. Then he sighed, looked me in the eye, and said that he couldn't provide me with cover on this one. I was a lost cause beyond even the powers of St. Jude.

But the commissioner was a good man and cut a deal with those who wanted me tried for murder. If I'd resign from the force and plead guilty to involuntary manslaughter, they'd figure that justice had been done. The district attorney wasn't keen on prosecuting a cop who'd saved a kid from a bunch of militants, and the do-gooders didn't figure that Jamal would emerge during a trial as a poster child for downtrodden blacks. When I was given a suspended sentence, the *Chronicle* ran the headline "Killer of Black Youth Set Free." A few protesters marched on City Hall, just four blocks from where the luck of the Irish had delivered Li'l Sly a month earlier.

I did my best to maintain a low profile, and the righteous activists were soon busy chasing after new affronts by the Man. I picked up work with Packard & Thomas Investigative Agency. Cy and Al had been first-rate co-operators when I'd been on the force, so we had a good working relationship. With my record, I couldn't qualify for a private investigator's license, so they mostly used me for surveillance. I put away a tank car's worth of cold coffee sitting outside apartments, houses, and businesses waiting for husbands, wives, and partners to arrive or leave. I put on twenty pounds watching my fellow humans cheating on each other. But it paid the bills, and I managed to hang on to my house. That, along with my record collection and insect boxes, kept me happy enough for a couple of years.

After my father died, I quit the detective agency and took over the family business. I liked the surveillance work that Cy and Al had given me. Some days it almost felt like I was a cop again. But my mother and brother needed help, and I could make a lot more money exterminating pests than watching people.

Chapter Eleven

The drive over to Berkeley at the end of the day was soothing, despite the snarled traffic on the Bay Bridge. I'd spent a hectic afternoon meeting with customers and drumming up business. So listening to a bit of Vivaldi on KDFC—even with the old truck's tinny speakers—put me at ease. Finding Laurie Odum's house wasn't difficult. Spruce Street climbs the hills east of the UC Berkeley campus, the prices going up with the elevation. Her house was about halfway to the top. College professors were doing better than I thought.

The house was a Spanish-style number, complete with red tile roof, stucco walls, and a courtyard plastered with those colorful tiles that Mexicans produce for about a penny each and decorators sell for a buck a pop. I went through the wrought-iron gate and, not seeing a doorbell, I used the ornate knocker. I heard voices from inside and waited. A cute kid pulled open the massive door. She looked up at me with jet-black eyes as if I were to introduce myself. So I did. The girl was polite, but I could see an impish spark in her. Our pleasant exchange was interrupted by the arrival of a heavyset woman with a beautiful olive complexion.

"Meester Riley, please come in," she said while gently moving the little girl aside. "Marissa, go downstairs and start the next load of laundry."

"Sí, Mama," the child answered and headed off with the half-skipping of a kid who didn't know how crappy it was to be poor.

"Meesus Odum is on the deck. Come with me, pleeze." She'd come up from Mexico not long ago—or so I figured from her thick accent. We walked through the tiled living room, which had Navajo rugs hanging from the walls and geometrically patterned pottery lining the shelf over an enormous fireplace. I can't understand why people put carpets on their walls and buy pots that just sit uselessly on shelves.

"Mr. Riley, so good of you to come out to see me on such short notice." A petite woman with an intense manner got up from the dark wooden table, on which there was a glass of red wine and a scattering of papers and file folders. "Thank you, Maria. Now please take care of the laundry first and then attend to the upstairs cleaning." The maid nodded obediently and went back into the house.

"It's no problem, Mrs. Odum," I answered, shaking her hand, which was thin and soft. She wasn't exactly attractive, but there was an engaging intensity in her narrow face, hazel eyes, and shoulder-length mousy brown hair. And, although I could just hear Carol scolding me, it didn't hurt the whole package that Mrs. Odum filled out her turquoise blouse nicely.

"Paul's clothes were delivered this morning by a courier service from the hotel. I don't know why I want them washed so badly. Maybe I'm trying to cleanse the sense of death from his things." She looked away from me and toward a sunset that was growing redder by the minute. The deck was perched on the hillside with a stunning view of the Bay across to downtown San Francisco, where the lights were just starting to come on in the buildings.

"I'm sorry for your loss," I said as we sat down at the table.

"Yes, of course," she answered almost dismissively, snapping back into the moment. Her intensity returned and she took control of the conversation. "Paul and I were soul mates. I know, people say that all the time, but our relationship was not merely about romance and bliss. It was based on a shared passion for justice."

"Justice?" I asked, knowing that not-quite-legal Mexican maids make a buck an hour and child labor is illegal.

"We both saw that the earth is dying. Our love of the planet fueled our love for one another. And our love was natural, as humans were meant to be. Without claiming to own the other person or control their body." I must've looked confused, so she was more explicit. "We had an open marriage in accord with natural love."

"I see," I said, but I didn't. Infidelity and righteousness seemed a strange foundation for a marriage. But whatever turns your crank.

"I chaired the 'Save the Redwoods' coalition. These trees have so much wisdom. I've heard their cries, and I would do anything to protect these magnificent beings."

"They sure are something," I offered, not quite knowing how to respond to a woman who could hear plants. She glared at me. "Really, I understand what you're saying," I tried. "I collect insects and most people don't know how fantastic they are."

"You kill creatures as a hobby, Mr. Riley? I don't see how this could allow you to connect with the spirituality of a redwood grove."

"I wouldn't put it quite that way." I wasn't off to a good start, so getting back on track with why the hell I was there seemed a wise move. "And what about your husband? Was he protecting the redwoods, too?"

"Paul took a similar path in his defense of Mother Nature." She took a sip of her wine and gathered up the papers on the table, mostly legal documents and insurance forms having to do with Odum's death. Dying in this country is no simple matter.

"Through his work at the university?"

"Yes. His research concerned developing new methods for restoring forests. He was replanting the lungs of our planet. He abhorred the forest industry, but his activism was directed at those who are trying to poison the earth."

"So, he was figuring out how to grow trees in his day job and battling polluters after work?"

"That's a rather flippant description, Mr. Riley. But perhaps that's what I might expect from a man who impales sentient creatures as a pastime." It was clear that we weren't going to be pals, but it was also evident that she needed me for something.

"Sorry, just trying to put things into terms I can understand. Please go on."

"Shortly after he was hired at Berkeley as an ecologist, Paul was studying the effects of insecticides on bird populations. A farmer failed to warn him that a field had been sprayed with chlordane. Do you know what that is?"

"Not really," I lied. I had a couple drums of the stuff in the warehouse for termite control, but I saw no need to add "planet-killer" to my dossier. She must've known I ran an extermination business already, so there was no point in aggravating her.

60

"It's a synthetic insecticide. These compounds kill anything with a nervous system."

"Sounds bad," I agreed. Of course, water kills creatures that need to breathe. Anything is deadly in sufficient quantity, and a lot more people drown than die of poisoning.

"It nearly killed Paul. He was on a ventilator in the hospital for weeks. Ever since then, he was hypersensitive to all man-made chemicals. Cleansers, soaps, perfumes, and every sort of fertilizer and pesticide. We ate only organically grown fruits and vegetables. We even installed a distillation unit in the house to purify the water."

"That must've been tough on you two." A water-and-salad diet would be a miserable life. But apparently toxins made by yeast were safe, as she was evidently enjoying her glass of wine. Perhaps alcohol passed muster, or maybe she'd lapsed with her husband gone. I might be able to make it for quite a while on my mother's oatcakes, potato farl, and cabbage soup if I could wash it down with a glass of single malt.

"No, not really. It brought us closer to the earth and one another. But even with these adjustments, Paul still suffered from terrible pain in his joints, intense headaches, and even seizures. Our herbalist helped him keep the seizures under control with valerian root and motherwort. But they'd still strike when he was stressed and didn't take his chamomile-and-passionflower tea to calm his nervous system."

"That's probably what happened to him in LA, eh?"

"I don't think so."

"Interesting. So, what do you think happened?"

"That's why I asked you to come here. Paul had taken a courageous and bold stand against the agrichemical companies. He was angry about what they'd done to him and so many others, including farm workers." So their sense of justice extended to other humans and not just redwoods and robins. I was relieved. "Paul provided expert testimony in lawsuits, filed briefs with the courts on cases of pesticide poisoning, and wrote extensively about how greedy corporate giants control the government and corrupt public agencies. He had enemies."

"You believe a chemical company had him killed?"

Before Laurie could answer, Maria came onto the deck. And she was in a panic.

Chapter Twelve

The maid wrung her hands and stammered, "I'm so sorry to interrupt, Mrs. Odum."

"What is it, Maria?" The question dripped with annoyance.

"Mrs. Odum, Marissa is sick. She is dizzy and trembling. I've cleaned up after her, but I must take her home. I don't know what is wrong."

"It's probably just the stomach flu, Maria. Is the laundry done or will I need to finish it?" She was clearly unhappy about the possibility of having to take on domestic chores. I guessed that the thought of a kid puking in her elegant house wasn't helping.

"I will come back tomorrow to finish. My sister can look after Marissa if she's still sick."

Laurie Odum waved her hand toward the maid as if to brush her out of the house, and sent her on her way. Apparently the environmentalist's compassion for native trees didn't translate well to immigrant girls.

Mrs. Odum took the chance to offer me a drink, which I accepted. While she was inside, I took the opportunity to look through the papers on the table. I learned long ago that people tell you only as much of a story as fits their purposes. She returned with a surprisingly decent whiskey—a bit too sweet for my taste but quite smooth. Probably one of Bushmills' mid-range blends.

"Now, where were we?" she asked, knowing fully that I was anxious to hear her theory of Paul Odum's death.

"I had just asked whether you thought the corporate bosses in the pesticide industry had taken out a hit on your husband."

"You can be brutally direct, Mr. Riley."

"I like to cut to the chase, Mrs. Odum. So if it's not too insensitive, your husband was not well. Why do you suspect that his death was not natural—or at least a result of his unfortunate condition?"

"I've seen what the chemical death brokers will do. The military-industrial complex will crush anyone in its way. Paul received death threats during court cases that he'd been involved with. I have no doubt that the corporations were trying to intimidate him." Her voice began to quiver, and I felt a pang of sympathy. Whatever her nutty ideas about the souls of trees, she'd lost her husband.

"Mrs. Odum, I don't want to add to your grief by doubting your story. But these corporate giants seem able and willing to trounce their enemies in court. I'm not so sure they'd resort to assassination."

"Any corporation that would slaughter a thousand-year-old tree to make picnic benches or poison a flock of doves to protect a cotton field would not hesitate to kill a human being. You've never dealt with them behind closed doors. They are evil, and if Paul got in their way and couldn't be beaten through our crooked legal system, they'd do whatever it took." She had a point. Greed had certainly been one of the most common motives in the murders I'd investigated. Most people killed for love or money, and only one of these mattered to corporate America.

"You sound like you might know something more that you're not telling me."

"Not really. Well, not exactly." She took a sip and stared into the wineglass. She had a way of bouncing between righteous anger and pathetic vulnerability. "It's just that Paul had been secretive of late. He usually told me about his projects, but he hadn't shared what he was working on for the last few weeks. Paul would spend hours every evening in his study. I think he had something important in the works, and maybe the corporations found out."

"That's a pretty imaginative leap. But I suppose it's possible." In my experience, complicated theories were usually wrong. Most people die in pretty simple ways. But I'd come across a few truly convoluted murders, so I couldn't dismiss the idea out of hand. "Let's say your suspicions are worth investigating. Why me?"

"I am a deeply intuitive person. In fact, I've cultivated this aspect of my being through meditation and herbal catalysts. I feel in my soul that Paul was killed, and I believe that you have the skills needed to find his killer."

"Hang on, Mrs. Odum."

"If we are going to be forming a partnership of sorts, you should call me Laurie."

"Okay, Laurie. And for that matter skip the 'Mister' and just call me 'Riley.' But let's not get ahead of ourselves in terms of what I can offer. I don't know what Howard told you when he dropped off the car, but I'm not a licensed investigator."

"Howard said you came across as very clever. He thought you probably had some background in law enforcement."

I nodded, thinking that the kid was pretty perceptive given the circumstances. "Yeah," I said, "I was a cop years ago."

"That's fine, even preferable. I don't need somebody with the endorsement of the corrupt system that governs us. I need cold-blooded competence."

"And you figure I'm your man?"

"You're not a particularly nice man. You spray poisons for a living and impale animals as a hobby. But I can tell from our conversation that you don't bullshit." The intense persona was back in spades. "I don't have to like you. It's enough that my instincts tell me that you can be trusted and that you deliver." She paused and her face softened. "Now then, can you help me?"

"I can't officially conduct an investigation, but I've sometimes provided 'pest management services' to people. And pests come in many forms."

"A lovely way of framing our prospective venture. And now it's my turn to be blunt. A solution to my husband's murder would be worth a great deal to me. I've lost my soul mate and I need to know who did it. I'll probably never get justice, but I need resolution." She finished her glass of wine and stared directly at me. The moment of truth had come.

&

The sun had set and the afterglow was giving way to night. A cool dampness had risen up the hills from the Bay. This was a passionate woman and her intensity was alluring. She was a bit wacky but at least she believed in something and had the guts to act on it. That's more than you can say for a whole lot of people with money who just float through life like jellyfish in the Bay.

"What's your offer?" I asked.

"Ten thousand dollars. But it's time-limited." That would keep Tommy's Fund going for a year. But I had an ace up my sleeve, a card that might put the program on its feet for good. First, however, I needed to know her conditions.

"Assuming that Paul was killed—and we're a long way from that conclusion—when do you need the proof?"

"Two weeks."

"That's incredibly fast, you understand. There's no evidence other than your vague impression that he was murdered. I'm starting with just about zero."

"Riley, the reason I'm willing to hire you is because I think you are a rare creature in this world. I'm sick of dealing with inept people telling me that solutions will take time. Bureaucrats, lawyers, and politicians say they'll change policies but 'it'll take time.'" She made quote marks with her fingers. "That's a code phrase for 'it'll never happen.' And it won't happen because these people are fucking incompetent." She was almost yelling now, and a dog started barking from across the fence.

"I get your point," I replied, hoping to keep our conversation from becoming neighborhood gossip. She dropped her voice and brushed the hair back from her face.

"People who know what they're doing get the job done quickly and efficiently using whatever means are necessary. And Riley, it strikes me that you are the sort who can bring effective—and perhaps unconventional—approaches to bear on a problem."

"So, I get two weeks to name the killer. And if I come up dry?"

"I'll pay you a thousand dollars for your time and hire a conventional detective agency. They probably won't be able to do any better, but I'm not going to give up on finding Paul's killer."

"I realize that you have cultivated your intuitive powers, but my experience suggests that it's a long shot that there's any killer to be found."

"Are you willing to try?"

"Maybe. Let's talk about money."

"My offer is very generous."

"Yes it is. But tell me a bit more about your husband's finances. This is quite a house for a university professor."

"Paul and I never spoke much about money. He provided a beautiful place for us to live and I never lacked for support in my battles against the timber industry and their government lackeys. I didn't ask where the money came from. I assume that he received some consulting fees for his expert testimony and supplemented his salary during the summer with grant funds." In other words, spoiled women ask few questions. Can't really blame them, except when things fall apart it's hard to generate much sympathy. And it was time to assure her my competence was, as she described, cold-blooded.

"And he left you a rather substantial life insurance policy, eh?"

"I don't see how that's any business of yours."

"Oh, it's very much my business if you want me to take this case. You see, I need to know as much as possible about him if there's any hope of determining whether he was murdered."

"I'm afraid I don't understand."

"Sure you do, Laurie. The papers you were working on when I arrived make it crystal clear. I don't doubt that Paul was your soul mate, but his death also means a financial windfall." Her jaw tightened, along with the tendons in her neck. I figured a slap was coming, but her icy stare was more vicious.

"I was mistaken. You can't be trusted." She began to sweep up the files as if I had disappeared. Then she looked up, seemingly surprised I was still there. "I rescind my offer. Please leave."

"Now slow down. You're half right. You shouldn't trust me until and unless we cut a deal. After that, my loyalty is unconditional. And as for my getting results, you're absolutely right."

"I should have expected as much from your sort. What is your counteroffer?"

"If Paul was murdered, it would be an accidental death and you'd be entitled to double indemnity. I think that works out to three hundred grand. I'll take half."

"You're a greedy son of a bitch."

"Not really. If it'll make you feel better, I don't want you to pay me a dime. Just make an anonymous donation to Tommy's Fund at St. Teresa's Church across the Bay." The $150,000 would endow the center and put it on firm footing for the rest of my brother's life.

"What a loutish, greedy, and complicated man you are, Riley. Underhanded tactics in the interest of charity—that's rather perverse. I won't ask why you want it played this way, but it makes your twisted offer palatable."

"Sometimes we can't make the world better by being nice. You're a strong woman who knows what she wants and how to get it. Do we have a deal?"

"You're a nasty opponent. And I trust that you'll be as valuable an ally. You have two weeks."

"Excellent." I knocked back the last of my drink and leaned forward. "Now I need two things from you and I won't bother you again until I return to deliver your answer or to collect my consolation prize."

"I sincerely hope you don't disappoint me. What do you need?" she asked impatiently, clearly wanting to be done with our conversation.

"First, when your husband's body is brought back here by the funeral home, don't have it embalmed, buried, or cremated. I'm pretty sure the LA coroner will sign the death certificate without an autopsy. Between the recession reducing staff and increasing crime there's a backlog of bodies. If Paul's death can be reasonably ruled as being due to natural causes, that's the way it'll be played. And I don't want potential evidence lost until we know what's what."

"Okay, the funeral director is an old friend of the family. I can surely get him to agree without having to give an involved explanation."

"Great. And I need to get a handle on who understood him and might've known what he was up to. I need to start somewhere."

"He wasn't on good terms with most of the faculty. His colleagues were petty like most academics, and they generally resented his research success. Most of them were ivory tower purists who thought that his environmental advocacy precluded his being an objective scientist."

"And his environmental work was pretty much on his own, or at least secretive, from what I gather. So, where do I begin? Who was close to him?"

"Start with his graduate students. He was a wonderful mentor, and they adored him. If anybody could provide some insight, it would be them."

"I've met Howard. Who else should I track down?"

"There's John Holling. He's almost done with his doctorate, so I think he'll be able to finish under another professor. And then there's Jen Tansley.

Jen is in her second year, so she'll be in a difficult spot. Go easy on them. They've worked so hard to please Paul, and I know they'll be feeling lost."

I thanked Laurie and saw myself out. On the drive back to San Francisco, the reflected lights of downtown dancing in the Bay mirrored my internal jitters. I doubted that I'd earn the big money, but the possibility had me on edge. I needed the detached focus that I'd cultivated when working a case on the force. Not so relaxed as to be inattentive, but in the calm zone where I could see and hear things that were not meant to be noticed.

And the best way to dispel the excess tension was a hard workout. When I got home, I changed into my sweats and headed down the hill to Marty's Gym, squeezed between the warehouses along 17th Street. The place was raw, dimly lit, frigid in the winter, stifling in the summer, and smelled of sweat and Marty's cigars.

It was heaven.

CHAPTER THIRTEEN

When I walked through the door of Goat Hill Extermination on Friday morning, Carol greeted me with a smile and then a scowl. "Put your hands over your head, Riley," she demanded.

"What's up, gorgeous?" She was looking luscious in a plaid wool skirt, and a forest-green sweater vest stretched over a starched white blouse. A woman doesn't need fancy clothes or makeup to be beautiful. And I was also hoping to distract her with my aesthetic assessment and evoke a short lecture rather than an inspection. It didn't work.

"Don't you 'gorgeous' me. Lift your arms, you stupid galoot." I got my hands up to my shoulders. They wouldn't go any higher. I grinned stupidly at her, knowing I was in trouble.

"Christ, Riley. When will you learn that you're not in your twenties? You can't treat your body like you're still a kid. Those guys at Marty's are in fighting shape."

"How'd you know I was at Marty's?" I'd gotten to know the place during my adolescent venture into Golden Gloves. Marty had managed to work me into a decent fighter, and he still enjoyed needling me. But his real joy was watching the fights, as long as they ended decisively. He loved the purity of a knockout—no referee making a call, no judges inventing a score, just one man's domination of another. I understood his desire for a place where things were clear and simple, a strange kind of sanctuary in a world that seemed to have more gray—and less black or white—every day.

"Hell, you're there two or three times a week. But you're not usually dumb enough to cripple yourself. You walked in here about as gracefully as a ninety-year-old man with gout. That was my first hint that you'd pushed too hard again." She was right. I'd alternated bouts of jump roping with working the heavy bag for an hour until I was drenched, and then I'd played sparring partner for one of Marty's prospects—a tough kid with a wickedly fast jab from the Potrero projects.

"I'll be okay. Just a little stiff."

"The old codger convinced you to serve as a punching bag for one of his up-and-comers, right?"

"Maybe." She was good, but maybe the puffiness under my eye where the kid landed a straight right was her second hint.

"I'd give you a rubdown, but it'd only frustrate you, seeing as you're both a sore and dirty old man."

"Maybe just work my shoulders a little?" I pleaded. Carol had incredibly strong hands, and I could certainly behave myself.

"Sit here, you dumbass." She got up and gestured to her office chair. I dropped into the seat and rested my forearms on her desk. She began to dig in, and a mixture of pain and pleasure flooded my body.

I would have been in better shape in the morning if I hadn't stopped by O'Donnell's Pub after my workout. But I was feeling drained after two hours in the gym, and I wanted to grab a bite and a drink.

Brian, the pub's owner and weeknight bartender, provided a running commentary on the Giants game which played without sound on the television at the end of the bar. He was an old friend of the family who'd helped my father get the loan to start Goat Hill Extermination. Brian didn't have much money, but he was highly respected in the neighborhood for being a discerning judge of character, so his vouching for my father at the bank made the difference. He was also Tommy's godfather, a relationship that I knew weighed heavily on Brian. He and Cynthia had a gaggle of their own kids, mostly grown but still struggling in one way or another. There was no money or time for Brian to contribute to Tommy's care. He always asked about Tommy, so I knew that he thought he should be doing something more in his role. Catholic guilt is a real burden, which is one reason I left the Church—it was worth exchanging the sure thing of a happier life for the long shot of eternal damnation. Last night I assured him that everything was all right, but I knew he'd be devastated if St. Teresa's had to shut down the daycare and leave my mother without help for Tommy.

I had a burger and fries and washed them down with a beer. Rejuvenated, I decided to pleasantly draw out my evening with dessert—a Bushmills sixteen-year-old single malt which set me back as much as the dinner. I no longer drank to get drunk—one of the benefits of leaving the stress of the force behind—so I drank less of the better stuff. But I also knew that my dehydrated body wouldn't appreciate the indulgence. I was right, which meant a headache and heartburn added to the rest of my pains the next morning. Nothing that a couple of Tylenol with an Alka-Seltzer chaser couldn't fix.

"Riley, are you dead or just not listening?"

I'd lapsed into a near coma, probably from the surge of lactic acid released from my muscles through Carol's kneading. "Sorry, babe, I just drifted off."

"Drop the pathetic attempt to get on my good side. I'm still pissed at you. Acting like a teenage kid." She dug her knuckles into the base of my neck, which made me wince in sweet agony.

"Christ, Carol," I gasped. "I think you're enjoying my pain."

"It'd be better if I was into S&M, but I'm not kinky—just gay. Now that I have your attention, what are you going to do about Isaac?"

"What do you suggest?" She'd obviously been talking to me about the kid, while I'd been in la-la land.

"You weren't listening, you oaf." Again with the neck to punctuate her annoyance. "Pay attention this time. I said that you needed to talk to Larry and Dennis or things are going to start unraveling. Now get your sorry ass out of my chair and see what you can do other than pretending to be a boxer."

"On my way." I got up to a swirling spell of lightheadedness. I managed to stagger down the hallway and into the warehouse.

"Whazzup, boss?" Dennis said as I pushed through the doors. Larry added, "You look like hell."

"I hit the gym a little hard last night, but I'm feeling good." I wasn't lying. The aches and pains focused me on the present, and I was ready to concentrate on finding Paul Odum's killer—if such a person existed. But first I needed to make sure the business would run smoothly while I was working the case. "Carol tells me that Isaac isn't shaping up like we hoped."

"I went out with him yesterday afternoon," Larry said. "The kid goes through the motions, but folks expect more. They can get a show of force cheaper with the big companies."

"Hate to say it, but Larry's right, boss," Dennis added. "Isaac is more interested in sketching shit in that notebook of his. He's not bad at drawing, but you can't kill pests with a pencil."

"The way I see it," Larry continued, "the kid doesn't have his heart in the job. He doesn't take pride in his poison." Dennis nodded. They were proud of their work. It wasn't the sort of job that won anybody public acclaim. But the two of them were very good at what they did. They understood the pests and the poisons—which is more than you could say for our corporate competitors.

"Where is he now?" I asked.

"He's out at the Morgans' place. It figured to be a simple job from what the old lady described, and we're slammed with a backlog of restaurant and warehouse treatments. This warm weather has the flies and roaches on a tear."

"I'll go out and have a talk with him. After that, I need to work on a project that'll take me out of the office most of the time for a couple of weeks. I know the timing's bad. But I'm asking you guys to see if you can bring him along. Maybe between my pep talk and your cutting him some slack, he'll come around. I think he's a good kid."

"Yeah, maybe he'll see the light. Is the project a big deal?" Larry was as much concerned as curious. And considering how long he'd been part of the family business, I owed him and Dennis an explanation. Besides, I hadn't had any great revelations on the Odum case, and I figured they might come up with something I was missing.

"It could be. If things go right, I may have Tommy set up for a long time. But there's a lot that has to fall into place. Which reminds me, what would you guys think about finding a fresh corpse in a hotel room with a bunch of dead flies?"

"Weird, man," Dennis offered. "Unless somebody had sprayed the room."

"It'd be like finding a pile of corpses at the end of the buffet line at Wyatt's Cafeteria," Larry observed in his sardonic way. "Either the old folks' home dropped off a busload of geezers for their farewell dinner or there was something nasty in the mac-and-cheese."

"My money's on the mac-and-cheese," Dennis observed, his brow deeply furrowed as he searched for another explanation.

"Good bet," Larry nodded. "Why's it matter, boss?"

"Just trying to put some puzzle pieces in place. And you two have been more helpful than you might imagine. Now, can you handle Isaac for a while longer?"

"Yessir, I be used to carrying the load. The Man has kept us brothers down for so long, it's part of our nature," Dennis answered in his best slave dialect to break the tension.

"Well, as long as you black brothers are used to the Man giving orders, how 'bout you take the Foodway warehouse job and I'll work the China-town gigs." Larry smiled mischievously, knowing that he'd probably score a free lunch at one of the Chinese restaurants.

As I headed out to the back door to the compound, I heard Dennis replying, "Sheeit, you honkeys are always shafting us black folk." I knew the two of them would try to work with Isaac, but they didn't have the time or inclination to babysit him. I figured it'd help for me to aim the kid in the right direction.

Chapter Fourteen

My reliable rust heap started up without a complaint. The warm fall weather agreed with the old truck. I headed out to the Morgans' house. They were a longtime customer that my father had landed not long after starting the business. The Morgans were wealthy, and from their recommendations we'd managed to build quite a list of customers in the Nob Hill area. Even rich people have problems with pests, especially when old Victorian mansions are built over dark, wet crawlspaces.

When I arrived, Mrs. Morgan let me in and told me that Isaac was in the conservatory at the rear of the house. She took me through the mahogany-floored entryway, down a hallway lined with Mr. Morgan's photographs of the mountain peaks he'd conquered, through the study which had more books than I suspected the Morgans could've read in their lifetimes, and into the glassed-in room that was Mrs. Morgan's pride and joy. She started pointing out the newest additions to her orchid collection, when she caught herself. "Oh dear, Mr. Riley, I am a prattling old dame, aren't I?"

"Not at all, Mrs. Morgan. I collect insects, so I appreciate your fascination with exotic flowers."

"You're too kind. And I know you're also a busy man, so I'll leave you with your helper to sort out those awful ants." Then she took me gently by the arm and whispered, "Mr. Riley, could you please send one of your other people next time. I'm afraid my husband wasn't too happy with this young man. He's not so fond of 'them.' I'm sure you understand." She headed back into the main house, leaving me with Isaac.

"How's it going?" I asked while he put down a thin spray of insecticide using a handheld pump.

"Fine, except for having to work for an anti-Semite. The old man answered the door, took one look at me, turned around, and walked back into the house. He left me standing there like a piece of trash until his wife came and showed me in." The kid did have a helluva nose and wavy black hair, but I hadn't known that Mr. Morgan had a problem with Jews.

"No sense stewing about it. You can't change them, so just do your job well."

"That sounds fine coming from a Gentile. You don't know what it's like to be a Jew. People driving by shout, 'Hey Hymie, you dirty Christ-killer,' or 'Go back to your own neighborhood, Yid.' I'm sick of ignorant bigots."

"Ok, you're a kike and I'm a mick. The Irish weren't exactly greeted with open arms when we showed up. All that 'Give me your tired, your poor, your huddled masses' stuff was a great come-on for cheap labor."

"Yeah, but your people didn't suffer a Holocaust. Nobody was out to exterminate you." Isaac was a spunky fellow, I'll give him that. But I wasn't going to buy into his self-pity.

"What is this? Some sort of a sick contest? Okay, you win. Your people got screwed big time. But all that matters in my world is whether I can count on a person. And I don't have much use for a whiny kid with lots of excuses." Until then, I hadn't laid it out to him in direct terms, but if there was any hope of his working out, Isaac had to know the deal.

"You don't know me or what I've gone through."

"I know enough about you. And I know that everyone's got a reason to complain. Hell, Dennis is black and Larry's a Vietnam vet. It's not like the world is giving them a big hug. And whether you figured it out or not, Carol's a lesbian. I got a nigger, a baby killer, and a dyke working for me."

"Sounds like you're something of a bigot yourself."

"Like I said, I judge people by what they deliver. If you give me an honest day's work and take pride in the quality of your product, I don't care if you're a Jew, an Arab, or a goddamn space alien."

"I'm sorry, Riley, it's just that the old codger set me off. It gets tiring." Isaac's bluster had waned and he looked spent.

"Listen kid, I get it. Life isn't fair and nobody said it would be. But from what I can see, you ended up with more than your fair share of smarts. It's

time to start using your head to solve problems instead of making excuses."
We'd both said our piece. It was time to get to work for the Morgans, what-
ever their prejudices. I gestured toward the baseboard along the glass panes.
"What're we looking at?"

"An infestation of flying ants," he answered without glancing down. I
bent over and plucked a specimen from the few dozen insects that were
staggering around. The poison had begun to do its job.

"I don't think so, Isaac."

"Why not?"

"Tell me what you know from the training manual."

"I read that ants often emerge in huge numbers after a rain. And it rained
here a few days ago."

"Good. Now look closely at these insects." I held my captive up to his
face. "Tell me whether you think this is an ant."

He squinted. "I see what you mean. It doesn't have the skinny waist like
an ant should."

"So what do you figure we've got here?"

"Termites?"

"Damn straight, kid. Now you're thinking, not just spraying. That's what
people pay us for. The rains bring out winged termites as well as ants. They're
all waiting at this time of year to start new colonies." In that moment, I
flashed back to Paul Odum's hotel room. That nagging sense of something
askew returned, and this time I wasn't going to let go of it. I stared into
space, recalling the details. The winged ants along the glass door. That was
the other piece that didn't fit. What the hell were they doing in the room?
Ants aren't attracted to dead bodies. Isaac gave me a strange look.

"You okay, Riley?"

"Yeah, Isaac, you just got me thinking about another customer. Where
were we?"

"The termites. Should I bother spraying? The queen will be down in the
wood under the greenhouse where the insecticide won't reach."

"Right again. I might just have to keep you. Here's the deal. Until I can get
Larry and Dennis out here for a foundation treatment, which takes a load
of experience and equipment, the Morgans will want to see some results. So
put down a barrier of insecticide to generate a body count and keep the ter-

mites from crawling all over the windows. I'll go tell Mrs. Morgan the good news and the bad news."

"Good news?"

"Yeah, her orchids are safe." I winked at Isaac and he seemed energized. I'd chewed his ass at the start, but that way he knew that my praise was genuine—not just happy fluff to make him think he was a 'valued employee.' I hate it when people pull that nonsense.

My father never gave gratuitous compliments, and he let me know when I screwed up. Like the time I sprayed a lady's house for flies. I was in high school and was just going through the motions to make some gas money. When he swung by to check on me, he looked at all the dead insects that had been clambering on the inside of the windows.

"So, what're you going to tell Miss Freeman?" he asked.

"That I solved her fly problem," I said.

"You treated the symptom, not the problem."

"What do you mean?"

"Those are fungus gnats, you knucklehead. They feed on the mold growing in the wet soil of her houseplants. If she doesn't water them so much, that'll put an end to the fungus and the gnats. And she won't be calling in a couple of weeks to tell me that the treatment didn't work."

His lesson stuck with me, especially when I was hitting the bottle while on the force. I'd wake up and take a handful of aspirin every morning. But I was just treating the symptom. Until I laid off the booze, the headaches were going to keep coming back. I probably should've quit entirely, but I'm no saint. Just a better sinner.

I told the Morgans that I'd have a crew out to treat for termites, and that it'd be pretty expensive. Mr. Morgan didn't flinch at the cost, but he asked who would be coming. I told him I'd send my most experienced technicians and left it at that. Isaac wouldn't be on that job, but I had no interest in giving Mr. Morgan the satisfaction of his bigotry.

&

I drove down Broadway toward Chinatown to grab some lunch. I picked out a bustling place on Hang Ah Street. The clatter of plates, the orders called out in Chinese, and the drone of pop music on a tinny radio blended into the background. I concentrate best when it's dead silent or chaotically noisy, and it's easier to find noise than quiet in the city. And I knew that people would be too busy to bother a guy looking at some glass vials while eating Sichuan chicken.

I'd taken the specimens that I'd collected from Odum's room out of the glove box and put them in my coat pocket before going into the House of Hong. I had to use a hand lens to be sure, but a close inspection revealed that the ants in the hotel room were not a species typically found inside of buildings. They were field ants that had probably emerged from the soil under shrubs that bordered the patio. I figured that after the rain, hundreds of them had poured out of the nest and dispersed. A few of them could've accidentally found their way into the room through the torn screen.

That all made sense, but according to Howard, the sliding glass door had been shut during the day. Even if they had forgotten to close it in the morning, the maid would've done so. In fact, the housekeeping staff kept closing my door, which I tried to leave open. And my room was on the third floor and opened onto a tiny balcony, so they'd surely not have left a guest's door open on the ground level. The flies obviously found their way into the room through the torn screen during the night, when the odor of death and filth rang the flies' dinner bell. But the ants wouldn't have been attracted to the stench, and in any case they weren't nocturnal.

I dug into my chicken, which was first-rate—fiery but not quite painful—and thought about what the ants might be telling me. Insects never lie. In fact, the six-legged bystanders make the best witnesses. And it pays to know where your witnesses come from. The difference between typical indoor ants and the field ants in Odum's room would be understandably lost on most people. But I had learned about the importance of small distinctions as a detective.

Like I'd told Tommy a couple nights ago, a rare butterfly stuck in the grille of a car had allowed us to catch a killer. What I'd left out of the bedtime story was that although the butterfly was a bit mutilated, it had looked and smelled much better than the building inspector when he was found. The dunes make for a challenging game of hide-and-seek, and I'd heard that the corpse had been found by following the stench of decomposition.

And something stank in Howard's story. I figured I needed to talk with his fellow students, John and Jen, but now I had some more questions for Howard. When it comes to getting at the truth, sometimes finding an ant on the carpet is just as good as being a fly on the wall.

CHAPTER FIFTEEN

I headed across the Bay to Berkeley, or as Larry calls it, Berserkly. Despite its politics, the university is first-rate. Mostly. Any college that offers courses in Bodies and Boundaries, Art and Meditation, Transcendental Peace Studies, and Black, Lesbian, and Womyn's Literature—all of which were listed in a recent article in the *Chronicle*—is a bit off its rocker. The traffic flowed reasonably well during the midafternoon, which was good because KDFC was playing classical guitar, which I don't particularly enjoy.

One of the advantages of driving a work truck is that the company logo usually allows me to park in restricted places without getting a ticket. Most cops cut some slack to construction and trade types, although an exterminator's truck in the granola capital of California was a riskier prospect than usual. I pulled into a "B permit only" zone along Durant Street, and put the "On Job" sign on the dashboard in the hope of some mercy. I'd been to the campus before, but I didn't know where to find the biology building. So I stopped to ask a group of long-haired students, who were holding antiwar signs on the plaza in front of a massive building at the gates to the campus.

They seemed stunned that I wanted simple directions rather than a political lecture. "Biology? Man, we're trying to find justice," one smartass carrying a "US out of Africa!" sign replied. He wore a black, red, and green headband and seemed quite taken with his cleverness. "Did you know that the United States government is providing arms to Somalia to prolong the killing fields of Africa?"

"Sounds bad. But can you tell me how to find the biology department?"

A spacey girl with a very tight "Stop the Killing" T-shirt answered, "The peaceful people of Ethiopia are being slaughtered on their own land." I nodded in my best imitation of sympathy, trying not to stare at what was jiggling under "Stop" and "Killing." This wasn't getting me anywhere. Fortunately a passing student overheard my question and suggested I try Hilgard or Mulford Hall.

I thanked him and started to walk away when the headband guy stepped in front of me and shouted, "Don't work for the Man, work for peace." A dopey-looking fellow with greasy blond hair and a pimply face was evidently emboldened and added, "Yeah, we're working for change."

I'd had enough. "Let's get clear on something, kid. What you're doing is standing in the sun, wasting your parents' money, holding a stupid sign, and making an ass of yourself. Instead of 'working for change' try *working* for a change. Once you've done some actual work, then we'll talk." I gave him a pat on the shoulder and headed through the archway onto campus. The protesters shouted slogans after me.

I should've just kept to myself without provoking the kids who had carved out a comfortable existence without being burdened with a job. But I held a special loathing for lazy bastards whose only effort went into figuring out how to avoid genuine labor and cut corners. Mostly because one of them had cost my father his life.

After Tommy had come home from the hospital, it was clear that expenses were going to be high. A father's first duty is to his family. So he'd been working weekends and taking some jobs in rough places. A lowlife landlord who owned a string of tenements had contracted him to spray for roaches because the city threatened to condemn the largest of his properties if the infestation wasn't brought under control. The sonofabitch hadn't lifted a hand to repair the place in years, just collected payments from the Housing Authority and rent from down-and-out folks who were hoping to stay dry and stash away a bit of money until they could find somewhere better to live.

On a Sunday afternoon, my father was heading down a dimly lit hallway with a heavy canister and spray hose when the bottom dropped out. The extra weight must've been enough to collapse the termite-riddled flooring. His leg plunged through the floorboard and became wedged. A nail had ripped open an artery, and he knew things were bad pretty quick. The splintered wood had him trapped, and he was losing blood fast.

Miss Cassie, a big black lady who I met afterward, took charge and told her nephew to call for help. A lot of people don't know that in run-down apartments, cockroaches seek out the warmth inside telephones, and their chewing and crapping destroys the inner workings. In any case, there wasn't a working phone in the building, so the kid ran a couple of blocks to a drug-store and called an ambulance. I suspect that rescue squads weren't much more enthusiastic about rushing into poor neighborhoods than the cops were when I was on the force.

By the time sirens wailed their way up the street, my father had bled to death. He died in the lap of Miss Cassie, who told him that everything was going to be all right. She was wrong, but that sort of faith must've sounded like my mother was there with him. I had to wonder about the wicked irony of my father being killed by a booby trap laid by termites in San Francisco, after avoiding landmines on the islands of the Pacific as he followed the American forces and battled mosquitoes.

I made my way toward a grassy opening amid the hodgepodge of architec-tural styles that made up the university. A sign said I was standing in Me-morial Glade, but it hardly felt like a mountain meadow. It was a lawn. The open space was surrounded by a monumental classical library, a modern ten-story block of concrete with rows of windows, and an old granite block building with a vestige of character. The most attractive things on the glade were the sunbathing co-eds. The Frisbee-tossing shirtless boys were doing their best to attract their attention. I found where I was on a campus map and headed down the hill to Hilgard Hall. Just inside, the building directory listed Paul Odum's office as room 214.

The second floor was a hive of activity, so it was easy to wander around without anyone bothering to ask if they could help. Next to Odum's office was the "Forest Ecology Laboratory" according to the sign above the open door. The room was dominated by an enormous black-topped table with wooden cabinets underneath. It was covered in various meters, instru-ments, and bags filled with leaves. Along the walls were gray metal shelves with glassware and bottles of chemicals, and on one side a bright yellow cabinet labeled "Flammable." A pair of deep sinks anchored the far end of the laboratory. Four doors were evenly spaced around the perimeter. The first door on my right was open, and a sign said "Instrument Room." What I guessed to be precision balances were set on marble-topped tables in a space that wasn't much more than a closet.

The other rooms had the names of Odum's graduate students stenciled on the translucent windows. Howard emerged from his tiny enclave, greeted me warmly, and asked what brought me to Berkeley. I explained that Mrs. Odum had asked me to poke around a bit regarding her husband's death. While we were talking, a fellow came out of the room next to Howard's. For my money, it looked like Jesus had emerged from the tomb.

"I thought I heard voices out here," he said. "I'm John Holling." He extended his hand and we shook. His grip was about what I expected.

"I'm Riley."

"Mr. Riley is the fellow who I told you about this morning," Howard explained.

"Ah, the curious exterminator. Nice to meet you. It's good that people are interested in the natural world, for whatever reason." He seemed remarkably mature and self-confident compared to Howard.

"I'm sorry about your professor," I began. "I was wondering if I might ask you a couple of questions. I've agreed to clear up some things about Professor Odum for his wife."

"I'd love to help you, Mr. Riley, but I'm a week behind in grading quizzes for the ecology laboratory that I teach. I have to get these back to the students early next week or they'll start complaining to the department chairman."

"How about this weekend?"

"Sorry again, but I have to finish a data analysis for a report to the International Forest Conservation Consortium. With Professor Odum . . ." he paused to find the right word, "well, gone, I'm hoping they'll continue funding my work under another adviser. I don't want to sound selfish at this difficult time, but I've worked hard to get this close to a doctorate."

"My questions shouldn't take long, seeing that I'm under some pressure myself. So when could you spare a bit of time?"

"How about midmorning on Monday? I'll have the quizzes graded by then, and I have to get the report to the departmental secretary for express mailing first thing that morning."

"I appreciate your willingness to squeeze me in. It must be pretty chaotic around here these days."

"Glad to help, although I doubt I'll do you much good." John smiled and returned to his office, half-closing the door.

"So Howard, I'd also like to talk to Jen Tansley. Is she around?"

"That's her office in the far corner. But she's out in the field working on her research today. She usually goes down the coast on the weekends, and Monday she teaches labs in the morning and tutors General Biology students all afternoon."

"So much for the lazy life of academics, eh?"

"At least the grad students. Some of the profs are another story."

"How can I find her to ask a few questions?"

"She'll be out in the field all day on Tuesday," he said, walking around the center table to her office door and examining the schedule she had posted. "And it looks like she has a grad council meeting Wednesday morning and a forestry seminar in the afternoon." He ran his finger down the page, which seemed to have entries in every slot.

"Like I told John, I'm under some time pressure to get answers for Mrs. Odum. Do you think I could meet up with her in the field on Tuesday?"

"That might work. Her research sites are in Tilden Park, so it's only a half hour or so outside of Berkeley. I'll draw you a map and leave her a note saying that you'll be visiting her." He sketched out a set of directions on a sheet of graph paper and penned a quick, almost undecipherable message that he taped to her door. He was either eager to help or anxious to send me on my way.

"Ok, I've got John on Monday and Jen on Tuesday." Things were coming together, although not as quickly as I'd hoped. "Now, would you have a few minutes? There are a couple of details that are bothering me."

Howard suddenly went from helpful assistant to evasive witness. "Uh, I don't know about that. I've got a lot of work. Grading, data reduction, getting ready for teaching next week. I told you everything I could down in LA. So I should really get after things here. Lots of stuff piled up while I was gone."

"Howard, this is important. It won't take long."

"I don't know," he began again.

"I think you do. And I think we need to talk." He sighed and glanced toward John's door. "Let's take a walk," I proposed. He followed me out of the laboratory, down the stairs, and out into elongating afternoon shadows. We didn't say anything until we were headed up the hill toward Memorial Glade. The halter-topped girls had disappeared and only a few students rested under trees with books in their laps. As we ambled along, I broke the silence.

"Howard, you didn't give me the whole story in LA."

"Why do you say that?"

"For one thing, I found flying ants in the room. They don't emerge at night and they're not attracted to human remains. So if the sliding glass door was shut all day as you described, I can't figure out how they got in."

"Some ants live inside, right?"

"Not these, Howard. The morning rain triggered their emergence, and they came into the room from outside. The door out to the courtyard was opened by somebody during the day."

"Maybe the maid."

"Nice try, but let's quit playing around. I'm not accusing you of anything, but you're not coming clean." Howard stopped walking, laced his fingers behind his neck, and stared at the sidewalk. "And if you don't tell me the truth, then I can't figure if there was foul play in your professor's death." For the first time, Howard looked scared. And it turned out he had a good reason.

Chapter Sixteen

Howard was frozen in place. We'd stopped in the shadows under a sprawling oak. It was a cool, quiet place with nobody around. His mentor was dead and it was a safe bet that he'd lied to the police. He didn't have any street smarts, but he was bright enough to know that he'd dug a hole. When intelligent people find themselves in a hole, they quit digging. And Howard was just now realizing that there might be a murder at the bottom of this hole.

"Is that what Mrs. Odum thinks?" he whispered. "That somebody killed her husband?"

"She's paranoid for sure. But that doesn't mean she's wrong. What's the real story about the day your professor died?"

"If I tell you, will you keep it just between us? I mean, it could be really bad for me if it got out. Not that I did anything to hurt Professor Odum. I'd never do anything like that."

"I know, Howard. And I'm not a cop, so I don't have to reveal anything you tell me. You have my word that whatever you tell me stays our secret." He started shuffling down the path. In my experience, people would often get up and pace the interrogation room when they finally decided to come clean. Somehow it's easier to spill your guts when you're moving—and avoiding eye contact.

"I couldn't tell anyone the whole story because I'm engaged, and if Melody ever found out, we'd be finished."

"Melody?"

"My fiancée."

"I understand. You have my word." We walked side by side at about the pace of a man heading to his execution.

"Okay, I wasn't at the meeting all day. I returned to the room around noon." Howard was staring ahead into space.

"And I suppose there was an awkward reason for that?"

"I'd met a woman the previous night while having a beer in the hotel lounge. She was gorgeous. Long blond hair, incredible body, and a sexy accent. I couldn't believe she was interested in me, but she kept asking questions about my work and touching my arm." He seemed to be relaxing into the story, and I didn't want to interrupt, but I wanted to get the details right.

"What kind of accent?"

"British, sort of. That wasn't quite it but along those lines. I figured she was attending the conference from some foreign country."

"I'm guessing that this woman was the reason you came back to the room the next day?"

"Yeah, Riley. It was like a dream or something. I'm not the kind that attracts a woman like Sarah."

At least he knew her first name. I was going to ask more about her but I sensed that Howard wanted to get the story out as quickly as possible. I'd seen this before, and I could always backtrack to fill in missing details. "I know what you mean, kid. I'm no Casanova either. Go on."

"Well, she caught up with me during a morning coffee break and one thing led to another. She could barely keep her hands off me. We headed back to my room because she said her roommate was still asleep." The pace of Howard's story and walking had picked up. "Oh man, Riley, I didn't know what I was in for. Sarah was into some kinky stuff."

"In what way?"

"Bondage. She pulled out these silk scarves from her purse. Then she asked me to tie her to the headboard. The sex was amazing. I'm glad it started to rain when we were going at it or her moaning would've been heard down the entire hallway. She was incredible. I still can't believe it all happened." His pace slowed down, and we strolled along like two old pals.

"Quite a story. What came next?"

"She asked me to untie her and she said she'd like a nice, steamy shower. I remember she said, 'Be a gentleman and run the water for us. I'll join you in a minute.' So I went into the bathroom and started the shower. She came in and we scrubbed each other. It was nearly as good as the sex. Her golden hair, the soap and the hot water." He almost came to a stop.

"Okay, Howard. You're not writing for *Playboy*. Just tell me what happened."

"Right, sorry. So she dried off, put her clothes back on, gave me a kiss on the cheek, and went back to the conference."

"Are you sure?"

"Of what?"

"Of where she went."

"Well, she headed in that direction. I didn't actually see her at the conference, but I figured that's why she was in the hotel. Anyway, I bundled up the sheets from the bed and stuffed them into a maid's cart in the hall. Then I called the front desk and asked for fresh bedding."

"How'd the sliding glass door get opened?"

"Given Professor Odum's sensitivity to odors, I was worried that he'd detect, well, you know."

"What?"

"The smell of sex. He was always commenting on the slightest scents. You know what I mean."

"Sure. So, you aired out the room?"

"Right. In fact, I opened both the glass door and the screen door to get some fresh air into the room. But I was so frazzled that I forgot that I left the doors open until the midafternoon break. So I hurried back to the room and closed them."

We kept walking together in silence as I put the pieces together. He'd opened the doors shortly after the rainstorm and they stayed open for a few hours. That would've matched the typical timeframe in which ants swarm from their nest—right after a heavy rain. It was then that the winged insects found their way into the room as they dispersed in search of their own sexual encounters. A few were trapped inside when Howard returned and closed the doors, where I found them the next day. So far, so good.

"All right Howard, now your story makes sense. So did you manage to catch up with Sarah later? Anything more you can tell me about her?"

"Well, I spent the rest of the day at the conference, but I don't remember any of the papers. The whole morning had been so surreal. Like I told you in LA, I went to the banquet that night. I was going out for some drinks afterward, and I saw Sarah in the lobby. I broke away from the group and tried to talk with her, but she was incredibly cold. Like she didn't even know me. I was really confused and hurt. That's probably why I got so hammered."

"Women will do that to a man. So you staggered back to your room after getting blitzed. What time was that?"

"Probably around three in the morning. I don't know exactly. But I remember looking at my watch and thinking that I was smart to be walking back to the hotel at two thirty a.m. with Marcelo. He was the guy from Brazil, a real bruiser. I figured it was a good idea to have him with me on the streets at that hour."

"So you snuck into your room so as to not disturb Odum, and slipped into bed?"

"Well, I used the bathroom light to see what I was doing. But I couldn't make out much."

"Right. Do you remember smelling anything?"

"No, but Professor Odum had left the back door open like I told you before. And I don't mean to be disrespectful, but he could pass some pretty strong gas. So I wouldn't have been alarmed in any case." Between his being smashed and the open door providing ventilation, Odum could well have been dead by the time Howard got back to the room, for all he knew.

"Can you add anything else? Anything about your professor that you might've overlooked before? Maybe some change in his behavior or mental state." Howard was quiet for a while, our feet scuffing along the asphalt path. Since he'd come this far, I figured he'd divulge anything else he knew if I just gave him some time.

"Maybe there was. He'd been acting wary in the last few weeks. You know, jumpy."

"How so?

"It's hard to say exactly. He just seemed kinda anxious. He didn't joke around much and he was always asking if I knew where John was. Professors guard their research, and he was pretty secretive about his work. Some of the other faculty members resented his success and probably would've been happy to steal his ideas. But I had the sense that he was worried about having real enemies, not just academic rivals."

"Thanks, Howard. You've been a huge help."

"Sure." He didn't sound sure at all. Howard stopped walking and looked directly at me for the first time that day. "I'm not really like how it sounds. I love Melody. It was just a one-time thing. You promise to keep this to yourself, right?"

"That was the deal."

"Riley, one last thing."

"Shoot."

"You figured out that I lied. Will the cops see the hole in my story?"

It was pretty clear by now that Howard didn't take me for merely a curious exterminator. His question and tone suggested that he figured me for some sort of investigator, which didn't matter much at this point. He'd given me the information I needed, so I assured him that the LAPD and the coroner would be looking to close this case, not seeking problems. I couldn't be positive that they'd buy his story. But he'd had me convinced that he was on the up-and-up until I realized that the ants undermined his alibi. Besides, there was nothing to be gained by having him frantic with worry. I might need him later, and it wouldn't help if he was a wreck.

Howard headed back toward Hilgard Hall with the beat-up shuffle of a fighter returning to the locker room after losing a ten-round bout. I strolled with my best imitation of a contemplative academic as I meandered my way across campus to where I'd parked. College campuses are good places to solve tough problems. The quiet pathways, massive buildings, and venerable trees encourage thinking. Fall has always been my favorite season, and in the late afternoon it was like having an oddly pleasant case of the fever and chills—in the open spaces the sun reflecting off the granite and concrete was uncomfortably hot, but in the long shadows the air was cool and humid enough to induce a shiver. As I wandered along, I sorted through what I knew—and what I suspected.

Howard had never been much of a suspect, and I figured he was now off the hook. His new story took care of the winged ants. But the insects were still telling me that I didn't have the whole picture. The dead flies didn't fit. Sarah was my best bet to fill in the gap, but tracking her down wouldn't be easy. This mysterious woman had become the lead—in fact, my only—suspect. But I still didn't have anything that came close to adding up to murder.

I walked through the archway and across the plaza, where the war protesters had been replaced by a group holding poster-sized photos of baby seals, men wielding clubs, and blood splatters on the snow. These activists weren't shouting slogans, as the pictures of cute animals being bashed were presumably supposed to speak for themselves and horrify the public. It's easy to make people who kill other creatures into villains. Rats and pigeons aren't baby seals, but soft-hearted folks are outraged about poisoning furry and feathered vermin. Especially when the problem is in somebody else's neighborhood. Just like do-gooders who get upset when a kidnapper is beaten. Especially when the hostage is somebody else's kid.

You don't have to like the cards you're holding, but your only choices are to play or fold. Exterminators and cops know that killing is part of the game. What I didn't know, as I crumpled the parking ticket that had been stuck under the wiper blade, was that a body cooling in the morgue would fill the inside straight I was holding.

Chapter Seventeen

On my way home, KDFC switched to playing the Brandenburg Concerto No. 5. Anything by Bach is preferable to classical guitar, but a little harpsichord goes a long way. Once over the bridge, I decided to swing by Tommaso's and grab a pizza to take home. Ever since leaving Howard on the Berkeley campus, I'd worked over Odum's death from as many angles as I could. No brilliant insights presented themselves, so it was time to just let the case incubate while I ended my week on a high note.

I pulled out a wooden box containing a particularly nice set of specimens from the freezer, laid out my mounting supplies, and set the sausage-and-onion pizza on the massive oak table that pretty much filled what might've been intended as a living room had I worried about such things. I suppose it's where I did most of my living in the house, with wooden cabinets to store my collection along one wall, and glass-topped boxes displaying my best material—and some of the beauties my father had brought back from the Pacific—mounted on the opposite wall above a bookcase of field guides. A battered recliner and a television completed the furnishings. The worktable faced a picture window that looked out onto the street. I could see some teenagers huddled under a streetlight, jostling one another, trying to look cool, and probably figuring out if they had enough money among them to get into trouble with a case of beer.

To round out my Friday night, I poured a glass of Black Bush—an excellent everyday whiskey that didn't dig too deep into my pocketbook—and put on the *Pastoral* Symphony. The music was the perfect antidote to the ugliness of the preceding days. Bruno Walter's conducting of Beethoven's Sixth was just the right background for pinning a series of gorgeous leaf beetles. As I pulled back each layer of cotton batting, I savored the spectacularly metallic insects. They were the treasure from a collecting trip that I'd taken to Mexico in June, when San Francisco was blanketed in fog and business had slowed. Writing the details of the collecting label for each specimen with a fine-tipped pen took me back to sunny days on the Yucatán. The jangling of the phone broke my reverie.

"Riley here," I answered with some annoyance.

"Oh, Mr. Riley, I finally reached you. This is Laurie Odum." She sounded just short of desperate.

"What's the problem?"

"It's Maria's little girl, Marissa."

"She's sicker than her mother thought, eh?" I wanted to say "than you thought" but resisted, which was good.

"Riley, she's dead."

"Shit," I mumbled half to myself. I'd taken a liking to the spunky kid. "What happened?"

"Maria called me and said that when she got home, Marissa was all twitchy and had problems breathing. So she took her to the hospital."

"Which one?"

"Does it matter?"

"It could." I was already trying to put this piece into the puzzle, although I didn't know whether or how it would fit.

"Highland Hospital. But it doesn't matter because they couldn't save her. This is just too much. I don't know what to think anymore. Could this be related to Paul's death?"

"Listen Laurie, your job is to take care of yourself. You're paying me to do the thinking. Don't go playing detective. Just tell me anything more that you learn."

"Okay, Riley." She paused. "I'm scared."

"Don't be scared, just be careful. Keep your windows and doors locked, and don't go hiring a replacement if Maria can't work for a while. Until I say otherwise, I want you to stay home and keep a low profile."

"What do you think happened to Marissa?"

"I don't know, but I have a first-rate contact who might shed some light on this. Now pour yourself a drink, watch a late movie, and go to bed. There's nothing you can do."

She thanked me and hung up. I pushed down the button on the phone cradle and called Information. In less than a minute, I'd lied to the hospital switchboard about being a doctor and managed to connect with the emergency room at Highland Hospital. I explained that I was looking for Beth Gilbert. I had to repeat myself to be heard over the wailing siren and shouting in the background. The ambiance of Friday night in Oakland. The harried nurse said that Beth was too busy to take a call and that she'd be back on duty Sunday night. I thanked her and went back to my pinning and labeling. But I couldn't concentrate, and I didn't want to damage the specimens.

I turned off the pair of high-intensity lights on my worktable and put the remaining insects back in the freezer and the leftover pizza in the fridge. Beethoven's Sixth was down to the final movement, so I settled into the motley recliner and nursed the last of my drink. Beth and I had had some great times together in my earlier life. She'd been my nurse in the ER when I came in with my nose splattered across my cheek. I told her that I'd been handsome up until that night, and she laughed. The Columbia Symphony's rendition of the allegretto stirred a memory of happiness that we'd shared for a while.

She was a good woman, tender and strong. But relationships between cops and nurses are about as stable as fire and gunpowder. We'd given it a good run, but we had too much in common. When both halves of a couple come together at the end of the day to tell their own stories of human suffering and inhuman brutality, there's nobody to listen. It helps if somebody in a relationship is sane. Or at least lives in a sane part of the world.

She was good at her job at San Francisco General, and I knew she'd gotten a plum offer from Highland Hospital. Nursing supervisor, or head nurse, or something like that. Highland was in a gritty part of Oakland, surrounded by working-class neighborhoods—not the best setting but far from the worst. She told me that the pay was great and the cases were "challenging," by which she meant lots of gunshot victims and other people clinging to life. Her move had put an end to a relationship that wasn't going anywhere. She'd sent me a sweet note when the Jamal thing was going down, but we hadn't talked for years.

It'd be good to see her again, although the circumstances didn't hold much promise of rekindling anything. I was more interested in finding some answers to a kid's death than seeking romance. At least Saturday had potential to lift my spirits before diving back into the grime. Tomorrow was my day with Tommy.

CHAPTER EIGHTEEN

After a paczki and cup of muddy coffee at Gustaw's, I drove over to my mother's to pick up Tommy. She was out in front, tending her flowers. Ever since I was a kid she'd had the most glorious garden in the neighborhood. The little patches of soil on either side of the steps leading up to the porch couldn't have been more than a hundred square feet, but they produced like a tropical paradise for her—much to the envy of the other ladies and to my mother's secret delight.

"Tommy was up before sunrise," she reported, looking up from thinning her bulbs. She'd once told me that growing plants in San Francisco was easy; the hard part was deciding what to yank up to keep a garden from becoming a jungle. "It's what you don't let grow that makes a garden," she'd said. My mother had on a well-worn flannel shirt that had been my father's, and a pair of baggy jeans—a fashion that caught me by surprise every time. Working in the garden was the only time she didn't wear a dress.

"By the time I came down, he'd had his oatmeal, cleaned up his dishes, dressed for your outing, packed his things, and was at the door," she said, shaking her head in disbelief. Saturdays were our "expedition days" and collecting insects was Tommy's favorite outing. He was sitting in the entryway with all of his insect-collecting gear in a backpack.

"Just a bit excited, eh sport?" I asked, and he nodded vigorously. My mother had brushed the dirt off her hands—she rejected garden gloves, saying that she wanted to feel God's good earth—and followed me inside. As we gathered up Tommy's supplies, she emerged from the kitchen.

"I packed you two a lunch," she said, handing me a basket of food that would've fed us for the week.

"Thanks Mom. Now, you have a good day and don't worry about us. I'll bring him back after dinner." If things went as usual, she'd spend the morning tending her plants and grocery shopping, and devote the afternoon to a long visit with Mrs. Flannigan to catch up on all the church news of who was sick, who had started dying her hair, and who had been added to the sacristy committee.

The September sky was piercingly blue and the air was crisp. Autumn is the best time in San Francisco, squeezed between the summer fog and the winter gloom. Golden Gate Park was humming with activity. The emaciated joggers were apparently succeeding in not enjoying themselves, while the beer-bellied softball players were evidently having a grand time. The healthy-and-miserable types reminded me of devout churchgoers.

Tommy and I strolled down to Metson Lake, where he carefully laid out his gear: illustrated field guide, magnifying glass, collecting net, forceps, and pill bottles for specimens. Being away from the ballfields and playgrounds, we managed to find a bit of solitude. I preferred to collect in more distant and natural settings, but Tommy wasn't keen on taking long drives. He spent a frenetic hour swinging his net along the lake in unrelenting pursuit of dragonflies and damselflies. I stretched out on the grass, closed my eyes, and soaked up the sun. The ground held on to the chill of the night, which perfectly balanced the slow roasting of my face. When he managed to snag an insect, he raced to me so I could put it in the killing jar.

"I like catching insects, Riley."

"You're really good at it, Tommy."

"No I'm not. You can catch them better than me." It was true, he'd only netted two specimens in an hour of mad dashing that made the joggers look sluggish by comparison. But he never complained about the hand he'd been dealt.

"Maybe I do, but you have more heart. And that's what counts. Hey, this green darner is gorgeous," I said, slipping the insect from his net into the cyanide-charged container.

"I don't like this part," he said, screwing up his face and then turning away from the insect flapping furiously in the jar.

"That's okay, pal. It kills them quickly and they don't feel much. Remember, we've talked about this. Everything dies. And most insects just rot away, but we preserve their beauty in our collection."

He nodded slowly. "So, killing the darner is a good thing?"

"Well, it can be if we do a nice job of pinning the ones we collect." The knowledge that good can come from killing is the reality understood by all exterminators, including soldiers and cops. The tree huggers and peaceniks are free to protest because others do the dirty work. But I didn't want to confuse Tommy with all of this.

He took a brief look at the insect thrashing in the jar. "I know, but I don't like to watch them get all twitchy."

Twitchy? That was how Maria had described Marissa's symptoms to Laurie Odum. What had been a serene morning plunged back into a bout of sifting through conversations and events over the last couple of days. My grim silence disturbed Tommy.

"What's wrong, Riley?"

"Nothing. I was just thinking. Are you worn out or are you up for some more collecting?"

"I want to catch some more. But I want to find some butterflies." We'd passed some flower beds on our way to the lake. The day had warmed enough that some late-season butterflies might be working the blossoms.

"All right, I think you might have some luck back toward the picnic area and the redwood trees. Butterflies love the sunny spots." I pointed back toward where we'd crossed earlier.

"I'll try over by the crillies," he declared.

"Where?"

"The crillies," he insisted, pointing toward a stretch of ferns interspersed with gaudy flowers atop tall stalks. We'd attended a walking tour led by a naturalist a couple weeks earlier, so I knew what he meant.

"The crinum lilies, pal. You almost had it."

"I hate getting words wrong," he grumbled in one of his rare moments of frustration. I knew better than to dwell on his mistake.

"Do you want me to come along with you?"

"No. I can do it myself," he announced, recovering quickly from his irritation. "Mom said I can do things if I'm careful."

"Fair enough, champ. But the deal is that you can't cross any streets. Understand?" We were in a section of the park bordered by Middle Drive and Metson Road, and both could be busy on the weekend.

"I won't cross any roads. I promise."

"Then it's a deal. I'm going to take a little walk. I'll circle back and find you in about an hour."

"How long is that?"

"About as long as you spent chasing dragonflies."

"Dragonflies *and* damselflies," he insisted. The kid knew his insects. Tommy stuffed his supplies into the backpack and lurched his way across the grass. I walked in the other direction, across the polo field and toward the police stables. There, I found Sergeant Ulatowski, an old buddy from the force who was spending his pre-retirement years in his version of police heaven. The sergeant had soured on what he called "street scum," but the man adored horses. He was fond of saying that "shoveling manure beats chasing thugs or pushing papers."

⸢

Just before noon, I headed back to find Tommy. The strip of land where he was supposed to be was only about a hundred by five hundred yards. Even with the trees and bushes, it should've been easy to pick out Tommy in his orange-and-black Giants sweatshirt.

I was starting to feel a twinge of anxiety when I was relieved to see his backpack outside the public restroom. He hated the dirtiness of the dimly lit facilities and he treasured his collecting gear, so I understood why the backpack was left next to the doorway. When I walked into the dank building, it took a few seconds for my eyes to adjust. It was almost enough time for the punks to adopt nonchalant postures of feigned innocence. But I could see that Tommy was backed into a corner and looked terrified.

"What's going on here?"

"They're being mean," he stammered. The biggest of the three, in his late teens and wearing a denim jacket, stepped toward me.

"Probably best to mind your own business," he sneered. The other two were more my size. One of them slouched against the opening of a stall and the other followed behind his leader.

"I am minding my business. He's my business." I nodded toward Tommy. "Now why don't you find some other way to occupy your Saturday?" Tommy had started to cry and the guy at the stall was mocking him by rubbing his eyes.

"Look, old man, we're just playing with the retard. But if you want to give us a little exercise, we'll be happy to rearrange your face." He stepped forward and pushed me in the chest. I stepped back and gave him one more chance.

"I don't want to ruin anybody's weekend. So if you leave now, we can all go back to enjoying ourselves." I stepped to the side as if to allow him and the others to get to the door. My real intent was to keep the big guy between me and his buddies. If things went bad, I wanted to give myself the chance to take them one at a time in the cramped space.

"I guess you don't want to do this the easy way," the head punk snarled and lifted his hands to deliver another push. I figured it was coming, knowing that this was just the sort of intimidation that bullies used to screw up their courage and impress groupies. As he leaned toward me, I caught him with a hard right to the solar plexus. He gasped and crumpled to his knees, which gave me access to his buddy. I needed to put him away quickly in case the third guy decided to go after Tommy.

Stepping around his indisposed pal, the guy threw a roundhouse left, which surprised me, although I shouldn't have supposed he was right-handed. I was a bit slow and it glanced off the top of my head as I ducked. But from my crouch, I had great leverage to throw a hard left hook into his exposed ribs. I was glad it was a body shot, as hitting him in the head would've really hurt. Me, that is. Dislocating that ring finger is unpleasant, but less painful than what he had coming. I felt a crunch as a couple of ribs gave way and a pop as my finger slid out of joint and then back into place. I figured he'd be out of commission, but I drove a right into his belly just to be sure. I considered doing some damage to his face. Although he was plenty deserving, it meant risking my hands. And I wasn't keen on not being able to work with my insect collection for a couple of weeks just for the satisfaction of rearranging this jerk's features.

The first guy had struggled to his feet, but he was still doubled up. A sharp knee sent him toppling backward. Tommy whimpered as blood gushed from the guy's nose. I stepped forward to put myself between Tommy and the last guy, but I needn't have worried. Having less fight or more brains than his buddies, the guy bolted past me and out the door. I might've punished the two guys on the floor, but I figured they hurt enough for my purposes. I know about busted noses and cracked ribs. They'd sustained enough damage to remember the consequences of picking on the weak, but not so much as to clog up the ER with their sorry asses.

Tommy was sobbing by now, asking if the bad guys were going to die. He wanted to call a doctor, but I convinced him they'd be okay. I knew that Tommy was enormously sensitive, but with him being trapped in the corner there was no way to spare him the violence. We went back to my house, and spent the afternoon working on the collection and listening to my assortment of Mozart's piano sonatas, violin concertos, and flute quartets.

I ordered takeout Chinese and we kept going through dinner, only pausing long enough to take a bite of egg roll or sweet-and-sour pork, which were Tommy's favorites. He can work for hours when Mozart is on the stereo, and I had quite a backlog of specimens in the freezer. It's amazing that the kid struggles so hard to walk and only by sheer persistence manages to net the occasional insect, but he can put an insect pin through a flea beetle. According to my mother we should thank God that Tommy survived and has retained at least some of his abilities. But if God's calling all the shots, I can't figure out why He decided to screw up the kid in the first place. Just so we could be grateful that things hadn't turned out worse? Seems perverse to me.

Chapter Nineteen

I picked up the Sunday *Chronicle* and walked down to Gustaw's. The sun was shining on Potrero Hill and illuminating the tops of skyscrapers down in the city. Ludwika cut an enormous slice of babka for me. The chocolaty cake went perfectly with my morning coffee. The sports page announced that Notre Dame had beaten Purdue 23-0. Seems that God was a Catholic after all. But it was hard to square a football victory with a little girl's body in the morgue. I knew that the clock was ticking on my deal with Laurie Odum, and I was frustrated that there wasn't anything I could do about it until this evening. My mood was becoming as black as Gustaw's coffee.

I hung around the bakery, idly reading the reports of economic recession and human depravity until eleven o'clock, then headed over to St. Teresa's to pick up Tommy. Mass was letting out when I got there, so I pulled into the driveway behind the church and slipped into the undercroft where Tommy spent the service "helping" Mrs. Polanski in the childcare room. I figured I'd slip out with him and avoid uncomfortable conversations with the faithful, but he insisted on finding our mother to show her a caterpillar he'd made out of an egg carton.

In the course of looking for her, we ran across Father Griesmaier, who took the chance to slyly mention that it was good to see me at church but it was too bad he hadn't seen me in the pews. He was in charge of all the religious mumbo jumbo, but I liked him anyway. A pudgy fellow with an Austrian accent, Father Griesmaier didn't have a mean bone in his body. He and his congregation looked after my mother and my brother, so I was deeply appreciative of their works, if not their faith. I gave him my best sheepish smile and promised that once things settled down at the business, I'd have more time for spiritual matters. He raised a dubious eyebrow. I managed to escape when Tommy pulled me toward our mother on the other side of the entryway.

"Mom, look at my caterpillar," Tommy announced, shoving the craft project toward her.

"That's wonderful, Tommy. Say, I'll bet Mrs. Nagy would love to see it. Why don't you show it to her?" Mrs. Nagy's son, Karsa, went to the adult daycare that looked after Tommy. The two of them were great pals. Karsa had eaten some rat poison when he was a toddler, and he'd not been quite right ever since. He'd been in the hospital the last couple of weeks—a regular happening in his life—and Tommy had missed him. So Tommy was delighted to share his creation with Mrs. Nagy, knowing that she'd tell Karsa all about it.

"Riley," said my mother, taking me aside. "What happened yesterday at the park?"

"Nothing much. Just a little tussle with some bullies."

"Tommy said you hit them and made one of them bleed. He couldn't stop talking about it this morning at breakfast."

"It was no big deal. A few punks were hassling Tommy and I stepped in."

"By beating them up?"

"Things got a little rough when they wouldn't leave. Nobody got hurt enough to worry about. You know how Tommy can exaggerate when he's excited."

"You're a good big brother, Riley. But he's so vulnerable. Please be careful with him, okay?"

"You know I will. Are you still on for lunch with the ladies?" I asked, hoping to change the conversation. "I have a plan for Tommy and me." She sighed and clenched her woolen coat. My mother was cold even on what passed for a warm day in San Francisco. "Come on now," I reassured her, "I'll stick close to Tommy." I took her coat and helped her into it. "We're just going to grab some lunch and then take in a free concert at Golden Gate Park."

"You'll eat something decent and have him home by midafternoon? With all the excitement, he'll do best with a nap."

I assured her that everything would be fine, and she left with her group of friends, who were busy critiquing Father Griesmaier's sermon and chattering about church politics.

At the park, Tommy and I grabbed some hot dogs with everything from a stand run by a cheery old man with a thick German accent, who seemed to think there was nothing better on earth than layering sauerkraut, pickle relish, onions, mustard, and ketchup on a bun. I gave Tommy an apple from my coat pocket to go with his hot dog, so that he had something of a decent lunch.

The concert was in the monumental amphitheater at the end of the mall between the art and science museums. We shared a bench under one of the trees near the orchestra. I couldn't sustain my dark mood. The sky was a bleached blue. The sparrows worked the crowd for crumbs. A ship's horn moaned in the distance. Even the music was a pleasant surprise. I'd read in the paper that they were going to play some of Philip Glass's minimalist compositions, so I didn't have high hopes. It was discordant, but not as bad as I'd expected. Tommy loved the repetitions, nodding and rocking like he was entranced. Edo de Waart conducted the ensemble, which made sense given his proclivity for contemporary music.

My mother could usually entice my father to attend the open-air concerts at Golden Gate Park. But after sitting and grumbling through a couple of performances conducted by Seiji Ozawa, my father refused to attend anything involving de Waart's Japanese predecessor. Nor would he walk through the park's Japanese Tea Gardens with her after the concert. He'd sit resolutely but patiently on a bench and read the paper or have a cigarette while she strolled through the gardens with Tommy.

After the concert Tommy and I meandered through the tea gardens behind the amphitheater. His lurching gait was less pronounced when he walked slowly, and he drew less attention from gawkers. Out of respect for my father, I had avoided the gardens for a year or so, but Tommy was so soothed by the sculpted plantings, tumbling waterfalls, and tranquil ponds that I ended up taking him regularly. I bought him some fish food, and he knelt down and slowly tossed one piece at a time into the water, watching the enormous white, gold, and calico koi rise to the surface.

I sat on a nearby bench, closed my eyes, listened for the plunking and soft splashing of Tommy's fish feeding, and recalled my father's explanation for why he refused to enter the tea gardens: "We Americans forgive too easily and forget too quickly." It wasn't that he hated the Japanese people, but he couldn't get past the things he'd seen during the war. He believed that people should be held responsible for their acts. The Japanese could start over, but only if they paid for what they'd done. It stuck in his craw that the Japanese imperial family avoided prosecution in the war crimes trials. The worst were executed, but the royalty was spared. And for my father, sometimes the dues that must be paid were death. He understood the samurai's view that it was better to die with honor than to live with shame—and he thought the Japanese should have lived up to their own ideal.

After all the years under English rule, an Irishman could appreciate that a man dying on his feet was preferable to living on his knees. And after all the killing he'd witnessed, he didn't find anything inherently bad about dying, only about dying badly. When I was under siege after killing Jamal, my father told me that he didn't see any difference between the death penalty on the streets or in the courts—as long as the killing was just. Cops had to make their judgments with less time to deliberate. "Why," he asked, "would I oppose capital punishment, when a man dying for his crime might be the only thing the fellow got right in his life? Don't take away a man's last chance to face responsibility."

I opened my eyes and watched Tommy throwing the last kibbles to the fish. He looked up and I gestured for him to join me on the path. The gravel crunched under my feet and his gait added a syncopated rhythm as we headed to the pagoda at the exit. I drove him back to my mother's house and spent the afternoon at the shop going over inventory and ordering supplies. I figured this could be a long week without much chance to keep up at work, so I wanted to leave things in good shape for Carol and the guys. I stuck with it until dark, then went home to reheat and relish the leftover lamb stew that my mother had given me when I'd dropped off Tommy. I tossed the dirty dishes in the sink and walked out into the chill of the night. I started up my truck and headed across the Bay to see what I could learn about a dead kid.

Chapter Twenty

Highland Hospital looked like a hospital should. Imposing white buildings in Spanish architecture with ornate touches and red tile roofs, all laid out in a grand geometric design reminiscent of a military complex. The stairway leading up the hill was flanked by towering trees, and the landscaping was meticulously clipped, trimmed, and mowed. The bucolic spell was broken the moment I pushed through the doors into the emergency department, which was basically a very long hallway packed with machines on carts and patients on gurneys. I worked my way down the medical obstacle course to the admissions desk.

Beth had her back to me, and it was still quite the backside. Her hair was tucked under her cap, but the starched whites couldn't hide her figure. But then a nurse's uniform had always done something for me. She sensed my movement and turned with the professional demeanor of someone expecting to be greeted with a spurting artery or a trembling junkie.

"Hey, stranger!" she said with evident relief, walking across to the counter and leaning over to give me a peck on the cheek.

"That's some nice first aid. But I think I may be more injured than you're assuming. Maybe we could sneak into one of the exam rooms for old times' sake?"

"Riley, you're incorrigible. Cute but hopeless."

"Ah, the curse of the Irish," I replied in my best brogue. "We're always dreaming of that pot o' gold," I leered.

"Stop it, or you'll get me in trouble." Another nurse sitting at the admissions desk was grinning and pretending not to overhear us.

"With who?"

"I've met somebody. A resident in orthopedics. He's handsome, kind, sensitive . . ."

"And rich?"

"Not yet. But he's got his act together, which is more than you can say for most doctors."

"Or cops. I'm happy for you. Really, you deserve a decent guy." She smiled, came around the counter, and took my arm.

"Let's go for a walk and catch up. Cindy, take me off the board for a half hour. Things are pretty slow." We headed out to the hospital grounds. "So, what's happening in your life these days?" she asked softly.

"Nothing by way of romance, if that's what you mean. A waitress at O'Donnell's and I were an item for a while, but she dropped me for a guy with a Corvette and a fat wallet." I liked how she held onto my arm. There was no chance of picking up where we'd left off, but the touch of a woman is a fine thing in any case. Beth let her head fall against my shoulder, and we walked quietly for a ways. "So, how's the job? I figured that with your seniority, you'd be able to get out of weekend duty."

She laughed. "Ah, there's value in knowing how the world of violence and perversion works. Sunday nights are usually a cushy shift. Most people manage to get themselves stabbed or shot earlier in the weekend."

"You were always a smart cookie." The night's cool dampness wrapped itself around us, so I slipped off my coat and draped it over her shoulders.

"And you've always been a gentleman, at least in public." She gave my arm a playful squeeze. "In the end you couldn't give me what I needed, but you were never cruel." We fell into quiet again, until the path divided, forcing a choice. "We should start heading back, and I'm assuming you came out here for something other than a lovely walk with an old girlfriend." I'd been enjoying the warmth of Beth's hands on my arm, but it was time to get to work.

"I'm looking into some matters for a friend."

"You're investigating a case without a license."

"You say potayto, I say potahto. Here's the deal. A little Mexican girl came into the ER on Friday night."

"Yeah, I had two nurses out, so I had to work the asylum shift. I remember her."

"Good, so I can cut to the chase. What killed her?"

Beth paused, and I knew she was violating confidentiality. But I also knew that she trusted me to never put a source at risk. "She came in with the classic symptoms of insecticide poisoning. Her mother reported vomiting and diarrhea, which she first thought was a bad case of the stomach flu. But when the girl started twitching, the mother understandably panicked. By the time we got to her, the poor thing was sweating and salivating excessively. Her pupils were constricted to pinpoints."

"Sounds bad."

"It was. While I was taking her history, her heartbeat became erratic and she started struggling to breathe. Given that she was Hispanic, the doctor figured this was a classic case of organophosphate intoxication."

"How so?"

"Farm workers' kids come into contact with their parents' contaminated clothing. We don't usually see such acute symptoms, but children are much more susceptible than adults due to their small bodies." Beth had begun to sound like a nursing school professor, which quashed any lingering sense of romance. Just as well.

"There's an antidote, right? At least that's what they tell us in the pesticide applicator's licensing course."

"Sure, but her mother insisted that the girl hadn't been in contact with clothing or anything else from a farm. Her husband is a custodian, not a picker. So we didn't administer atropine until we had ruled out other poisons. If you give atropine to a person who's not suffering from one of the nerve toxins, the cure can be deadly." We'd reached the double glass doors into the emergency department. She let go of my arm and slipped my coat off her shoulders.

"But you figure it was a neurotoxin?"

"I suspect so, but there're a lot of chemicals out there. And some infections can cause symptoms like hers."

"So why figure she was poisoned?"

"That's where things pointed. She started having seizures and her vital signs were crashing, so the doctor gave her a dose of atropine. Her heart rate responded and she seemed to be improving for a few minutes. But then she stopped breathing. We bagged her and gave her another dose, but it was too late."

"I hate that this is why I came to see you. But thanks for helping me out."

"It's like when we were together, Riley. By the time we shared our screwed-up days, there was never a chance to talk about us." She kissed me on the cheek and plunged into the glare of the fluorescent lights and white walls. I put on my coat and savored her lingering warmth.

◆

Across the street and down a block, I found Emiliano's Bar & Grill. I didn't know the place, but there were a handful of patrons that looked like a mix of off-duty hospital staff and locals. I ordered a Jameson, stared at the rows of liquor lined up against a mirror behind the bar, and tried to make sense of what Beth had told me.

I imagined that the struggle to save Marissa had been like what the doctors and nurses had done for Tommy years earlier. There's a price we pay for having poisons in the world, just like there's a cost to bullets and bombs. As for pesticides, unless we want to feed our crops to cutworms and cede our homes to cockroaches, accidents will be a part of life. But how did Marissa come across a deadly chemical? The timeframe suggested that she'd been poisoned while in the Odums' house. But given Paul Odum's sensitivity, they never would've tolerated having a pesticide around. Unless.

I threw back the rest of my drink and headed for the pay phone in the back. The bartender grunted that it was next to the men's room. I didn't need further directions. Even in the dimly lit interior, I could've found it by heading toward the bouquet of ammonia and industrial cleanser. I dialed Laurie Odum and she answered after a dozen rings.

"Hello?" she said groggily.

"It's Riley. Sorry to wake you, but I need to ask you a question."

"Now?"

"Yes, now. Did you finish doing Paul's laundry?"

"No, it's still in the basement by the washing machine. I did a load of sheets and towels today. I was going to take care of his things tomorrow. Riley, why are you calling in the middle of the night to ask about laundry?"

"I have an idea about what might've happened to Paul."

"Oh God, what? Tell me." Her voice was no longer gravelly but clear and demanding.

"I don't know for sure. It's still mostly speculation, and it won't do either of us any good for me to share my half-baked theory. Just don't wash Paul's clothes."

"Should I do anything with them?"

"No. Don't touch them. I'll be over tomorrow morning."

"Okay." Her voice was tired again.

I hung up and walked back to where I'd parked. On the way back to San Francisco, I turned KDFC on low, and a program of Schubert's piano sonatas provided a perfect background for churning my way through everything I knew. So far, I had a few dozen dead flies, a dead university professor, and a dead kid. None of which I could explain, all of which might be somehow linked—or not. As for the humans, their last minutes were not dissimilar. And the only connection was Paul Odum's clothing. I doubted that he'd somehow contaminated his clothes with an organophosphate insecticide while at a professional meeting in a hotel. But perhaps some other toxin was involved. Like Beth said, poisonings are difficult to diagnose. I drifted from what I knew into the realm of imagination.

My theory left open the question of how a poison got onto Odum's clothing. It might've happened while he was at the meeting, given that hotels use all sorts of pesticides, solvents, and cleaning solutions. However, he hadn't exhibited any symptoms during the day, so it seemed more likely that the chemical was in his room. The hotel maids and Howard were possible sources, but they seemed like long shots in terms of an accident, given that they knew of Odum's sensitivity. And as killers, they had no motive. Maybe Odum had finally gotten tired of being sick and poisoned himself to provide his wife with a nice insurance windfall, but that seemed unlikely given his enthusiasm for his work and the conference.

There was another possibility worth mulling. The only other person in Odum's hotel room was Howard's passionate lover, Sarah. However, I couldn't come up with either a plausible motive or an accidental scenario involving her. Without more information, my speculations were going nowhere.

There was nothing more to do until morning. But I was wired from playing out the possibilities. I changed and swung by Marty's Gym. A light was on, so I pounded on the door. Marty opened and I asked if I could work the heavy bag for a half hour or so. He shrugged, shifted an unlit cigar to the other side of his mouth, and said sure, as he was up late working on the books. He told me to have at it and shuffled to his office in the back of the warehouse. I knew the dull thud of leather on leather soothed the old codger, like Schubert's sonatas did for me. I pounded the bag in the dim glow coming from the light in Marty's office mixed with the streetlight that filtered through the grimy, grate-covered windows. Once I was dripping and panting, I headed back up the hill to my house. The night's chill had just worked its way through my sweatshirt by the time I got to my porch.

Chapter Twenty-One

I wolfed down a bowl of cornflakes and a giant mug of instant coffee, then swung by the office. Carol's pop station was playing some insipid song which was supposedly revealing fifty ways to leave a lover. I could only decipher five while thumbing through the mail on the corner of her desk. Which was fine, as I was presumably saved from hearing another forty-five lines of the awful rhyme scheme that passed as lyrics. We chatted a bit about her weekend, which involved "a gnarly party" in the Castro. I wasn't sure what made the party "gnarly" in her estimation, but I was pretty sure I didn't want to know. When I heard the garage door opening in the warehouse, I headed to the back. Larry was putting his lunchbox in the locker and Dennis was changing into his work overalls when I pushed through the doors.

"What's up, boss?" Larry asked.

"I have a favor to ask of you guys."

"Nothing's too much for our fearless leader," Dennis saluted, letting his overalls drop around his ankles.

"Your respect for authority is truly moving, Dennis," I replied. He smiled and pulled up his pants. "I need a dozen mice."

"Should we take them dead or alive, Commander?" Dennis was enjoying himself and poking fun at Larry's military background at the same time. Larry hated the army, but he felt that only a grunt could badmouth the military.

"If you send Dennis on rodent patrol, it's likely Goat Hill Extermination will chalk up a KIA," Larry broke in.

"No mutherfuckin' mouse could take this bad boy."

"Okay, you two listen up. It's a simple job. Just set some live traps down by the docks this morning, dump the mice in a couple of ten-gallon buckets, and leave them in my office. Can you handle that?"

"When do you need the little POWs?" asked Dennis.

"By late this afternoon, if possible."

"They're a lot easier to catch overnight, boss," Larry suggested.

"Yeah, I know. But time's not on my side. Set out thirty or forty traps and bait 'em with peanut butter. That should catch a dozen or so by the end of the day."

"Sounds like a plan," Larry said.

"Great. By the way, where's Isaac?" I'd been too involved arranging for the mice to notice him missing.

"He said he had an appointment with the art department at San Francisco State," Dennis answered. "I figure he's too smart, or creative, or something to stay long with this gig."

"Don't worry boss, we have him covered," Larry said. "He's no more scatterbrained than I was at his age."

"Sheeit, like you're Zen now," Dennis replied. "C'mon, we hafta jump some mice and then get after the nasty cockroach job at the warehouse on Pier 36."

The two of them began gathering up chemicals and spray equipment, and I headed to the front. Carol was talking on the phone and gave me a wave as I passed her desk. My next stop was Laurie Odum's house, where a pile of laundry promised to take me one step closer to figuring out whether I had bought into a case of paranoia or murder.

❧

I parked in front of the house, and knocked with the iron ring. No answer. The door was unlocked, so I pushed it open and called out. Still no answer. The hum of an electric motor came from the back of the house. I headed through the living room and saw that the glass door to the deck was open. Laurie Odum was lying on a towel, next to a hot tub with furiously bubbling water. I hadn't noticed the hot tub when I met with her last week. It was sunken into the far end of the deck and had probably been covered. But now neither the tub nor the lady had a top on.

Even though she was lying on her back, I could tell she had maintained the firmness of youth, including a flat belly. Paul had been a lucky man until a few days ago.

I stepped back into the middle of the living room and called out, "Anybody home?"

"Hold on," she shouted and came to the door wrapped in the towel. "I didn't hear you come in."

"You left the front door open. Until I know what's up, it'd be a really good idea to keep things locked."

"I must've forgotten when I got the paper this morning."

"Okay, just be careful for a while."

"Do you really think that whoever killed Paul will come after me?" She pulled the towel tightly around her.

"Slow down. I'm still not sure that your husband was murdered. The case has more holes than a Teddy Kennedy alibi." She scowled. "But a pile of laundry might fill a big gap in the story with some physical evidence."

"It's down in the basement." She nodded toward the stairway on the other side of the room. "And you might also see if there's anything in his study that could be useful in your investigation."

"Can't hurt to look. Where is it?"

"Over the garage. You have to go out the front and around the side of the house. I don't know where he kept the key, but there are a bunch of keys in the drawer under the kitchen telephone."

"You didn't go in there, I gather."

"No, it was off-limits. We each had our own spaces, which suited both of us. My office is upstairs. While you figure out how to get into his study, I'll get dressed." She padded across the tile floor toward the terracotta staircase that presumably led up to the bedrooms.

I grabbed the pile of keys from the kitchen and headed around the house. A set of stairs led up to a rickety landing attached to the garage. The door was locked, and a deadbolt above the handle made breaking it down a messy proposition. After a bit of trial and error, I found the right keys and went into a shag-carpeted loft that extended the width of the garage. The ceiling slanted at a sharp angle, so you couldn't stand up in half of the room. This was evidently no problem for Odum because that part of the floor held a built-in desk buried in stacks of papers, a worktable covered with scientific journals, and bookcases stuffed to capacity. The walls were plastered with graphs and charts, and the far side of the room was lined with filing cabinets. The only sign of comfort was a beanbag chair in the corner with a swag lamp overhead.

I rifled through the notebooks and papers that were scattered about and read the notes pinned to a corkboard over the desk. There wasn't much of interest, other than some phone numbers and names that I jotted down. The desk drawers were cluttered, but the filing cabinets seemed to be meticulously organized. I worked my way through all the files, finding reams of tabulated numbers, pages of calculations, and entire drawers of computer punch cards and printouts. I'd pretty much given up on coming across anything of importance when I pulled the handle of the last filing cabinet, a small two-drawer unit in the far corner of the room. This was the only locked drawer in the loft, which meant it was worth getting into. I retrieved a drill from the toolbox in my truck and polished off the lock in a few seconds.

The top drawer had a sheaf of papers inside a folder, and the bottom drawer was packed with baggies of marijuana. I didn't figure Odum to have been a pothead, so I was doubly intrigued. The papers had variously dated and rather cryptic notes, a checklist of what appeared to be construction supplies, a list of first names and last initials, and a set of hand-drawn maps. I turned on the desk lamp and examined the plastic bags. Each had a four-letter code followed by a series of numbers. I couldn't make heads or tails of what this all meant, but I did find one particularly interesting bag. In the bottom were a couple of ladybird beetles, larger than those I'd seen in this region, and oddly colored, black with a couple of red spots. I picked out the beetles, dropped them into a vial, and put the bags back in the filing cabinet. I decided to take the papers from the top drawer for further study. I didn't have much hope of deciphering anything useful from Odum's scrawled notes and drawings, but maybe the beetles could tell me something. So far, insects were my most reliable witnesses in this case.

I gathered up the booty from my pillaging, locked the door, and headed to my truck. From the storage box in the bed, I retrieved a pair of protective vinyl gloves and a plastic garbage bag that we use for our contaminated overalls after a spray job. As I came through the front door, Laurie emerged from the kitchen with a tray of sandwiches and glasses of iced tea. She'd changed into a floral sundress.

"I made us something to eat and brewed up a pitcher of chamomile tea with ginseng," she announced.

"I thought you had concluded that I was not a nice man."

"You aren't, but I'm used to having people around. With your warning, I've not had anyone over to the house and I'm getting lonely. Even the company of a man who kills things for work and pleasure is better than rattling around here in silence."

"Gee, that's quite the compliment."

"Besides, I figured you'd worked up an appetite with whatever you were doing in Paul's study. What was all that noise?"

"Turned out that getting in was a challenge," I lied. "I had to jimmy the lock. I managed to get things locked up when I was done, but you'll need to call a locksmith to get the door re-keyed once I tell you that it's safe to have people in the house."

"So none of the keys worked?" she asked over her bare shoulder, carrying the tray out to the back deck.

"No luck. I'll put the keys back where I found them," I answered. I went into the kitchen and returned all but the ones for the handle and deadbolt. I didn't want Laurie going up there and finding the pot, wondering about the empty drawer in the same cabinet, or coming up with questions.

"Did you find anything useful?" she asked. She'd laid out a nice spread on the table where we'd negotiated our deal.

"Nothing really." I took a bite of my sandwich, which looked better than it tasted. I shouldn't have been surprised to find it stuffed with sprouts, tomatoes, and cucumbers, but lacking in meat.

"So you really do think he was killed?"

"Let's just say that I've come to believe it's a valid question. But I'm a long way from having an answer." I directed our conversation toward the Indian artifacts in the house, and she launched into a rambling account of the various trips she'd taken with her husband to the pueblos of the southwest and the art galleries of Santa Fe. It was reasonably interesting, but I didn't have time for social niceties.

So I finished my lunch, thanked Laurie for her hospitality, and started to get up. She seemed a bit peeved with my cutting short her walk down memory lane. I apologized for having to eat and run, but suggested that I was working under a bit of pressure. She caught my drift but didn't offer to extend the deadline.

While she cleaned up the lunch dishes, I went down to the basement. Paul's clothing was piled on the floor. I slipped on the protective gloves and stuffed his things into the plastic bag. When I came back up, Laurie was at the kitchen sink, so I shouted my good-bye from the entryway and headed back down the hill to the Berkeley campus.

So far the case was getting messier with each step. But eventually the pieces had to start coming together. Or so I told myself. I hoped that a visit with John Holling might be the turning point. Maybe Odum's student could help put a frame around this poisonous puzzle.

Chapter Twenty-Two

I managed to find a parking space on Telegraph Street—Berkeley's version of Haight-Ashbury. Tie-dye and head shops on every corner. After feeding the meter, I grabbed a liverwurst-and-onion sandwich from Foley's Deli and ate it while walking toward campus and marveling at the street vendors, record shops, and organic diners. I suppose a person can be amazed by a remote village in the Amazon jungle, but I'm just as dumbfounded in my own country sometimes.

On my way to Hilgard Hall, I passed through the main plaza where the students had gathered for their daily protest. This time a group of pleasantly braless co-eds held up signs demanding the passage of the ERA while a middle-aged woman with long, straight hair and a pair of aviator sunglasses shouted into a microphone. For some reason, nobody asked me to join in.

I found Howard reading a book on one of the benches in front of the biology building. "Whatcha reading?" I asked. He shut the book, holding the place with his finger, and read from the cover.

"*Ecological Methods with Particular Reference to the Study of Insect Populations.*"

"Sounds spellbinding. What's the plot?"

He smiled. "I'm trying to figure out how to use capture-recapture techniques as a way of estimating the size of populations."

"Ah, so you can tell me how many cockroaches are in a warehouse?"

"That's the idea. We'd catch a bunch of roaches, mark them with paint, turn them loose, collect another sample later, count how many marked individuals are recaptured, and from that we could figure out how many are in the whole population." He sounded genuinely excited by all of this. I was lost.

"Great idea. Of course, you'll have to explain to the customer why you're turning loose the first batch of cockroaches so you can catch them again. Just count 'em the first time and kill them."

"It's more complicated than that," he replied and ran his fingers through his curly hair, obviously wondering how to explain this to me. I saved him the trouble.

"Don't worry, Howard. I trust that you scientists know what the hell you're doing. Otherwise, you wouldn't have come up with insecticides, and I wouldn't have a business."

"I suppose that a lot of what we do seems pretty mysterious."

"Since you brought up mysteries, I have one more question for you." The spark went out of his eyes, like I'd just told a child that his dog had been run over.

"I thought I was done with that."

"You are, for the most part. It's just that this woman you met might be more important than I first thought."

"Look, Riley, it seems to me that the more you try to find out about her, the less likely it is that I'm going to keep the whole thing quiet."

"Don't worry, kid, I have no intention of exposing your fling. I'm sure I can get what I need and keep our little secret. I just want to know whether you can tell me anything more about her."

"Like what?"

"You said she had an accent that was British or something like that. Right?"

"Yeah, it was definitely foreign, but there is a professor in the department who's British, as well as one of the lab techs, and Sarah's accent wasn't quite the same."

"All right. Did she use any words or phrases that were unique? You know, like how the Brits say 'bloody good' and call an apartment a 'flat.'"

"Sure, now that you mention it, she did have a couple of strange expressions. When we were at the bar, she asked the bartender for a dop. He was confused and probably figured she'd said another drop but he'd misunderstood her accent. Anyway, she held up her empty glass so he poured her beer. I guess that's what she was asking for."

"Good. Now think, anything else?"

"Well, she'd say 'is it?' during our conversations. It was like a way of encouraging me to say more."

"That might be useful. What else?"

"I only remember one other term, and it's kind of embarrassing, but I guess we've come this far, eh?"

"Sure, go ahead."

"Well, after sex we'd lain there for a bit when she turned toward me and looked at my, uh, penis."

"And?"

"Well, she said something like, 'Looking slup there, Howard. Think we might be able to get you going again?' I know what she meant, but I'd never heard it called that before."

"It's a new one for me, too. Thanks for the help. Hey, do you know if John is around? I'm supposed to meet up with him."

"Yeah, I saw him go into the building with an armload of books about a half hour ago."

⬩

I let Howard get back to reading about capturing and counting insects and headed inside. It wasn't hard to figure out why students hung around on the lawns between classes. Old university buildings can have nice exteriors, but in my limited experience they all have interiors like some sort of third-world hospital. Long corridors lit with flickering fluorescent lights, drab walls, cheap linoleum, and unidentifiable odors. The door to Odum's lab was open, so I stuck my head in and called out to John.

"In here," he replied from the cramped, windowless closet that served as his office. There was enough room for his desk, a spare chair, and a bookshelf. At least, the shelving was designed to hold books, although John had filled it with stacks of punch cards held together with rubber bands. The walls sported posters featuring plants ("The Trees of California" with a bunch of different trees surrounding a sequoia) and environmental slogans ("Forests: The Lungs of the Planet" with some trees arranged in the shape of lungs across a map of the world). He spun around in his chair and gestured toward the empty seat. With the stacks of green-and-white lined computer printouts covering the floor, there was no room to push the chair back, so our knees almost touched when I sat down.

"My filing system takes up a lot of space, but at least I can find things when I need them," he said.

"Whatever works," I replied, turning my chair sideways to gain a little legroom. "Looks like you're a busy fellow."

"Yeah, Dr. Odum and I had some big plans for a research project. Now it's fallen into my lap to find another faculty member who will take over the supervisory role, at least on paper." He swung his arm over the stacks of papers. "All this is what ecologists think we know about nutrient cycling in Asian forests."

"Looks like you fellas have it pretty much worked out."

"Not even close. Our project was going to be a study of how to restore clear-cut forests in acidic, nitrogen-poor soils. Nobody understands the full complexity of these ecosystems."

"So, Professor Odum hadn't done much along these lines?"

"He was the leading expert on restoring coastal forests, like here in California. But the tropics are another world. He had some really cool models that we were going to adapt to Thailand. These programs were our first attempts." He waved his hand toward the bookshelf and paused. He sighed deeply and slumped a bit. "Now it's all up in the air."

"You have a lot to deal with, so I won't take much of your time. What can you tell me about Professor Odum? I'm particularly curious about any recent changes in his demeanor."

"I don't know what you're getting at."

"Was he unusually tired, happy, or distracted in the last few weeks?"

"I can't really help you, there. He seemed his typical self."

"Any changes in his pattern of movement, when he came or left?"

"Nothing noticeable." John gave off plenty of signals that he was being less than forthcoming. He kept his eyes on one of the posters to avoid looking at me. His left arm was across his belly, propping up his right elbow so he could rub his beard along the jawline. Academic types are supposedly seeking the truth—maybe that's why they make awful liars.

"So, there wasn't anything about him that struck you as out of the ordinary?"

120

"No, not really." He continued to silently proclaim his acute discomfort. It was time to press.

"Look, John, I'm not playing a game. There are two corpses, and I'm trying to make sure there aren't more."

"Two?"

"That's right. Don't worry about the other one, but there's good reason to think that another death is connected to Odum's."

"I don't know if you're some kind of private investigator, but I know that you're not a cop. So I don't have to answer your questions. I'm busy with a ton of crap." He turned back to his desk and started rummaging through some papers.

"That's right, I'm not here in any official capacity. But the way things are unfolding, I wouldn't be surprised if somebody shows up with a badge. Now, if you and I can have a chat, then maybe I can get things figured out before they spin out of control."

"Jeez, I don't know," he said, swiveling halfway between his desk and me. "It's not like I have much to offer. But being dragged into some criminal investigation will be the deathblow for any chance of getting on with another faculty member." I reached over to the door and swung it shut.

"Just tell me what you know. Whatever you say is between us."

"Shit," he whispered. "I guess there's not much choice. Here's the thing. Dr. Odum was obsessed with Ed Abbey's new book, *The Monkey Wrench Gang*. Do you know it?"

"No, what's it about?"

"A bunch of regular people who are sick of corporate greed go out and destroy the machines and infrastructure that rape and pillage the natural world. They throw a monkey wrench into the engine of 'progress.' Get it?"

"I see. So Odum wanted to give it a try himself?"

"Something like that. At first, we had these longs talks about what we might do. It was like daydreaming or something. We weren't serious, just imagining how to monkey-wrench around here. But the more we talked, the more he moved from fantasy to reality."

"How so?"

"Okay, this would get my butt kicked out of the university, but a couple times he and I did some stuff."

"Go on."

"Nothing major, just some small-time sabotage. One night, we pulled up the survey stakes for a new road through Tilden Park. And another time, he torched a couple of billboards along Highway 1 while I kept a lookout. He wanted to put sugar in the gas tanks of some backhoes parked at Ocean Beach where they were putting in storm drains, but I chickened out. There were too many people around, even in the middle of the night."

"So a few acts of vandalism. Probably not enough damage to add up to a felony, except maybe the billboards. It'd be a bit problematic if somebody found out, which they won't. But I take it there's more." John was rubbing the back of his neck and stopped to stare up at the ceiling.

"I can't be sure, but I think Dr. Odum was planning something really big. After I bailed on the backhoe job, he became much more reticent. He stopped talking to me about monkey-wrenching, and things went pretty much back to normal for us. But as time went on he'd drop hints that he wasn't done."

"Do you have any idea about what he had in the works?"

"No. He was very cryptic. Saying things like, 'You have to cherish knowledge to be a good scientist, but a fellow has to cultivate courage to make a really big impact in the world,' and 'In the end, we only really regret the things we didn't do.' He'd also allude to the Hindu god Vishnu, calling him ecology's deity because I guess he was the destroyer of worlds. Sometimes he scared me, but mostly he just made these tangential references." John's veneer of confidence had melted away. Now he turned toward me and just looked lost.

"I can see why you were keeping this to yourself. It couldn't have been easy to be both his student and co-conspirator. You were in a tough spot, and I'm not looking to make things any worse." He was as fragile as Howard had been at the hotel. I could see why universities coddle the eggheads. They wouldn't last a day on the streets.

"I appreciate that, Mr. Riley. I don't know what all you've found out about Dr. Odum's death, but I'm afraid he might've been out of his league."

"In what way?"

"Look, I'm no expert on politics and economics or whether environmentalists are really a threat to industry. But I suspect that things can get pretty nasty when somebody puts a company's profit or equipment or whatever at risk. There's a reason that these people have armed guards at their plants and factories."

"You think Odum's plan might've leaked out and somebody decided that the best defense was a good offense?"

"God, I don't know. I don't know anything really. It's just fiction, but read *The Monkey Wrench Gang*. I think maybe Ed Abbey comes closer to reality in some ways than many people imagine."

I thanked him again and gave him a reassuring pat on the shoulder. The tiny office had become unbearably stuffy, and it felt good to be outside and walk across campus. I made my way to the university bookstore and picked up a copy of Abbey's book. The protesters had dispersed, leaving their chalked slogans on the plaza: "The Personal is Political," "ERA NOW," and "Hear me Roar!"

On the way back across the Bay Bridge, I caught the end of Puccini's *Tosca*. It matched my increasingly dark mood. I tuned in as the hero was being led off to prison. As I made the turn onto the Embarcadero to avoid the freeway congestion, the heroine realized that what she thought was the faked execution of her lover was actually the real deal. As I pulled into the fenced lot behind the shop, Tosca leapt to her death when the double-crossing villain came for her. Things weren't going quite that bad for me. Yet.

Chapter Twenty-Three

When I got back to the office, something resembling music was coming from Carol's radio.

"What's playing?"

"Riley, you're hopeless. That's the theme from *S.W.A.T.*"

"Well, it's better than those songs with the asinine lyrics. Maybe there's hope for pop if it sticks with instrumentals."

"Right. And you're surely just the right person to be advising the American music industry." She nodded in mock sincerity, then handed me a message. "Your mom called earlier and asked me to pass this along to you."

I thanked her and read the note on the way back to my office. She wanted me to pick up Tommy and her at the church this evening after a special program. I remembered that a visiting organist was going to play some Bach fugues, which would've been great to attend, but I had more pressing matters. My mother didn't like walking even the couple of blocks from the church to her house in the evening. She wasn't so much worried about crime in the neighborhood, but her night vision was getting worse all the time and Tommy was easily frightened in the dark.

As I flicked on the lights in my office, I heard the frantic scurrying of tiny feet. The guys had delivered the mice in a couple of deep plastic pails. The rodents couldn't get out, despite their desperate attempts. If Carol came into the office, I didn't feel like explaining what I was doing with a garbage bag of clothing and buckets of mice, so I looked through some mail until I heard her call out a good-bye and leave for the day.

Then I went back to the shop and grabbed three more buckets for my experiment. I lined up the containers along the wall of my office and deposited a couple of mice in each one. No longer feeding off the group's panic, the pairs were much calmer. Next, I retrieved the bag with Odum's laundry from the truck and put on a pair of rubber gloves. It seemed most sensible to divide the clothes into types. So I put his underwear into one pail. The other mice were given his T-shirts, socks, pants, or shirts. I was concerned that rather than rummaging through their newfound bedding, the mice might use the clothing to launch escapes. So, I cut some wire mesh from a roll in the shop and covered the buckets. I wanted the little guys to have plenty of contact with Odum's laundry. If there was a chemical on his clothing that was potent enough to poison him and Marissa, I figured the mice would let me know by tomorrow which of the garments were guilty.

I headed over to Tommaso's for a plate of pasta and a glass of Chianti. I liked the North Beach area almost as much as Potrero; it had the same sense of ethnic identity and pride. The Italians are happier than the Irish, having once ruled the civilized world and having avoided famine in modern times. They live on as if the Roman Empire still calls the shots and their duty is to introduce good food and wine to the barbarians. Maybe they're not so far off. The homemade ravioli with a simple marinara sauce was unbeatable, and the din of shouted orders, animated conversations, and clinking plates was soothing. I'd brought along *The Monkey Wrench Gang* and read through the first few chapters over dinner. Exploding bridges, burning billboards, and George Washington Hayduke's defiance made for a helluva start to a book. I could see how Odum might've been drawn into the crazy world of Edward Abbey. Even in my police days, I had more respect for the criminal who acted out of his own sense of right and wrong—however twisted it might be—than for the by-the-book cop who followed orders without thinking for himself.

After dinner, I headed to St. Teresa's. I stood in the back of the sanctuary, happy to have arrived in time for the last strains of Bach's Great Fantasia and Fugue in G Minor. Father Griesmaier was standing placidly outside the confessionals. I hated to disturb him, but given the diverse ethnicities of his parish, I figured he might be able to shed some light on the nationality of Howard's mysterious lover. I caught his eye and nodded toward the rear doors. He smiled and followed me into the entryway.

"And what can I do for you this fine evening, Riley? Having called me away from the confessionals, I assume that you'll not be seeking absolution tonight?" he teased.

"Uh no, Father. Not that I couldn't use some forgiveness, but it'll have to wait until a better time."

"My son, that could be difficult to explain before the Lord should you find yourself in His presence. Not having time for the sacraments may not go over so well." He shook his head in semi-serious disappointment. I would've loved to please the gentle and well-meaning priest by going through the motions, but pretending about things that were so important to him and my mother would have been disrespectful. If what seemed like mumbo jumbo to me brought meaning to him and serenity to my mother, then I wasn't going to make a mockery of their faith.

"I'm hoping that the Almighty is mighty forgiving," I tried.

"Sometimes you understand more than you know, Riley. Now then, you didn't come for catechism class, so how can I help you?"

"Father, I'm trying to help out a friend."

"I see. Go on."

"And, well, to help her with this problem, I need to figure out the identity of another woman."

"Ah, infidelity. How sad." He sounded genuinely hurt.

"No Father, it's more about finding a woman who might have some answers about a tragic death."

"I see. It's all a bit distasteful, eh? I trust that you are acting out of compassion. After all, you are Marie Riley's son." The priest gave me such an intense look that if I had been scamming him I would've confessed.

"I am truly trying to do the right thing. My mother says you've served other churches with lots of immigrant parishioners, and St. Teresa's certainly has its assortment of folks."

"So this person you're seeking has some feature that might be associated with a foreign nationality?"

"Exactly, Father. She used the term 'dop' when asking for a drink. And she sprinkled her conversation with the expression 'is it?' when the other person was speaking."

"It sounds like she is South African. I served with Father Walsh, a priest from Johannesburg, when I was at Our Lady of Sorrows in Chicago. He liked his evening libation and often said he'd have a dop. It was weeks before I realized that he was not mispronouncing 'drop.' His glass certainly held more than a drop."

"That's great, Father."

"And like the woman you're seeking, he would also intersperse 'izit?' during a conversation. Enough so that the altar boys took to calling him Father Frog when he wasn't around because they thought it sounded like 'ribbit.' Any other quirks that might confirm my identification?" I wanted to be sure, but I didn't know how to tactfully broach the other term.

"Maybe just one last thing."

"Maybe?"

"It's a bit awkward, and I'm pretty sure I understand the meaning. But I want to be positive."

"Ah, something lewd, eh? I've taken a vow of chastity, but I manage to keep up with such matters in the course of hearing confessions," he smiled.

"Okay. She referred to a man's organ as 'slup.' I'm sorry if I'm being offensive." Instead of being offended, the priest laughed explosively. The last notes of the fugue drowned out his howl.

"Oh dear, Riley," he panted, clasping his hands as if in prayer. "I hadn't heard it used that way."

"Whaddya mean, Father?"

"Well, Father Walsh used to rave about the french fries he'd get from a fish-and-chips place a couple blocks from the rectory. He'd say they were 'slup chips,' which I thought was just his term for fries. But a parishioner from Cape Town told me that he was praising the sogginess of the fries."

"I'm not sure I get it."

He chuckled at the thought of a priest having to explain such matters to another man. "You see, Riley, 'slup' means limp in Afrikaans. The woman was evidently unimpressed when she rendered that judgment."

"Well, that seals it. She must be South African." The audience was beginning to come through into the entryway, pulling on jackets and sweaters. "Thanks so much, Father."

"I'm happy to help, as long as you use what you know to help a person in need. And I'd also be happy to see you in a pew some Sunday." My mother and Tommy emerged from the sanctuary just in time to save me from trying to offer an excuse. Tommy was excited to tell me about the music, which he described as filling his head and shaking his stomach. Father Griesmaier turned to visit with an elderly fellow who seemed to have some pressing matter. I took my mother and brother back to their house, with Tommy chattering the whole way. My mother didn't say a word. It was clear that she was basking in Tommy's joy.

When I got to my house, I heated up some leftovers and poured a tumbler of Black Bush. I laid out Odum's files on my worktable and then looked for Mendelssohn's Octet for Strings in E Flat. Chamber music was an ideal background for reading, but I couldn't find the record. So I opted for Brahms's Sonatas in E Minor and F. The cellist was Jacqueline du Pré, with her husband, Daniel Barenboim, playing piano accompaniment. At the time of the recordings, they were in their early twenties and taking the world by storm. Sometimes it seems that God deals from the bottom of the deck. At least du Pré and Barenboim knew they were holding royal flushes and shared their winnings with the rest of us.

Odum's papers were mostly scrawled, telegraphic notes that made little or no sense. However, there were three lists that suggested John might have been right about his professor planning something big. On a sheet of notebook paper with a ragged edge torn from a spiral binding, he'd drawn up a table with three columns. The first entry in each row was the name and address of an industrial plant in the Bay Area, the second entry was a series of chemical names, and the third was a number between 1 and 10. Most of the plants had numbers between 3 and 6, but he'd put a star next to the names of two locations with scores of 9 and 10: CalAgri and AmeriChem Industries. And in the column next to AmeriChem, he'd repeatedly circled one chemical: chlordane. The next several pages were hand-drawn maps of a factory site labeled ACI along Oakland's inner harbor.

On another sheet, Odum had typed a list of names. Each name had a parenthetical notation and a dollar figure:

Frank Moffett (NE gatehouse) $2000
Ed Colter (grounds maint) $1000
Bill Jackson (shift supvsr) $5000

Steve Reiners (tank maint) $1000
Scott VanDyke (bldg eng) $3000
Kirk Schell (shift guard) $2000

I also found a half sheet of newspaper. Odum had filed away the used vehicle section of the *Chronicle* from August 22. He'd circled four ads for VW
vans and two for panel vans.

The most intriguing and worrisome list was handwritten on paper torn
from a yellow legal pad. It was a series of items that were each innocent
enough, but together told a chilling story:

ammonium nitrate (farm supply), 500 lbs
nitromethane (campus chem store?) or diesel fuel (7 gal)
methylammonium nitrate (campus chem store?)
powdered aluminum?
nitric acid (9 qt)
potassium perchlorate + sulfur + white glue
22 gauge wire
nichrome wire (from toaster)

I'm no expert in chemistry, but a dog-eared booklet in Odum's files from
the Wisconsin Conservation Department left no doubt as to the professor's
plans. The document was titled *Pothole Blasting for Wildlife* and described
how a conservation officer could blast craters in marshy soils that would fill
with water to entice ducks and geese. For about $3.50 worth of chemicals
you could create a pit four feet deep and twenty feet in diameter.

I poured myself another drink, which I hadn't been planning on, but
the most sensible explanation of the evidence was unnerving even for me.
Odum was evidently planning to bomb the AmeriChem Industries plant in
Oakland. This was the company that had manufactured chlordane, the insecticide which Laurie said had poisoned him years ago. And he was going
to even the score. I surmised that he was paying off several of the security
and maintenance people at the site in order to gain access and position an
explosive-filled van within the grounds. The bomb was cheap, but the entire
operation was going to cost him a bundle—enough to put a sizable dent
in the finances of even an overpaid professor at Berkeley. Paul Odum was
plenty serious.

I knew some of the guys at AmeriChem from training programs they'd provided to exterminators. And an old pal, Bino Mancini, had retired from the force in the late '60s and taken a position as chief of security at the company. Nobody knew his real name because, as he was the last of ten children, his mother had called him her 'little bambino,' which had been mercifully shortened by his father to Bino. I'd talked to him a couple times in the intervening years, and he was always happy to describe his job as the cushiest gig of all time. "Nobody wants to steal pesticides," he'd told me. But now it looked like things were becoming a lot dicier for the folks at AmeriChem.

If Laurie was right and the top dogs had gotten wind of Odum's plan, then maybe the stupid bastard really had been the victim of a corporate hit. Considering the scope of the bombing that he had in the works, the stakes might've been high enough. I doubted that Bino would know anything about an assassination, or whether he'd tell me if he did. But with the right sorts of questions, I might learn something from a visit. Like whether Odum was even on the company's radar.

Bino might well lie, but at least there was one informant I could trust. I dug into my jacket, which was hanging by the front door. At first I couldn't find the vial with the beetles that I'd collected from Odum's bag of dope, but it had slipped through a tear in the pocket and into the liner of my coat. I made a mental note to sew up the hole, but it had about the same chance of getting done as my scraping and painting the porch or putting new linoleum in the kitchen.

The beetles weren't in great shape. One was missing a head, and there were only three legs among them. However, it was possible to identify them as ladybird beetles based on their tarsal features. From there, I went to my books. However, nothing in *Peterson's Field Guide to the Beetles of North America* or *The Beetles of the United States* seemed to match their size and color. Now I had another visit to add to my list if I was going to be generating more answers than questions. If anybody could identify these beetles, it would be Scott Fortier at the Essig Museum of Entomology. It'd mean another drive over to Berkeley, but I was planning to catch up with Odum's other student at Tilden Park tomorrow afternoon anyway.

I threw back the last of my Black Bush and headed to bed. With four days down and ten to go, the case was looking more interesting. And less solvable.

Chapter Twenty-Four

I didn't get up until midmorning. All night I'd alternated between strange dreams and fitful bouts of trying to piece together dead flies, unidentified beetles, poisonous chemicals, exploding vans, bags of pot, and a South African temptress. And nothing was working, including sleep. In an effort to stop my imagination from churning, I picked up where I'd left off reading *The Monkey Wrench Gang*. I figured that after a couple chapters, I'd nod off, but Abbey was too good of a storyteller. Having finished the book around four a.m., I drifted into a dreamless and unsatisfying sleep. At least I had developed a better understanding of Paul Odum's passion for attacking AmeriChem Industries. I knew that the story was fiction, but I couldn't shake the sense that corporate assassination of troublemaking environmentalists was more plausible than I'd initially assumed. I also concluded that Mormons are even wackier than Catholics.

After a quick breakfast, I headed down the hill to my home away from home. As I came through the door and greeted Carol, whatever hope I had for popular music evaporated. Most of the lyrics were unintelligible, and the only line I could discern was "Play that funky music, white boy." Given this, I couldn't imagine that the other words, had they been understandable, would have salvaged the song. Carol was bobbing to the music and looking very nice in a fuzzy, low-cut sweater. She greeted me without missing a beat and blew me a kiss as I headed to my office.

The screens over the buckets with Odum's clothing were still in place, but I couldn't see any of the mice. They'd evidently made themselves at home in the laundry piles. Before I could check on them, Carol forwarded a call to my phone. She knew I was in the middle of a mess, and would've taken a message if the caller wasn't important.

"Riley here," I answered.

"Nuthin' like the voice of my best friend's kid."

"Mr. Hale, it's good to hear from you." Tom Hale wasn't important in terms of being a major contract, but he'd been one of my father's first customers and had become a friend of the family. He operated a couple of motels, and even though they were from a bygone era, he took pride in his accommodations and made sure they were vermin-free.

"Tell ya what, kid, I got a problem at my place on Fulton. One of the maids said she saw roaches in a bathroom. I checked it out and found a couple earwigs under the sink where a pipe was leaking." Mr. Hale knew his business and his pests. Most clients couldn't tell the difference between a cockroach and an earwig.

"Those damp areas are heaven for earwigs, Mr. Hale. I'll bet if you fix that pipe, hit the area with some Raid, and let the flooring dry out, that'll take care of the problem."

"That might work, but we're due for a treatment at the end of next month. So maybe you could come and spray this week."

"I could send one of my guys out, if that'd be okay." I knew it wasn't, but I couldn't spare the time.

"Nah. I'd rather you did the job. I know you have good workers, but I trust the guy who owns the business." He'd always insisted that my father take care of treating his places. Now that I was the boss, he wanted me to take care of things. Although it was much more efficient to send out one of my technicians, I didn't mind doing the job for him. In fact, it was nice to keep my hands in the real side of the business.

"I'm sorry Mr. Hale, but my schedule is packed this month. I could come out two weeks from today but not any earlier."

"That's what I like about you, kid. You're like your old man was. No sorry-ass excuses, just telling me the way it is. I called an electrician last week, and he gave me the royal runaround. Promised to come that day and never showed up. His girl called me the next day saying he'd be there in the afternoon. He came the following morning when I was in the middle of installing some new drapes. The idiot said his secretary hadn't put the appointment on his calendar. I told him I was too busy to deal with him and he left." This was going to keep on for a while unless I cut in.

"The world's going to hell these days, Mr. Hale. But I have you on my schedule for the twenty-fifth at ten a.m. Will that work for you?"

"Sure, cuz I know you'll be there. You're not just stringing me along like that goddamn electrician. I prefer to wait a couple weeks and know a fellow's going to show up rather than be told some guy will do his best to get here 'as soon as possible' only to have the asshole feed me some line of bullshit about a crisis when he's been banging his secretary all afternoon." He was on a roll, so I broke in and told him he could count on Goat Hill Extermination. Mr. Hale's tirade was defused, and he finished by telling me to give his best to my mother and to "that hot little number you have working the front desk."

I hung up and found Bino's number in my Rolodex. An officious secretary said he was in meetings all day, but that he had some time tomorrow afternoon. Would I like to schedule an appointment with Mr. Mancini, she wanted to know. I said yes and she asked what my matter with Mr. Mancini concerned. When I told her it was a subject that didn't involve her, she turned snippy and said she'd work me into his calendar for three o'clock.

Having dealt with my fellow humans, I got up and went around my desk to the row of buckets to check on my mice. I pulled on a pair of gloves and lifted the screens from the improvised cages. Most of the rodents were hiding under the clothing, but a few had to be shaken out of the folds of his shirt and pants. All of the test animals looked hale and hearty, until I came to the pail with Odum's underwear. Both mice were lying dead beneath the pile of white cotton briefs. I tore last month's page from the oversized calendar hanging on my wall and laid it on my desktop. No sense risking contamination of my personal space. I laid the underwear on the photo of a bikini-clad babe wearing a backpack sprayer and carefully looked for residue that might reveal the presence of a chemical. Not seeing anything at first, I went back into the shop and rummaged around for the magnifier that I use to read the fine print on pesticide labels—reading glasses being for old men.

When I returned to my office, I didn't need any help to find the chemical culprit. In the intervening minutes an oily stain had appeared on the paper. I ran my gloved fingers over the underwear, feeling for slickness. There was a clear, greasy substance along the elasticized leg openings. Using a knife, I scraped the material from the fabric and transferred it to a glass vial for safekeeping. I was about to wipe off the knife on the paper, but I wanted to be sure that my suspicions were correct. So I grabbed a mouse from the nearest bucket. As it struggled and dangled from my fingers, I wiped the residue from the blade onto its naked tail and set it back with its partner.

By the time I'd returned to my office from tossing the paper and gloves into the contaminated materials drum, the mouse was in bad shape. It would stagger a few steps and then fall over, struggling to right itself. After another ten minutes it stayed on its side, gasping and kicking its legs. I reached in and broke its neck, careful to avoid touching the tail.

The pieces were starting to fall into place. Odum had returned to his room, showered, pulled on what he took to be a clean pair of briefs, and sealed his fate. This also explained the dead flies. The poor bastard had been converted into fly bait. As with Marissa, the poison caused him to vomit and lose control of his bowels. When the flies moved in for a fecal feast, a few of them crawled over his poisoned underwear, picked up a toxic dose, and died with their dinner.

I turned the surviving mice loose on the steep slope that stretched from Goat Hill Extermination up the Potrero projects—one of the few places that might've been too steep for even San Franciscans to build on or pave over. I'd once collected an exquisite California Sister, one of the rarest and most beautiful butterflies found inside the city, from that hillside. The mice might find something to keep them fed among the trash that dotted the crispy brown grass. In any case, I didn't see any point in killing them. They'd done me a favor, and the little fellas represented job security.

While washing out the buckets and stuffing Odum's other clothing into the dumpster, I mulled over how and when the deadly ointment had been applied. Everything pointed to Sarah, who'd been in the room earlier that day. Maybe she'd been a hired assassin for AmeriChem Industries, but that sounded more like an Edward Abbey storyline than a plausible theory. I needed to find this woman rather than conjuring up wild conspiracies. I could come up with only one thin connection that might lead me to her. But making that link would have to wait, because I had an appointment in the forest outside of Berkeley.

I wasn't hopeful that Jen would be able to add much to what Odum's other students had told me, but then, both Howard and John had surprised me. My image of a campus full of harmless, absentminded professors, working with their students on academic problems that nobody else cared about, was fast dissolving.

CHAPTER TWENTY-FIVE

I rummaged around in the glove box and found the map that John had drawn for me. Tilden Park covers a couple thousand acres in the rugged hills above Berkeley, and it would've been impossible to track down Jen without directions. John's map took me to a turnoff from the Wildcat Canyon Road, which became a poorly maintained dirt road for a half mile before I saw a truck parked under a sprawling live oak. I found an opening into the underbrush, and the dried grass was crushed down well enough that I could follow a path that headed steeply uphill into the hot afternoon sun. Between my perspiration and the fragrant oils of the pines and eucalyptus it started to smell like Marty's Gym—sweat and liniment. After a few hundred yards, the forest opened into a field of knee-high grass.

I'd made enough noise shuffling through the dried bark and leaves to announce my arrival. Jen was coming to greet me as I emerged from the tree line. She was a thin but not skinny woman with straight brown hair in a ponytail that reached to the small of her back. There was a cheery bounce in her step and a pleasing, if not voluminous, bounce beneath her T-shirt. She wore a pair of khaki shorts that covered very little of her long, brown legs. Damn, if women don't want to be objects, they sure make the objects they have hard to ignore. I apparently needed a tutorial from Carol, but I'd have to make do with my manly befuddlement for now.

"Mr. Riley, I presume," she smiled.

"Just 'Riley' is fine. And you must be Jen Tansley," I replied.

"John's note said you were coming and that you had some questions regarding Dr. Odum. An 'unofficial investigation' is what he called it."

"I do, but first tell me about your work out here."

I wanted to put her at ease before broaching the topic of Odum's increasingly strange life and death. And I was enjoying her vitality. She told me about her work on forest regeneration. The grassy field had been planted with Monterey pines and California bay trees to simulate the conditions of restarting a forest after clear-cutting. She was measuring the growth rates after various rates of fertilization. I'd not imagined that someone could be quite so enthusiastic about trees. She took me by the arm and led me to her saplings, stroking their branches as if petting a cat as she spoke. As the heat became too intense, we moved to the shade.

"Watch out for poison oak," she advised as we approached the underbrush. "It's everywhere in this forest."

"Thanks for the warning." I stretched out my legs and rested my back against the smooth trunk of a towering eucalyptus. The soft bark that had been shed by the tree made for comfortable seating. Jen sat cross-legged, with her knee resting on the toe of my work boot.

"Well, I'm sure you didn't come out here for my lecture on reforestation. What do you really want to know?"

I gave her the same story I'd provided to John. Enough to make sense without offering too much detail. She seemed genuinely interested, which made getting down to work much easier.

"I'm not sure that I have anything to offer. I was busy with classes and fieldwork the week before Dr. Odum left for the meeting in Los Angeles."

"Just tell me what you know about him and his work."

"Let's see, he has, or had," she sighed briefly, "three students. John, Howard, and me. John's just a nerd who lives for his punch cards and wouldn't know a plant from an animal. He was developing forest growth models. Saving the world through math. Howard's a nice guy, a little naïve but well-meaning. Dr. Odum was planning to put him on the forest project in Thailand. The idea was to compare regeneration in temperate and tropical ecosystems."

"Was the project a done deal?"

"No. It's hard to get grant money for overseas work. But Dr. Odum had spent time in Thailand and established a good contact in the Ministry of

Forests and Wildlife in Bangkok. The fellow had already coordinated the shipment of samples to our lab for a pilot study."

"So, you have tropical trees sitting around?"

"Not whole trees, silly. Bales of leaves for nutrient analysis. We need a lot of material even for the preliminary work that Dr. Odum hoped to parlay into big funding. The idea was to start by looking at nitrogen levels, which he figured might be key to regeneration."

"That sort of research sounds like it would be expensive. Lots of sophisticated equipment, I suppose?" The man seemed to have plenty of dough—for a fine house, museum-quality artwork, research projects—and a major sabotage operation.

"Yeah, time on the GC-mass spec isn't cheap. New columns can run you hundreds of bucks, and then there's the cost of gases and reagents." I nodded, as if I had a clue what she'd said.

"So, without a grant, how was Professor Odum funding the preliminary research and his international travel?"

Jen smiled in a conspiratorial way and gave a soft laugh. She put her hand on my boot and pushed herself up. I stood up as well, and she leaned close to me, the softness of her breast pressing against my bicep. It didn't seem like she noticed. I did.

"You don't look like an exterminator," she declared, gently poking me in the chest. "Are you sure you're not a cop?"

"I used to be, but I traded in my .38 for a spray nozzle years ago." She briefly pressed herself harder against me and then drew away mischievously.

"Well then, if you'll come by my apartment Thursday morning, I'll take you to one of Dr. Odum's field sites that will answer your question."

"I'm intrigued." Which was true in more ways than one. I wondered who had been objectified, to borrow Carol's term. It wasn't clear to me whose body had been used—and what it would mean for each of us in a couple of days.

"Good. I have the upstairs apartment at 410 Dana, a couple blocks south of campus. Be there by seven or I'll leave without you," she called over her shoulder as she walked back to her tiny trees.

⧉

I headed into the forest, the return to my truck being easier on the lungs and harder on the knees. I had one more stop to make on this side of the Bay before calling it a day. I drove back down to the Berkeley campus and made my way to Wellman Hall, an impressive granite building. This was the one place I could find without asking directions, as I'd been there several times.

The Essig Museum of Entomology hosted "Insect Safaris" at various sites around the Bay, and Tommy loved these outings. The museum staff would bring display cases of fantastic insects, along with some live hissing roaches and giant millipedes to get people fired up. Then they'd provide a brief description of the habitat and its insect community and send folks out with nets for a couple hours of collecting, after which the entomologists would identify the specimens. Tommy had befriended an energetic young fellow from the museum—unlike most taxonomists, who seem to have been somehow born as sixty-year-old men—who had a remarkable knack for working with kids. So Tommy and I had made it part of our routine to check out the public displays at the Essig at least a couple times a year and drop in on his pal.

Once in the building, it was easy to find the museum by following the scent of naphthalene. A series of dark-stained office doors with pebbled glass lined the hallway across from the insect collection, and I knocked on the one with the name "Scott Fortier, Associate Curator" stenciled on the glass.

"Come in," he called, and I poked my head through the door. Scott unfolded himself from his chair. The man must have been at least six foot four and couldn't have weighed more than 170 pounds. "Riley! It's great to see you. Where's Tommy?" he asked, coming around his desk, which was buried in piles of papers and unopened mail. Scott had a crooked-toothed grin on his long, horselike face. His hair looked like blond steel wool. He was homely as hell but irresistible in his warmth and enthusiasm.

"He's at home, Scott. We were just here a few weeks ago, so I didn't bring him along."

"That's right, you two dropped by in July. It was the weekend of the Fourth, if I remember correctly."

"You're good." How a fellow could keep track of such details amid the utter chaos of his office was beyond me. Tables on either side of his overflowing desk were covered in wooden boxes, cardboard trays for pinning insects, microscope slides, and books opened to elegant line drawings of insect anatomy.

"So what brings you to this side of the Bay?" he asked, shuffling sideways between his desk and a waist-high stack of scientific journals, the top one being *The Coleopterists Bulletin* with a photograph of a dung beetle on the cover.

"I found a beetle that I'm struggling with," I offered, knowing that Scott loved a challenge almost as much as he adored beetles. He led me down the hall, past the public displays, to the main collection. The room was filled, floor to ceiling, with wooden cabinets forming a maze of narrow walkways. There must've been several hundred thousand insects perfectly pinned, carefully labeled, and lovingly stored. Scott sat down at one of the dissecting microscopes, and I pulled up a chair.

"Okay, let's see your tricky insect," he said. I pulled out the vial and handed it to him.

"They're pretty banged up, but at least there're enough pieces to work with," I said. He scowled, placed them in a glass dish, and pushed them under the microscope.

"The tarsal formula is that of the coccinellids," he murmured.

"That's where I got stumped," I said, not wanting to equate my amateurism with his expertise.

"These aren't typical ladybirds, but I think I've seen them before." He pushed back from the microscope and stared at the ceiling, as if the fluorescent fixture would provide the answer. Then he closed his eyes and it looked like he was in pain. I remained dead still, hoping he was deep in concentration rather than having a migraine. Suddenly he jumped out of his chair, sending it crashing backward to the floor. I set it back on its legs and followed him into the maze of cabinets. He began running his finger down the labels on the drawers and pulling them out to peer inside, each time shaking his head in annoyance. Finally, he pulled out a drawer at about chin height for him and peeked over the edge.

"That's the one. I had the genus as *Harmonia*, but I couldn't remember the species." He lifted the glass cover from the drawer and removed a tray of beetles from somewhere near the back corner. Now I could see about two dozen specimens neatly aligned on pins. Scott carried the tray back to the microscope in his office and set my beetles next to the museum mounts. I waited while he examined the insects and hummed happily, if not melodiously.

"Are they the same species?" I finally asked.

Scott leaned back in the chair, clearly pleased with himself. "Yes, they're all *Harmonia axyridis*. But the species has three color forms." He explained that some were reddish orange with black spots, others were black with four red spots, and a few were black with two red spots. My beetles were a perfect match to the last ones.

"Are they rare?"

"Not really, at least in a global sense. The only reason I remembered this species is because the Department of Agriculture sent us a series of specimens a few months ago. My assistant was on vacation so I worked them into the collection myself."

"So they're pests?" It seemed peculiar for ladybird beetles, but I knew that a few species attacked crops.

"Quite the opposite. The boys at the USDA are planning to import them from Southeast Asia as predators of aphids, and they wanted to let us know so we wouldn't be caught off guard. Where'd you get these?" Now I was in a tough spot. So I fibbed enough to avoid the messy details of my investigation. It's always best to evade with a half-truth, as it is very difficult to create a convincing full-blown lie without careful planning—as plenty of suspects have discovered in the course of an interrogation.

"Well, it's a bit awkward. Let's just say a friend of a friend found these in a baggie of dope."

"Ah, the old 'friend of a friend' eh?" He figured I was being evasive, but no harm there. "Well, it makes sense. Marijuana is a great food source for aphids and whiteflies. And these beetles would find easy pickings in a field of pot."

"So you know about pests of marijuana, eh?" I teased in return.

"That's what I've been told by a friend," he replied, giving me a knowing smile. "And it looks like your friend has latched onto some pretty good stuff."

"How so?"

"The stuff from Burma, Cambodia, and Thailand is pretty choice. Or so I've been told by those who have experience with these sorts of things." I didn't know what Scott thought about me, but it wasn't important. What mattered was that he'd added a piece to the puzzle. I thanked him and promised that next time I'd have my kid brother with me. He seemed delighted at having solved my entomological mystery and at the prospect of a visit from Tommy.

As I drove back to San Francisco, KDFC was playing a program of modern classical music. This made it easy to think because I have no problem disengaging from the works of John Cage and Philip Glass. The ladybird beetles had ratted out Odum as having dope from Southeast Asia. This might somehow fit with his project in Thailand, but it didn't help to link him with the woman from South Africa. And none of this helped explain the poisoning. At least tomorrow held the promise of making some progress on what role AmeriChem might've had in Odum's death. I had plenty of pieces and some even fit together, but I still couldn't see the whole picture.

I was frustrated, so I grabbed a quick bite and spent the evening pounding the heavy bag, working the speed bag, and heaving a medicine ball with an aging has-been who'd once dominated the local fight scene. During a break, I leaned on the apron of the ring and watched a couple of young turks bang away. Marty came over, an unlit cigar stub clenched in his teeth.

"The white kid's strong," I said.

"Sure is. And his footwork is top-notch," Marty replied without a hint of enthusiasm.

"But?"

Marty shifted the cigar to the other side of his mouth. "But the Mexican kid has heart." The white guy had landed a wicked jab-and-hook combination that sent his opponent against the ropes.

"Doesn't look like heart's going to help him tonight," I observed as the Mexican fighter tried to cover up.

"Nope, but my money's on him for the long haul," Marty rasped.

"If he survives."

"He'll survive all right. He's just like you were when you came here as a kid. Except he has talent."

"Gee, thanks, Marty."

"I don't mean it in a bad way. Look, you didn't have hand speed and you were forever crossing up your feet. But if you survived the first two rounds of a fight, then there'd be hell to pay in the third."

"Fair enough."

"I can teach technique, but heart has to come from the fighter. The white kid, he's had lots of coaching in a fancy gym in Pacific Heights. He's just here cuz they're closed for remodeling."

"When are you going to remodel, Marty?"

"And lose this ambiance? Never," he grunted. "But you see, that kid'll go back to his hoity-toity trainer and equipment where he'll apply his skills in the ring every week so he can win some trophies and add a line to his college application. Luis will stay here and use his skills in the streets and maybe win enough money to buy his way out of being a dishwasher at his uncle's restaurant." The bell rang, and the fighters headed to their corners.

"So you wanna bet on Luis? I got five bucks that says he'll be on the canvas in the next round."

"No bet. But give it a year. And if these guys meet and it goes past the second round, the smart money will be on Luis."

Marty turned and shuffled back toward his office. I went back to the heavy bag and wondered whether the smart money was on me when it came to solving Odum's murder before time ran out.

Chapter Twenty-Six

I rolled out of bed with that deep and pleasant soreness that reminds a guy he can still push his body hard. A scalding shower melted some of the ache out of my neck and shoulders. I figured this could be a long day, so I fried up four eggs and toasted a stack of bread. My coffee wasn't as stout as Gustaw's but it did the trick. I glanced through the paper—the Communists were busy launching cosmonauts and burying Mao Tse Tung. Good riddance on both counts if you ask me. Meanwhile, NASA had unveiled its space shuttle, demonstrating that the American government has no clue about the value of money in a recession. Space isn't going anywhere, so what's the rush? Maybe the world was going to hell, but it turned out that in my little corner of the universe, things were working out. I dialed my favorite hotel in Los Angeles and got lucky.

"Thank you for calling the Hyatt Regency, this is Linda. How may I help you?" she intoned.

"Drive up to San Francisco and have dinner with me."

"Excuse me?"

"You wouldn't disappoint your old friend Riley, would you?"

"Riley!" I could hear the excitement in her voice, and then she whispered, "I can't take personal calls at work. You'll get me in trouble. What are you doing calling me?"

"Just wanted to hear your lovely voice," I tried.

"Save it, Casanova. What do you need, and make it quick before the manager catches me talking with you."

"Okay sweetie, Odum's death has gotten complicated, but nothing that will make trouble for your hotel. I need you to pull the registry for the week of that science convention and see if you can find a guest named Sarah."

"You're such a romantic."

"Sorry, you said to make it quick."

"Yeah, just like a typical man—only too happy to make it quick. Hang on, let me see what I can find." She put me on hold and I listened to an orchestrated version of a Beatles tune. Leave it to the music industry to take one of the few pop groups with a modicum of talent and make their songs unlistenable.

"You're lucky. My manager is tied up with a guest who managed to scald himself in the shower and is threatening to sue."

"Thank God for stupid people. What did you find?"

"There were no guests registered as 'Sarah' for that meeting. However, there was a Sarie Botha who paid the conference rate."

"Can you spell that?" She did and then struck gold.

"Hold on, there's more. She had a reservation through Friday, but she checked out on Wednesday." Linda's voice trailed off.

"The day Odum was found dead."

"So it would appear. Do you think she's connected to his death?"

"Maybe. At least I'd love to ask her some questions. Do you have her address or phone number in your records?"

"Sorry, I can't help on that one. We give guests a card at check-in, but most folks don't fill it out."

"You've been a huge help. And I was serious about the dinner. I'll be back in LA sometime. And San Francisco is a very romantic city just a few hours to your north, if you're looking to get out of the smog."

"I don't know what I see in you. But inscrutable exterminators have always been a weakness of mine." I laughed and her voice dropped in pitch. "Riley?"

"Yes?"

"Be careful. This whole thing sounds like it's getting creepy. Remember curiosity killed the cat."

"Don't worry about me. I'm an old alley cat. It's the mice that need to watch out." In more ways than she imagined. We said our good-byes and I headed out the door, hoping that my luck would hold when it came to finding Sarie Botha.

I drove over to the Mission Station, where I'd been assigned in my early days on the force. Some of my best buddies, including a fair number who stood behind me in the tough times, were still there. I dropped by every so often to catch up on news and remember just how bad police station coffee could be. The grimy gray stonework, and the palm trees flanking the heavy columns leading to the entrance, made the place look like it had been lifted straight out of Havana and plunked down on Valencia Street. I went in and told the desk officer that I was looking for Kelly Madsen. Without looking up from his crossword puzzle, he waved me down the hall.

Kelly was a fiery redhead who worked in the Records Division, and we'd had a brief but intense affair. Neither of us found what we were looking for, except in bed where she was incredible and I managed to barely keep up with her inventiveness. But we didn't have much else in common, so our dates consisted of stilted conversation over a rushed dinner followed by a luscious dessert in her bedroom, or kitchen, or even the elevator. It'd been a while since I'd seen her, but there were no hard feelings, so I hoped I might be able to plead for a favor.

"Hey doll, how's life treating you?" I asked, admiring the way she stretched the buttons on a police-issue blouse.

"Well, well," she replied, her green eyes sparkling. "To what do I owe the honor of a visit from my favorite Irishman?"

"I need a favor, Kelly. I'm trying to find a person." She liked to get down to business—at work and in bed.

"And why, pray tell, would I use police equipment for a private matter?" she purred, just to remind me of what I'd given up years ago.

"For old times' sake?"

"Mmmm. There were some fine times, Riley."

"So how 'bout it?"

"Maybe I can sneak in a special favor without getting caught," she said coyly. "The sergeant has been on the phone all morning arguing with his wife's lawyer about who gets the boat, so I have a bit of latitude if you know what I mean. What's up?"

"I'm trying to find a woman named Sarie Botha. She's likely a foreign national from South Africa." Kelly was jotting notes on the back of a punch card.

"What else have you got?"

"That's it," I admitted.

"Not much to go on, but I'll give it a run." She started clacking away on her keyboard, punch cards rolling across the face of the machine. Watching those long freckled legs unfold from beneath her desk brought back some very fond memories. She took the cards and dropped them off at a window on the far side of the room and sashayed back. Kelly sat back down, crossed her legs, and rotated her foot in long slow circles. I leaned against her desk and we managed to talk about life—her vacation to San Diego last month and my collecting trip to Mexico in June—in a way that we'd never managed when we were together. A buzzer sounded on her desk and she headed back to the window. Kelly returned looking disappointed.

"Nothing," she said. "Didn't find a match, but I didn't think it'd be easy."

"I know, it's not much. But it's pretty important to me. Well, to a friend of mine."

"Don't try to explain or you'll just end up lying. I only ran her name through outstanding warrants. There're a bunch of tricks I can use—different spellings, immigration records, things like that."

"So, you can keep trying?"

"You know me, Riley, I was never one to quit when things got hard." She leered at me. I was tempted, but I knew as good as it'd be for a while, I'd get burned by this rekindled flame.

"That's for sure, doll." I glanced at my watch. "Hey, I have to run. Give me a call if you find anything?" She looked disappointed that I hadn't taken the bait, but her pout was too perfect to be authentic.

"It may take a while, but I'll let you know." She stood up, put her hands on my shoulders, and gave me a kiss on the cheek. "It was really good to see you, Riley." At least that felt genuine.

I headed back down the long hallway, feeling that maybe the world was going to give me a break after all. And I knew I'd need some luck if my meeting with Bino at AmeriChem Industries was going to get me any closer to a payday with Laurie Odum.

Chapter Twenty-Seven

I grabbed an early lunch at a diner where I used to get free food as a cop, a couple blocks down Valencia. There were new owners and staff, so nobody knew me, but I liked soaking up the old atmosphere—vinyl bench seats, chipped linoleum, and a brushed stainless steel counter. I went over various approaches to my conversation with Bino. I needed to give him enough to entice him into talking, but not so much as to make him suspicious. I'd learned long ago that rather than scripting an interview, a good detective let the witness take the lead. But Bino had been a cop too, so I didn't know if he'd be drawn into this ploy.

I swung by the shop to pick up the vial of toxic goo that I'd scraped from Odum's underwear. The chemists at AmeriChem could probably identify the stuff, and I'd even worked out a cover story as to how I'd acquired it and why I needed to know. Adaptability is fine but you can anticipate a few moves. At least a bit of planning paid off in the short term—I managed to get the vial and Odum's papers from my desk and stuff it all into one of those expandable envelopes while Carol was out to lunch. My timing meant I didn't have to suffer her wrath for the phone messages stacked on the corner of my desk. She'd left a note on top of the pile: "See you after work at O'Donnell's. Or else!" I couldn't miss Wednesday night beers two weeks in a row or there'd be hell to pay.

On the way over to Oakland, I listened to a program of Beethoven's piano sonatas and wondered whether Bino's loyalty would favor his corporate employer or an old pal. Probably the former, unless I played things just right or my lucky streak continued. The plant was surrounded by a chain link fence with razor wire, and the guard shack at the entrance made it clear that AmeriChem took security seriously. The uniformed guard wanted to see my driver's license, then called to be sure my appointment was for real.

I was assigned a parking spot in front of the main building—a stark, concrete tribute to Soviet architecture, which struck me as ironic since the headquarters was packed with some of the nation's most fervent capitalists. I had to check in with another guard in the lobby, who showed no interest in the contents of the envelope I carried. I took an elevator to the fifth floor, checked out the map on the wall, and walked down a spotless, gleaming corridor to room 5780—which was quite a contrast to the building's exterior. The reception area was decked out in cherrywood furniture, the hardware was all polished brass, and the walls were lined with expensively framed aerial photographs of AmeriChem factories around the world.

A gray-haired receptionist wearing a classy women's business suit nodded when I introduced myself. She gave me a stern look and buzzed Bino. A moment later, the door off to the side of her desk opened. My old friend stood there with his loosened tie hanging askew over a wrinkled white shirt that had probably been tucked when he arrived at work. I gathered that he'd been enjoying his pasta and Chianti. Bino looked like a well-fed disheveled accountant from the neck down. But with his square jaw, intense eyes, and heavy brow he looked like a mafioso from the neck up.

"Come in, Riley, you old dog!" He waved me into his office and closed the door. We shook hands heartily and he latched onto my shoulder. "Feels like you've stayed in shape," he said, giving my arm an appreciative squeeze. He pulled up a chair for me that I could've sworn he'd swiped from the precinct's interrogation room. Bino's office couldn't have been a greater contrast to the anteroom, which was decorated for the eyes of the public and corporate types. He went to sit behind his desk, one of those gray steel jobs that weigh a ton. "Sorry I don't have much furniture for hosting visitors. The bigwigs tried to give me a bunch of that froufrou furniture, but I worked with the facilities guys to set me up with something that made it feel more like the old squad room." It showed.

The office was spacious, with a wide window looking out to a gargantuan jungle gym of pipes, tanks, and steel structures. Below the window was a row of mismatched filing cabinets. On the opposite wall was a bank of television monitors, and lining the wall behind me were green army-issue bookcases stuffed with binders bearing labels such as "Security and Blast Barrier Designs."

"It's good to see you, Bino," I said, waving off his apology for the furnishings. In fact, the room felt remarkably comfortable, not unlike my office but five times larger.

"Tell me, Riley, how've ya been?"

I assured him that I'd landed on my feet—Goat Hill Extermination was flourishing and I enjoyed the business and my people. I filled him in on my mother and Tommy, saying that everything was working out for us. In return, Bino seemed overjoyed to tell me about his deep-sea fishing trips and a boat-building project he had going in his garage. Chitchat having paved the way, I moved the conversation toward the reason for my visit.

"Sounds like your weekends are great, Bino. But how's the job? You told me a while back that you had a cushy gig going around here."

He leaned his elbows on the desk and rubbed his temples. "Riley, the world is changin'. I figured maybe some crackpots would want to mess with a chemical plant. Nothin' too serious—a few sign-wavers and maybe a fence-jumper. But security has become a friggin' nightmare in the last few months."

"How so? You got people pinching drums of benzene?" I teased, trying to keep him talking.

"Christ, if it was only that easy. I got corporate espionage comin' at me from every direction. Our competitors are after the formula for a new insecticide that's supposed to revolutionize agriculture accordin' to the AmeriChem brainiacs in the lab coats. Then there's a Dutch company sniffin' around, and our management is worried that they're preparin' for a hostile takeover. Hell, I don't even know what that means, but I'm supposed to do somethin' about it. And last week a Japanese guy takin' a tour of the plant had a camera hidden in his briefcase like some sort of slant-eyed James Bond."

"Sounds like a circus."

"That's not the half of it. I got environmental wackos who'd love to embarrass the company by creatin' an accident or screwin' with our production system." That was the opening I'd hoped for. I tried not to sound too interested.

"No kidding? There're people who'd attack your plant in the name of saving the planet?"

"Yeah, somethin' like that. But hey, ya didn't come out here to hear about my problems," he said, leaning back in his chair. "What's up?" Bino was clearly a busy man—more so than he'd originally bargained for. So rather than being too cutesy, I combined a bit of evasion with an honest appeal.

"I'm helping out a friend, and there might be a link to AmeriChem."

"Oh yeah? And ya think I can help?" I was hoping that by laying one of my cards on the table, Bino might be willing to play along.

"Maybe. Ever hear about a fellow named Paul Odum?" Bino's face hardened momentarily, like I'd mentioned his ex-wife. It had been an ugly divorce.

"Sure. We know about him." Bino went to the filing cabinet nearest his desk, pulled out a drawer, grabbed a file, and laid it open on his desk. I was happy to see that there didn't look to be more than a few pages of typed notes. If my raid on Odum's office gave me information that AmeriChem lacked, I might work it to my advantage. "But it seems that this little problem is no longer with us." He pointed to a fax on company letterhead. "My counterpart at our Bakersfield plant reported that Odum died in his sleep in an LA hotel room. What's yer connection to the guy?"

"It's a bit convoluted," I lied. "But the bottom line is that this friend of mine knew Odum and had some questions about the cause of death."

"Good riddance, if ya ask me."

"Why's that?"

"I bet ya already know, but I'll play along. We had reason to believe that he was plannin' some sort of attack on the plant. We been trackin' him for a while, but there wasn't enough evidence to turn over to the police." This wasn't sounding like a corporate hit, at least not one that Bino knew anything about.

"So that'd be the normal course of action? AmeriChem security wouldn't, you know, take care of things on its own?"

"Like what—contract a hit? C'mon, Riley, ya been readin' too many of those San Francisco leftist newspapers. Hell, the corporate bigwigs have the politicians and bankers eatin' outta their hands. AmeriChem is worth a couple billion dollars and we employ a thousand people. If we want a troublemaker shut down, we don't need to mess with private contractors. The police chief is a political appointee who works for the city—and we stuff the coffers of government. See what I'm sayin'?"

"Yeah, I didn't really think the company was involved. But like you say, the world is getting weirder all the time." By this time, I'd crossed off Ameri-Chem from my list of suspects. If they'd been involved, their head of security would've been in the loop and Bino never would've admitted knowing about Odum or his shenanigans.

"Ain't that the truth," he sighed and leaned back in his chair. "Ya know that I'd love to give ya access to our files on Odum, but the corporate boys want to keep these investigations quiet."

"Maybe I could add something of interest to your files in exchange for a favor." I hadn't planned to play things this way, but I was pretty sure Bino would love to have the notes I'd acquired from Odum's study.

"Riley, ya haven't changed a bit. Always figurin' an angle. I remember how ya worked witnesses and suspects to get what ya needed. Now that I think about it, I'm feelin' a little like one of 'em." He smiled, letting me know he didn't harbor any resentment. Bino was savvy enough to know I was gaming him. "So, what's the offer?"

"I can give you the details of the attack Odum had planned, including his weapon of choice."

"That might be of interest."

"There's more. I can also provide the names of six guys in AmeriChem who he either paid or was planning to pay off."

"Now yer talkin'. Is the information good?"

"It's in his own handwriting."

"I'm impressed. We figured he had somethin' in the works, and I knew that he'd made contact with Frank Moffett at the gatehouse. In fact, Frank came to me after Odum approached him at a bar with a generous offer to look the other way and let a van pass onto the grounds. I thought he was plannin' to crash the van into a storage tank or the lobby. But it sounds like maybe he had somethin' bigger in mind."

"Would five hundred pounds of ammonium nitrate give you a hint as to what something bigger might've been?"

"Holy shit. The guy must've been nuts. And yeah, I'd like to know who he had targeted for payoffs inside the company other than Frank. I'll show ya what we got on the guy, but it's soundin' like ya got more on him than we do.

So I'm guessin' yer after somethin' else. What's it gunna cost me?" he asked, rubbing the back of his neck. I picked up the envelope from where I'd left it under my chair.

"I want to know what's in this," I said, pulling out the vial and setting it on the desk. He lifted the glass container to eye level and squinted.

"Looks like Vaseline or glue." He started to unscrew the cap.

"Don't! Whatever's in there is pretty toxic."

"Okay," he said, setting it down gingerly. "I can get the eggheads in the residue lab to do their magic, but I have to give 'em a reason. The bean counters need a justification for everything." I'd worked out my story in advance, so this was easy.

"I have a competitor who's applying this stuff along baseboards of people's houses for cockroach control. I suspect that he's formulating it himself, and I'm sure he doesn't know what he's doing. I had a disgruntled technician from his company tell one of my guys that customers' pets were showing up dead along with the cockroaches."

"I can see where that'd be a problem for him. But what's it to you?"

"The environmental kooks have launched a crusade against exterminators. We are Satan's soldiers, and AmeriChem is the headquarters of hell. I don't need some idiot poisoning puppies and kittens—or God forbid, some kid—to make things any worse for those of us who know what we're doing."

"So, if it turns out that this stuff is a cheap backroom formulation, yer gunna report the guy?"

"Nah. Imagine the fallout if the press finds out that an exterminator killed Fido or Fluffy with a homemade concoction. Those healthier-than-thou zealots would have a field day."

"A slaughter of the heathens, eh?"

"Exactly. Let's just say that if your chemists come back with the right answer, I'll be having a come-to-Jesus meeting with my colleague. He'll have converted to another line of business before I'm through."

"All right, I think I can put this in terms that'll satisfy the lab director. We hafta make sure that insecticides are used safely for the industry's reputation, even if yer pal's concoction doesn't involve an AmeriChem product. Now, what about the information on Odum?"

I pulled out the sheaf of papers from the envelope and slid them across his desk. Bino looked at them, taking enough time to get a sense of what they meant. He nodded and grunted after turning each page, trying to hide his rising interest, but he couldn't keep his bushy eyebrows from arching when he got to the booklet on pothole blasting and Odum's list of ingredients. He pressed the intercom button on his desk.

"Mrs. Brubaker, could ya please come here. I have some papers to be copied." The door opened and his secretary strode stiffly into the room. He handed her the materials and she made a point of glaring down her nose at me. He shrugged and grinned, like a kid behind the teacher's back. Once she had closed the door behind her, he smiled mischievously. "That should give us just about enough time to toast our reunion. This is strictly against corporate policy and she'd just love to report me to the vice president and score some points for a promotion out of this purgatory, so stash the evidence when ya hear her comin' back."

"No problem." I felt like I was back in high school sneaking a smoke in the boys' room.

"I'd offer you a good cigar, but that's against the rules too. The old bat would sniff me out in a heartbeat. I can only enjoy a smoke after she's gone for the day and I spray some of that perfumy deodorizer shit around so's the place smells of lemon lilacs or whatever by morning."

Bino unlocked the lowest drawer of his desk and extracted a pair of high-ball glasses along with a bottle of Wild Turkey. Thanks to Mrs. Brubaker's speedy work—which was surely a function of her evident desire to see me leave—I was limited to just one drink. It was just as well since I knew that my crew would be waiting for me at O'Donnell's Pub.

Chapter Twenty-Eight

After a long day, there was nothing better than downing a cold one with my crew—a Wednesday tradition since I'd taken over Goat Hill Extermination after my father's death. He would've approved, believing that next to family, friends are a man's most important assets (God and country came after, but I'm not sure in which order). My father had dozens of business associates and acquaintances but only a handful of close friends. As I came through the doors of the pub, the gang raised their mugs in mock salute, Isaac looking uncomfortable with his insubordination.

"Hail to the chief," Larry proclaimed, and the four of them drank deeply and facetiously in my honor.

I nodded to Brian, who was behind the bar pulling another pitcher of Anchor Porter for the table. "I suppose they have you putting that on my tab?" I asked.

"Sure enough, Riley. They said you were a generous boss, always givin' of himself to others." He laughed and handed me the pitcher. At least the gang had good taste. The deep amber ale had a thick creamy head—just to my liking, if not my pocketbook's.

"Glad you could make it, boss," Dennis said, as I refilled their glasses and settled into a chair that was as comfortable as it was battered.

"Yeah, Dennis, who'd buy your beer if I didn't show up?" I replied.

"It's no problem, Riley," Carol answered. "When you were in LA last week, we just put the drinks on your tab. But I suppose you'd have to drop in sometime or Brian would quit serving us."

"I'm truly touched," I said. The conversation meandered from Harvey Milk (according to Carol, the first openly gay man to be a city commissioner), to Patty Hearst (who finally got a seven-year sentence for bank robbery, "as if the spoiled bitch needed the money," noted Larry), to Elvis Presley (who Dennis announced would be giving a concert at the Cow Palace in November, which seemed to excite everyone except me), to Jackie (Larry's serious girlfriend, who Carol thought should become his fiancée over Dennis's strenuous objections while Isaac wisely chose neutrality). Finally, I had to break in.

"Okay, Carol tells me if I'm going to deduct these little gatherings from my taxes, we have to talk business for at least a few minutes. So how're things going at Goat Hill?" Larry and Dennis recounted a particularly nasty job in the bowels of a cockroach-infested warehouse, and Carol gave me a rundown on a couple of new leads for contracts with landlords and restaurateurs who'd gotten tired of slapdash treatments by the big boys.

"What about you, Isaac? Getting the feel of this crazy line of work?" I asked, hoping he'd been fitting in a bit better.

"Yeah, I guess so," he replied, idly dragging his finger through the water ring his mug had left on the table.

"Ah, c'mon, Isaac, you're getting it," Larry encouraged. "You and Dennis handled that flour beetle infestation at Dockside Bakery with panache."

Isaac perked up a bit and then leaned forward, resting his forearms on the table. "Can I ask you guys something?"

"Sure," Dennis answered for everyone. "We's all friends at Goat Hill," he offered in his most Southern black accent.

"I've been reading about chemicals. You know, insecticides and stuff like that." He paused. "Can I be honest with you?"

"Go ahead," I said.

"Well, there's a pretty ugly history behind what we do. Poisoning isn't the most honorable way of making money. What keeps you guys going in this business?"

"Cuz Riley buys the beer," Carol proposed. Everyone laughed and drank to that, while I caught Brian's eye and ordered another pitcher.

"No, really. I'm serious," Isaac said, looking somehow sad for us.

"It's easy," Dennis said, dropping any of his hip, black jive. It was as serious as I'd seen him. "For me, it's about getting out of the projects and getting even."

"What do you mean about getting even?" Isaac asked.

"I saw a baby killed by rats," Dennis said in almost a whisper.

"Jesus," Larry said. "You never told me that."

"I don't like remembering," Dennis answered. "When I was fifteen, a neighbor lady set to screaming in the middle of the night. The whole hallway was woke up. My old man pounded on her door, but she wouldn't answer so he kicked it in thinking she was dying or something. I followed behind to a bedroom where she was holding this baby that had been chewed up. Its crib was all bloody and its body looked like it had been slashed. There were gouges across the baby's face." He paused and took a deep breath. "They'd eaten its ears."

"Shit, Dennis," Larry said. "That must've messed you up." Carol looked like she was about to cry. I reached under the table and gave her leg a reassuring pat. She gripped my hand and leaned against my shoulder.

"The lady had worked the late shift and gotten home late. Her sister was supposed to check on the baby, but she'd gotten drunk and passed out. We called an ambulance, but the baby was hardly moving. I saw it quit breathing as the sirens came up the street." He took a deep draw on his beer. "I told myself then that I wasn't going to spend my life in the projects and that I'd kill anything that would hurt a baby."

"Geez, that's terrible. So you figure insects and rats are all about the same?" Isaac asked.

"I've seen poor folks' kitchens crawling with roaches. The kids in these places are always sick, and I know that the filth those insects carry around isn't helping. I know that things like that aren't right. And I know that I can fix it," Dennis said.

"So how about you?" Isaac turned to Larry, who was just nodding silently, taking in what he'd heard.

"I don't have a reason as good as Dennis does," Larry said. "For me it's pretty simple."

"How so?" Isaac asked.

"Some things just need killing. It's just like in 'Nam." Larry poured himself another beer and then filled Carol's glass.

"Quite the gentleman," she said approvingly. Dennis got up and went to the bar to grab a bowl of peanuts. For as skinny as he was, he could pack away bar food like a bottomless pit.

As he came back, one of the guys at the next table made his distaste for blacks evident with a sneer. His pal was too busy ogling Carol to join in the silent but conspicuous insult. She was a pleasant sight with a V-neck sweater that drew a man's eye to her freckled—and utterly off-limits—cleavage. The two guys looked like middle-aged salesmen passing through the neighborhood, with Brylcreemed hair, loosened neckties, and blazers draped over the backs of their chairs. They weren't regulars and they were fast becoming unwelcome visitors.

CHAPTER TWENTY-NINE

As Dennis sat down, the smaller of the two guys caught Carol's eye and his leer became a lewd wink as he puckered his lips. She flashed a look of disgust and turned back to our table—and I understood the objectification thing, which is usually complicated in my mind, but this time seemed repulsively simple. The pig's buddy continued to stare at Dennis like he was filth, until his buddy said something under his breath and they both started laughing. Then the two of them went back to their drinks and muffled conversation.

"Like I was saying," Larry started up again, "I don't claim to have known all that goes into figuring out which people need killing. That was up to the government and the officers. But I can tell you that after I saw what the VC did to a buddy of mine, those gooks went to the top of my 'to kill' list." He fell quiet, as if he could see the guy with his balls stuffed into his mouth—Larry had told me about this a year ago when he'd missed a couple days of work because nightmares kept him from sleeping. But he couldn't bring himself to describe it again, so he just said, "You don't do those things to another human without paying a price."

"And the Viet Cong were like cockroaches?" Isaac prompted.

"Not exactly. But what it comes down to is that one needed killing in the jungles and the other needs killing in the cities. Part of life is killing, and most people want someone else to do the killing for them," he said, punctuating his summary with a long draw on his beer.

"You want simple reasons?" Carol asked, putting her elbows on the table and resting her chin in her hands.

"Sure," Isaac answered, "this whole thing is getting weird." The kid looked a little shell-shocked, but between the beer and the intimacy of our regular table at O'Donnell's we were less inhibited than at work. That was the idea.

"It's a good job with a bunch of guys who know how to work and don't cheat people. That's a combination that's not easy to find. I've managed offices for contractors, food suppliers, cleaning companies, you name it. And everyone in those places was either stealing from the business or lying to customers."

"So, the poisoning doesn't bother you?" Isaac pushed further. It was obvious that something about the insecticides was not sitting right with him.

"I'll take working for decent people doing a shitty job that needs doing." She drained the last of her beer and slammed down the mug to make the point. The guy at the next table took advantage of the bang to grab another eyeful of Carol.

"How about you, Isaac? What's your stake in this game?" Larry asked.

"I appreciate the way you people approach this work. I really do. But I'm not sure it's for me."

"Listen, Isaac, if this gig isn't your thing, that's cool. But what's the hang-up, man? Maybe extermination has bad vibes for the sensitive arteest?" Dennis put his hand over his heart and closed his eyes. He was teasing, mostly.

"I liked how Riley told me this isn't paint by numbers," Isaac answered. "That we have to decide in each case which is the right paint to create the effect we want. I liked thinking that way, since I want to be an artist."

"Very nice, Riley, so now I have to put up with these two claiming to be the Picasso and Rembrandt of insecticides," Carol said, waving dismissively toward Larry and Dennis and rolling her eyes. She was back to her old self.

"It's just that I've been doing some reading about insecticides, and I found out stuff that makes it really disturbing to use these chemicals. You know that the Nazis discovered the nerve gases while trying to find new insecticides? We're basically spraying a form of the chemical that they developed to kill humans."

"Okay," I said, "I can see where that might be upsetting for a Jewish kid."

"That's not all. In the extermination camps—and I can't get over that we're exterminators—they used Zyklon B to gas my people. And that compound was originally used as a pesticide."

There was a moment of silence and then Larry piped up, "Harsh bong, dude—as they say in LA." A nice try, but it didn't break the tension.

"Who are we to judge who lives and who dies, even if we're talking about insects?" Isaac stared at the empty pitcher in the middle of the table.

I'd stayed out of the conversation so far. Listening is more my style on our beer nights. But I couldn't resist any longer. "Who are we to not judge? Remember, Isaac, when the Nazis came for the Jews, it was those who failed to judge between right and wrong who let their neighbors be taken away. Nobody asked to live in the Warsaw ghettos, or to fight in 'Nam, or to grow up in the projects. But you can either let others do your judging, and fighting, and killing, or you can take it on yourself. The thing is, either way it ends up being your decision."

"Whoa, that's heavy." Dennis shook his head. Isaac looked confused.

I got up for a last refill, and by the time I got back the conversation had made a turn toward a decidedly lighter topic, the Giants. They were debating the future of Ed Halicki, who'd just beaten the Dodgers in a complete game. Isaac and Dennis were arguing that he had great potential, having thrown a no-hitter against the Mets a year ago, while Carol and Larry had joined up to declare him a flash in the pan.

The folks on Potrero Hill have a special attachment to the ball club, given that the team played its first two seasons in our neighborhood at the old San Francisco Seals stadium along 16th Street while Candlestick Park was being built. When I was a high school senior and more trouble than I was worth, my father took Tommy and me to a game. Not that he was a baseball fan, but he wanted his kids to be proud that Potrero was the home of a major league team.

We finished off the last pitcher and Larry headed out with Isaac, as they'd come together in Larry's '69 Buick Electra, a copper-brown abomination that made my junker look respectable. Carol asked Dennis to walk her to her car. He offered his arm and she gracefully accepted. I chatted with Brian for a few minutes and then started to walk home. But when I came to the corner and was about to head up the hill, I looked down Connecticut and saw trouble.

A thin fog had drifted up from the Bay, but I could see four figures a half block away under a streetlight. And from the silhouette of an Afro and the sound of scuffling, it was my guess that Dennis and Carol had run into a problem. I headed toward them and realized that the two jerks from the pub had made their move. They were standing beside Carol's car, which she'd parked along the curb. As I got near them, I saw that the bigger guy had Dennis's arm pulled up behind his back, and from the look on his face the fellow was applying some serious pressure. The other guy had his arm around Carol and was saying, "A pretty girl like you shouldn't be interested in a nigger."

"Well, fellas," I interrupted, "I hate to break up this little party, but I think it's time everyone said good night." I'd stayed in the shadows along the buildings, and the two guys had been so intent on their victims that they were obviously surprised.

"Just keep walking, if you know what's good for you," sneered the guy who had Carol.

I was a bit tired, a bit drunk, and plenty angry. A bad combination. I stepped into the yellow haze of the streetlight. Carol stood in the way of a right jab, which was my preferred approach to ending this fiasco. So I opted for a left hook, my second-best punch—although I knew I'd probably regret not having my hands taped. The left would leave me open for a shot from the guy holding Dennis. But I figured he'd have his hands full. I was wrong.

My left hook connected solidly with the one guy's jaw, and a moment later the side of my head felt like it had been split open. Dennis's assailant had thrown him against the building and freed his hands to deliver a wicked shot to my ear. I lurched sideways and fell to one knee, bracing for the next blow. But out of the corner of my eye, I saw Dennis grab the back of the guy's collar with both hands. And then came the dull, hollow sound of a head being slammed into the side of Carol's car. As I struggled to my feet, Dennis pulled the guy back and repeated the facial treatment two more times, aiming for the edge of the car roof for maximum punishment. The guy slid down the windshield, leaving a smear of blood and draping himself across the hood. His buddy was on his hands and knees, looking dazed.

"You okay?" I asked Carol, who looked nearly as stunned as the jerk on the sidewalk.

"Yeah, thanks to you," she answered, her voice sounding far away and her face just now coming into focus.

"And I'm feelin' much better, bro," said Dennis, wiping his hands on his faux leather coat. Now that my head was clearing, I began to regret having delivered the left hook. My ring finger was hanging limp at an unnatural angle. Carol looked at my hand and winced as I gritted my teeth and yanked on the finger to pop it back into place. My pain triggered something in her, and she looked down at the guy on all fours.

"And are you okay, you chauvinist pig?" she asked, delivering a fierce kick to the man's face. His head snapped back, and he collapsed onto his stomach. Carol kicked him again in the side, and I could hear the meaty crunch of ribs giving way. Then she turned to the guy lying on the hood. "And how about you, you racist bastard?" she asked between clenched teeth. I could see what was coming, what with the guy's legs spread apart to prop him up against the car. He groaned in agony as her foot sank into his crotch, and he slid onto the sidewalk.

"Shit, you are one bad chick," Dennis murmured, nodding approvingly.

"Hey, what's going on there?" Brian shouted from the corner. He'd come out of the pub and started down the hill toward us.

"Just a little pest control operation," I said.

He looked at the two guys and the blood on the car. "I didn't like the looks of those two," he said. "And they're looking a mite worse now. Should I call the cops?"

"Yeah, these boys might be needing a bit of patching up at San Francisco General," I answered. He headed back up to the pub. Carol offered Dennis and me a ride home, but I said that I needed the walk. Dennis gave me a weak smile. I could tell that the surge of excitement was no longer blocking the pain in his shoulder. I helped him into the passenger seat, and they pulled away into the night.

I headed back up the hill, hoping I'd make it home and sack out before the beer and adrenaline gave way to the aching in my head and hand.

CHAPTER THIRTY

My alarm clock jolted me awake at five thirty. I felt awful. After a hot shower, I felt wide awake and awful. My head was pounding and my hand was throbbing. I had just enough time to swallow a few aspirin before heading over to meet Jen in Berkeley. Last night's unseasonal fog had persisted, and the dankness matched my mood.

As the fog was lifting, I pulled up to a Victorian house that had been cut up into apartments a few blocks from the university. The front door was unlocked and led to an entryway with two more doors, labeled "S. Buskirk" and "J. Tansley." The latter opened to a steep flight of stairs. I called out a greeting and headed up.

As I got to the landing, Jen shouted, "I'm back here." A narrow hallway led through a cramped kitchen and out to a nook that had been converted from a back porch into a sun room just large enough for an old-fashioned cupboard, a white-painted wooden table, and a couple of mismatched chairs. She was wearing a short terry cloth robe and had her hair in a ponytail. "Grab a cup," she said, gesturing to the mugs hanging on the wall. "The coffee's in the kitchen." I poured myself a cup and settled into one of the chairs.

We talked about the unusual weather, and Jen explained something about ocean temperatures and currents. I was distracted by the inability of her robe to stay closed and the glimpses of a small, daintily upturned breast. When it comes to sensual pleasures, I've always favored quality over quantity. Jen asked about my time as a cop. She seemed keenly interested, and I figured she was still trying to decide whether to trust me. I offered some vague answers as she finished her bowl of Grape-Nuts, birdseed, or whatever passed as breakfast for the healthy set. As she carried her bowl out to the kitchen, I followed with my mug.

"I'm going to take a shower," she said, taking a step toward me. "There's lots of hot water in this old house, so I may be a while. It's one of my guilty pleasures." She turned quickly so that her ponytail swung across my chest. Jen headed down the hall, and as she turned into what I took to be the bathroom, her robe slid from her shoulders and she added, "You can enjoy another cup of coffee or whatever turns you on."

The coffee was strong and it seemed to be helping my headache. It would've been pleasant to join her, but I figured she was playing a game and I dislike being a woman's pawn. Besides, I figured that her next move would involve far fewer complications than the gambit she'd just offered.

As I was finishing the dregs of my third cup and rubbing the back of my neck, she came into the sun room dressed in a halter top and jeans. I was surprised—and somewhat disappointed—that she wasn't wearing shorts. "You're looking a bit tense," she said.

"Am I?" I replied. "And what might you prescribe for that?"

"I have just the thing," she answered, pulling out a drawer from the cupboard. She held a joint between her fingers and struck a match. She inhaled slowly with her eyes closed and then passed it to me. "Go ahead, it'll take the edge off," she said, letting the smoke slowly leak from her mouth.

Having declined her first test, I figured that if I refused this one there'd be no seeing whatever she had to show me out in the field. There's a common belief that undercover cops aren't allowed to have sex or use drugs with informants. Bedding a healthy young woman had much more appeal than smoking pot. But I wasn't keen on her terms. Call me old-fashioned, but sex should be about love, or lust, but not passing an identity test. I understood her anxiety about taking an ex-cop—who might just still be on the job—on this morning's field trip. So I proved myself.

After I took a couple of perfunctory hits and she finished the joint, we headed out to the university truck parked in front of the house. Jen drove into Tilden Park and then down a series of winding dirt tracks to a dead end in a eucalyptus grove. She took a walking stick out of the truck bed and handed one to me. I followed her along a barely discernible trail through the underbrush. After a hundred feet or so, she veered to her left.

"Be careful. This is all poison oak," she warned, gesturing toward the shiny green shrubs that stretched up a hillside. Now I understood why shorts would've been a very bad idea. "Use your stick to push aside the branches." We made our way to the top of a low ridge and the vegetation changed markedly. The climb convinced my head and hand to join in a bout of synchronized throbbing.

"Here's Dr. Odum's little secret," Jen announced. Sunlight drenched an opening in the trees, allowing the marijuana to grow in green profusion.

"Not bad. This must've provided a nice little income, eh?" I asked, pushing my way into the chest-high tangle of plants.

"I'd guess we harvested nearly a hundred pounds last year."

"We?"

"Yeah, he cut me in on the deal after coming to trust me. First he sold me a couple of lids. When I was cool with that, he showed me his plots. I handled sales on campus. It wasn't the big time by any means, but after expenses my share was nearly a thousand bucks."

"Not bad."

"The best part is that I knew this weed was safe. After the paraquat fiasco a few years ago, I preferred to grow my own rather than risk being poisoned." She pulled a joint out of her pocket and lit up. "Wanna share another?" she asked.

"No thanks. I was tempted by your first test, but I think I passed the second one this morning." She looked hurt, knowing that I knew.

"Sorry, Riley. I had to be sure," she said, taking a deep drag and holding her breath. She sighed and released the sweet smoke. "You know, that first offer wasn't just a test. I like mature guys and you're really cute. There's a nice grassy patch under that oak." She nodded toward the far side of the clearing.

"I'm flattered, but let's keep things simple. There are plenty of students—and probably quite a few faculty—that'd be delighted to accept your offer." The aspirin were wearing off and the sun was making my head pound, so the prospect of a romp in the forest was less than enticing at the moment.

She stroked my arm and said, "But they're not a challenge, and I like challenges."

"I'll bet John would be a challenge."

"Yeah," she laughed. "Luring him away from his punch cards would be a test of any woman's seductive skills."

She finished the joint and we waded back into the poison oak. On the walk to the truck, I mulled over Odum's hobby farm. He wasn't making enough from his little operation to cover the costs of his attack on AmeriChem. Bribing the security and maintenance crews wasn't cheap when you're expecting a guy to put his job on the line for a one-time payment. But maybe a larger supply of high-quality pot would've funded his monkey-wrenching—say, a few bales of first-rate Asian dope. I asked Jen if she could take me to where Odum had stored the plant samples sent from Thailand.

&

Jen drove onto campus and parked at a loading ramp behind Hilgard Hall. It sure was easier to access the university when you drove a truck with their logo on it. We went through an unmarked door and down a cool, dimly lit hall. A room had a sign in large block letters. "Do Not Enter: Biological Material Under Quarantine."

"This is Dr. Odum's cold storage," she said, producing a key and unlocking the door. She led me into a long, narrow room with racks of wire shelves. "The vegetation samples from Thailand are in these packages." She swept her arm across three racks holding plastic-bound bales about two feet on a side. Each bore a label with a four-letter code followed by a series of numbers, along with "M. Srisai, Chief Scientist, Forest Regeneration Project, Ministry of Forests & Wildlife, Atsadang Road, Bangkok, Thailand, 10330." Jen hugged herself against the chill, so I suggested she wait outside. She seemed reluctant to leave me alone with the samples, but her shivering drove her out into the hallway.

I pulled out my pocketknife, cut through the plastic of one of the packages, and pulled back the flaps. The bale was stuffed with enormous glossy leaves of various shapes. I was going to try another, but making a mess of the storeroom didn't seem fair to Odum's students, since I wasn't sure of finding what I was looking for. So instead I dug through the leaves on the open side of the bale, piling the vegetation on the shelf. By now my fingers were getting numb, but the cold was relieving the throbbing in my hand, so I pressed on.

After pulling out a few inches of tropical tree leaves, I discovered another plastic package. Cutting into this, I hit pay dirt: a tightly packed mass of marijuana. I figured the inner package of pot had a street value of at least a grand. With twenty bales in cold storage Odum had plenty to finance his project at AmeriChem. Now I was shivering, so I stuffed the outer leaves back into the package and turned the cut side to the wall to keep the contents from spilling out.

"So what did you find?" Jen asked as I emerged. Her question seemed utterly genuine.

"Nothing," I lied and watched her face carefully. She gave no hint of surprise or relief. "Just bales of leaves that I presume are valuable to the world of science."

She laughed, "One man's detritus is another man's treasure. Dr. Odum processed the first shipment a few weeks ago, but I don't know when or if anyone will ever get to analyzing the rest."

"Can I buy you lunch?" I asked as we emerged into the sunlight. The sudden warmth momentarily melted the aching in my body.

"That's sweet of you, but I have to get back out to my field plots. The scientific ones," she said with a wink. "I'm still hoping that my thesis research is going to work out. Wanna ride back to my apartment to get your truck?"

"No, I've taken up enough of your morning." And a walk across campus sounded like good medicine to me.

"It was my pleasure. At least almost." She gave me a peck on the cheek and climbed into the cab of the truck.

As I headed across campus, I tried to fit the new pieces into the puzzle. It seemed that Odum had kept his new import business to himself, probably because he didn't want to explain to Jen why he was getting into the big leagues. I presumed that he was wholesaling the dope to distributors, since even at Berkeley a professor selling bags of pot from his office might catch the eye of campus authorities. With his supply line to Thailand and a great cover story, he could easily fund his extracurricular monkey-wrenching and underwrite his wife's environmental projects for years.

The problem for Odum was that while small-time growers weren't a threat to the major players, his new venture was sure to have attracted attention. Bino had convinced me that the companies dealing in legal chemicals weren't behind Odum's death. But the bigwigs in the illicit chemical industry don't like competition any more than their corporate counterparts. Maybe in his effort to save the world, Odum had made himself worth killing.

CHAPTER THIRTY-ONE

On the way across the bridge, KDFC was playing a marathon of Haydn's London symphonies, with one of my favorites, No. 96—better known as *The Miracle*—being featured on my drive back. By the time I reached Goat Hill Extermination, my aches had returned with a vengeance. But learning that Carol and Dennis were feeling fine did me a lot of good. And thanks to a handful of aspirin from the bottle in the top drawer of Carol's filing cabinet, life was improving by the minute.

The most painful part of coming to the office was being accosted by the inanity of a man and woman singing about muskrat love. There is simply no musical context which justifies lyrics about rodent passion. Carol mercifully turned down the radio and filled me in on events at work. Larry and Dennis were working on a big rat control job on the docks, so Isaac was handling a bunch of little assignments. She told me that Isaac looked preoccupied when he came to work, so I might want to check on him, "if you can afford time away from your project." I assured her that I'd be back full-time within a week. In fact, I had exactly seven days to come up with an answer for Laurie Odum. I was on my way out the door when the phone rang.

"It's Officer Madsen from the San Francisco Police," Carol said, covering the mouthpiece with her free hand. "You want to take it?"

"I'd better see what's up," I said. "Can you forward it to my office?" A few seconds later, the phone on my desk rang.

"Riley here, what's up, Kelly?"

"I have what you want," she said provocatively. Kelly could sound as tempting on the phone as she appeared in person.

"I know you do, but did you find out anything about Sarie Botha?" I answered, playing along.

"I had to dig around quite a bit, but the summer crime flurry is over so it's easier to work on special projects like yours. You know it's not easy for a busy girl to slip in these requests."

"And?" Kelly had always been good at drawing out the suspense, which was one of the qualities that made her so good in the sack.

"Your Miss Botha lives in Berkeley."

"No kidding?" I replied. The wheels were spinning.

"I have more," she cooed.

"You always did."

She snickered appreciatively. "I pulled the institutional directories and found that she works at the university in the anthropology department."

"Kelly, this is great work. I owe you, doll."

"Yes, you do, Riley."

We left it there, and I headed out to find Isaac. It was lucky that I could navigate the city without thinking, as my mind was churning. Either Howard had misunderstood his mysterious lover's name, or she'd used an amateurish alias. If she was Odum's killer, she certainly would have wanted to cover her tracks. She could've been a brilliant anthropologist for all I knew, but she certainly wasn't an experienced criminal. It hadn't been all that hard to trace her—or at least someone with a remarkably similar name. I'd have to get back over to Berkeley tomorrow to see if she matched Howard's description. With nearly five million people in the Bay Area, it was amazing how often names and identities got mismatched. And if Sarie Botha was a blond bombshell, then there was the little matter of figuring out a motive.

◊

I pulled up in front of Simon's Seafood, on the north side of the Castro. As I walked into the entryway, Simon came mincing from the back of the tentable restaurant. The lunch rush was over, so there were only a few lingering diners to fully appreciate his lavender silk shirt and the pair of white bellbottoms he must've painted on. No wonder the poor guy pranced rather than walked. But Simon made some of the best calamari in the city and his steamed clams Bordelaise was untouchable. As was Simon, at least if you were a woman.

"Riley, ith just awful," he lisped, taking my hand in his. "Thoth flieth will be the death of me," he declared with all the drama he could muster. Simon ran a first-class establishment. I'd taken Kelly there for a candlelight dinner a couple of times because it was one of the nicest restaurants I could afford on a cop's salary. So I knew his anxiety was real.

"Don't worry, Simon, we'll take care of them." I patted his hand, extricated mine, and headed through the kitchen. I found Isaac in the alley spraying the sunlit side of the building. A cloud of flies hovered overhead.

I stood there for a minute, then interrupted. "What's up, Isaac?"

He was so startled that he nearly sprayed me with the pyrethrin. "Sorry! You startled me, Riley. It's just a fly infestation. I should be done in a few minutes."

The concrete apron along the base of the wall was peppered with dead and dying flies. "Looks like you're cleaning up the adults pretty well. But do you think there's more where they came from?"

"More flies? Sure."

"No, I mean what's the source of these? Unless you treat the cause of the problem and not just the symptoms, you'll have to be back here in a few days."

Having finished coating the brick wall with insecticide, Isaac stepped back to inspect his work and consider my question. "I dunno. I suppose they come from the dumpsters back here."

"But then, wouldn't every alley be filled with flies, if all it took was a dumpster filled with garbage?"

"I suppose."

"So, check out the dumpsters and see if one of them has anything special happening." I had a pretty good sense of what he'd find based on the whiff I'd caught when I came into the alley. But it was a better lesson if he found out for himself. Isaac started working his way down the dumpsters, lifting the lids and letting them drop with a clang that made me wince. The aspirin were wearing off again.

"Oh gawd." He turned his head and screwed up his face.

"What'd you find, sport?"

He lifted his hand to his mouth and retched, but managed to keep his breakfast down. "In the bottom," he said through clenched teeth.

I held my breath, lifted the lid, and saw the remains of a pretty good-sized dog seething with maggots in the back corner of the dumpster. As I'd suspected, the oozing fluids had glued the carcass in place so the flies had an ongoing feast despite the efforts of San Francisco garbage trucks to periodically disgorge the contents of the dumpster.

"What now?" he asked.

"Time to act like an artful assassin instead of a mobster from the twenties with a tommy gun." Isaac looked quizzical. "The Orkin types rely on brute force. We rely on a tactical hit. So instead of repeatedly drenching a building with insecticide, lift the lid and soak the hell out of that maggot mine. And then get a shovel from the truck, take a really deep breath, climb in there, and scrape that mess loose so it'll fall out with the trash the next time a garbage truck happens to come by."

"It's not going to be pretty, but I can handle it."

"Good. And remember, kid, if it was pretty, nobody would pay us to do it."

He gave me a lopsided smile, and I headed back through the kitchen. I assured Simon that his fly problem was solved, and he was beside himself with relief. I was worried he'd try to hug me. To my relief, he conveyed his delight by offering me a platter of grilled shrimp. Squeezing some fresh lemon onto my meal was far more appealing than being squeezed by Simon.

⬥

I spent the afternoon at the main public library, a massive gray edifice in the city center that seems more of a tribute to utilitarian geometry than great books. But I wasn't there to peruse literature. With the help of a dumpy reference librarian who seemed utterly thrilled to be of assistance, I pored over university bulletins and course catalogues to get some idea of who Sarie Botha was and how she fit into the anthropology department. I needed a plan for tomorrow—I couldn't just walk into her office and ask why she'd poisoned Paul Odum. I'm not much for pretentious shushing in libraries, although I had a pretty lucrative contract to exterminate a silverfish infestation from one of the branch libraries a few years back. So after a bit of research on archaeology—which turned out to be Miss Botha's speciality—I was more than happy to hit Marty's for a short, intense right-handed work-out.

Afterward, I showered and picked up Tommy so my mother could have an evening with the ladies from church. We ate the Dublin coddle she insisted on packing up for our dinner. I poured Tommy a Coke and myself a Black Bush after cleaning up the dishes, and we got down to work. I penned labels while he spread and pinned a gorgeous series of morpho butterflies that I'd collected from Mexico. Between the warmth of the whiskey and the tranquilizing strains of Mozart's Serenade in G Major, which Tommy picked to start the evening, I lapsed into a contemplative mood.

It struck me how much like tropical butterflies we humans can be. The upper surface of the morpho's wing is the most iridescent blue imaginable, while the lower surface is a dull, spotted brown. The blue is important for attracting mates, and the brown for avoiding predators. Love and death. In the end we aren't all that different than the insects. And so far, there seemed to be two sides to everyone involved in Odum's death—one beautiful and the other ugly. I wondered about Sarie Botha.

CHAPTER THIRTY-TWO

The morning drive to Berkeley reminded me why I would never be a commuter. I could leave my house, stroll down the hill, and be at Goat Hill Extermination in ten minutes. My walk to work was sheer heaven compared to the chaos of morning rush hour on the San Francisco-Oakland Bay Bridge. I might've thought I'd died and gone to hell had it not been for a cup of Gustaw's coffee on the dash and Chopin's piano concertos on the radio. I parked next to a sign that declared "Permit Parking, Zone A" on College Avenue and put the "On Job" sign on the dashboard.

Kroeber Hall housed the anthropology department. I gathered from yesterday's reading that Alfred Kroeber had been a real big shot in the field, working with the Indians before their cultures were completely screwed up by the modern world. It's ironic that I feel sympathy for the Indians, given that European immigrants like my family were the reason for their dying out. But I look back on the values from the Old World that my parents brought with them, and I understand that just because something's new and shiny doesn't mean it's better. Maybe the Indians and I have something in common. We're both outdated.

The building was apparently designed by the same architect who drew up the plans for the city library. It seems the guy only had a straightedge on his drafting table and loved the color gray. Once inside, I passed the entrance to the Hearst Museum of Anthropology, which was across from the main office for the anthropology department. I headed up to the second floor and worked my way down the hall. Sarie Botha's office was next to the one with

Rene Morley's name on the door. I'd learned from my library work that she was his assistant. The calendar posted on his door indicated that he had a meeting all morning, but I couldn't tell if Miss Botha was in her office. There were no lights on in either one. Pleased that the first element of my plan had fallen into place, I returned to the main office.

The waiting area consisted of a couple of chairs next to a low table, all arranged in front of a counter. The walls on the public side of the counter featured George Caitlin prints of Indian life in the 1800s, or so I gathered from the little brass labels. Behind the counter, the room was lined with bookcases packed with leather-bound volumes and rows of rather uniformly sized documents which I took to be students' theses. A massive wooden table surrounded by elegantly carved captain's chairs gave the room an air of dignity. Along the left wall were two closed doors, the painted signs on their frosted windows indicating that one was the department head's office and the other was the mail room.

A doorway to the right of the counter opened into a room with at least four secretaries, from what I could make out from the voices. From what I'd read about the size of the department, I figured there'd be a stable of secretaries. In fact, I was relying on it.

Between the clatter of typewriters, the ringing of a phone, and the chatter of women, nobody noticed me. Resting on the counter was an ornate brass bell, which I took to be the signal to announce one's presence. I gave it a ring. A stern older woman with her hair in a tortuously tight bun strode from the office. She reminded me of Sister Mary Leon in elementary school—the only teacher capable of instilling terror in a smartass kid like me.

"May I help you?" she asked. Glancing through the doorway, I could see a couple of very pretty women at the other desks. Too bad one of them wasn't the departmental receptionist, as my story wasn't all that brilliant and this biddy didn't look like she'd be easily snowed.

"I'm looking for Dr. Rene Morley."

"He's in a curriculum committee meeting until noon today," she replied curtly. "Is there something I can help you with?"

"I'm Cedric O'Toole. I'm from Santa Barbara, but I had some business in the area so I thought I'd stop by your fine university. As a private collector of pre-Columbian art, I'm quite familiar with the Hearst Museum. I am also very much impressed with the quality of Dr. Morley's research."

"Yes?" she said with a hint of impatience.

"And I am considering a sizable donation of Mayan ceramics and jade carvings which I'd like to discuss with him."

"Oh, I see, Mr. O'Toole. I'm sure that Dr. Morley will be delighted to speak with you." Her voice was suddenly chummy, and she introduced herself as "Miss Betty Hoshor, the administrative assistant to the chairman," which I took to mean that she was his secretary. Nothing like the possibility of some treasure to endear oneself to an institution of higher education. "I'm sorry that he's not available. Dr. Sylvester, our department head, will be in shortly, but he has a nine thirty meeting. Perhaps you can come back later this morning?"

"That might work. But you know, I'd also be delighted to discuss this matter with Dr. Botha." The secretary's eyebrows lifted just a moment, then she regained her composure. As if on cue, the typing in the next room also slowed to a few tentative taps. I'd evidently struck a nerve.

"I'm afraid that Miss Botha will not be in until later." She emphasized the "Miss" to correct my intentional error. "And I'm not sure that she's really in a position to be of much assistance in such a matter."

"Well, I understand that she's currently Dr. Morley's research associate. My mother has a close friend on the university's board of regents." I leaned forward and dropped my voice to a conspiratorial whisper. "And I gather that Miss Botha's archaeological research and academic reputation are impressive enough for serious discussion of offering her a faculty position." At this, I saw a pretty secretary in the other room put her hand to her mouth in surprise. She turned to the girl next to her, who opened her gorgeous brown eyes as wide as they'd go and bit her lip. My fabrication was working, so I continued.

"She'd be the first female professor in the archaeology program, as I understand it. I suppose that this is all pretty hush-hush, so maybe I shouldn't have said anything." My matronly confidant pursed her lips, evidently torn between politeness and outrage. But before she could formulate a response, a short serious fellow in a tweed coat—with leather elbow patches, of course—strode into the office. He was trying hard to look like an Ivy League professor in the slovenly informality of Berkeley.

"Miss Hoshor, can you pull the file on faculty teaching loads for the central committee meeting? We need to be there in fifteen minutes." He didn't seem to see me at all, either singularly focused on his administrative duties or wholly lacking in social skills. Probably both.

"Dr. Sylvester," she said, "this is Mr. O'Toole, a private collector who is considering a donation to our collection. He was hoping to meet with Dr. Morley this morning, and I explained that you'd be happy to talk with him except that you're meeting with the central committee." Her mentioning my generosity had the same effect on him that it had on her. He was suddenly interested in me.

"A donation, Mr. O'Toole?" He reached to shake my hand. "I'd love to visit with you, but this meeting will take up my whole morning. If I weren't the chairman of the committee, I could duck out. It's mostly academic politics, but one never knows when the dean will come up with some new and inane idea for allocating faculty positions or teaching responsibilities."

"Oh, it's no problem. I'm sure Dr. Morley will fill you in on my offer. I suspect that a jade death mask and a ceramic figurine from Jaina Island would complement your museum holdings nicely." I was relieved that Sylvester was pressed for time, as I'd read just enough at the library for an initial bluff that would fall apart with much further conversation.

"Sounds remarkable. I am truly sorry to miss chatting with you." He called into the secretaries' office, where his assistant was sorting through an open filing cabinet drawer. "Miss Hoshor, do you have that file? We need to be there a few minutes early if you're going to be taking the minutes." He turned back to me. "Is there anything we can get you? There's coffee behind the counter and even a couple of clean cups."

"Thanks so much, Dr. Sylvester. I'll help myself and perhaps peruse some of your students' theses while I wait for Dr. Morley, if that's all right with you." I wanted to get closer to the inner office, and the chairs in front of the counter were not a great place to eavesdrop.

"By all means, make yourself comfortable." Sylvester and his assistant hurried out the door and down the stairs. I went around the counter, poured myself a cup of coffee, pulled a bound volume off the shelf at random, and sat down at the table. I chose a chair that was out of view of the secretaries but close enough to overhear the gossip I had catalyzed.

"Can you believe that?" one of the women whispered to the others, evidently unsure of whether I was within earshot but unable to contain herself.

"Sarie Botha, a faculty member? That'd put the department into chaos," another answered. I lost track of who was speaking, but there was no confusion as to what these ladies thought.

"She's such a bitch."

"Ellen!"

"Well, she is."

"Yes, but that sounds so crude."

"She acts like she's better than everyone. Driving that fancy convertible."

"Did you see what she wore yesterday? An Yves Saint Laurent peasant dress."

"That'd cost me a month's salary."

"At least."

"And the way she was showing off her naked shoulders was just slutty."

"Oh, don't be such a prude, Clayleen."

"I'm not."

"Well it was better than that micromini she had on last week."

"That look is fine for students, but it's hardly professional."

"Speaking of which, can you imagine having to do her typing?"

"I'd quit if she was assigned to me."

"Me too, or at least I'd make enough mistakes to get her assigned to one of you."

"You wouldn't!"

"I couldn't stand being told what to do by her in that accent."

"She's no more obnoxious than her boss."

"I suppose you're right. Dr. Morley is no easy man to work for."

"He was in a good mood last term."

"And he's been a monster this fall. When he's in one of his funks it's awful."

"He's nice enough to me."

"Sure, because he thinks you're a slave. He's such a chauvinist pig."

"And a prima donna. When he needs something typed, nothing else matters."

"Maybe that's why Sarie had that makeover. She's trying to please Dr. Morley."

"I suspect she already does. If you know what I mean."

"Oh, *now* who's being crude?"

"Well, I bet it's true. Where there's smoke, there's fire, you know."

"I'll bet she's trying to impress some guy at the Savoy."

"She goes there?"

"Every weekend from what I've heard."

"I heard they only let certain people in, and the drinks are like five dollars apiece."

"It's not the drinks that people go for."

"What then, the glamour?"

"I've heard there's a back room with orgies."

"That can't be true. How do you know?"

"A friend of a girl who used to waitress there told me. That place is wild."

"Well, she won't be there tonight."

"How do you know?"

"I'm typing a grant proposal that she and Dr. Morley need to have by five p.m."

"So?"

"So, they're planning to work on revisions tonight."

"How do you know? Maybe they're going to work over the weekend."

"I know because I have to come in Saturday morning to make the final changes."

"Can't it wait until Monday?"

"No, it has to be in the mail first thing Monday morning."

"So you have to work for Botha and Morley on your Saturday?"

"Dr. Sylvester told me I could take off a day next week to make up for it."

"I'd ask for two days to make up for working for those two."

"Yeah, the manic-depressive egomaniac and his rich, slutty mistress."

"Now you don't know that."

"No, but I know we'd better get to work."

"You're right, or else Miss Hoshor will read us the riot act when she gets back."

The sound of typewriters replaced the chatter of the women, but I'd heard plenty to give me a sense of how to proceed. First, I wanted to see Miss Botha for myself, so I quietly slipped out of the office and headed back upstairs. Even bankers get to work by ten o'clock. Her door was open, so I slowed and glanced in as I passed. I was stunned.

Sarie Botha was not a blonde. In fact, she looked remarkably like the brunette on *Charlie's Angels* played by Kate Jackson. I couldn't remember the character's name, but then I'd only seen the silly program a couple of times when I was too tired to work on my collection in the evening. The secretaries were right about Miss Botha. She was pulling a book off a shelf, and in profile her skirt and sweater were plenty tight to reveal a supple, athletic body, very nicely proportioned. I kept moving so she wouldn't notice me in the otherwise empty hallway.

I'd imagined a Farrah Fawcett from Howard's description of his temptress. The secretaries had mentioned a makeover, and I wondered if the dark-haired Sarie in Berkeley had been the blond Sarah in Los Angeles. Maybe she'd changed her name in LA and changed her hair upon returning, so that Howard wouldn't recognize her if their paths crossed on campus. If Sarie Botha was Paul Odum's killer, she was no professional assassin, but neither was she stupid. She'd either tried to cover her tracks—or I had the wrong woman. I considered asking Howard to identify her. It would only be a five-minute walk from Hilgard Hall. If she'd dyed her hair, he could surely still recognize her, but I couldn't risk drawing him further into this. The kid was already at the ragged edge of anxiety and there was no telling what he'd do. I was on my own.

On the way back to the city, I began to formulate a plan. With a week to go, I had to make my move if I was going to hit it big for Tommy. Sarie Botha was my best—okay, my only—suspect. I had to figure out how to extract the truth from her, and there wasn't time for lots of nuance. As I ruminated, KDFC played a set of Samuel Barber's compositions. By the time they got to his dark and disturbing Adagio for Strings, Op. 11, I had the outline of a plan. My approach had a kind of grim justice, if not elegant subtlety, going for it. And my mood matched Barber's composition.

Chapter Thirty-Three

At the office, Carol had taped to my door pink "While You Were Out" slips with the high-priority calls. She suggested that my "project" had better be over soon or we were going to have some grumpy customers. I promised her I'd take the afternoon to make the most urgent contacts. I closed the door, sat down heavily at my desk, and leaned back. A high-pitched squeal came from either the aging springs in my chair or the muscles in my lower back. I breathed in deeply and rubbed my temples, shifting gears from a murder investigation to the Housing Authority, which topped Carol's list. The jangling of the phone undid my moment of tranquility.

"A Mr. Mancini is on the phone," Carol said. "It sounds important."

"Thanks, I'll take it." There were a couple of sharp clicks.

"Riley, Bino here."

"Hey, thanks again for getting together. That Wild Turkey sure hit the spot."

"Anything for an old pal, even a wily bastard like you. Speakin' of which, the boys in residue analysis identified your sample."

"That's great."

"Not really. Turns out that yer fellow exterminator is using a very high concentration of parathion in a petroleum-based carrier."

"And that's bad?"

"It is for puppies, kittens, and any little brats who get this stuff on 'em. Parathion's about as hot as organophosphates get. The Rachel Carsons of

181

the world couldn't find a better chemical to motivate their call for bannin' insecticides."

"Any more reasons to worry?"

"Yeah, the industry has been takin' heat for the deaths of some cotton workers in Egypt and sugarcane cutters in Brazil. They entered fields too soon after parathion treatments and managed to off themselves. If some moron runs into a burnin' building and roasts hisself, I suppose we should ban fire."

"Sounds like a couple of isolated incidents. Not enough to get the environmentalists in a tizzy."

"It doesn't take much, and we're catchin' wind of some pretty nasty stuff that might really push things along for the tree huggers. The European press is reportin' that right-wing fanatics have used parathion to assassinate anti-apartheid activists in South Africa. I don't have the details, but if somebody's usin' insecticides to kill blacks it's not gonna help our image."

"Does AmeriChem manufacture parathion?"

"No, but people don't know one chemical from another. The earth muffins are only too happy to encourage the confusion so that folks are scared of everything from DDT to the preservatives in their breakfast cereal. Goddamn political radicals in Africa are fuelin' the environmental radicals in America. It's a nutjob cluster fuck out there."

We commiserated about the state of the world for a while, and then Bino had a meeting. I imagined him wearing a coat and tie, explaining security to a bunch of middle managers in a conference room, which convinced me that there were worse ways for an ex-cop to make a living than owning an extermination business. After I hung up, I pushed aside the pile of phone messages and headed back to the warehouse. I needed to digest Bino's news and fold it into my plan.

Sarie Botha had to be Howard's seductress—and Paul Odum's killer. This all made sense in terms of how, but it made no sense with respect to why. What reason did a beautiful archaeologist have to poison a radical ecologist at the same university? There was no connection, and without a reason for such an elaborate scheme, my theory elegantly connected a bunch of dots to form an incoherent picture. I couldn't go to Laurie Odum and claim that this woman had intentionally poisoned her husband, and incidentally killed her maid's daughter, without offering a motive. So I was back to the question: How to get Miss Botha to talk?

I wandered back between the shelves in the warehouse, scanning the products and contemplating an approach that I just couldn't bring myself to seriously consider. It was too close to home. These chemicals were supposed to make the world less ugly. I knew how Isaac felt.

As I passed by the lockers and dilapidated chairs next to the rickety coffee table, the sulfurous odor of the insecticides was suddenly replaced by a pleasant earthy smell. The guys hung out here after work, and on Fridays they had a tradition of smoking a cigar before calling it a week. The thick, sweet scent of tobacco wafted up from the box on the table, and with it came the solution to my problem.

I nabbed a couple of cigars, filled a beaker with water, and headed to my office. There, I pulled out the binder of notes we'd been given at the meeting in Los Angeles. Some extension agent from UC Davis had given a presentation about home gardeners accidentally poisoning themselves with "nicotine tea." Seems that these suburban hippies decided to control their hornworms by soaking cigarettes in a pail of water and sprinkling the concoction on infested tomato plants. Like all hippies they imagined that Mother Nature provided safe solutions to the world's problems. They didn't figure that nicotine was absorbed by the skin and carried to the nervous system, where it was every bit as dangerous as those nasty, synthetic chemicals. The symptoms were most unpleasant, but the modern wonders of an emergency room kept the back-to-nature gardeners from becoming compost.

After reviewing the details of the cases and guessing how many cigarettes would equal a cigar, I broke up one of the stogies and part of a second, and dropped the mess into the water. I pulled out a heating pad that I kept around for days when my back was hurting. Then I set the beaker on the pad and turned it to its lowest setting. The antidote used by the ER doctors had rung a bell and provided me with a Plan B, in case my solution generated its own problem. I went back into the warehouse and opened the refrigerator, where we kept various chemicals but mostly beer. Shoved toward the back behind a six-pack I found a thick glass vial.

A couple years ago, while I was doing a treatment in a cramped basement, the rubber gasket in my sprayer failed and I was soaked with insecticide. I hurried back to work, showered, and changed clothes. I felt dizzy and nauseous for a few hours. Nothing bad enough to go to the hospital, but I made the mistake of telling Beth about it. She called me a "macho idiot," saying that if I'd been far from a hospital and hit with a bigger dose, I'd be dead.

The next day Beth gave me a vial of atropine and a couple of syringes that she swiped from the hospital. She insisted I keep this stuff in a cooler when I went out on jobs, which I did for a few weeks. Eventually it became too much of a hassle so I stored it in the fridge. Beth also wrote a note card with simple instructions on how much of the antidote to inject in case of acute poisoning. Atropine didn't counteract every insecticide, but it worked for the most toxic ones I used—and it was this medicine that the doctors had used to reverse the stupidity of the organic gardeners. I figured it was probably still good since it had been kept cold. At least that's what Miss Botha and I would be counting on if things went badly.

On my way out to solve some "While You Were Out" crises, Carol's radio was blaring a singularly artless account of sexual exploits that featured the lyrics "afternoon delight." This struck me as painfully ironic, since the first stop was at the projects in Pacific Heights to check out a rat bite. I detoured through Chinatown and grabbed a few egg rolls from the House of Hong. I finished the last one just as I double-parked behind a city car at the projects.

A representative from the San Francisco Housing Authority had a handful of unhappy people gathered around him. The tired-looking, middle-aged black man introduced himself as Leon Jones. The fellow had the look of an idealist worn down by bureaucracy. The mother of the child who'd been bitten was a three-hundred-pound mountain of black fury demanding that "something be done." She was holding a crying child in one arm while waving the other menacingly. The little boy, who was sobbing either out of pain or fear of his mother's rage, had a series of bloody gouges on his thigh. The mother might've been hysterical but she had a good reason. There was no question that the kid had rat bites. His cries increased as his mother grew intent on inciting a riot.

The woman's neighbors began to trickle out onto the sidewalk to see what the commotion was about, and things started to degenerate. Jones tried to calm the situation by assuring the crowd that the Housing Authority would be "assessing the situation and taking appropriate action."

"We don' want no 'propriate action, we wanna live in our homes without being attacked by rats," she shouted. I thought she had a point, and given that folks were getting more fractious by the minute, I tried to defuse the situation.

"Ma'am, I think that's why I'm here."

"Who you be?" she sneered.

"I'm an exterminator. I kill rats. And I think the Housing Authority is going to hire me to clean up your apartments. Isn't that right?" I asked Jones, who seemed relieved to have an ally.

"Yes, absolutely," he said, nodding with grave authority.

I opened the binder I was holding. "And right here is the contract between my company and the city. Let's get this paperwork taken care of, and then I'll have my crew out here as soon as possible." I filled in a few blanks with my eyeball estimate of the job and passed the binder to Jones, who nervously scanned the documents.

"I'm supposed to get a second bid," he whispered.

"Just sign the contract," I murmured. "If you get a better bid by next week, I'll let you off the hook. But for now let's save our skins and worry about the niceties of administrative policies later."

As he signed the papers, I announced to the crowd, "So when you see a truck from Goat Hill Extermination, remember these guys are on your side." I knew how unfamiliar vehicles in the projects could sometimes fare, so I thought I'd lay a bit of diplomatic groundwork for Larry and Dennis.

The mob dispersed amid grumbles and curses. Jones got back into his city car, and the mother lumbered back toward the apartments with the sobbing kid, hopefully to find some merthiolate or iodine. Nobody was happy. I wasn't keen about killing rats—bleeding to death internally from warfarin poisoning can't be a great way to go. But there was a job to be done and I wouldn't shed any more tears for rodents than I did for the criminals I put away. Exterminators and cops understand the reality of necessary evil. It's nothing personal. Rats are just being rodents and sociopaths are just being humans. But somebody has to make sure that innocent people aren't hurt by these creatures, and that means using force. Sometimes even deadly force. The more I thought about it, the more I settled into my plan for Sarie Botha.

I swung by the library at the end of the day to see if the foreign papers had any more on the South African poisonings. They added some details, but Bino's account was on the mark. The assassins broke into the hotel rooms of their political enemies, applied a thin layer of parathion-laced petroleum jelly to their undergarments, and waited for the poison to do its work. The symptoms were diffuse enough for physicians to attribute the deaths to metabolic syndromes, heart attacks, and unspecified infections. After one of the activists flew to England for a lecture and collapsed, a doctor in London figured out the scheme by collaborating with South African authorities. Nobody knew how many anti-apartheid leaders had been killed.

That evening I reheated leftovers and poured a full glass of Black Bush after doing the dishes. I put on Mahler's Ninth Symphony—a selection that fit the task before me. I made some calculations based on my best estimate of body weight and nicotine concentration, then repeated them twice to be sure. I was used to having a more precise sense of a job, and I could've figured out an exact dose if I'd been willing to use one of the insecticides in the warehouse. But I couldn't bring myself to consider using a product of my trade for the purpose I had planned.

Satisfied with my mathematics, I sipped the whiskey and began to make a list of materials I'd need for tomorrow night in addition to the tobacco extract and atropine.

The last notes in Mahler's final movement were slowly dying away. The orchestra took heartrending minutes to play the few final notes which are said to prophesy the composer's death without him ever having heard his final symphony performed.

Chapter Thirty-Four

I slept remarkably well, given what I had planned for the day. At least the morning would give me a chance to feel human. I began with an early breakfast at Gustaw's Bakery. Ludwika cut me an enormous slice of mazurek.

"It should only be for Easter," she apologized, "but we are now Americans, and our customers adore this cake."

Gustaw poured some of his thick coffee for me and noted, "There is reason to celebrate with a special treat."

"What's the occasion?" I asked.

"Monday marks the thirty-seventh anniversary of the Polish Underground State," he said with pride. "The resistance never surrendered to the Nazis. The Soviets will fare no better."

Ludwika scowled. She'd often scolded Gustaw for mixing politics with business. I thought it wise to let the subject drop, although I was confident that not many of the locals enjoying a Saturday breakfast were going to side with the commies. I wiped up the marzipan and drained my coffee. Then I paid my bill and headed down the hill to get my truck from the fenced lot behind Goat Hill Extermination.

The day was crystal clear and Tommy was waiting on the front porch with his collecting gear. We headed out to Baker Beach. It isn't my favorite spot, although it has some great views to the north. That end of the beach has been taken over by nudists, and a mile further is the Golden Gate Bridge. What mattered this morning, however, was that Tommy and I had found at least three species of tiger beetles lurking in the beach grass back in July.

I spread out a blanket below the dunes while Tommy stalked the beetles. Tiger beetles are as nimble as they are beautiful, and it takes either phenomenal quickness or heroic patience to net them. Tommy's awkward dives and frequent tumbles into the sand made it clear that he couldn't rely on agility. But what my brother lacked in athleticism he made up for in perseverance. I'd brought along Ludlum's latest book, *The Gemini Contenders*. The story was pretty engaging, what with the elements of religion, politics, and family. It probably wasn't great literature, but I could escape into an imaginary world where, however messy things got, in the end good triumphed. I couldn't help but think about the Odums, Paul's students, and Sarie Botha— and I wasn't at all sure who was a hero and who was a villain. Or who was going to triumph.

My reverie was broken by shouts from Tommy, who'd finally nabbed a beetle. He came lurching down the dune with his net wadded up. "I got one, Riley!"

"Let's see, pal." He showed me the pouch at the bottom of the net, below his clenched fist. "I'm impressed. That's a beaut!" And it was quite an insect, with long spindly legs, bulging eyes, and an iridescent green body sporting vivid yellow spots around the edge.

"Do you want me to put it in the killing jar for you?" I asked.

"No, I can do it."

"It won't bother you?"

"Not so much," he said as I unscrewed the lid and he slipped the net over the mouth of the jar. He held it up and the sun glinted off the insect.

"Why not?"

"Cuz it's not a butterfly. It's an etter."

"An etter?"

"Yeah, that's what Scott from the museum told me." He set his jaw defiantly, and I knew we had to work this out.

"Hmmm. Did he maybe say 'editor'?" I couldn't figure out what editors had to do with insects, but it was the closest thing to Tommy's word.

"That's it," he announced. "The ones that eat others. Editors."

"Ah, you mean 'predators.' They eat other insects."

"Predators," he repeated, furrowing his brow in deep concentration. "I'm not good with new words, Riley."

"Don't worry, pal. We figured it out, and you'll remember it next time."

"I'm going to catch another one," he shouted, stumbling back up the hill. His right leg swung wide and carved arcs into the sand. It was late morning by the time I finished a couple more chapters and Tommy scored another tiger beetle—a rust-colored specimen with ivory swirls. He had an important event to attend at eleven, and I knew he wouldn't want to be late.

We headed back to the neighborhood and stopped just up the street from the church at a pink stuccoed house with white-framed windows. A brass plate on the front identified it as St. Teresa's Rectory. I'd not reminded Tommy of Father Griesmaier's invitation, as the kid would've been too distracted to enjoy his morning at the beach. But when we pulled up, it was clear that he knew what was up. Tommy jumped out of the truck just as I came to a stop, hit the sidewalk in a jumble, struggled to his feet, and lurched his way toward the open front door.

"Father, Karsa, I'm here!" he shouted as I caught up to him. The jovial priest and Tommy's best friend from the adult daycare met him at the door. Karsa was blinking hard and rolling his shoulders, signs that he was as excited as Tommy.

"Come in, Tommy," the priest said with undisguised delight. "I have the couch set up for you and Karsa, so you won't miss a minute of the game."

"And snacks?" Tommy asked.

"Of course. Hot dogs, popcorn, chips, and root beer." The priest stepped aside to let the two men hug and head into the living room with their arms draped over each other's shoulders.

"Thanks, Father, this means so much to him."

"It's my pleasure, Riley. They're fine fellows doing the very best they can. We could all learn something from their approach to life."

"Just the same, I know that aside from Mass, watching Notre Dame football is as sacred as it gets." I didn't add that he would also have to forgo his Trumer Pils in the presence of Tommy and Karsa. Trading root beer for his beloved Austrian beer on game day was as close to martyrdom as it got these days around St. Teresa's. But he insisted that a man of the cloth needed to set a good example.

"Indeed," he smiled. "And your mother will be by to pick him up around two, right?"

"Yes, but I don't think he'll last that long. We had a busy morning at the beach, so he'll probably doze off by halftime."

"Ah, the Fighting Irish will keep him enthralled," the priest assured me. He headed into the house and Tommy came to the doorway to tell me good-bye. I drew him aside.

"What's the word for animals that eat other animals?" I asked in a whisper. He closed his eyes and clenched his fists. I was starting to wish that I'd left him to enjoy Karsa and the party, but I knew he'd be thrilled if he could remember.

"Predators," he declared triumphantly. I gave him a hug and he headed back into the living room shouting, "Notre Dame is going to be the predators today, Father!" The priest laughed uproariously. I headed back to the truck, wondering how predators were going to fare in my slice of the world.

I grabbed a quick lunch at my old hangout on Valencia. The diner took me back to my police days, which got me into the right frame of mind for what was to come. I swung by my house and dug through the bedroom closet. In the dark recesses, I found the outfit that Kelly had bought for me when we were tapping into the San Francisco nightlife. I pretty much hated the clothes as much as she adored the disco music. But to be fair, she couldn't stand going to the symphony with me even though she was a knockout in an evening dress. I suppose I should have figured out sooner that any relationship built on mutual, alternating martyrdom couldn't last, no matter how good the sex. In any case, a green leisure suit and a wide-collared polyester shirt with a Picasso-like print in yellow, brown, and burnt orange was the best I could do on short notice. I zipped the clothes into a suit bag and headed down the hill.

At the office, I found that my little chemistry experiment had worked well. The heating pad had evaporated the water in the beaker down to what looked like a strong tea. I poured the liquid into a vial and tossed the tobacco residue in the trash. Then I filled out the rest of my list—atropine, cotton balls, rubber tubing, syringes, and latex gloves.

Out at the truck, I transferred the supplies to the pocket of my suit coat, rezipped the bag, and headed toward the Bay Bridge and switched off the radio. I hated to miss Peter Allen announcing the Texaco-Metropolitan Opera broadcast of Verdi's *Aida*, but I needed to carefully think through my next steps. I had two important visits to make before playing my gambit with Sarie Botha.

Chapter Thirty-Five

As a detective, I'd learned that to understand a suspect you had to get a sense of their family, friends, and coworkers. From what I could tell, Sarie Botha didn't have many of the first two, but at least I could make firsthand contact with her evidently unlikable boss. So, my first stop was on Spruce Street, a half mile beyond and at least a hundred feet above the Odums' house. If Paul Odum had parlayed his extracurricular agricultural project into better digs, it was clear that Rene Morley had figured out an even better angle. Whatever his racket, this guy was living well beyond the means of a university professor.

The Tudor-style mansion was faced in exquisite stonework and featured turrets and a glassed-in conservatory overlooking a sweep of perfectly manicured lawn. I parked on the circular drive, under a sprawling oak, where the truck could be seen but at an angle that the sign on the cab door wasn't readable. No sense leaving a calling card.

I headed through a stone arch and rang the bell alongside a massive front door. I'd picked off the name of Morley's neighbor from a burnished brass sign announcing that the Pearlman Residence was next door. With that information, the shtick I'd worked out on my way across the Bay, and a bit of luck, I figured I'd get a sense of Sarie Botha's boss—and maybe gain some insight about her. I was met by a dumpy, balding man with an air of utter disdain. He was dressed in a silk smoking jacket with a pipe stem poking out from the side pocket, khaki pants with a crisp crease, and leather slippers worth more than any pair of shoes I'd ever owned. The guy looked like a cross between Danny DeVito and Hugh Hefner.

"What is your business?" he demanded.

"Funny you should put it that way," I replied in my most accommodating tone. "I'm with Golden Bear Extermination." I extended my hand. Morley looked past me toward the derelict truck and began to close the door. "Hold on, sir, your house may be at dire risk. At least, the Pearlmans wished they'd had an inspection before things got so bad." He paused just a moment. I knew I had him.

"What about the Pearlmans?" He opened the door a bit further.

"Well, I know how sensitive these matters can be, so please say nothing to them. But my company is conducting a termite extermination of their house. Lots of subfloor damage, and they'll have to call in a structural engineer."

"So?"

"Well, termites are not good at staying put. And there's a good chance they've worked their way into your house." Morley looked annoyed and concerned.

"What do you propose?"

"A quick examination of the side of your house that faces your unfortunate neighbors should tell us if you have visitors."

"What'll this cost me?"

"An exterior inspection is twenty-five dollars. We'll bill you, if that's okay."

Morley sighed deeply and rolled his eyes in disgust. He flicked his hand at me. "Go, do whatever you do, but be discreet. I expect you to be gone in fifteen minutes, and should you find anything you will call before coming to my door again. Do you understand?"

"Completely, sir," I said in a conciliatory voice.

He closed the door without another word, and I headed to the side of the house. I conducted a quick inspection just in case Morley was watching. However, there was almost no chance that the pretentious runt would be wasting his time spying on the servant class. Between short man's syndrome and being named Rene, his arrogance was probably the only hope he had of salvaging his ego. I didn't know where he fit into the whole scheme, but at least I had a sense of what Sarie Botha's professional life entailed.

On my way back down the hill, I swung past Laurie Odum's house for no good reason other than a vague unease that came from having dealt with Morley. As I drove by, I saw a man on the landing outside the door to Paul Odum's study. I'd told Laurie to wait to call a locksmith until I was sure things were safe. And when I didn't see a service vehicle parked on the street, my alarm bells went off. I turned at the corner, parked my truck, and wished I had a gun. I walked back toward the house at a leisurely pace. As I approached, I could hear the racket of a drill and then the banging of a hammer. Whoever the guy was, he wasn't worried about making noise and drawing attention to his work. And there was no sign of Laurie Odum—or the cops.

I crossed to the other side of the street and found a garden along the sidewalk, where I could kneel down and keep an eye on the handyman while giving a passable impression of weeding the flowerbed. The guy looked to be in his sixties and was wearing jeans and a yellow sweatshirt emblazoned with a blue oval and the letter C. He sure wasn't trying to hide, unless he was heading to a Cal football game after his project was completed. He managed to get the door open, but he didn't go into the loft office. Instead, he installed a new handle, after which he stood up and admired his work. The guy closed up his toolbox and walked heavily down the stairs. He headed up the driveway and then turned up the street.

I thought about following him, but just then the lady of the house whose garden I was "weeding" came out and shouted, "What are you doing in my flowers?" The handyman turned to see what the commotion was about as I waved to the woman and replied that I was just going to pick one flower for my girlfriend. "Go to a florist, you cheapskate!" she shouted with all the generosity of the rich. I muttered an apology and headed down the street toward my truck. There was no point in trying to tail the guy now, and he didn't look to be dangerous.

Driving back into Berkeley, I wondered why Laurie had called a repairman and why he didn't have a company vehicle. But I couldn't afford to be distracted given the challenges already on my schedule. My last stop was the Hearst Museum of Anthropology. At least parking next to campus was unrestricted on the weekends. On a sunny September afternoon, the residents of Berkeley were apparently out picnicking or tending their pot fields, so I had the museum to myself. I wasn't sure exactly what I was looking for, other than some background to engage Miss Botha in some witty banter this evening. Anthropology exhibits are not the best places for developing pickup lines, but I was never much good at such things, and she was not your typical nightclub target.

I wandered through a special collection of Mayan artifacts. There was a faded but evidently rare painting of a market scene and lots of intricately decorated clay pots. The jade masks were impressive and suggested that, for all their glory, the Mayans were not a happy bunch. What really caught my eye was a stone slab with a detailed carving of a ritual bloodletting. I supposed that piercing a person's tongue was a step up from human sacrifice. It was the sort of tradeoff that I was hoping to make if everything went according to plan.

I chatted with the only other person in the museum, the guy assigned to keep watch, man the counter, and answer questions on Saturdays when nobody else wanted to be indoors. He told me he was a new curator at the museum. Seems that rookies don't get a break in any field. Our conversation started with a lecture on pre-Columbian culture. I eventually steered him toward my less academic interests.

"I understand that Professor Morley is quite an expert on the Mayans," I said.

"Sure is. Berkeley managed to steal him from Yale with an endowed professorship."

"I'll bet the students were thrilled to have a professor of his caliber."

"Not really. Morley was pretty much given free rein to pursue his research. He doesn't have any use for undergrads. Called them 'stupid, idealistic sheep.'"

"Well, he must have a following among the upper-level students."

"Yeah, riding his coattails is not a bad strategy. In fact, he was on my graduate committee."

"Must've been great having a fellow like that to learn from, eh?"

"At times."

"I suppose big-name professors can be difficult even for advanced students."

"That's a nice way of putting it. Just between us, the man was a goddamn tyrant. More of a tormentor than a mentor. Oh, he was a brilliant scientist and his productivity was incredible during his up periods."

194

"But?"

"But during the dark times, his rage was legendary. So if you're interested in meeting him, it'd be best to wait a few weeks. The anthropology students say he's been in one of the worst moods on record since the start of the semester."

From there, he walked me through the galleries and provided a series of lessons on the various exhibits, a tour which lasted an hour past the posted closing. I had nowhere to be until evening, so I enjoyed the private tutorial. The most enchanting lesson was on the artwork from the Pueblo Indians. I'm not much for omens, but the Hopi creation story of the kachinas struck home.

As I understood the Hopis' account—which is much more interesting than the whole Garden of Eden thing—the first world to be created was populated by insect-like creatures that scrambled around in dark caves. Probably a good thing there were no exterminators at the time. Then Grandmother Spider took the creatures to the second world, where they grew fur and became bears and wolves and whatnot. From there, the old Spider took them to the third world, where they became humans. But some evil spirits invaded, so a fourth and final world was made. And there, Grandmother Spider created a pair of mountains which were home to the kachinas. The amazing thing is that this place in Arizona is called the San Francisco Peaks. Insects, spiders, and San Francisco—an eerie coincidence.

Stopping by the gift counter on my way out, I couldn't help but notice that they were selling some knockoff kachina dolls. As I read their tags, my guide was more than willing to expound on each of the dolls. I decided that one of them just might make a perfect way of endearing myself to Sarie Botha. With a bit of dark irony, I picked the Kokopelli figurine. It had an absurd turquoise head with a long beak. It was a trickster god with a mischievous—even dark—sense of humor, a flute player that brought good luck to hunters, and a fertility deity often depicted with a huge penis (this last tidbit courtesy of the curator). Deception, music, and sex all seemed to resonate with my plans for the evening. I plunked down seven fifty for the doll, dropped it into my pocket, and headed out into the dusk.

I drove to the Savoy, Miss Botha's weekend playground. It was still too early for much action, so I parked down the block and had a couple beers at a joint that was more my speed. I avoided the hard stuff, both because they didn't have any decent whiskey and because I wanted to be sharp for later. After a couple of hours, I went out to the truck, grabbed my suit bag, and headed back into the bar for a quick change in the restroom. I went in looking like a working stiff and came out looking like a character from *Saturday Night Fever*. A few eyebrows went up from the guys perched on stools, and at the far end of the bar, a buxom blonde in her forties—trying to look like she remembered her twenties—nodded approvingly. I gave her a wink and headed out the door. My hope was that Sarie Botha would be just as impressed. I had my doubts.

Chapter Thirty-Six

A light mist had begun to fall. The neon lights of the bars and clubs colored the night air and reflected from the wet street, giving the scene a carnival atmosphere. As I approached the Savoy, there was a gaggle of men and women in their early twenties dressed to kill. My getup was tame compared to the guys in garish polyester shirts with nine-inch dog-ear collars and one decked out in a silver jumpsuit unzipped to his navel. He actually fit in with the women posing in halter tops with flared, sparkling pants and a leggy girl in a remarkably short skirt with tall, vinyl boots as white as the fellow's jumpsuit. To add to the fashion show, there was a bizarre couple with the guy wearing torn jeans and a leather jacket studded with about a pound of metal, his partner sporting a short plaid skirt, a black T-shirt, and what for all the world looked like a dog collar.

I walked up to the bouncer, a strapping fellow with a military haircut. He was the only one dressed like a normal person—suede jacket over a black turtleneck and tan slacks. The bouncer was half-sitting on a brushed aluminum stool, one leg resting on the middle rung and the other firmly set on the sidewalk. It was clear that he was ready to move powerfully from his perch if trouble developed under the lavender awning that proclaimed "The Savoy" in gold script.

"What's up with those two?" I asked to open the conversation, nodding toward the leather-and-collar couple.

"Punk rockers. It's the new fad."

"Looks to me like they shopped the Salvation Army's reject racks." Maybe I should have skipped my disco duds and just gone with my rattiest work clothes.

"I don't even try to understand it." He looked me over and kept an eye on the unruly crowd on the sidewalk. In particular, the aptly described punk couple seemed to be looking for trouble.

"Kind of rowdy out here, eh?"

"Yeah, I don't need a disturbance messing with my evening."

"Well, I'd like to get out of the way. Got any space inside tonight?" I asked, looking toward the door. He gave what I took to be an apologetic wince, like he wasn't happy with the answer.

"Don't think so. The Orchid Oasis is a couple blocks over. It's a nice place. Less of a youth crowd, if you catch my drift." I did, and I wasn't offended. It was clear that I didn't fit the Savoy profile. What I needed was an angle—and the bouncer had tipped me off. He'd said "disturbance" rather than "fight" or some other common term, and he'd been able to watch me and monitor the crowd at the same time. These added up to his being an off-duty cop making a few extra bucks.

"Thanks for the recommendation, pal. Use code zero with this crowd." His eyebrows lifted in recognition of being advised to use caution.

"You a cop?" he asked.

"I was. Had to quit to take over my father's business after he died."

"Where'd you work?" Before I could answer, he stood and took a step toward the punk rocker, who was sneering at a guy who towered over him in four-inch platform shoes. The kid was trying to look tough, but the bouncer's move convinced him to melt back into the scenery. When my new pal sat back down, I continued our little chat.

"I was out of the Potrero Station in San Francisco."

"That covers Bayview and Hunters Point, right?"

"Sure does."

"Tough precinct." A couple came out of the club. He was struggling to keep her upright as they weaved down the sidewalk.

"Looks like they got an early start."

"Yeah," he grinned sardonically. "So it looks like there's room inside after all." He nodded toward the door, and I heard some grumbling behind me.

The inside of the nightclub was a purple, pulsing pandemonium. The walls and ceiling were jet-black and the dance floor was snow-white, so the lilac lighting mixed with the cigarette smoke to create a sensual purple haze. The erotic feel was enhanced by a low throbbing from enormous speakers in the corners—as well as the sweaty crush of half-clad bodies squirming on the dance floor and around the glass bar that glowed violet.

I worked my way through the crowd and spotted my target at the bar, talking with a guy in a sky-blue leisure suit and a geometrically patterned shirt unbuttoned to show off a tangle of gold chains and a crop of chest hair. She was wearing a red catsuit with a deeply cut halter top. She wasn't overly well endowed, but the plunging neckline made what she had impossible to ignore. I hung back and caught a few snippets of their—mostly his—conversation. It wasn't long until he figured out that she really was as bored as she looked.

When the guy slid off his stool and melted into the crowd, I took his place. Sarie Botha showed no interest in me—I was hardly one of the young studs. She looked into her drink, a vodka martini from what I'd overhead. At least it wasn't some fruity concoction. A point in her favor. The bartender, a guy with primped hair and sideburns to match, came over and asked me what I wanted. I scanned the array of bottles.

"A Glenlivet for me," I answered, delighted to see a single malt on the glass shelf. When they put their minds to it, the Scots could make a decent whisky. The bartender started to turn and I added, "And one for my friend, here."

I reached into my pocket and put the kachina on the bar. The movement caught Sarie Botha's eye. She looked at the doll and then over at me.

"Do you even know what you have there?" she asked.

"Sure. He's my sidekick. We go way back."

"To some people, scaling religious figures of other cultures might seem offensive." Her accent was enchanting, but I'd have to do a bit a translating—I figured she was accusing me of stealing.

"I could see how somebody might think that. Are you Hopi or Zuni? Or perhaps an anthropologist?" Her eyebrows shot up and she took the bait.

"An anthropologist, if you must know." She sounded put off, but her body language belied her tone. It was time to set the hook.

"Well, Kokopelli and me are pals. We both like music and enjoy a good laugh—or at least we share a sense of irony about the world." I didn't mention the phallic feature, figuring that a bit of discretion was needed even in this carnal setting.

"At least you know something about kachinas. I'm almost impressed."

"Why thank you, I think. It would be easier to impress you if I knew your name." She paused and cocked her head, as if deciding whether I had potential for the evening.

"Sarie," she replied, turning to face me and offering her hand. "I took you for a dodgy oke, but buy me a dop and we'll see if maybe I was mistaken."

I figured it was bad to be whatever it was she said and that I was invited to buy her a drink. But after that, things became much easier. I asked about her accent, and she told me about growing up in Johannesburg and coming to California to study with the famed Professor Rene Morley. It was easy to get her talking about her fieldwork in Mexico, the Mayan culture, and the politics of anthropology. She was smart and sassy with an enchanting smile which crinkled her nose and spread to her deep green eyes. All the while, she'd drained a half-dozen vodka martinis and I'd managed to keep up. We were in our own world—the frenzy around us was just so much background noise and motion, in the way that two lovers can walk down a bustling city street and ignore the honking taxis and jostling pedestrians. Every time she leaned forward to laugh, her halter top gapped just enough to flash a swollen pink halo at the peak of her breast.

Despite my best efforts, the conversation eventually came around to me.

"So, Riley, you know all about me and I don't know a thing about you. Other than you take kachina dolls out for drinks."

"There's not much to tell. I'm a former cop." I've always been better at questions than answers, and I'd had enough to drink that keeping a series of half-truths from getting tangled wouldn't be easy. So I decided it was time to make my move and take my ploy to the next level. Sarie had invested the last hour in me, so I figured she wasn't going to cut bait.

"Izit?" she encouraged.

"Yeah, but now I run the family business. And I like to find something to spice up life on the weekends." She slid her hand across the bar and let it come to rest on mine.

"Some spice, eh? Ex-cops can be pretty unrestrained, I've heard." Her fingers stroked the back of my hand.

"Or restraining, if you know what I mean." I had no doubt that she did.

"And perhaps you and Kokopelli, share another quality?" One long, thin eyebrow arched in interest.

"Only one way to find out."

"Oweh," she responded with evident delight—at least that's how I took her phrase. Sarie gently bit her lower lip and suggested that we drive back to her apartment to continue getting to know one another. I slipped the Kokopelli doll into a coat pocket and patted the other to be sure that my supplies were in place. It was nearly time for the trickster. The bartender retrieved her fur coat—waist-length, black mink—and we headed out. The drizzle had stopped and wisps of clouds were drifting across the moon. The breeze was cool, so we walked quickly to her car, a lipstick-red Corvette Stingray convertible that matched her outfit perfectly.

Her place—she called it her "pozzie"—was opulent. White leather couches and chairs, the deepest white shag carpet I've ever sunk into, a black lacquered coffee table, and erotic ebony carvings on the walls. The only color was a pair of jade masks, one with a terrible grimace and the other with a look of shocked surprise. They reminded me of the Mayan carving of a ritual bloodletting at the museum. There were at least four levels of flooring in the enormous room that included the entryway, living room, dining room, bar, and lounging areas, all of which surrounded a "conversation pit" featuring a white marble fireplace edged in polished onyx.

I poured us a couple of drinks while Sarie went to work on the coffee table with a razor blade and a packet of white powder. Her hedonism seemed limitless. I brought our drinks over and declined her offer, so she sniffed the lines of coke herself. Our conversation drifted to what it took to feel alive. And then we drifted to her bedroom.

CHAPTER THIRTY-SEVEN

The bedroom walls were decorated with zebra skins and black-and-white photos of African landscapes. An enormous round bed, set atop a platform in the middle of the room, completed the decadent setting. Sarie turned back the covers and down the lights. In the soft glow, she wriggled out of her catsuit. She was left with a pair of red satin panties. As she slid into bed, her brown hair fell onto the pillow and framed the most seductive expression that it's been my pleasure to encounter. I shed my clothes and stretched out on the cool silk sheets. After some preliminaries that started off gently and escalated to involve teeth and nails, she pulled a pair of black silk ropes from the nightstand drawer.

"Not too tight," she murmured, lifting her hands over her head. I tied a slipknot into each rope, then tied the other end to a rail above the head-board. She slid her hands into the loops and lay back with a quiver. However, my desires were less primal and more principled. I saw her as an object, not of desire but truth.

"Sarie, it's time for a bit of honesty," I said, rolling off the bed and turning up the lights. I'd seen a man's robe in her bathroom when I'd washed up earlier, so I took it off the hook and put it on. The thick white terry cloth felt warm and soft, in stark contrast to the final move of my gambit. When I came back into the bedroom, she looked more intrigued than worried.

"Oweh!" There it was again. She dropped her voice to a sultry purr. "What have you planned for us?" She was still unaware that the tryst was over—at least in terms of what she'd hoped for.

"A confession," I answered, sitting on the edge of the bed. She turned her head to look at me.

"Of what?" An edgy impatience began to replace the lust in her voice.

"Let's start with you and Paul Odum."

"Ag, I have no idea what you're talking about."

"In Los Angeles. At the Hyatt Regency."

"You're mal!"

"I suppose that means I'm crazy. But my dear Sarie, I know that you seduced Odum's student to gain access to his hotel room. And while there, you applied Vaseline laced with parathion to the crotch of his underwear. A rather effective approach to poisoning since, according to the London *Times*, your countrymen figured out that the organophosphates rapidly enter the body through hair follicles. I understand that the South African assassins were targeting anti-apartheid activists. But I can't figure out why you wanted Odum dead. Help me out, sweetheart."

She laughed mockingly. "You can't prove a thing. Untie me and get out, you bastard."

"Perhaps a bit of your own medicine might convince you to share more than your body with me. I'm afraid, however, that you're much prettier than what's coming." I went out to the living room and returned with the contents of my coat pocket. Her face went from rage to dread when I dumped the supplies on the nightstand.

"What are you doing?" Her voice had a slight tremble as she struggled against the silk ropes.

"Nothing that you didn't do yourself in LA. Are you up to a chat or should I proceed?"

"If you kill me you won't have any answers. Besides, you're bluffing with the vials and props. You don't scare me." She was back to defiance, but her tone was rather less convincing.

"Fine. Have it your way, doll." I pulled on the latex gloves and uncapped the vial of tobacco extract. A cotton ball soaked up the liquid, which was a reasonable approximation of the amber that she might've recognized as parathion. Then I leaned over and pulled her panties off. I wanted her to think that her fate was the same as Odum's if she didn't cooperate. Applying the extract in this way had the added advantage of removing all doubt that

Sarie Botha was Howard's blond seductress. When she dyed her hair, she didn't count on anyone checking more than her scalp.

For a minute or so, nothing happened. Sarie gave a little mocking laugh and sneered at me. I was about to dab on some more of the extract, when she took a couple of deep breaths and swallowed hard. She started to roll her head back and forth.

"You maniac, what are you doing?" she gasped, looking pale and panicked.

"Ah, my dear Sarie, turnabout is fair play. I have some antidote here, which is more than you offered to Paul Odum. I can give you this or add some more parathion. It's up to you."

"I'll talk, just give me the antidote."

"Not so fast. You're not going to die in the next few minutes, and I think a bit of suffering might help you focus. And maybe you'll even build some character, which you could use nearly as much as I could use some answers. Now, start talking." Not only did I want answers, but I wasn't sure what course the chemical brew of alcohol, cocaine, and nicotine would take—and exactly how the atropine would work in her jangled nervous system.

Over the next hour, she sweated and struggled against bouts of nausea. In between, her story came out in fragmented bursts that I managed to piece together along with what I already knew. At least for a while, her growing discomfort seemed to provide the motivation she needed to come clean. It turned out that Sarie had been working with Morley on more than anthropology.

The professor was running one of the largest drug rings in the Bay Area, with a network of dealers providing high-grade 'dagga'—marijuana, or so I surmised—throughout Berkeley, parts of Oakland, and the east side of San Francisco. Which would've included Potrero. When Sarie found out about his venture, she blackmailed him into letting her into the business.

But the power play backfired. She proved quite useful to him in terms of his lust for both sex and power, not that the two are necessarily that far apart. The professor soon had her under his control. From what I could tell, when his capacity for rage and violence weren't sufficient to force her obedience, he could ensure that his beautiful assistant would follow his orders by threatening to destroy her career and have her deported. She had no doubt that Morley was both influential and vicious enough to do so.

She arranged shipments of marijuana to his warehouse of archaeological relics, thoughtfully provided by the university. Field trips to the Mayan sites offered opportunities for him to consummate his business deals, and between his reputation and Sarie's impeccable paperwork, customs inspectors never bothered with the crates of artifacts. It seemed that everything was going smoothly until the paraquat scare, after which sales of Mexican dope nosedived, as dealers and users wanted no part of poisoned pot. It was entirely possible, even likely, that Morley had supplied the pot that poisoned Tommy—and from what I knew of Morley, he wouldn't have cared. After the bottom fell out, some small-time producers, such as Paul Odum, began to fill the gap. However, Morley found a reliable source of "clean" dope in Guatemala. In the last year, he was well on his way to building back his dominance of the Bay Area drug market.

Reading between the lines, it seemed that Morley would have ignored Odum as a minor annoyance had he stuck to growing his local supply. But when he began importing first-rate pot from Thailand to bankroll his sabotage of AmeriChem, the ecology professor became a problem that needed to be solved. Morley ordered Sarie to take Odum out of the picture, and made it clear that dithering or failure would mean the end of her career and life in the States—or perhaps altogether. She'd learned not to ask too many questions or defy him, having found that rebuffing his sexual advances got her "donnered"—beaten to within an inch of her life.

Sarie Botha was in way over her head and could either drown or pull Odum under. She might've figured a way to return to South Africa on her own—even rats and roaches find a crack to escape when things get too hot. And her family had the money and connections to help her. They'd clung desperately to the privileges of apartheid and provided financing to right-wing organizations. These associations explained how she'd learned about the use of parathion-laced ointment for assassination. She hadn't planned on it killing Odum so quickly. There was supposed to have been much more distance between them before he succumbed to a set of mysterious symptoms. But she didn't know about his chemical hypersensitivity. So the trail—and poison—were still fresh when I arrived at his hotel room.

She also didn't plan on her caper leading to anyone else's death. When I told her about having killed a little girl, she became more alert and clear-eyed than any time the entire evening. She shook her head as I described

Marissa's poisoning. Tears came, and then deep sobs, which triggered a series of tremors building toward a full-blown seizure. When her breathing started to come in labored gasps, I knew it was time to decide if she would suffer the same fate as Odum. I had the antidote with me to ensure that the nicotine intoxication could be reversed if she became unable to keep talking, but now I had her whole story.

This woman was a deadly pest. She'd chosen to get rich by teaming up with Morley. To protect herself, she'd murdered Paul Odum—and she'd killed a child out of thoughtless disregard for whoever else might contact her poison. It all unfolded because she wanted what most people desire. Fine clothes, a sports car, and a luxurious condo. But she'd picked the wrong partner and the wrong approach in running drugs. In some ways Sarie Botha—a rich, educated, voluptuous white woman—was much like Jamal Watson, a poor, dumb, scrawny black man. Both of them bought into an ugly game, chose the wrong partners, got dealt bad hands, and decided how to play their cards.

But I had no reason to kill Jamal. That was just an unfortunate consequence of his decision to try bluffing. And I had no reason to see Sarie die. Backed into a corner, she'd struck out. There was nothing inherent in her or rats that made extermination necessary. In the right context, either could live peacefully. She'd retained a core of human compassion, as I'd seen with her sobs for Marissa. I've seen my share of faked tears during questioning, but Sarie's were genuine. And anyone under Morley's thumb had to evoke at least a shred of sympathy.

So I untied her hands and she stared wildly at me, unsure of what was coming. Just as Beth had instructed—and made me practice with saline, much to my displeasure—I drew a syringe of the atropine, tied a ligature, found a vein in her forearm, and injected the drug. I left the supplies within easy reach in case her condition didn't improve. I stroked her hair, which had become tangled and damp with sweat. She began to relax. After fifteen minutes, her breathing grew regular and she closed her eyes.

I got up and pulled the sheet over her. She rolled onto her side and curled into a fetal position. I turned out the lights and went into the living room, leaving the bedroom door open to listen for her. After pouring a nightcap, I stretched out on her leather couch and mulled over my next move.

Chapter Thirty-Eight

The light pouring through the sheer drapes in the living room woke me up at sunrise. Piercing light to match my searing headache. I went into the bedroom, where Sarie was breathing deeply in a sound sleep. I grabbed some aspirin in the medicine cabinet and headed to the kitchen to rustle up some breakfast. I got the coffee started, found some eggs, bacon, and bread, and set to work.

I'd been up half the night weighing my options. At first, I figured I'd just wipe the place for my prints, head home for a good night's sleep, and report my findings a few days early to the grieving widow. Case closed, payment made, everyone happy.

Except I knew that Laurie Odum wouldn't be satisfied, let alone happy. She'd want to go after Sarie and Morley. If she went to the cops, it'd be just about impossible for me to remain behind the scenes—and unlicensed investigators are highly unappreciated. Even if Laurie didn't give them my name, the detectives would haul Howard in for questioning. And I had no doubt he'd spill his guts. Or maybe Laurie would try to handle things privately, but given the usual bumbling of most PIs, there'd be a good chance that a trail of crumbs would lead to my door.

My next plan was to just go to the cops myself with the whole story—or most of it. But the evidence was pretty thin. The underwear and an autopsy would show that Odum had been poisoned, but the link to Sarie and Morley was circumstantial at best. She'd been in his hotel room, but without her confession they'd have nothing. A detective wouldn't have silk ropes and nicotine tea during questioning. If Sarie just kept quiet, there'd be no way to link her to the murder. And Morley would be even tougher to nail.

Around three in the morning, I'd come to the conclusion that this was my mess to clean up. I wasn't done with Sarie Botha. In one sense, I'd found Paul Odum's killers—Sarie and Morley were both guilty the way I figured it—which was all his wife had wanted. Sarie had been a means to my ends, and I could discard her if she was nothing more than an object to satisfy my need for information.

But I wanted more—for her and myself. Morley had used Sarie for his purposes, both financial and physical. I couldn't lower myself to his level. I believed that Sarie might salvage a worthwhile future if she could be protected from Morley—and take responsibility for her past.

My concern turned to the question of who would warn the next Tommy about Morley. Sure, we all have to live with our decisions, but there's no reason that scum like Morley should be allowed to make the consequences horrific. Justice requires a sense of proportionality. We don't shoot people for double-parking. I could picture a confused kid from Potrero buying into Morley's next shipment of contaminated dope. Stepping away from this case without dealing with him was like Isaac spraying for flies and leaving the rotting dog in the dumpster.

I heard Sarie stirring at about the time the eggs were scrambled and the bacon was crispy. She came into the kitchen looking remarkably lovely for last night's ordeal. Her black full-length silk robe draped sumptuously in all the right spots.

"Hungry?" I asked, pulling toast from the toaster.

"Ag! You torture a confession from a girl and then offer her breakfast? You're a piece of work, Riley."

"No reason for a rough night to mess up a sunny morning. Cream or sugar?" I asked, setting a couple of mugs on the table beside a bay window with a panoramic view of the city.

"I don't know whether to try to kill you or kiss you, but I don't have the strength for either at the moment. I'm famished, you bastard." She sat, alternately rubbing her temples and sipping her coffee.

"Feeling better?" I asked after she'd wolfed down half of her breakfast.

"Thanks, the graze is tops. My stomach is recovering, but the rest of me is kussed out." I gathered that she felt awful. "What you did was terrible, but at least now somebody else knows. It's a relief that I'm not alone. But the whole thing is worse than I thought."

"Worse? I thought you said that telling the truth helped."

"It did, except the truth is more dreadful than I'd imagined. Now I know what it was like for Paul Odum." She paused and drew a deep breath that caught in her chest. "And I know about the little girl." She fell silent again and ran her fingers through her hair, letting the strands fall on her face. "Riley, what was she like?"

"Her name was Marissa. I just met her once for a few minutes. She was a spunky Mexican girl with satiny hair. She was very polite, but not timid. You could see a fire behind those jet-black eyes."

"Shit," she said, her own eyes filling with tears. "Shit, shit, shit. I'm trapped in a nightmare that keeps getting worse." She wiped her cheeks angrily. "I don't know how to get out. I thought I was glad to have survived your interrogation last night. Now, I'm not so sure."

"Slow down. I can help you escape."

"Why would you?"

"I have my reasons," I said, wiping my plate with a slice of toast. "But I'd like to know something about you before we get any further."

"Didn't I tell you everything last night? I can't actually remember most of what I said," she sighed.

"I know you hooked up with Morley's dope ring, but what I don't understand is why."

Sarie launched into a halting explanation of how she'd learned that her mother was seriously ill with a rare blood disorder, and that the family's best bet was to get her under the care of American specialists. Her father had a lucrative art export business, specializing in selling African artifacts to European collectors without anyone asking too many questions. Sarie had helped fund her American education by smuggling smaller pieces from the archaeological sites in Mexico back home to the family business. Things had been very comfortable in Johannesburg, but her mother's medical treatments couldn't be covered with the sale of a few Mayan pots and jade figurines.

"I rationalized that the drug money would be going to save my mum. She was a good and gentle woman." She drew a deep breath. "But she died before the necessary visas, financial confirmations, and medical arrangements could be obtained."

"Let me guess, you'd filled your bank account in the meantime and it didn't make sense to throw away all that money."

"You can be so harsh. Yes, I enjoyed being rich," she said defiantly. Then she looked into her empty cup and slumped into the chair. "I liked the things that money provided."

I got up and refilled the coffee mugs. She took hers from me, brushing her fingers across the back of my hand.

"So now you know what I'm about. But who are you? Why are you willing to help me?

"Like I told you last night, I'm an ex-cop. When my father died, I took over the family business to support my mother and my brother, who has medical problems. I run an extermination company across the Bay." The caffeine was working along with the aspirin, and I almost felt human for the first time since going into the Savoy.

"Okay, but how'd you get involved with Paul Odum?"

"I do a little unconventional but discreet pest management on the side. Odum's wife hired me to find his killer."

"So you're done. You found me . . ."

"And Morley," I added.

"Yes, he's evil. I suppose I am too, but not down deep. Not really. Do you believe me?" She looked desperate, lost.

"It's not about what I believe. But I figure that you know about people by what they do, not what they say." She looked utterly defeated.

"Why don't you just go and tell Odum's wife that you've solved the case?"

"Because Morley is like a maggoty dog and his flies are spreading filth." I paused and considered how much to reveal. "And some of that filth may have poisoned someone important to me." She looked up quizzically. "Sorry honey, not you. This person made some bad calls too, but he didn't deserve what he got."

A long silence. I could see her struggling, trying to choose between self-pity and courage. When people reach bottom, they can either quit or start clawing their way back up. I've seen boxers hit the canvas, and I've watched the same struggle in their eyes. It's easier to stay down. There's a damn good chance that if they get up, a brutal beating is coming. Not many fighters win a bout after kissing the canvas.

"What can I do?" She had heart, enough to stay in the ring, and perhaps enough to win.

"I've been working on that. But I need some information before my plan can come together."

"This isn't going to involve another round of better answers through chemistry, is it?"

I gave her a grim smile. "I much prefer to have beautiful women talk to me without needing alcohol, drugs—or poisons. So, tell me about Morley's schedule. When does he come and go? What's his routine?"

Sarie explained that her boss's week was unpredictable, except on the days he taught. Morley didn't like having to deal with students, so he'd reduced his classes to Tuesday and Thursday mornings. He'd arrive in a foul mood at seven thirty, pull out his lecture notes from the files, and teach from eight until ten. Then he'd come back to his office and expect Sarie to have his coffee—cream and two sugars—ready for him. Their offices shared an interior door, so she was to listen for his arrival and serve her master promptly. He liked to schedule meetings for the late mornings on these days, so he'd have the rest of the week available for research, writing, and extracurricular work.

When she'd finished her account of Morley's routine, I poured the rest of the coffee into our mugs and headed into the living room. While I worked my way through these details, Sarie cleaned up the dishes. It felt almost domestic, except that the man of the house was plotting a murder while the little lady was shaking off the effects of his having tied her up and poisoned her.

She came out from the kitchen and settled into an overstuffed chair that looked like it had been upholstered in polar bear skin. The bathrobe tie had loosened, and when she crossed her legs, the silk slid aside to reveal a length of thigh. My plan was simple, which is invariably a virtue in these matters. I had her write a short note to Morley explaining in a clear, simple, dispassionate way that "It's over between us." She objected that there wasn't anything to end in terms of romance, but I explained that it didn't matter because Morley would never actually see the note. She looked confused, but she did as I asked and handed me the paper. Then I explained the plan—or at least as much as she needed to know.

"On Monday, I'll drop off a vial containing a couple tablespoons of a bluish-green liquid. Tuesday morning will be show time."

"What's my role?" Her foot began swinging like an anxious metronome.

"Simple. You'll make Morley's coffee and add the stuff I give you. I'll be waiting in his office when he returns from class. All you need to do is listen for your cue."

"Which is?"

"When you hear me say, 'I don't want to be a pest,' you knock on the door and deliver his drink. Then leave."

"We're poisoning him, right?"

"Not just any poison. One that ensures a measure of justice."

"I'm not sure I'm up to this." She sighed, shaking her head. Her foot came to a rest, and the bathrobe ended its sensual migration.

"You were up to killing Odum. Maybe he wasn't a saint. Like you, he figured to use the drug money for what he thought was a noble purpose. But on the way, you both ended up with some pretty posh lives."

Sarie looked around the room with its stylish furnishings and high-end art. "But …" she began. I could tell she was going to make a last-ditch effort at justifying her duplicity.

"Hold on sweetheart, I'm not done. There's a little girl who died a miserable death and a family that will live with that loss."

"I didn't know that would happen. I didn't know." Her voice quavered.

"Here's how it works in my business. You put poison into the world, and it's your responsibility. Things go wrong, you fix them." She put her face in her hands, as if she might be able to hide from it all. "Cleaning up the mess is a small price to pay for getting away with murder, doll."

"But I don't see how this is all going to work. It all seems so dodgy." Eyes glistening with tears, her face was a strained mixture of grief, confusion, and hope.

"Relax. The less you know before we're done, the less likely it is that you'll over-think your role and make a mistake. You have plenty of book smarts. But let's face it, your criminal smarts aren't so hot. It wasn't that hard for me to find you, so trust me on this one."

"You're the fundi tsotsi." She paused and gave a weary smile, knowing she had me flummoxed with that expression. "You're the expert on how to be a hoodlum."

"I've gone up against some of the best. Do as I say and you'll get out of this."

"I'll never get away from Marissa. That was her name, right? Every time I see a Mexican girl . . ." Her voice trailed off.

"Look, I'm an exterminator, not an exorcist. I'll take care of pests. You'll have to deal with your own demons."

She took a deep breath, wiped away a tear, and smiled weakly. I wasn't sure what to make of her vulnerability and grit. All I knew was that Rene Morley was vermin, and Sarie Botha was the most alluring pesticide I'd ever handled. I got up and went to get dressed in the hope of salvaging what was left of the weekend. As I was hanging up the bathrobe, Sarie stood in the doorway and let her robe slide to the floor.

"Help me forget. Just for a little while," she pleaded.

I was tempted. But it would just be her using me for an hour of amnesia and me using her for something that wasn't even lust but some adrenaline-fueled struggle for control with handcuffs, ropes, and flesh. "Not now, not here," I said. "Let's focus on cleaning up a mess before we make another one."

She gave a sad smile and slipped back into bed, saying, "I'm here if you change your mind."

I showered and dry-shaved with one of those worthless pink plastic razors that women use for their legs. The scraping was worth the sense of being clean-shaven and starting afresh after last night. When I came out of the bathroom, Sarie had fallen asleep. I dressed, gathered my things, and headed through the living room. Then I stopped and went into the kitchen. I left the Kokopelli doll with a note: "It's your turn to be the trickster." I hoped that she'd be up to the role when the time came.

I walked a mile or so back to where I'd parked. I wasn't dressed for a Sunday morning, which got me a few curious looks, but I managed to clear my head in the crisp September air. On the way back to San Francisco, I caught a sports report on the radio. Notre Dame had throttled Northwestern, 48-0. I had to wonder how much confidence you could derive from beating a weaker team. The announcer shared my concern, suggesting that the Irish might find it a rougher go against Alabama and USC later in the season. I switched to classical music and wondered about my next opponent. Morley was no Northwestern.

CHAPTER THIRTY-NINE

When I got home, I put on a threadbare sweatshirt and worn-out khakis, then went down to the kitchen and made a ham sandwich (on soda bread, accompanied by an enormous dill pickle and a handful of chips—as it should be). There was nothing I could do about Morley until tomorrow, so I tried to distract myself with my idea of a perfect Sunday afternoon. I threw open the curtains on the front window and let the sunlight illuminate my worktable. I decided against putting a record on, as I had a ticket for the symphony in the evening. Like a juicy steak, a concert is that much better after fasting. Then I got down to working on my favorite part of my collection.

Most insect collectors organize their specimens according to taxonomic groupings, and most of my cabinets were arranged that way. But I also had a cabinet that my father had given me when I graduated from the police academy, and the specimens were organized to reflect my own peculiar interests. Most of the drawers held insects that I'd collected from corpses—flies, beetles, and a variety of other species that occasionally show up. And then I had my "criminal collection"—a drawer devoted to insects that were guilty of murder, theft, vice, and fraud. Well, not so much guilty (they didn't really choose a life of crime) as exemplifying the dark side of nature, including our own.

I'd begun with the murderers, after reading about insects that killed members of their own species. That tray included a very fine series of female mantids, who were well known for consuming their mates. Perhaps the most spectacular specimens were the female black widows, one of which was nearly the size of a marble with a blood-red hourglass set against a velvety black. I had to keep the spiders in vials of alcohol because their bodies shriveled into ugly raisins when they dried. I fully realized that they weren't insects, but their murderous tendencies were too fascinating to overlook.

It took more careful reading to figure out which insects were thieves. I'd put together several stunning rows of cuckoo bees and wasps, shimmering in metallic blues and greens. These little jewels are notorious for sneaking into the nests of other bees and wasps, and laying eggs so their offspring can poach their victim's food and shelter. I was particularly proud of two rather blandly colored flies. I'd gotten these from one of my father's army buddies who'd been in the mosquito control unit and collected insects along with my father. After the war, he'd stayed behind to become an embassy guard in New Delhi. I'd traded him a few common but beautiful Californian butterflies for these uncommon and ugly flies, which make their living by hanging out along ant trails and mugging the unsuspecting workers returning to their nests with bits of food.

My trays devoted to vice crimes held a particularly strange assortment of insects. Scott Fortier at the entomology museum put me onto some books about reproduction that were perfect for filling out this part of the collection. I had a fine series of bed bugs, in which the male inseminates the female by violently puncturing her body wall rather than using her genital opening. This approach qualified as sexual assault in my estimation. When I was in Mexico, I caught some tropical butterflies that are pedophiles—the males mate with females before they even emerge from the cocoon. I also figured that insects conspicuously copulating in public qualified as exhibitionists or pornographers, so I included a series of March flies, stink bugs, dragonflies, and grasshoppers all caught and preserved *in flagrante delicto*, as the prosecutor's office liked to say. And finally, I had my prostitutes— insects that paid for sex. These included dance flies that wouldn't turn a trick unless the male provided a meal, and crickets that paid for services by allowing females to consume the john's wings. (I had several males with chewed-up wings as evidence of payment.)

My favorite section was the frauds, grifters, and con artists. It had been easy to nab some toxic monarch butterflies but more of a challenge to collect a nice series of queens and viceroys—the harmless mimics that defraud birds into thinking they are also dangerous. Likewise, there were sets of swallowtails and tropical butterflies with both the genuinely nasty species and its fraudulent copycat. In midsummer, I'd received a package from one of my father's old pals who was a county extension agent in Iowa. In exchange for some Californian pests of various plants, he'd sent me two species to fill out my con artist series. For the last couple of weeks, I'd been keeping the specimens in a cigar humidor to slowly moisten their tissues so they wouldn't crumble when I pinned them.

He had carefully laid a couple dozen fireflies between layers of the cotton. These were a species in which females flash signals to dupe males of a different species into thinking that they are prospective mates. When the males show up hoping for a little action, the females attack and eat them. There was also a very nice set of ash borers—a kind of moth that is the spitting image of a wasp. I had some beetles and flies that resembled bees, but these moths were such incredible counterfeits that I had to look closely to be sure he hadn't sent me actual wasps. The moths required extremely careful handling to avoid tearing the delicate wings. I'm always amazed that such easily damaged creatures can survive the rigors of the world while alive.

After an intense hour, I leaned back and admired my work. Next to the smaller males, I'd pinned some of the female fireflies on their backs. This unconventional orientation highlighted the greenish-yellow patch underneath the abdomen—the source of the light which the femme fatale uses to entice her victim. And I'd mounted a few of the waspy moths with their wings in a natural position, rather than spread out as usual. This made their deceptive appearance all the more authentic and convincing.

I wondered where Sarie Botha would fit. On the one hand, she belonged among the fireflies, deceiving with the promise of sex, only to prove lethal. But on the other hand she was much like the ash borers, vulnerable despite her appearance of danger.

As for Morley, I considered him more of a parasite than a criminal. I could admire the work of a good assassin, a skilled thief, a talented prostitute, or a clever grifter. I remember a hit man who, after the district attorney promised to leave his family alone, came clean about having been the gun behind more than a dozen contract killings on the West Coast and as many in Chicago and New York. He didn't so much confess as take credit for his work. The man didn't brag, but his pride showed—all the way to the gas chamber at San Quentin. He'd screwed up on the hit that I investigated and he knew the deal. There were no weaseling lawyers or last-minute pleas for forgiveness. He deserved his punishment, but I felt no sense of satisfaction when he was executed.

Morley was a different case. If he had an insect equivalent, it was the screwworm fly. My father had a half-dozen of these in his collection. He'd gotten them from the Texas hill country when he was stationed at Fort Hood after returning from the Pacific. He told me that one day they'd be valuable because the Department of Agriculture was going to drive them to extinction. They are such vile creatures that even the eco nuts haven't come up with any reason to object to the government's wholesale extermination program. Nobody's going to miss them. The maggots infest the wounds of animals, expanding the opening into a gory mess that causes horrible suffering until the poor beast dies of an infection—or gets put out of its misery. My father told me about a cow with an open sore the size of a dinner plate filled with writhing maggots. But even these awful insects can't be blamed for inflicting such pain on the world. Yes, Morley was another matter—a vermin that knew what it was doing.

As evening settled in, I changed into my best—actually my only real—suit, a conservative dark gray number with a blue silk tie that had been my father's favorite. I was overdressed for driving my rust bucket, and the old truck didn't blend into the parking lot at the War Memorial Opera House. I arrived almost an hour early to take in the setting. The Opera House is a grand building featuring Roman columns and a gorgeous entrance hall with one of those vaulted ceilings that belongs in the Vatican. I wasn't in the class of the tuxedoed and gowned patrons, but at least I had something in common with those who were there to hear the concert rather than to be seen by the others.

I found my way to the side of the balcony—the almost affordable seating. I couldn't imagine that the music sounded all that much better in the premium orchestra section on the floor. The warm glow from the gilded arches, the enormous chandelier, and the soft lighting reflecting off the blue vaulted ceiling succeeded in taking me far away from the ugliness of the last two days. At least until Edo de Waart lifted his baton.

The San Francisco Symphony was playing Tchaikovsky's *Pathétique*, perhaps the most tragic of all classical works. He composed it as a kind of rebuttal to the uplifting feeling of Beethoven's Ninth. I think I know how the Russian felt—the world isn't always or mostly a place of joy. The opening movement began with a despairing bassoon solo accompanied by the low strings, all of which drew me in and set the tone for the evening. The rest of the strings provided a lighter response, but this time I could feel a sort of free-floating anxiety, as if Tchaikovsky had been following me for the last few days. By the time the orchestra had built to a dark crescendo, courtesy of the brass section, I couldn't tell whether the music was coming from the stage or from inside my head.

At least the second and third movements provided a bit of relief. They were upbeat, but even so, the work had a kind of jittery feeling that is lost in many recordings. Actually the undertone is missed in plenty of live performances as well, but it came through thanks to my mood and de Waart's conducting. He didn't have Ozawa's flamboyance, which my father disliked almost as much as his being Japanese. (After a performance, my father grumbled that "The job should speak for itself. A concert is about the music, not the man. I don't prance around when I'm spraying a house.") But for his part, the young Dutchman had a demanding precision that worked especially well for less exuberant symphonies.

Lots of people hearing *Pathétique* for the first time think it's over after the chorus. But I knew better. The finale is dark and brooding, and the orchestra was in fine form. The ending was more eerie, even nightmarish, than I'd remembered. Maybe it was because the previous movement had been so manic—or because I knew the concert was coming to a close and thoughts of tomorrow were creeping in. The symphony closed with the sense of desolation and despair that Tchaikovsky sought—and found—so powerfully.

On the way home I dropped by O'Donnell's Pub for a quick bite and to close the day with a glass of Connemara single malt. I considered the Bushmills twenty-one-year-old. I've always found it odd that a good whiskey is as old as the people who can legally drink it—and there's something screwy in a country where you can be sent to die in a war before you can have a drink to toast your own descent into hell. As smooth and tempting as the Bushmills was, it only offered 80-proof therapy, and I needed 120. Brian served me a generous pour and we chatted for a while, as old friends will. But he sensed that my heart wasn't in it and graciously went back to polishing the glassware. The Connemara was a perfect match to Cynthia's shepherd's pie. She cooked with the simple grace of the home country. Modern life has its advantages, but new isn't always better when it comes to what a woman cooks. Or what a man values.

CHAPTER FORTY

The morning was crystal clear, the sort of San Francisco day that makes you forget about the summer that never lives up to its name—at least in terms of warmth. A chance for postcard photographers to frame the Golden Gate Bridge, the Transamerica Building, or Alcatraz Island against a blue sky. A chance for the Chamber of Commerce to deceive tourists. A chance for residents to delude themselves that the thick winter fog and days of gray drizzle are not our fate for the next five months. It's the lies that make life bearable for most people.

When I got to the office, Carol was on the phone. She had on a sweater with horizontal stripes of fall colors. It only took a moment to decide that the burnt orange stripe was my favorite, at least in terms of location. Had she noticed, Carol would've given me a failing grade in Sexism 101, but the quiz was unreasonably difficult. I'd never be an A-student, but I had passed the test with Sarie—if a guy is allowed partial credit.

I went to my office and looked up some figures in a four-inch-thick handbook that had everything you'd want to know about pesticides—including how to avoid (or ensure) poisoning. I grabbed a vial from the warehouse and headed to the front door. It didn't feel right to rush out without checking in with Carol. She'd been carrying the ball around here, and I wanted to be sure that nothing important was falling between the cracks.

"Look, here's how it works," Carol was explaining to the caller. "There's fast, there's good, and there's cheap. You can pick any two of these, ma'am. If you want one of my guys out there this morning doing a good job, it won't be cheap. If you can wait to the end of the month, we can clean up the infestation for about half the price I quoted. And if you want somebody who can come right away at the low price that your neighbor told you about, then I can give you the name of some other exterminators, but I won't guarantee the quality of their work."

There was a pause, as Carol listened and rolled her eyes in my direction.

"Okay, ma'am. I can see where you can't stand having fleas in your carpet for another day. You're right, the bites are terribly itchy and it's kinda gross knowing that they're sucking your blood."

Another pause.

"Yes, we guarantee our work."

Pause.

"All right then, just give me your address and I'll have a technician there before noon." She filled out the work order, hung up, and looked at me expectantly.

"How're things going around the shop?" I asked.

"Better than when you're here to muck up schedules and orders. There are some potential customers that need your attention, but they can wait for a day or two. Do you have a sense of when your project will be done?"

"It'll all be over by midweek, one way or another."

"I should be able to keep things rolling until then." She cocked her head. "Especially with some musical encouragement." She had turned down the radio to take the call, but not far enough to mute the insistently repeated request to "Shake your booty"

"Gotta love KC and the Sunshine Band, eh?" she teased.

"No, I don't."

"C'mon Riley, these are the guys who gave us 'Get Down Tonight.'" She did one of those disco dance moves in her chair and sang, "Make a little love, do a little dance, get down tonight."

It was almost palatable coming from Carol. "Ah, yes," I interrupted. "I remember hearing those lyrics over and over again, which seemed to be the entirety of what KC and his untalented group managed to commit to memory and foist upon the world."

"You're just a sourpuss on a Monday." She frowned and turned up the radio again, but it was just an ad with a bunch of flower children singing about wanting to buy Coke to bring utopia to the world. I couldn't follow the logic. At least KC wasn't suggesting that booty-shaking was the path to world peace.

"Sorry." I pulled up a chair and leaned my elbows on her desk. She came around behind me and dug her fingers into the base of my neck.

"Geez, you're tense," she said, kneading the muscles into something between excruciating pain and exquisite pleasure.

"Long weekend. But the ball is rolling and everything will come together or fall apart soon." I winced between her massage and my anticipation. "Then I can get back to work around here. You've been great covering for me."

"I know you're just doing what you figure you have to. From what I know of you, Riley, whatever it is won't be pretty, but somehow things'll be a little more right than they were before you got involved. Not perfect, but better. And that's something. Besides, business is going well, what with Isaac's attitude improving."

"That's good news. The kid just has to get over the great American lie."

"Which is?" Her thumbs were now busy trying to separate ligaments from muscles in my shoulders.

"Follow your dreams and you'll be rewarded with money and glory. Here's how it works: do whatever you think is right, but don't count on anyone giving a damn, paying you for it, or praising your work. The world doesn't care what you think and you should return the favor. Do it because it needs doing."

"You are a grump." She squeezed hard enough to make me flinch. "It's probably best that you're not around impressionable young people anyway. Get out of here and go do what 'needs doing.'" She'd lowered her voice to imitate me and then pushed me toward the door.

          ◊

I started up my truck and drove to the east end of Warehouse Row on 17th, where I knew a guy who wholesaled pesticides to the smaller exterminators. I had my own warehouse, so I didn't have to rely on him for my usual chemicals. But this morning I was after something that wasn't in my inventory. Using an organophosphate would have been just punishment, but I respected the tools of my trade. On the other hand, herbicides weren't part of my business. To some, a pesticide is a pesticide, but that's like saying Jameson Limited Reserve is the same as Schlitz beer. I had my professional principles, and my plan would have its own poetic justice.

I parked next to the loading dock and went into the cramped sales room, which was furnished with a dust-coated artificial plant, a fading poster promising "Better Living . . . Through Chemistry," a battered folding chair with "First Baptist" stenciled on the back, and a cracked Formica counter running the length of the room. Nobody was there, but a buzzer had sounded when I came in. Norm pushed open a swinging door behind the counter and shuffled in looking annoyed. I'd known him for years, and he'd always looked like he was about seventy and needed a shave—or a drink. He took a drag on his cigarette and grumbled, "Whaddya need?"

"Nice to see you too, Norm," I replied, leaning on the counter.

"Riley? Shit, sorry, I didn't see it was you." He squinted and ran his fingers through the wisps of yellowing white hair on either side of his head, as if that would somehow improve his vision.

"Don't worry about it, Norm. I just came in to get some paraquat."

"Paraquat, eh? That's not a product in yer line of business. Or've ya conquered the roaches and rats and decided to expand into weed control?"

"No, I have my hands full with the beasts. I need it for a little job of my own."

"That's good, cuz y'know they're talkin' about makin' it a restricted-use pesticide. Wouldn't be able to sell it to someone without their havin' a license. Supposed to be dangerous, but hell, more people drown in the Bay than get killed by paraquat. Maybe the government oughta require a license before tourists go in the ocean." He gave a raspy laugh, which sent him off on a coughing binge that ended with his hawking up a wad of mucus and spitting it somewhere behind the counter. "Sorry, kid. So whatcha planning for the stuff?"

"I'm going to spray a swath of hillside along the fence behind my shop," I lied. I had an answer ready, because I knew that Norm would have questions. He was a crusty old bastard, and though he wouldn't admit it, he was lonely. Ever since his wife died in a car accident on Route 17, he'd been coming into O'Donnell's three or four times a week. At first I wondered if he was taking up booze, but he'd nurse a couple of beers for an hour. Norm would start up conversations with whoever was on the next barstool. Baseball, fishing, politics—anything was fair game. It wasn't about getting into an argument. Just the opposite, in fact. I'd seen him one night agreeing that Gerald Ford was the man to lead the country and the next week slapping a guy on the back and shouting, "Carter's the man!" He wanted someone to talk to and disagreement tended to end conversations.

"Whatcha got against some grass and weeds?" he asked, flicking his ashes onto the floor behind the counter.

"Kids have been hanging out there after school. It's their new smoking place."

"Cigarettes?" he asked with a wink.

"Mostly. Doesn't really matter to me, but they're going to set the hillside on fire someday. And the last thing I need is to have those drums that I store inside the fence go up in flames."

"Kinda late in the year for using a herbicide, doncha think?"

"There's still plenty of green. At least it'll help to spray now, and I can hit it again next spring." He wasn't giving me a hard time, just hoping to keep the discussion going.

"That makes some sense, I guess. Easier than tryin' to keep kids from smokin' and dopin'." He started with a gurgling chuckle but stopped before it could degenerate into another coughing fit. "How much you need?"

"A pint should be plenty for now, and then I'll just hang on to the rest."

He shuffled back through the door behind the counter and returned with a translucent plastic bottle. "Stuff's a beautiful blue," he said, holding it up. "But sea snakes are the prettiest reptiles you'll ever see and deadly as hell. I ever tell ya about the time a guy in my platoon got bit during an amphibious landing on New Guinea? The poor sonofabitch . . ."

"Norm, I have to run, but next time I see you at O'Donnell's I want the whole story. Okay?"

"Sure thing, Riley. It's a helluva story, lemme tell ya."

"Send Carol the bill for the paraquat," I called over my shoulder. In the cab of the truck, I transferred some of the pesticide to a vial and headed out to make a delivery. To Sarie Botha.

CHAPTER FORTY-ONE

Midmorning traffic over the bridge was light, and I was at the doors of Kroeber Hall in under an hour. It was nearly ten a.m., so I figured classes would be out soon. Right on cue, a mass of students began to pour out of the building, giving me the perfect chance to make my way up to Sarie's office unseen by anyone in the main office who I'd met last week. The last thing I needed was to run into one of the secretaries or the department head and get drawn into faking my way through discussing a donation of artifacts to the anthropology museum.

Morley's office was dark, but I could see light through the frosted glass in the door of Sarie's adjoining office. I knocked softly, the flow of students down the hall having diminished to a trickle.

"Come in," she called. Sarie looked up from her desk with an odd mixture of relief and anxiety. The sort of expression that I imagine a doctor sees every time he walks into an examination room. I closed the door behind me. The morning sunlight streamed through the south-facing window, making the scraggly plants on the sill look like a verdant jungle.

"This won't take long," I said reassuringly. "Let's go over the plan."

"Riley, I don't know if I'm up to this. I've been thinking. What if something goes wrong? If he finds out, he'll kill me."

"Do as I say and nothing will go wrong." She shook her head. Whether it was denial or confusion, I couldn't tell.

"Look, doll, like I said at breakfast yesterday, you bought into his scummy world. You're a big girl and it was your choice to make. But getting out isn't free. At least what I have planned is simpler than what you pulled off in LA. And if your conscience is acting up, consider that Odum deserved your toxic touch less than Morley does."

"And the little girl, Marissa. She didn't deserve anything." Sarie sounded wistful, like it had all been a bad dream. "How do I know it'll stop with Morley? That nobody else will . . ." She trailed off.

"Get killed? It won't happen. We're preventing deaths, not spreading them like he does."

"Isn't there another way?"

"Sure. But you'll just be getting somebody else to clean up your mess. Morley's at the core of this and you're an accessory. You want to start making up for what's happened, then now's the time."

Her head dropped forward and she drew a deep breath. "You're right. It's my cuck, so what do I need to do?"

"Let me have a look at Morley's layout, for starters." She got up and unlocked the door between their offices and flipped on the light. The room smelled of old leather, furniture polish, and expensive pipe tobacco. His office was meticulously organized. The bookshelves lining the walls were perfectly arranged. Every item on his massive desk was evenly spaced, letters and papers were all tucked into precisely stacked trays, and a Tiffany glass lamp was perched on the corner. I tucked away his compulsion for neatness, thinking that it could prove useful when the time came.

Lying open beneath the lamp was his schedule book, opened to this week's appointments. He had class tomorrow at eight a.m., and then he'd noted "CAS directorate meeting @ 11:00, Morrison Planetarium." I knew from having taken Tommy to star shows on the weekends that the planetarium was part of the California Academy of Sciences museum in Golden Gate Park. The timing couldn't have been better. Morley would have just enough time to host my unexpected visit before wanting to hurry off to his meeting in San Francisco.

A floor-to-ceiling bookcase with glass doors loomed behind his desk and held an imposing collection of antiquarian volumes. Wooden blinds covered the windows on either side of the bookcase, keeping out all but the thinnest slits of sunlight. A small table to one side of his desk held a mechanical typewriter. Morley had opted to keep one of those heavy black throwbacks, rather than an electric model that might diminish the aura of sophistication.

His choice suggested that anything longer than a letter would be passed to a secretary. The great man's time was too valuable for such plebeian tasks. As with his need for order, I figured that the typewriter would come in handy tomorrow.

Morley's view of people was evident in his furniture. There was an uncushioned, armless wooden chair in front of his desk—the sort you'd expect in a Catholic school principal's office. And behind the desk loomed a deep red, tufted leather-upholstered chair, complete with brass nails lining the woodwork. Intimidation was the game.

We returned to Sarie's office. I cleared a stack of papers from a chair and motioned for her to sit at her desk. I wanted to look into her eyes and assure myself that she was onboard. She looked resigned but attentive when I said, "Let's review the plan."

"Okay, I'm ready," she replied, picking up a pencil and pulling a notepad in front of her.

"Don't write anything down, for God's sake," I said, pulling the pencil from her hand. Her grip on it was fierce, as if the pencil somehow kept her anchored to the world.

"Relax, sweetheart." I took her hand and felt the tension release as she gave a weak smile. "There're only two things to remember. First, I'll get here as class lets out, just like this morning. That way I can slip up here without being noticed. You'll need to let me into Morley's office. I figure it takes him at least a few minutes to get here from his class, eh?"

"Yes, that's exactly right." She seemed to perk up now that we were talking about the nuts and bolts of tomorrow's plan. "In his mind, the world waits for him. Only unimportant people need to hurry places."

"Very good. Once Morley arrives, you just make his coffee like usual." There was a coffee maker on the long wooden table beside the door, and one of those tiny refrigerators underneath, presumably for her lunch and his cream. "Then all you need to do is listen for your cue."

"Which is when you say, 'I don't want to be a pest,' right?"

"Well done. You remembered from yesterday." I pulled the vial of paraquat from my jacket pocket and set it on the desk. "Just pour this into his coffee, stir, and serve." I'd noticed a slight ammonia odor when I filled the vial. I didn't think Morley would notice, but I figured it'd be smart to cover it a bit. "You might make his coffee a bit stronger than usual and add some extra cream and sugar. That should mask any telltale taste. Plus, I'll time things so he's in a bit of a hurry and unlikely to be savoring his coffee. Is there any chance that he won't drain the whole thing?"

"None. He can be bloomin' stroppy without his caffeine. And the man's such a creature of habit that he's constitutionally unable to move on with his morning until he's had his coffee. He'll drink it."

"That was my last concern. Our little drama should come off without a hitch."

"But Riley, I'm still not clear on how this whole thing is going to work. Won't there be an investigation? Surely the medical examiner will discover that he was poisoned." She gripped my hand harder and harder as she went on. "They'll figure out that I did it. And then what—we make a plan?" The woman sure had some odd ways of putting things. I guessed that she was talking about coming up with some alternative approach. But that wasn't going to be necessary.

"Slow down. There's nothing to worry about. Nothing. It'll all be clear tomorrow after he leaves. Like I told you yesterday, I don't want you fretting over details and getting distracted. The more you know at this point, the more likely that you appear unnatural or say something to raise suspicion." I stroked the back of her hand with my thumb, trying to soothe her.

"But what happens when the police show up?"

"The way I have it worked out, you'll be asked a few simple questions. You simply deliver the lines that I'll give you tomorrow, they'll applaud, the curtain drops, and you walk away."

"Are you sure?"

"I know how these guys think. I was one of them. If there're a couple pieces of evidence that match up with a sensible story, they're only too happy to close a case and move on. I just need you to focus on the next act."

Sarie sighed deeply, reached for the vial, and put it into a desk drawer. I must've looked worried because she said, "I can do it, Riley. There's nothing to worry about." She smiled at having turned around my words. I kissed her forehead and closed the door softly. On my way out of Kroeber Hall I ran into a gaggle of wide-eyed high school kids taking a tour of the university, in the hope that they might gain access to such a virtuous institution filled with noble scholars.

I spent the rest of the day back in the city. Too preoccupied to schmooze with prospective clients, I changed into work clothes at the shop and caught up with my crew. They were on a big job in a grain warehouse on Pier 30. This was the real San Francisco, where the smell of sweat and diesel mixed with the salty stench of rotting kelp. This morning, the seagulls were rioting over the remains of some greasy mound of hair—most likely a wharf rat or an alley cat—their angry squawks filling the air along with their frantic flapping.

I'd always liked the South of Market neighborhood. At least when I was growing up, this was where a tough kid could find trouble among the transients, sailors, and working-class men who lived and drank hard. The old Victorians with the stable residents provided a sense of nineteenth-century affluence, which was tempered by a skid row of dingy streets and trash-filled alleys.

The fancy developers with an eye toward gentrification began to clean up the Embarcadero about ten years ago, which pushed the gays into this neighborhood. Living on the margins, they'd built their own gritty community among the warehouses and industrial sites. I couldn't care less what they were doing behind closed doors. What mattered is that these guys had managed to fend off the city's redevelopment efforts and keep South of Market from turning into another prettified neighborhood for the tourists and financiers. I'll take a leather-clad homo who can hold his own over a suited-up banker who lives off the poverty of others.

When I got to the warehouse, Dennis and Isaac were laying out the fumigation tarps and Larry was busy running numbers to figure out the right amount of gas. I leaned across the hood of the truck and double-checked his calculations. You don't want to screw up with methyl bromide.

Grain beetles are tough little bastards, and cleaning them out requires good, airtight seals. Climbing into the rafters to tape ventilators and ducts was hard work. And wading through the cavernous bins to break up the grain crust was just plain dirty as the dust turned into a thin layer of muddy sweat. It felt good. Once the fumigation commenced, there wasn't much to do but stand around to watch for leaks and make sure that no idiots ignored the warning signs posted all over the place. Isaac and Dennis called it a day and headed back to the shop.

Larry insisted that he'd watch over the site until the gas had dissipated. I grabbed some fried chicken for him at a not-so-savory takeout joint a few blocks away. At least he'd have something for dinner because I was sure he wouldn't leave until the place was safe. A buddy of his from 'Nam working for another exterminator had been the one to find a dead runaway kid who'd snuck into a warehouse during a fumigation a year ago. They'd seen plenty of death in the jungles of Southeast Asia, but seeing a fifteen-year-old girl who'd vomited and drowned in her own fluids, skin blistering as she left scratch marks inside the door that locked behind her, was pretty hard to take.

I headed home, showered, and wandered down to O'Donnell's Pub for a burger. Brian was in the back doing inventory so his nephew was bartending. What the kid lacked in conversation he more than made up for with his ability to pull a beer with a perfect head. The place was quiet, except for the Monday Night Football game on television. It just doesn't seem right that baseball and football should overlap, but America had bigger problems to solve with unemployment, nuclear arms, and the prospect of a peanut farmer as President. Between Fran Tarkenton's aging arm and Walter Payton's explosive legs, Howard Cosell had more than enough raw material to drown out Gifford and Meredith's commentary. The Vikings and Bears were evenly matched, but I couldn't stay interested in the game. The television chatter faded into the background, and for the first time all day, I had a chance to mull over and refine my plan.

In one sense, I had everything I needed for my agreement with Laurie Odum. I could drive over to Berkeley, deliver the goods, and demand payment. With what I had, she could turn the case over to the police, who would have to conclude that poisoned underwear combined with the death scene and an autopsy added up to murder. Then she'd score the double indemnity, I'd get my cut, and Tommy's Fund would be in the black for years. There'd be an investigation, but the story that Howard first gave to me would be believed (the dead flies and winged ants were long gone) and the case would sit in the files until the report turned yellow and the detectives turned gray. And assuming that Sarie's confession was on the up-and-up, Morley would reassert control of the dope network for the Bay Area. The cops and courts do their best and it's usually enough, but they only claim to enforce the law—not to provide justice.

The alternative was my plan. If Sarie came through, Morley would be exterminated and she could move on. I could go to Laurie with what I had (or at least the parts of the story that she needed to know), and we'd all live happily ever after. Except, of course, for the corpses of a drug-smuggling ecology professor, an innocent Mexican girl, a slimeball anthropologist— and a slew of paraquat-poisoned kids. So much for fairy tales. But if Sarie blew it, things could get ugly. I played out various scenarios and none had happy endings. Morley would surely punish her disloyalty after he extracted what she knew about me. Depending on how the tangled mess unfolded, she'd likely end up on the wrong end of a bullet and I could find myself on the wrong side of a desk in a police interrogation room. Or Sarie could choke at the last minute, go back under Morley's control, and it wouldn't be long before he knew that I had the information to bring him down—a most undesirable situation. I was just getting all twisted up, so I headed over to Marty's Gym.

After breaking a good sweat jumping rope, I saw Marty in the doorway of what passed as his office, watching a couple of skinny Mexican teens wailing on each other in the ring while their trainer scowled. The fighters had plenty of piss and vinegar but a decided lack of skill. The bare bulb in his office didn't provide much light, but it looked like the side of Marty's face was purple and swollen. I wrapped a towel around my neck to stay warm, and detoured by his office on the way to the bags. Marty started to shift the cigar to the other side of his mouth, and then flinched.

"You run into a truck, Marty?" He squinted through his black eye. I could tell he was deciding whether to send me on my way with a quick lie, or come clean.

"Nah," he croaked, tilting his head toward the inside of the office. He went in and I followed. Marty leaned against his desk, which was covered in rolls of athletic tape, wads of Ace bandages, folders with their contents leaking out, sporting goods catalogues, and a collection of ashtrays emblazoned with the names of Vegas casinos from his days in the big time.

"I'm telling most people that I tripped over a mop bucket in the locker room, but them's that need to know are already getting the word." I looked him over, and it was pretty evident that the old guy hadn't fallen, unless he'd managed to land on his knuckles as well as his face.

"Got into it with somebody, eh?"

"I lent one of the up-and-comers a C-note. Probably shouldn't have, but his manager was a real piece of work. Wouldn't advance the kid enough for a suit and bus ticket to his father's funeral."

"So what happened?" I asked, wiping my face with the end of the towel.

"Turns out there wasn't no funeral. I was the sap. The kid needed the money to pay off a bookie and figured he'd stiff me for the loan." Marty rubbed the backs of his bruised hands.

"And you collected."

"Never lend money that you can't collect yourself."

"Bet the kid didn't count on you still having your stuff," I smiled, imagining the surprise when the grizzled has-been gave the hotshot a lesson outside the gym.

"Wasn't sure I did," he grinned and gingerly touched his swollen cheek. "The world's gone soft, Riley. People figure that somebody will solve their problems. They hire a strong-arm to collect on a debt, or even worse, some candy-ass lawyer to sue the guy."

"Everyone wants the cops or the courts to make things right," I agreed, thinking about my own desire to pass off Morley to the system.

"Damn right, Riley. And half the time what's right and what's legal don't line up. Laws are written by politicians. You ain't gonna get gold nuggets outta the rear end of a horse," he chuckled. "And you ain't gettin' fit by listening to an old crank. Better start on the bags before you cool off." He ushered me out of his office, and I started pounding away.

Tomorrow wasn't about saving the world. It was personal. Laurie's money would make things right for Tommy in the future. But for what Morley had already done, somebody had to make things right. That is, if Sarie was telling the truth. Her story was credible, but it was all I had—and I'd learned that a smart suspect can weave a convincing lie. I wanted to lure Morley into either affirming or refuting her account, and then I could be satisfied with what he had coming.

When I finally called it a night and headed up the hill, my shoulders were burning and my arms were like lead. I'd sweated out the booze and never felt better.

CHAPTER FORTY-TWO

The morning promised another crisp and sunny fall day. No clouds, no drizzle, no fog, no gray. Not exactly weather to fit what I had in the works. I stood under the shower until the hot water ran out, steaming the soreness out of my shoulders. Then, I pulled my suit out from where I'd hung it Sunday night after the concert. Dressing up twice in three days was some sort of a record for me. But I wanted to create the right impression with Morley. I decided to wear the blue silk tie again. My father would not have taken any pleasure in what I was planning. Neither did I, for that matter. However, he knew the importance of duty, of a man doing work that needed to be done, even—maybe especially—when it was not a pretty task.

I walked down to Goat Hill Extermination, hoping to slip in before Carol got to work. No such luck. She gave me a hard time, asking if I was going to a funeral. I couldn't help but give an ironic smile, and she let the subject drop. In my office, I pulled a briefcase from on top of the bookshelves and blew off the dust. I didn't carry one of these things unless I was visiting a potential client who was the sort to expect a business owner to have one. I'm pretty much a take-it-or-leave-it guy when it comes to offering my services, but I can appreciate the formality of the old-school types. And I'm happy to accommodate their expectations, especially when a big contract is at stake.

I thoroughly wiped the bottle of paraquat for prints and put it in the briefcase along with a pair of rubber gloves. There was a stack of city maps for northern California, some blank pads of paper, and a pair of black dress socks that had somehow been left in the briefcase. I didn't need the maps or socks, but they came in handy to keep the bottle from banging around. I went through the expandable folders in the lid of the briefcase, looking for business cards, receipts, or anything that could link me to the contents if I had to abandon the thing for any reason. Satisfied of anonymity, I pulled from my desk drawer the note that I'd had Sarie write to Morley, slipped it into a pocket in the lid, and latched the briefcase.

Then I unlocked the filing cabinet and pulled out the bottom drawer, where I kept my snubnose .38. It had been my personal weapon while I was on the force. Plenty of guys preferred a bigger piece, but I'd found that it was much faster to clear a holster with this gun. And working the streets in plainclothes, the snubnose was comfortable to carry and easy to conceal. Sure, you give up some accuracy, but all of my encounters involving guns were close-range affairs. And if, by some chance, things went completely awry and I needed to draw down on Morley, it wouldn't be from more than a few feet. I slipped the gun into the holster inside my waistband. My suit-coat covered the bulge nicely.

My father had given me the holster as a Christmas present when I made detective. He'd used his connections with Mr. Guicciardini—an old guy down the hill from us who had emigrated from Tuscany—to locate his brother, who hand-tooled the most gorgeous leather goods in the city. As good luck would have it, when my father arrived at the fellow's shop, he saw some dermestid beetles crawling inside the store window. He warned Mr. Guicciardini's brother that his leather was probably infested. I don't know how my father could've afforded the custom holster without the man insisting that it was his gift for saving his stockpile from terrible damage. So that's how I became the only cop toting a full-grain Italian leather holster with "Erin Go Bragh" tooled into the side. It was too bad that such a fine piece of craftsmanship was hidden away, but it felt good to have it pressed up against my body.

I waved to Carol, who was on the phone, fired up the old Ford, and headed across the Bay. Traffic was heavy, but I'd left plenty of time. Why everyone was in such a rush to get to work was beyond me. Most of the poor slobs were heading to the financial district or some other prison masquerading as an office. I suppose the work put bread on the table, which, given the country's economic mess, was saying something. I'd loved being a cop, but not the hierarchy, which more often reflected department politics than professional competence. I had to say that being your own boss had lots going for it in terms of freedom and control. The biggest downside was that there's nobody to blame when things fall apart.

That's not quite true. I knew plenty of guys who blamed the city hall, tax collectors, and state inspectors when their businesses failed. But I didn't have any government fall guys this morning—if anything spun out of control, it would be my screw-up. Even relying on Sarie was my call. I could've taken care of Morley on my own and done so with far less uncertainty. But it's not just about getting the right outcome. It matters how you close the deal.

In Berkeley, I parked a few blocks from campus in a legal spot where the ratty apartments for students ceded real estate to ranch-style homes with big picture windows looking onto a not-very-picturesque street. No sense drawing the attention of the campus parking patrol and having my license recorded by some ticket-happy rent-a-cop. It's always the small stuff that gets overlooked and comes back to bite you. Setting aside incompetent criminals, who account for the majority of arrests, most cases are made on the details—an eyewitness across the street, a movie ticket in a coat pocket, a fingerprint on a windowsill, a dead fly on a mattress. Not that I was planning to have Morley's death trigger a murder investigation. But my father was fond of declaring that "an ounce of prevention is worth a pound of cure"—and this held true whether exterminating cockroaches or their human counterparts.

The campus was quiet, either because classes were in session or the students were still recovering from the weekend. Probably some of both. On the plaza in front of the administration building was a single longhair whose sign showed a map of the world under a photo of the Pentagon, along with the caption, "Humility. Don't leave home without it." A clever play on the credit card slogan, all in all. I gave him a nod and walked through the archway onto campus. The September day was just the way I like it—too cool in the shade, too warm in the sun. It made a fellow feel alive, at least for the moment.

I got to Kroeber Hall and stopped at the top of the stairs to read the announcements of university lectures pinned to a bulletin board. Not that I was terribly interested in or could even fathom what might be addressed by talks on: "Dynamics of Protons in Hydrogen Bonds through Vibrational Spectroscopy," "A Linguistic Survey of Sandaun: The Politics of Enumeration," or "The Significance of the Rose as a Symbol of Male Hegemony in 18th Century British Literature." However, perusing the flyers gave a natural excuse to be loitering in the hallway, along with the perfect angle to see into the anthropology office. Miss Hoshor was behind the counter, facing away from the door. I could hear the chatter of women's voices along with the clatter of an electric typewriter. The odds of her turning and recognizing me as I passed were slim, but I had a few minutes to spare and continued to study the announcements, halfway expecting to find a lecture on a new technique for counting the number of angels that could dance on the head of a pin. When Miss Hoshor went into the next room to admonish the other secretaries to buckle down with their work, it was a simple matter to slip past the doorway and head upstairs.

Most of the faculty apparently shared the students' disdain for mornings. Only a few offices had lights on. Sarie's was one of them. I knocked softly and went in. She was wearing a sleeveless pale blue dress and a white cashmere sweater as if to stave off the morning's chill, despite the sun pouring through the window. She smiled like a scared girl trying to appear brave. For all of her bravado in bed and her homicidal adventure in Los Angeles, Sarie now looked incredibly vulnerable. She got up to unlock the door between her office and Morley's. As she turned back to her desk, I took her hand and gave it a reassuring squeeze. She responded with a forced smile. Neither of us spoke. There was nothing to say—no pep talk or review of the plan would help. I had to trust that she'd come through.

I went into Morley's office, opened the blinds just enough to cast some light into the room, and put my briefcase on his desk. I pulled the oldest-looking book from his shelves and sank into his plush chair. The book was bound in maroon leather with the title in gold lettering: *The Holy Land, Syria, Idumea, Arabia, Egypt & Nubia*. The pages were brittle, which I took to mean that the book was really old and probably valuable. The illustrations of ancient temples were quite impressive and the text was surprisingly readable, as opposed to what passed for interesting lecture topics at the university. Maybe today's academics could learn something from the old guard. I'd begun to settle into the author's enchanting account of the temple at Luxor, when I heard a key in the lock.

Morley came into the room and turned on the overhead light in one continuous movement. A caricature of a professor, the pompous ass was decked out in a tweed jacket complete with elbow patches, maroon bow tie, and brown corduroy pants. Just the sort of pansy to require both cream and sugar in his coffee. Morley started toward his desk, but when he saw me in his chair he stopped mid-stride. For a fleeting moment, a look of surprise— maybe even fear—crossed his face. But this was quickly replaced by a sneer. He continued toward the desk, set a pile of books on the edge, put his hands on either side of the stack, and leaned forward.

"Who the hell are you?"

So, he didn't remember me as his friendly neighborhood exterminator, which had been a concern. I could've worked around it by saying something about having scoped him out earlier, but this made things neater. I smiled warmly. "Who let you in?" he asked menacingly, which struck me as funny, so now I was grinning. "Sarie!" he shouted. I hoped she wouldn't answer, as I wanted to keep her role in this little drama to a minimum. Either she didn't hear him, which seemed unlikely, or she had the good sense not to respond.

"My dear Mr. Morley, please slow down. There's no reason to be upset. Your assistant let me into your office after I explained that I was an old friend who wanted to surprise you." He leaned further over the desk and glared.

"I have no idea who you are. What do you want?" Before I could begin to answer, he continued, "No, better yet just leave." He stood up and gestured toward the open door.

"You don't know me or the syndicate that sent me, but I think you'll want to hear their offer." He raised an eyebrow, suggesting that I had his attention.

"Put down that book and get out of my chair," he hissed, closing the office door and coming around to the side of the desk.

"I just love a good travelogue. And the pictures are great," I added, snapping the volume shut and rising to my feet.

"Careful, you cretin. That book is more than a century old and is worth a thousand dollars, at least." Good to know that my powers of deduction were on the mark. "The pictures, as you call them, are the artwork of David Roberts, one of the most important painters of Egyptian archaeological sites."

"Right. But let's talk about real money." As Morley sank into the leather seat, I ignored the low chair intended for visitors and perched on the edge of his desk. He was used to being in control, so I wanted to put him on the defensive. I knew that being both close to and above him would make his type uncomfortable. To add to a sense of my contempt, I toyed with an ostentatious cherrywood pen holder inset with a brass medallion from the Society for American Archaeology. Morley pushed his little treasure to the other side of the desk.

"Get to the point. I'm a busy man," he snarled.

"The point is that I represent a business interest in the Bay Area that has a keen understanding of your little extracurricular enterprise. My employers know that your reputation was—how should I put it?—tarnished by some contaminated inventory," I said in the most condescending way possible.

"I don't know what you're talking about, Mr. . . . ?"

"O'Toole," I lied.

"A mick. I should have figured." So, Morley was a bigot who wanted to play games. No surprise. I slid my briefcase across his desk and popped the latch. It was time to up the ante.

CHAPTER FORTY-THREE

Rene Morley was used to being treated with deference by students and colleagues. And if Sarie's account was true, then he'd been one of the biggest fish in the pond when it came to the drug trade in this area. But I'd seen a flash of apprehension when I mentioned "my employers." He'd been able to intimidate little fish, but Morley knew there were sharks in the water—and when they smelled blood, things could go bad in a hurry. At least that was the story I was selling to get him talking.

People interest me, especially criminals. Most of them are simpering cowards, anxious to blame society, their childhood, or anything else for their crimes. Every so often, though, I'd come across an assassin or a thief who decided for himself that this was who he was. These sorts warranted respect. Not forgiveness, but a kind of appreciation for a man who learned a craft and refused to cut corners. I didn't figure Rene Morley for such a man, as I'd never met an honorable drug dealer. I was curious how ivory tower intelligence translated into street smarts, and I wanted to hear Morley in his own words. I wanted to know that he deserved what was coming.

Morley glared at the briefcase I'd laid on his desk, as if it was an affront to his tidy world. He certainly didn't appreciate my intrusion on his morning. But he was the one who'd decided to play games.

"Perhaps this will remind you of your little problem," I said, lifting the bottle of paraquat by the lid and setting it between us. "It seems that your customers were a bit put off by being poisoned."

"It wasn't my doing. The goddamn U.S. government took it upon themselves to douse Mexican fields with herbicide."

"Let's be frank, shall we? Those planes sprayed fields of pot, Mr. Morley. The ATF boys weren't going after avocados."

"They had no business being there. The whole program was a monumental disaster. Nobody knew which fields had been sprayed, so contaminated dope was mixed in with hundreds of shipments."

"I'm not sure the government was much worried about the quality of your product. I imagine their goal was to reduce the quantity."

"The program didn't even put a dent in the supply. Okay, a few of the beaners might've gone out of business and decided to crawl across the border to scrub toilets in San Diego. But most of the greasers are back to producing like before." The real Morley was showing through beneath the tweed.

"The only result that concerns my employer is the gap—let's call it a business opportunity—that was created when people figured out that your pot was making them sick."

"Yes, eventually those stupid college fucks put together enough of their surviving brain cells to associate my product with their breathing problems and coughing fits." He chuckled in contempt. "For a while it was working itself out. The college potheads could take a few hits and if their lungs burned, they'd just sell the rest to even dumber high school dopers."

"No problem there, eh?" I gave him enough rope to hang—or redeem—himself.

"Problem? Hell, I was making the world a better place. The country would save a bundle on welfare payments if a few of those worthless punks scorched their lungs before they grew into full-blown junkies." As far as I was concerned, Morley had taken the rope, tied a noose, and stepped onto the trapdoor. I wasn't going to enjoy killing this vermin, but neither was I going to regret it.

"But as you say, even the dopeheads put two and two together. While you were scrambling to find another source, somebody had to fill the demand and restore our industry's reputation. That's when the syndicate stepped in."

"Tell your bosses that they have my gratitude for keeping the customers high and happy. I worked long and hard to build that market. And now that I've found a reliable source, I'm back in business."

"And that, Mr. Morley, is the problem. You're trying to muscle into turf that's no longer yours. Now please understand that my employers appreciate the entrepreneurial spirit, the dreams of the small businessman." I knew that he'd broken into the big leagues and would consider this an insult. As he started to object, I raised my hand to silence him. Morley was fuming. "You've done an admirable job for an amateur," I assured him in my most patronizing tone while leaning over his desk, "but I'm afraid that others are much better positioned to meet the growing demand." If he was intimidated, he didn't show it. I would've taken his disdain for guts, except I knew that it grew from pure arrogance.

"Make your point, so I can send you on your way." Morley sighed, leaning back in his chair as if he'd grown tired of a dimwitted student.

"I'm prepared to offer you a generous buyout. You take the money and get out of the business. I assure you it's enough, if well managed, to sustain the standard of living to which you've become accustomed."

"Not interested," he sniffed.

"Ah, Mr. Morley, please don't be so hasty." I reached across the desk, took a pen from the fancy holder, and pulled one of his business cards from a monogrammed silver tray. I wrote "$250,000" on the back of the card and slid it to him.

His eyes dropped for a moment and then he scoffed, "If this wasn't a joke, I'd be insulted."

"My employers are generous and patient men. I'm sure they wouldn't want to see you dealt with in the same way you handled your competitors, but they have their limits."

"What do you mean by that?" Morley stole a glance at his wristwatch—a gold-toned Rolex with a jet-black face.

"I believe that a colleague of yours on campus suffered a most sudden and tragic death in Los Angeles. I don't believe that he threatened your professional status at the university based on what I've learned about your rather eminent position. Rather, it's my understanding that his outside interests conflicted with yours."

"How do you know about Los Angeles?" I said nothing. Sometimes silence is power. I'd induced more confessions by remaining quiet than most of my fellow detectives pried out through harsh questioning. "That bitch," he spat, "I'll deal with her later." He'd lost the veneer of a cultivated academic and confirmed Sarie's story in one move. "So you're threatening me, eh?"

"That's such a harsh way of phrasing a business offer. Let's put it this way. We can imagine that a big cockroach might not put up with a little silverfish eating his crumbs. Fair enough. What I'm saying is that the cockroach might want to think about whether he should stand his ground when the homeowner hires an exterminator."

"Very clever, Mr. O'Toole. You may leave now." He flicked his hand dismissively. "But let your boss know two things. I have no intentions of abandoning a lucrative venture."

"And?"

"And I don't entertain offers from messenger boys." He had salvaged a veneer of power, but it was a petty insult. I could tell he was rattled. When he looked at his watch again, I figured it was time to bring down the curtain.

"Look, Mr. Morley." I cleared my throat. "I don't want to be a pest. I just came to extend an offer." I rose slowly from the edge of his desk and closed my briefcase. Just as I was beginning to think that Sarie had missed her cue or lost her nerve, there was a soft knock at the door between her office and his.

"Come in," he snapped.

"I'm sorry about your coffee being late, Professor Morley. I knew you had a visitor and didn't want to disturb you." Sarie set the mug on his desk blotter, careful not to risk leaving a ring on his furniture. She turned to me. "Would you like some coffee?"

"He's leaving," Morley answered.

"Will there be anything else?" she asked.

"Yes, Miss Botha. I gather that you've been talking about confidential matters concerning my affairs."

"I don't know what you mean." She looked scared, even knowing that he'd soon be unable to hurt her.

"Go." He gave her the same dismissive flick. "I'll deal with you later." She backed out of the room and shut the door.

Morley swiveled to face me. "She'll pay for her disloyalty."

"That's no concern of mine," I shrugged. "I've done my job, and I'll let the syndicate know that their offer was rejected."

Morley lifted his coffee cup and took a sip to test the temperature. Satisfied, he took a deep draw and looked at his watch. "I have important matters to attend to, Mr. O'Toole," he said and began gathering some papers. I'd started to head to the door, as he rose from his chair. "Hold on there. Take this with you." He held out the bottle of paraquat that I'd left on his desk.

My ploy had worked nicely. I figured that with his compulsion for neatness, he wouldn't tolerate the bottle on his organized desktop. Things would've been fine if he hadn't grabbed the container, but his fingerprints would make a nice touch for the investigators. I took the bottle by the cap, put it into my briefcase, and gave Morley a nod on my way out. He was too busy gulping down his coffee to bother acknowledging my departure.

I headed down the hall, slipped into the men's room, and listened at the door. A couple minutes later I heard footsteps and a metallic ding announcing the arrival of the elevator. I figured Morley wouldn't take the stairs. His sort expected to be carried. I returned to Sarie's office and found her standing at the window. I put my arm around her. The sweater was nearly as silky soft as her skin.

"Well done," I said with a reassuring squeeze of her shoulder. She gave me a wan smile and turned back to the window. The morning sun painted elongated shadows of trees across the sidewalk running along the east side of the quad. A few students were strolling with books tucked under their arms. Two guys in cutoff jeans and T-shirts were tossing a Frisbee on the green, while their girlfriends sat in the sun pretending to enjoy the boys' antics.

Morley was making his way deliberately along the sunny sidewalk that bordered the west side of the lawn. He slowed and stopped. The famed archaeologist took a handkerchief—silk, no doubt—from his pocket and wiped his face. He took another few steps, then paused and looked about, trying to decide whether to go on or return to his office. He looked lost. A group of students passed by and he stepped onto the grass. Morley took a few weaving steps back in the direction of Kroeber Hall. Dropping his embossed leather briefcase, he started to lurch toward the center of the quad.

The students who had passed him stopped to stare, and the girls watching the Frisbee game shifted their attention toward the staggering professor. Morley raised his face toward the window, as if seeing his office would allow him to escape his fate. His head cocked ever so slightly and his eyes settled on the two of us. A fleeting moment of surprise, followed by recognition. His face twisted in rage.

Morley teetered and fell to his knees, the handkerchief pressed to his mouth. As the students—the "stupid sheep" whom he'd been so cavalier about poisoning—approached him, Morley vomited and began convulsing. Through the window we could hear the shouts for help. A couple of the young men ran toward the nearest building.

CHAPTER FORTY-FOUR

Sarie turned away from her tormentor's writhing on the lawn and looked to me for reassurance. I couldn't tell whether she was more horrified or relieved. In any case, her sensitivities would have to wait. There was little chance that anyone would be coming to Morley's office soon, but I wanted to be sure things were ready just in case. I guided her through the doorway and put the finishing touches on the scene. He had, of course, put the expensive book back on the shelf, so the office was just as I'd found it first thing this morning. Nothing was out of place to catch the eye of a savvy investigator or snoopy secretary. Snapping open the briefcase, I pulled the rubber gloves from beneath the maps and pads of paper. While Sarie watched over my shoulder, I took a piece of paper from Morley's drawer and loaded it into his typewriter. Then I hammered out the sort of note that suicidal people tend to leave behind:

My Dear Sarie,

My fame and the adulation of lesser scholars is not enough to sustain me. I cannot live without you. You say that you cannot continue your work here knowing of my love. But without you, life is unbearable. This is the best way for a man of my stature and dignity.

Rene

I pulled the sheet from the typewriter and positioned it squarely on his blotter—the sort of thing he'd be sure to do. Next, I pulled the note that Sarie had written from the briefcase. I was glad I'd had her write it in her apartment, as she wasn't in any shape for composing rejection letters to supposed lovers right now. I tore it crudely into pieces that could be readily reassembled and dropped them into the trash can behind his desk. One fluttered to the floor, and I decided to leave it there as a dramatic flourish. Anyone who knew Morley would infer that he must have been utterly distraught to leave a scrap of paper out of place. And the fragment would draw a person's eye to the trash can, allowing even a bumbling detective to discover the letter, which would provide physical evidence to corroborate Sarie's story.

I found the final element particularly clever. I lifted the container of paraquat from the briefcase and wiped the lid with a handkerchief to remove my prints. Morley's would be all over the bottle, which would provide a nice touch if the detective wanted to dot an *i* or cross a *t* in his report. Morley had set his coffee mug on a coaster alongside the blotter, so I left the bottle neatly positioned next to it. The dregs in his cup would show that the distraught would-be lover had mixed the poison with his coffee—not an implausible approach to suicide at all. I took a moment to wipe my fingerprints from the obvious places that an overly curious technician might dust—the arms of the chair and edge of the desk. Everything was in place for the final scene. All that remained was to give Sarie her closing lines.

"Well, doll, it looks like it's just about all over." She stared into space, breathing deeply.

"At least for you," she sighed. I grabbed her shoulders gently but firmly and turned her to face me.

"Pay attention. There're only a couple things you need to focus on when the cops arrive. My guess is that they'll be up here this afternoon, once the hospital reports that Morley was poisoned."

"Poisoned," she repeated as if trying to affirm what had happened.

"That's going to be their first question. And what they'll find is a bottle with his prints on it and traces of paraquat in his coffee cup. They might ask about why he used this chemical. You just explain that paraquat poisoning is a popular suicide method in the Third World. I got this from a presentation at the meeting in Los Angeles."

"That seems so long ago," she said.

"It was, and if you listen to me it can disappear into the past. The use of this pesticide is the sort of thing you could've learned about in your work with Morley in Mexico. Just shrug a bit and speculate that he probably heard the same stories and that's where he got the idea."

"They'll believe that?"

"Sure, just don't volunteer the information or go on too long with an explanation. Stick with answering the questions they ask. The other thing they're going to want is a motive. Between your note in the trash and his note to you on the desk, there won't be much of a mystery. Just tell them that you broke off an affair and that you were planning to seek a position at another university. Keep it simple. He was controlling and had become abusive and you wanted out. Based on his reputation around here, that story will have plenty of support. Don't talk about there being another man or offer any other details because you'll end up digging a hole. Got it?"

"Sure. But is it all too neat? Will the police be suspicious?"

"Of course they will. That's their job. But the detective won't be looking for more work. He'll be happy to close a case if everything points in the same direction, which it does. Just don't come across as too devastated or distant. Aim for shocked regret and you'll be fine."

"The gogga had it coming," she murmured.

"Gogga?"

"Yes. It's a South African term for a disgusting insect."

"Like a cockroach?"

"Exactly. That's what he was, you know. A nasty creature leaving filth wherever he went. He got what he deserved." I put my arm around her shoulders and walked her back into her office.

"Maybe that's all any of us can really expect."

"What do you mean?"

"I mean, the best we should hope for is to get what we deserve."

"I suppose most of us get more than we deserve. Like second chances and peaceful deaths."

"The real question is how to live. But if our lives don't mean something, maybe our deaths should. Like that old saying about living by the sword and dying by the sword. Or in Morley's case, poison. There's a kind of justice in a fitting death."

"Even a kind of poetry." She looked at me with bottomless sad eyes the color of the jade carvings she had brought back from Mexico. "But I'm not sure that the last stanza has been written."

"Meaning?"

"My own poetic justice. I smuggled artifacts to South Africa and dope to America, I helped Morley distribute his filth, and I have three deaths on my hands. I need to find meaning in my life or—"

"Or?"

"Never mind, Riley. Like you said back in my apartment, things go wrong, you fix them. What matters is what people do, not what they say." She smiled unconvincingly.

I took her face in my hands and leaned down to kiss her forehead. She closed her eyes. "Figure out what's right. You don't have to worry about Morley or me, sweetheart. We're both out of your life."

&

As I headed out of the building, sirens wailed toward campus. On the way back to San Francisco, I turned on the radio and let Chopin's nocturnes fill the cab. Sweet, slow, and sad—somehow the perfect complement and counterpoint to the morning. I considered heading to work and catching up on my calls, but there'd be plenty of time later this week. Instead, I went home, stashed the gun in my top dresser drawer, changed into jeans and a flannel shirt, gassed up the truck, and headed south to Pacific Grove.

Based on monarchs I'd seen flitting through San Francisco, I figured the migration was under way. It was still a bit early for the spectacle, but that meant fewer people underfoot. Once the crowds arrive in October, I usually opt for Andrew Molera State Park near Big Sur. It adds an hour and a half to the trip, but the site is all but unknown to the gawking tourists and busloads of school kids.

At Pacific Grove, I parked by a brick-red building and found an empty bench alongside the gravel path through the eucalyptus and pine. I sat back and pulled out the sandwich I'd brought—dark rye with spicy German mustard slathering the leftover corned beef that my mother had given me on Saturday when I picked up Tommy. The sun was pouring through the trees and the black-and-orange clumps in the branches looked like enormous masses of hanging fruit.

A sign in the parking lot had the current number of monarchs at 10,000, although I had no idea how anyone came up with this estimate. By the end of October, that number would quadruple, according to the official butterfly counters. Coming from as far north as Canada and as far east as the spine of the Rockies, the monarchs gathered every winter in these groves. These butterflies had never seen this place. Months ago their great-grandparents had left California, and somehow these insects knew exactly how to return to the groves of their ancestors.

That sense of tradition took me back to my parochial school days. If nothing else, the Catholics tapped into a deep and ancient sense of ritual that could make the hair on your neck stand up during High Mass. But the black-and-orange flitting through the treetops reminded me of a less profound—maybe even profane—tradition: plaid jumpers on Catholic schoolgirls. One wouldn't think that such a uniform, designed as it was to mask individuality and sensuality, would do much for adolescent boys. But Ann Murphy proved otherwise. She tucked her skirt up into the waistband to bring the hem halfway up her thighs. This stylish refinement provoked the wrath of the nuns and the lust of the guys in my ninth-grade class. And the steadfast refusal of the top button on her intriguingly thin white blouse to stay fastened reportedly led to some very long talks with Mother Bernadette. So you couldn't really blame me for having my hand under the back of her skirt in the cloakroom one September afternoon. Ann had an exquisite rear end, and when Sister Catherine caught me, I knew that my rear end was in for a much less gentle treatment. She hauled me off to the Mother Superior, who sentenced me to Father Mahoney's paddle. What Ann Murphy was to temptation, Father Mahoney was to punishment.

While I waited in the hallway outside the priest's office, Deacon Roland walked by in his starched white robe. He'd led my confirmation class the year before, and was a young, hip, soon-to-be priest. Or at least that's how we understood it. He could be both cool and serious, which impressed even the hooligans like me. In confirmation training, Deacon Roland had told us that our childhood was over, that we were moving beyond following rules to avoid punishment, that being an adult meant doing what's right because it's right. Seeing me in the hall, he stopped to inquire what I was doing there, as I was the sort of kid that might be up to something.

"Aren't you supposed to be in class, Mr. Riley?" He called all the boys "Mr." after their confirmation, which made an impression on us.

"Mother Bernadette sent me to see Father Mahoney," I replied. The Catholic hierarchy sounded like some sort of big family, except nobody could produce children. The Irish and Italian families in my neighborhood did their best to make up for this shortcoming in the Church.

"Ah, I heard that you might be in for a bit of straightening out," he smiled with what I took to be sympathy. I considered suggesting that upon confirmation, the deal was supposed to be that I didn't do things to avoid punishment. By this adolescent logic, there should have been no place for paddling if the sacrament had done its work. But I didn't figure that this appeal would have much hope with Deacon Roland. Moreover, he didn't seem to carry much weight in the school.

"Seems so," I replied.

He moved next to me and dropped his voice. "You have a choice, you know."

"I can get out of the spanking?" I tried hopefully.

"No, you already chose that through your actions."

"What then?"

"You can choose whether or not to cry. If you do, it won't last as long."

"And if I don't?"

He put his hand on my shoulder. "You'll have chosen to take your flogging and to keep your dignity." He gave a gentle squeeze and headed down the hallway.

When I was called into the office a couple of minutes later, Father Mahoney looked me in the eye. He held a long wooden paddle that looked like a flattened baseball bat. The priest told me that if he didn't respect me he wouldn't be delivering the punishment. I learned some important lessons that day. But probably not the ones that anyone was hoping to teach. With the possible exception of Ann Murphy.

CHAPTER FORTY-FIVE

The next morning I was only too happy to return to my familiar world. Real work with real people sounded like just the antidote to yesterday's drama. I woke early and stopped by Gustaw's Bakery. It felt like the old days on the force, with my .38 pressing against my body beneath my jacket and reminding me that there were evil people while I had breakfast with good people. I wanted to return the gun to my office, as having it in the house with Tommy around wasn't a good idea. Besides, I was more likely to need it to deal with some burglar hitting the shop than at home, since only a truly desperate punk would think there was anything worth stealing in my neighborhood.

While savoring one of Ludwika's apple-filled paczkis and sipping a mug of her husband's thick coffee, I scoured the *Chronicle* for news about Morley. The paper claims to cover the region, although the coverage of East Bay happenings is spotty compared to San Francisco events. So I was surprised to find a headline in the Bay Area section: "Berkeley Professor Kills Self." According to police, Morley had been distraught over a failed romance and had taken his life using poison. Sarie must have played her part effectively. The piece went on to say that he'd been a highly respected anthropologist with an international reputation in the study of Mesoamerican cultures. The university had issued a statement saying that "Professor Morley was a valued member of the faculty, and his tragic death has stunned the university community." I supposed it depended on who you asked.

I got to Goat Hill Extermination just after Carol had unlocked the front door and mercifully just before she'd had a chance to turn on her pop music station. She was happy to hear that my project was completed except for one last trip across the Bay to close the deal. I spent the morning returning messages and driving around the city to meet with prospective clients. It felt good to be busy, and after lunch I stopped off to see how the guys were getting on with a pigeon job at Ghirardelli Square.

Most exterminators don't want to mess with cleaning out birds, so we pretty much have these operations to ourselves. The merchants were getting fed up with pigeons crapping on the tourists and the outdoor cafés. Couldn't really blame them. When I got there, Larry was on a ladder jamming wire mesh into gaps between the buildings where the birds were nesting. I could hear him cursing under his breath as dried pigeon crap showered onto his head. Dennis was carrying lengths of sheet metal that the guys had cut and shaped back at the shop.

"How's it going?" I asked him as he struggled.

"I'd rather be spraying for roaches, Riley. Sheeit, this here nigger would rather be pickin' cotton than messing with birds."

"Dennis, you're a city boy. You wouldn't know cotton from begonias."

"True 'nuff. But I know that pigeons are nasty. And working with this sheet metal is a drag. I got nicks all over my arms and I nearly cut off my own head unloading a stack from the van."

"Where's Isaac?"

"On the roof. Larry's got him up there with a shovel, moving gravel to fill in the low spots. Keep the birds from getting water, he says."

"You headed up?"

"Yeah, we cut these to fit into the freight elevator. I'll mount them along the edge of the roof. Sure is a lot of work to harass the pigeons into finding new digs." The sheet metal would form a steep slope along the parapet to prevent the birds from roosting.

"Need a hand?"

"This is the last load, but you could grab a couple bags of that poisoned corn." He nodded toward the open doors of the utility van. I loaded up and followed Dennis into the elevator. On the rooftop, Isaac was leaning on his shovel and staring toward the *Balclutha*, a beautiful three-masted square-rigged sailing ship moored near Fisherman's Wharf.

"Looks good," I said.

"The ship?" he asked wistfully.

"I meant the roof. I don't see any puddles, so that should keep the pigeons from enjoying their penthouse arrangements." I set down the bags.

"Well, I'm done here," he said, looking anxiously toward the deadly grain and heading toward the door.

"What's up with him?" I asked Dennis, who was slathering epoxy along the edge of the roofline.

"Don't know, Riley," he replied. "He's been real funky since we did that rat gig last week. Won't go near the chemicals."

"That's okay on this rooftop job, but he's not going to be much good otherwise."

"You ain't jiving, man."

I left them to their work and headed up Van Ness toward City Hall. Carol had asked me to drop off a bunch of paperwork and pick up some forms from the Housing Authority. On most days I couldn't stand dealing with bureaucracy, but I looked forward to the mindless errand as an opportunity to think through what I would tell Laurie Odum.

Tomorrow was the deadline, and I had solved the murder of her husband. She needed enough to provide the police with evidence to convince them that Paul Odum had been murdered. We needed the district attorney to call his death a homicide for the insurance company to pay on the double indemnity clause—and for me to get my money. But I didn't want to give her so much that if things got messy with Morley's death—or Sarie's life—I would be dragged into an investigation. The most worrisome complication was the very real possibility that if I gave Laurie the name of her husband's killer, she'd seek revenge. Whether she'd try a do-it-yourself job or try to hire professional (and usually inept) assistance, whatever happened could likely also lead back to me. What I needed was a clean ending to a dirty saga.

Playing out various scenarios while standing in lines and waiting for clerks made the afternoon seem productive. By the time the enormous woman waddled back from the files clutching a copy of "Vendor Approval Form 928c: Landscaping, Refuse Disposal, and Extermination Services," I'd worked out my story for the widow Odum. It would take some ducking and weaving, but I had an idea how to convince her that I'd fulfilled my side of the bargain without her wanting to even the score.

Since it was Wednesday, I met the gang at O'Donnell's Pub. Brian was behind the bar. He reached across to give me a slap on the shoulder and ask about Tommy. I told him that the kid was doing great—still chasing insects like his old man. I didn't see Cynthia in the back, so I asked if everything was all right with his family. The poor guy shook his head and explained that his wife had to drive up to Sacramento, where their second-oldest boy had gotten himself into some trouble.

"Crosswise with the law?" I asked sympathetically.

"Nay, that'd be easier. His brother Kevin learned that lesson after a stint in jail and passed it on to the others. Seems that Sean's managed to get himself fired and his girlfriend pregnant."

"Makes you understand why some animals eat their young, eh?" Brian threw back his head and laughed. There was nothing that the guy wouldn't do for family, including knocking his sons in the head if they needed it. And no matter how bad it got, he'd find a way to keep things together.

"Better join your crew before they bankrupt you with their bar tab." He nodded toward our table, where Carol, Larry, and Dennis were dividing the last of a pitcher among their glasses. I walked over and Dennis handed me a full glass and the empty pitcher.

"Gee thanks. That's mighty polite of you to offer me some of my own suds." He gave me a "gee shucks" grin while I took a deep drink, then set the half-empty glass at my traditional place at the table, the chair beneath the autographed photo of O. J. Simpson—the greatest communal treasure at the pub. O. J. had grown up in the Potrero projects. He was the neighborhood's most famous product. Everything on the Hill shuts down when he's playing in a televised game. Except, of course, O'Donnell's, where it's standing room only.

I asked Brian to pull a pitcher of Anchor Porter. It wasn't the cheapest beer by a long shot. But I liked supporting local businesses, and Anchor Brewing had been a part of Potrero since the 1890s. Besides, I was in the mood to celebrate. I was looking forward to wrapping up the Odum case and revitalizing Tommy's Fund. So Carol's bad news wasn't on my radar.

"Where's Isaac?" I asked, settling into my chair. Larry and Dennis took long, serious pulls on their brews.

"He quit at the end of today," Carol said.

"He quit? Why didn't he tell *me* that he was leaving?"

"Uh, Riley," Larry answered, "you're a great guy, but when it comes to warm and fuzzy reactions, I think I'd go to Carol too."

"You be one bitchin' boss, Riley. But the cat's not jiving," Dennis added, pointing at Larry. "You dig it?"

"No I don't. That's not the way a man quits."

"Chill out, bro, and have some of this primo beer." Dennis refilled my glass.

"I don't think it was about you," Larry offered. "The dude was freaked out by the warehouse fumigation on Monday. I don't know what was going on in his head—"

"Larry's right," Carol interjected. "Isaac told me he'd come in tomorrow for his last paycheck. When I asked him why, he said that he'd decided to enroll in the art program at San Francisco State. So I pushed a little and he mumbled something about not being cut out for judging and gassing other living things."

"Sheeit, the problem was that he was always either drawing or thinking," Dennis said, draining his glass.

"It's dangerous if you think too little," Carol tried in defense of Isaac.

"And you're worthless if you think too much," Larry replied.

"He'll be happy in art school." It was easy to see why Carol's sympathetic side made her the person to talk to about bailing on us. But I couldn't get past the way he'd quit.

"Not a bad move. Ol' Isaac gets to paint nudes and scores a student deferment. Not a bad way to keep out of the next war," Larry observed.

"It's not a bad way to stay out of this whacked world," Dennis echoed. The conversation drifted to how screwed-up society had become, but I'd become lost in my own thoughts about throwing in the towel.

"Riley?" Carol brought me back to Wednesday night at O'Donnell's.

"On no, the dude's remembering one of his stories," Dennis said.

"Five bucks says it's a boxing story." Larry put a five-spot on the table.

"I'm betting it's from his days with the fuzz," said Dennis, putting his money down.

"Stop it, you two," Carol scolded. "I like Riley's stories."

"Don't really matter. Once the cat's on a roll, he's gonna lay one on us in any case," Dennis answered.

"Okay, it's a short one. And I'd keep it to myself, except telling it means that Dennis is out five bucks and that's worth it." I smiled as Larry grabbed the money off the table. "I was fighting in a Golden Gloves tournament in about '57. I'm not positive of the year but I am certain that I was getting thrashed. After the second round my nose was bleeding so bad I couldn't breathe, and the blood was running down my throat and choking me. The guy had hit me so hard with a left hook that I was deaf in one ear and tilted to the side like a drunken sailor. He'd dropped me at the end of the round with a body shot that cracked a couple ribs. If the bell hadn't rung it would've been over."

"Wicked." Dennis nodded his approval.

"What'd you do?" Carol asked.

"I told Marty—he was my trainer and corner man—that I wanted to answer the bell. He had to prop me up on the stool to wipe the blood off my face. Marty grabbed my chin and looked me in the eye. 'There's no shame in gettin' beat,' he told me. 'Only a damned fool would let his fighter go back in there. And there's no shame in quitting, as long as you do it right.'"

"I bet you were pissed," Larry said, refilling the glasses and lifting the pitcher to catch Brian's eye for a refill.

"I was, but Marty taught me something more that night. 'Riley,' he said, 'here's how it works. When the bell rings, I'm going to throw in the towel, but I'm not quitting for you. That's your job. You're going to go to the center of the ring and touch that guy's gloves. Let him know that you lost the fight but you're keeping your dignity. There's no dishonor if you respect your opponent and the sport.' I never forgot staggering out from my corner with the ring spinning and tilting. That guy touched my gloves and said, 'Nice fight,' like he meant it. I'd quit but I wasn't a quitter."

The conversation headed off into various tales of people who quit too easily and didn't know when to quit. Carol took the chance to suggest that the problem with men, according to her straight friends, was that guys couldn't commit to anything. Then she went on a tear that ended with a warning that Larry had better not quit on Jackie, so it was about time to pop the question. He promised he'd think about it and she rolled her eyes as if he'd made her point. The discussion of quitting moved into politics, and the ensuing argument over Agnew and Nixon drew in some of the regulars at the bar until it threatened to become a regular donnybrook. Brian had the good sense to offer free pub fries for the house if we'd talk about something else. All I know is that I should've quit after the sixth pitcher.

CHAPTER FORTY-SIX

Thursday morning was the deadline—an appropriate term, considering how I felt. Between the beer and pub fries, my gut was in bad shape. A scalding shower helped some, although the piercing sun wasn't doing me any good. I walked down the hill to Gustaw's Bakery, hoping the fresh air would help. It didn't. I must've looked miserable because I'd barely sat down before Ludwika gave me a scolding look and came over to my table.

"Riley, you've been drinking, haven't you?" she accused.

"That obvious, eh?"

"My Gustaw has provided me many mornings to show how a man looks after too much to drink." She glared at her husband as if my hangover was his fault. "Wait here. I give you Polish cure."

I wasn't going anywhere. Gustaw came over with a cup of his muddy coffee and a sympathetic look suggesting that Ludwika's remedy wouldn't be much more pleasant than my current condition. She came back with a glass of milky liquid.

"Here," she said, pushing the glass into my hand. "Drink."

"What is it?" The contents smelled slightly rancid.

"Kefir. It is my breakfast with buckwheat groats every morning. All Poles know that kefir is good for the sickness."

Gustaw leaned over. "It's sour milk, my friend. Be thankful. If she didn't have any in the kitchen, she'd have made you drink sour pickle juice." He nodded knowingly.

I drained the glass as quickly as possible, figuring the best approach was to empty the contents before I could taste the stuff. While I read the *Chronicle* and kept down the milk, Ludwika went into the kitchen and scrambled some eggs, grilled a slab of *boczek*—the fattiest, tastiest bacon on the planet—and fried cabbage-stuffed pierogis in the grease.

"Here," she declared, putting the plate in front of me as Gustaw refilled my mug. "Sour, then fat. This is how we cure your head and stomach."

By the time I left, I was feeling almost human. The crisp fall breeze on the walk to work finished the transformation. I came through the front door to find Carol looking about how Ludwika's sour milk tasted. She squinted as the sun sliced into the office and explained that she'd closed down O'Donnell's with Larry and Dennis. They had yet to make it to work, but I knew they'd drag themselves in if there was a job on the schedule. Most of our Wednesday-night affairs were lower key, but every so often it was good to let loose—and remember why I'd given up on heavy drinking. As Carol winced at the ringing of her phone, I headed back to my office.

I closed the door, pulled the plastic bag with Paul Odum's poisoned briefs from my bottom desk drawer, and jammed the evidence into my jacket pocket. Then I called Laurie Odum. She seemed relieved to hear from me but annoyed that I'd not been in contact. She'd been hiding out since we last spoke, just as I'd ordered. And she was none too happy about having been sequestered. I told her it was safe to go back into Berkeley and that I'd explain everything when I got to her house in the afternoon.

I spent the rest of the morning catching up on inventory in the warehouse. I'd have asked Dennis or Larry to do it, but I wanted a mindless task so I could rehearse my story to Laurie Odum and prepare for various directions that she might take the conversation. As a detective, I'd found that it was often easy to catch a person in a lie because they'd only anticipate the questions that they'd ask of themselves—and cops think in very different ways than most suspects. Trying to think like a rich, artsy, tree-hugging, sexually liberated vegetarian was no small task. I wasn't planning to lie to Laurie, but I needed to withhold some information if I was going to close the book on this case and convince her to pay for the story.

I grabbed lunch at Simon's Seafood. The Castro was not on my way to the Bay Bridge, but Ludwika's remedy had done the trick and I was famished. I was also thinking it'd be a good idea to make sure our fly extermination had done its trick. And maybe score a free lunch. Simon was in fine, fruity form—a pale pink muscle shirt with a pair of hip-hugger jeans. He squealed my name when I came into the tiny restaurant, causing the rest of the patrons to look up from their meals with quizzical expressions.

"Thith ith the man who thaved me from a plague of flieth," Simon lisped, ushering me to a table by the window and dropping a napkin into my lap with an effeminate flourish. "Jutht like in the Bible, God wath trying to punish this thinful fairy but Mr. Riley would have none of it. Would you, dear?"

"That's right, Simon," I answered, hoping that the diners would go back to their meals. I had to hand it to the guy, he was who he was and made no apologies for it. Simon's authenticity was refreshing in a world of pretenders, although I could've done without his exuberance. But it was a small price to pay for a plate of his grilled calamari swimming in olive oil and garlic.

I was getting tired of the drive to Berkeley, but if things went as planned, this would be the last time for a while. That is, until Scott Fortier led another "Insect Safari," which Tommy would not miss for the world. The trip was pleasant enough, with light traffic and KDFC playing Rachmaninoff's piano sonatas. Classical music listeners might not seem the sort to get easily agitated, but the afternoon selections fueled a fierce debate on the call-in show as to whether his first or second sonata was superior. I had to lean to the latter, based on my love for Vladimir Horowitz's performance on the RCA record. Say what you want about the godless Soviets, but that Ukrainian Jew played with the soul of a man who believed in something greater than himself.

I parked in the Odums' driveway, went through the wrought-iron gate, and knocked on the door. There was no immediate answer, so I admired the lavender flourishing in the courtyard. Just as I was about to give it another try, I heard a deadbolt being drawn back. That was a new addition to the house, so it seemed that Laurie Odum had taken my warning seriously.

"Come in, Riley," she said. "Sorry to keep you waiting. I had my neighbor Mr. Baine put in this new lock a week ago, and he even replaced the door handle to Paul's study. He's very handy—and he offered to help when I explained that I wanted some extra protection now that I'm alone. It's one of those locks that only opens with a key from the inside or outside. And I'm forever misplacing the thing."

"That was a smart move—a deadbolt installed by someone you trust." At least that explained the repairman without a truck. I smiled. "And I'm happy to say that you don't have any reason to be afraid." She didn't look scared, but her white linen dress with Mexican embroidery made her look young and vulnerable. There was nothing alluring about the dress itself. That is, until she headed toward the deck and the sunlight backlit her figure, making it evident that the dress was all she had on.

"I want to hear everything from the beginning," she said, waiting for me to catch up and then taking me by the arm out to the deck, where she'd set the heavy walnut table for an afternoon shindig. There were bowls with pistachios, almonds, olives, tortilla chips, and guacamole. She'd put out a platter piled with empanadas and a tall blue-rimmed glass pitcher filled with sangria.

"That's some spread," I noted, taking a few of the nuts. "I would've skipped lunch if I knew you were throwing a party."

"I'm sorry. It's just that I haven't seen anybody other than Mr. Baine and Maria since you left. She came by for the first time yesterday and made the food, as if you couldn't have guessed. Maybe it's all too festive given what you've come to tell me." She paused to sip her sangria. "And what I've learned."

That caught me off guard. I couldn't imagine what she had discovered without leaving the house. "Which is what?" I asked, wanting to know the terrain before making my move.

"Oh, you first. It's just something that came in the mail, and I'm not even sure what it means or whether it has anything to do with what you found." I wasn't keen on possibly walking into a trap, but she was paying the bill so I didn't have much choice. I went through my findings, giving her most of the story. She wasn't surprised Odum had been making money on the side. Marijuana was a natural medicinal plant, she explained. Then she got all riled up, telling me that a government conspiracy was beneath the whole paraquat program. I didn't follow her rant, but it had something to do with organized crime being in cahoots with politicians.

When she was done, I went over her husband's move into the big leagues with Thai dope as a way of funding his monkey-wrenching gambit. This part of the story barely caused a lift of her eyebrows, followed by what I took to be a nod of admiration and approval. Seems they really had been nutty environmentalist soul mates. When I got to the poisoning of her husband, she stopped sipping sangria and looked incredulous.

"Let me understand this. You're telling me that a major drug dealer paid a hit man to sneak into my husband's hotel room in Los Angeles and apply Vaseline laced with a deadly insecticide to his underwear?"

"I know it sounds bizarre," I answered, pulling the baggie from the pocket of my jacket, which I'd hung over the back of the chair. "These are his. I suggest you turn them over to the police, who will find a high concentration of parathion." I set the evidence on the deck next to her chair. She didn't look down. "Along with the underwear, the coroner will find toxic residue on his skin. And if the funeral home has followed your directions, it'll probably be possible to detect the poison in his blood. That should be plenty to establish a homicide, which will trigger the accidental death benefit."

I refilled our glasses, grabbed a couple of the olives, and waited. Laurie turned away from me and stared out over the Bay. The weather had stayed clear, and the sunlight on the water was dazzling even from high on the hill where the house was perched. With the Golden Gate Bridge in the distance, a person could've imagined that the world was a beautiful place filled with marvels of human ingenuity. Only one reminder of reality intruded—the blocky, whitewashed walls of Alcatraz Prison squatting on a tiny island in the Bay.

"A pesticide, how ironic," she whispered bitterly. Then, turning back to me with a glare: "I want justice." I figured this was coming. All this earth-loving tripe didn't convert into singing Kumbaya with your husband's killer. So I played it carefully, hoping she'd be satisfied.

"Laurie, it's over. The kingpin who ordered the killing is dead."

"How do you know?"

"Because I took care of it. I knew you couldn't move on and I wouldn't be satisfied until your husband's murder had been avenged." It was a lie. Paul Odum played the game and lost. Tough luck. He knew the rules. Killing Morley was about Tommy and other kids too defiant or confused or naïve to understand the game.

"Why didn't you just let the police handle it?" She sounded suspicious.

"I don't have to remind you why you hired me instead of going to the cops."

"Fine," she said, emptying her glass. The warm afternoon sun made the ice-cold sangria extremely refreshing. I'd have to watch myself. "But how do I know that you actually 'took care of it,' as you claim?"

"Check out yesterday's paper. There's a story about a Berkeley professor committing suicide. If you doubt my story, then I suspect you have contacts who can confirm that this fellow was heavily involved in the drug trade. But if I were you, I wouldn't go around asking too many questions. You're safe right now, but it's possible to put yourself in danger by letting on what you know to the wrong people."

Maria's empanadas were fantastic, even if they lacked meat. I didn't need to be eating after Simon's cooking, but I figured a hard night at Marty's would have me sweating out today's indulgences along with the remnants of last night's binge. Besides, I didn't want it to look like I was rushing through the story that she was paying so handsomely to hear. I figured that coming next was a demand for the name of the killer or evidence that I'd also taken care of this matter. But things took a very strange turn. Laurie Odum already knew who'd killed her husband.

CHAPTER FORTY-SEVEN

"I have something you need to see," Laurie Odum said, rising from the table and heading a bit unsteadily into the house. Five or six sangrias will do that to a small woman. She returned a minute later with a manila envelope. Laurie set it on the table, leaned against the deck railing, and stared vacantly toward the Bay. The sun backlit her thin dress in a most distracting way.

I cleared a space on the table in front of me and examined the envelope. It was addressed to Mrs. Dr. Paul Odum—a rarely used title. Either somebody with an old-fashioned sense of etiquette or an un-American appreciation of formality had written it. There was no return address and no postage, so I assumed the sender had put it into the mailbox directly. The envelope was wrinkled along the edges, as if its contents had made it bulge with something more than a letter. Now it held just a single sheet of expensive-looking paper, the heavy bond stuff with a fibrous texture. The note was handwritten in black ink with a felt-tipped pen. Even so, there was a light touch to the odd script of printed letters irregularly joined together with cursive forms. It didn't take a handwriting analyst to recognize that a foreigner had composed the message:

Dear Mrs. Odum,

You don't know me. I killed your husband. I want to believe that I had no choice. But that's a lie. I was a coward and because of me your husband is dead and so is an innocent child. I hate what I've become. My life has not meant any-thing. Except money. Please accept the enclosed cash. Take what you consider fair and give the rest to Marissa's family.

With deepest sorrow,

SB

I slipped the letter back into the deformed envelope and looked at Laurie Odum. From behind she could almost pass as a naïve young girl. But I knew better—she'd held back the letter to check my account up to this point. And she was too savvy for a happily-ever-after ending. Until now, I hadn't been entirely satisfied with how I was going to finish off the deal. I'd come to the house with a plan, but the letter gave me a better idea. The underwear and autopsy would ensure that Odum's death would be ruled a homicide and that she'd collect the insurance money. But I didn't want the police to follow the leads back to Howard—I'd made the kid a promise to keep him out of this. More to the point, I didn't want the case being traced to me, given my problematic history and conspicuous lack of a private investigator's license. No, I needed a way to have the official investigation stop with Sarie. And the letter provided just what I needed. But before I could lay out my plan, Laurie broke from her reverie, leaned her hands on the table, and hissed, "Who is SB?"

"Why does it matter?"

"I want him dead. Money isn't going to buy my forgiveness."

"So you want to contract a hit? That seems to have all the potential of pulling you into a mess that I won't be able to help you get out of."

"At least I want him arrested. Then he can rot in prison or die in the gas chamber, whatever the system decides."

"I don't think that'll be necessary."

"Why not?"

"I suspect that your husband's killer is already dead."

"I want proof."

"If I'm right, I should have something in the next day or two. And re-member, my satisfying your lust for vengeance wasn't part of our deal. You wanted to know if your husband was murdered, as I recall."

"Don't be cute with me."

"I'm not being cute. In fact, I'm not even going to be polite. It's my turn to tell you how this is going to play out." She glared at me, but the tension in her face melted into a pitiable confusion. Laurie Odum was in way over her head and she knew it. "Sit down," I said flatly. She settled heavily into a chair, looking bone-tired.

"I just want it to be over," she sighed. I could see that she was emotionally wrung out from days of worrying about whether she was the next target of whoever killed her husband. And I suspected that she was also anxious to collect the insurance money for her next crusade to save the dolphins or daisies or whatever.

"So do I, and here's how it's going to happen. First of all, the note came from a woman, not a man."

Laurie looked puzzled. "A woman?"

"Don't be so surprised. Women's liberation includes the capacity to murder."

"So who is SB?"

"Sarie Botha. She was Morley's assistant and became entangled in his drug business. As she indicated, she had options, but it was easier to follow orders. Aside from the money, her letter provides just what the cops need to close the case and put an end to your nightmare."

"It does?"

"Sure, with you providing them a creative but entirely plausible framework to hold the whole thing together."

"Go on."

"The note doesn't mention Morley or anything that could get you dragged into an investigation as an accessory to your husband's plans for blowing up a chemical plant or expanding his drug operation. If somebody didn't know any better, it reads like a suicide note along with a confession for a killing motivated by greed. So, just go along with it."

"That she killed him for money?"

"Sure. What difference does it make if it means you get on with your life and the work that meant so much to your husband?" I was milking it, but she was coming along.

"Okay, I suppose. So what do I tell them?"

"First of all, you give them the poisoned clothing, and they'll get the corroborating evidence from your husband's remains. They'll ask how you came up with the evidence, and you tell them that you found the greasy substance on his underwear just the other day. You decided to do the laundry yourself because you'd given Maria time off after Marissa became sick and died. Right after you touched the residue, you became dizzy, nauseous—and suspicious."

"Then what? How does the letter fit in?"

"Simple. You tell the cops that Paul was interested in buying Mexican art. That'll be an easy story to sell, given how your house is decorated. He found out that an anthropologist on campus, Sarie Botha, could provide some beautiful pieces. That element of your account will fit nicely with her research travel. You'll also want to suggest that their relationship might've been more than business. That angle will match up with the romantic betrayal that led to Morley's apparent suicide. The cops will figure her for something of a campus femme fatale."

"But why should I make it look like Paul was having a fling with her?"

"Because that'll explain how she had access to his underwear. Otherwise, things get complicated."

"All right. But how does the artwork come into the picture?"

"Sarie Botha was, in fact, shipping pieces to her father, who is an art dealer in South Africa with connections to the black market. You'll tell the police that your husband had revealed to you that he had evidence proving that Miss Botha was engaged in a lucrative smuggling ring, and he was planning to report her to the authorities. That provides motive, means, and opportunity."

"Do you think they'll buy it?"

"Sure. It matches the physical evidence, including her sumptuous apartment. And it fits an established pattern. Plus, there'll be nobody to contradict your account." At least if I was reading Sarie's message right. That was the only wild card. But I was confident that she'd finally decided to play her hand on her own terms, rather than blaming others for what she'd been dealt. Too bad she'd chosen to fold, but at least she'd made the choice for herself.

"You're sure?"

"I know from experience. There's nothing better than a clean—but not too neat—story to close a homicide case." I took a satisfied swig of sangria.

"Just give me a day to confirm Miss Botha's departure. Then you can call the police with the evidence and your account of events."

"I trust that you're right. Cops have never impressed me as the smartest of the Man's puppets. I hate associating Paul with that woman, but he would've wanted to keep me out of the legal entanglements so I could continue our work on behalf of Mother Earth." The afternoon sun combined with the wine had a soothing effect. Laurie Odum closed her eyes and breathed deeply.

"So, we're square?" I asked.

"If by that you mean that you've fulfilled your end of the deal, yes. And I know what to do in order to meet my half of the bargain."

As I got up to leave, she took my arm and leaned against me as we walked into the house. I thought she'd had enough sangria that she needed some support. But she had more in mind. Once inside, Laurie turned and pressed herself against me. She reached behind my neck and pulled my head down to her waiting mouth, her pelvis pushing against my thigh. She moaned softly at the end of our kiss. Things were primed to develop quickly given the urgency of her grasp. As much as I would've enjoyed a desperate tangle of naked bodies on her overstuffed couch, I just didn't want Laurie Odum. I derived much more satisfaction from deciding not to be her means of satisfaction. She was too used to getting what she wanted. When it comes to power and sex, it's usually the man calling the shots—as Carol would hasten to point out.

And for the first time in a very long time, I found that the chorus to one of Carol's beloved pop songs made sense. We'd briefly found common musical ground nearly a year ago when I realized that this song opened with London's Bach Choir—a group founded in 1876 for the sole purpose of performing Bach's Mass in B Minor. Of course, she'd fawned over Mick Jagger's voice, rather than the choir.

I gently pushed Laurie away. "As good as it'd be," I said, "you can't always get what you want." Then I kissed her on the cheek and left. The drive back in late afternoon traffic was tedious, and it didn't help that KDFC was playing classical guitar. Tense and tired, I skipped dinner and headed to the gym.

It took a full hour on the heavy bag at Marty's before I sweated out last night's booze, worked off today's food, and wore out my lingering libido.

CHAPTER FORTY-EIGHT

While Gustaw poured my coffee, I opened the *Chronicle* and scanned the headlines. After scowling at the softness of my belly in the mirror that morning, I had promised myself I'd limit myself to Ludwika's pastries no more than once a week. But given the last few days, one of her paczkis seemed justified. The sunlight coming through the bakery window was filtered through wispy clouds and the weather was looking a bit unsettled. The gloriously sunny days of fall were coming to an end. And San Francisco's dreary, wet winter wasn't far behind. Sarie Botha had chosen a good time to call it quits.

The article was on page B-2, alongside a story about a psychic claiming to have a new lead on the Zodiac Killer. I'm sure my pals at the station appreciated having their investigation trumped by a crystal-ball-gazing nutcase. The headline for Sarie proclaimed, "27th Jumper Takes Fatal Leap." According to the story:

A twenty-six-year-old woman that police have identified as a scientist at the University of California Berkeley leapt to her death off the east side of the Golden Gate Bridge. The woman, Sarie Botha, was associated with a faculty member who killed himself earlier this week over a failed romantic relationship. Police were called to the scene, just past the San Francisco tower at 4 PM on Thursday. Eyewitnesses said that Botha sat on the railing and placed a small Indian doll beside her. Then she stood up and calmly stepped into empty space.

The story went on about a politician calling for a barrier to be built and a sociologist contending that more people commit suicide during tough economic times. What I couldn't get out of my head was the doll. Sarie had brought along the kachina I'd left at her apartment. Kokopelli, the trickster. She'd managed to fool almost everyone in her life, until she could no longer fool herself.

I walked down the hill to work. Carol was looking as perky as ever and her music was as inane as ever, with some guy asking what's wrong with singing silly love songs. The song itself seemed to provide a more than ample answer. I told Carol that my project was complete, which seemed a great relief to her. She was always concerned that my outside ventures would get me killed or jailed. Maybe she was right to be worried. Like I'd told Sarie, the best we should hope for is to get what we deserve. I gave Carol a kiss on the top of her head on the way to my office.

After closing the door, I called Laurie Odum and told her to contact the police and tell them that she had evidence that her husband had been murdered. I made her go over the story with me, much to her annoyance, but I wanted to be sure she wasn't going to mess up an open-and-shut case for the detective assigned to the investigation. When she asked about Sarie, I said she could pick up the *Chronicle* if she wanted confirmation that her husband's killer was dead. There was a long pause and she said softly, "So you and I are really done, eh?" I'll never understand women.

I spent the rest of the morning and into the afternoon reading through job applications. It'd only been a few months since we'd hired Isaac, so I figured that most of the applicants were probably still looking for work, given eight percent unemployment in the city. I was reading the resume of a guy who'd done everything from mopping floors at a nursing home to selling used cars, when there was a tentative knock. Before I could answer, the door opened. I looked up and there was Isaac, looking embarrassed as a schoolboy buying condoms.

"Come in," I said, leaning back and gesturing for him to sit. He carefully cleared the catalogues off the chair in the corner and took a seat. "I'd been told you quit, so what brings you back?"

"I came to collect my last paycheck. I wasn't even going to come into the building if I saw your truck parked in the back."

"I walked in this morning, so I guess your detective skills need a little work."

He smiled weakly and said, "Well, I was still going to slip out without you seeing me until Carol shared the story you told the guys about quitting." He paused, hoping that I'd fill the silence. I didn't. "You know, the one you told the other night at the pub. The one about how you quit that boxing match when you were younger. About how you respected the other guy and kept your dignity."

"Okay. And so?" I was making it rough on the kid for a reason. I wanted him to remember this day.

"And so I decided that I needed to come to you and quit. To your face." He hesitated. I sat there waiting. "Like a man." He started to drop his eyes but then caught himself and looked right at me.

"But I'm not your opponent, Isaac. I didn't beat you."

"No. Well not directly. I was beaten by the work, by being too weak to keep going."

"What do you mean? You were doing fine."

"Not after that warehouse fumigation. I just couldn't get it out of my head how much sealing that building and releasing the gas was like the stories my grandfather told about what the Nazis did to our people. Riley, they called the Jews 'Ungeziefer'—vermin." He shook his head and rubbed his temples, as if he couldn't get a picture out of his mind.

"Sounds like you were beaten by your own history and imagination, Isaac. Maybe that's why being an artist is the right thing for you."

"It's more than that. I don't have what it takes to kill, even grain beetles. I'm weaker than Larry or Dennis. I'm the sort who pays others to do what I'm unwilling to do myself."

"No, you're a different sort, Isaac. You know who you are and what you can't do. And you admit it. There's no shame in recognizing and owning up to your limits." I half-believed this myself. At least the part about figuring out what you're capable of doing, although I wasn't sure that Isaac had taken himself to the limit.

"I didn't want to disappoint you. I know there were lots of other guys you could've hired." He nodded toward the applications that I had spread across my desk.

"I appreciate your sense of duty, kid. That's an admirable trait. But in the end, it's about not disappointing yourself." I grabbed a few of the applications from my desk, stood up, and led Isaac down the hall to the front office. Carol looked up and smiled approvingly.

"I see that things have cleared up a bit," she said, taking the applications from me and handing Isaac an envelope with his last payment. "I just know that you'll do great in art school," she gushed and gave Isaac a hug. I couldn't stand all this sappy nonsense. In all likelihood the kid would never make a dime painting pictures, but at least he'd made the decision for himself. It didn't guarantee that the world would pat him on the back. He'd probably end up spending his nights waiting tables and wasting his days on Fisherman's Wharf, sketching caricatures of tourists with cartoon silhouettes of the Golden Gate Bridge in the background or pastel portraits of honeymooners adorned with little hearts and streetcars to evoke Tony Bennett's god-awful song.

"And when you're famous, Isaac," I said, "you can come back and draw us a logo that doesn't look like a cross between Satan and Billy Goat Gruff armed with a sprayer."

"Riley!" Carol scolded. "My friend Dwayne designed that for Goat Hill Extermination and everyone but you likes it."

Isaac and I shook hands and he headed out the door. I turned back to Carol. "Hey, doll, you got a minute to look over some of these applications with me?"

"Depends on whether you're going to apologize about our logo," she pouted.

I said I was sorry and we worked our way through a half-dozen of the files. We ended up debating the merits of two applicants we'd interviewed earlier. There was an Italian kid who Dennis had thought was too scrawny—which was saying something—but Larry thought the guy had grit. And there was a dyke who Larry figured could kick his butt, but Dennis had reservations about her reliability. All I cared about was that whoever we hired would deliver an honest day's work.

"So, who would you hire?" I asked.

"Neither of them today," Carol answered. "It's five o'clock on a Friday and we can let the decision sit until Monday morning." She got up and started turning off lights and shutting down for the weekend. I went back to my office and put away the leftover files, checked the warehouse to be sure that Larry and Dennis had locked up, and met Carol at the front door.

"You know," she said, turning the deadbolt, "if you're worried about who to hire, we can run it by the guys tomorrow night."

"Tomorrow night?"

"Think, Riley, it's the last Saturday of the month. I know you've been frazzled with your project, but that won't get an Irish boy off the hook if he forgets his mother's family dinner."

I shook my head and offered my everlasting thanks. She smiled and patted me on the cheek with something between pity and understanding. Carol had saved me from being in the doghouse for weeks. I watched until she'd pulled out of the back lot, then I locked the gate behind her and headed up the hill to my house. The clouds had thickened to a gray matte. A stiff breeze was coming off the Bay.

As I walked, I found some solace in playing out how tomorrow night was likely to go. It would be just like every other dinner for the gang at my mother's house. Dennis would be there early and Larry would bring Jackie if things really were getting serious. If all went as expected, my mother would tell Carol that she's so pretty and personable that it's hard to believe she hadn't settled down with a good man. Carol, knowing the concern was heartfelt, wouldn't turn my mother's world upside-down by explaining that lesbians and marriage don't mix. So she'd once again offer the excuse that she was just too busy at work. This would cause my mother to scold me while Carol smiled slyly over her shoulder. Larry and Dennis would find all of this hysterical, but hide their mirth from my mother. She'd ask about "that nice Jewish boy" and we'd have to tell her that he decided to go to art school, which would make her happy because art and music are callings almost as virtuous as becoming a priest.

True to form, we'd sit down to an enormous meal of poached salmon, baked ham (or roast lamb, if the butcher at Mission Market had a good cut in the shop), mounds of colcannon (or poundies, depending on which version of potatoes went best with the meat), glazed carrots, dressed cabbage, sweet potato bake, and piles of soda bread. At some point, Tommy would spill his drink, which wouldn't matter. After dinner, I'd share a bottle of Jameson's finest with the guys (saving a glass for Carol and giving a bottle of Coke to Tommy) while the women did the dishes. Larry and Dennis would take turns losing to Tommy in checkers. We'd end the evening early because Tommy would fall asleep, probably with his head on Carol's lap, and my mother would begin to nod off, having spent the entire day preparing the feast.

My mother hosted these monthly dinners because she saw us all as family. Larry, Dennis, Carol, and whoever else was connected to the business kept her and Tommy with a roof over their heads and food on the table. Killing things might seem like an ugly way to hold a family together, but the Irish know from experience that the world is not an easy or pretty place. The Old World folks on Potrero Hill understood that butchers, exterminators, soldiers, and cops kept the rest of society believing that things are clean, safe, and decent. Coming away from an evening with my mother and Tommy always reminded me of the honor in a job well done, whether it was transplanting hearts or spraying cockroaches. Both took guts because most people didn't want the burden of what it meant when something went wrong with a scalpel or a poison.

By the time I got to the house, a cold drizzle had begun to fall and downtown San Francisco had disappeared in the mist. I poured myself a Black Bush, put on Beethoven's *Moonlight Sonata*, and prepared some butterflies for pinning. The monarchs would need to hurry if they were going to make it to their overwintering grounds.

Chapter Forty-Nine

By late October, the damp of winter in San Francisco had arrived. As in earlier years, I reluctantly gave up insect collecting with Tommy to spend our weekend afternoons prepping and pinning specimens while a bone-chilling fog lurked outside. But the weatherman had predicted that the weekend might provide a final gasp of Indian summer.

So I told my mother I'd pick up Tommy after church for an outing. She, in her own gently insistent way, suggested that I might join them for the Mass. I failed to come up with a plausible excuse on the fly. What's more, I could see the hope on her face—an irrepressible belief that I was one of the lost sheep that the shepherd would bring back to the fold. When I was a rebellious teen, I'd once told her that the Church was no better than organized crime, that both rackets shook down people who they'd managed to scare. Her face fell and I could hear her sobbing as my father lifted me off my feet by my upper arm and dragged me up to my room. My bicep was black and blue for a week—it was as close as he ever came to beating me. "You want to hurt somebody," he snarled, "then you come after me. We'll settle it like men." I sensed that with the anniversary of my father's death upcoming, she needed to believe. And my being at Mass was vital to her.

The scripted ritual was as superficially elegant and personally empty as ever, although Father Griesmaier's sermon was almost interesting. The gospel reading was about Jesus picking his apostles, which I figured was something like my hiring employees. This led me to think about the past month and take some pride in having hired Nicole ("Nick"), who was one tough piece of work and took no crap from either Larry or Dennis. She worked as hard as the guys and was earning their respect. To my delight, Nick treated customers with the sort of genuine politeness that had people like old Mrs. Morgan calling Carol to say that they didn't think this was the sort of work that a lady should be doing but they appreciated her courtesy, "which is so lacking in young people today."

When I drifted back to Father Griesmaier's sermon, he was admonishing the congregants that while St. Jude is the patron saint of lost causes, nothing is hopeless in the eyes of the Lord. He insisted that "despair is the greatest sin, for it is the opposite of faith, the forsaking of God."

I didn't buy the whole God-can-do-anything line (if the big guy can do anything, then why make a world with so much suffering?). But the priest got me thinking about fighting against long odds. I'd gone to the Roxie to watch *Rocky* earlier in the week, which turned out to be a great movie. Maybe the Catholics would attract more people if they used action-packed movies with vibrant soundtracks rather than dusty old stories and hymns that nobody sings. By this time, I'd lost interest in the service and started thinking about a new organizational plan for the warehouse while alternately sitting, standing, and kneeling in concert with the congregation.

When the Mass was over, the folks filed through the double doors at the back of the sanctuary and made their way around the building to the undercroft where a lunch spread was waiting. According to some mysterious liturgical calendar, this was the Feast Day for Saints Simon and Jude, which translated into a sumptuous feed put on by the church ladies. I knew that Jude was my mother's favorite saint, a commitment sealed when they built St. Jude Children's Hospital in Memphis a few years after Tommy's poisoning. She and Mrs. Flannigan organized a bingo night and silent auction every year to raise funds for the hospital.

My mother was busy chatting with her friends in the sanctuary, as they'd delivered their covered dishes to the basement before the Mass and gossip trumped hunger. It was a perfect day for her—I'd been at church, St. Jude had been celebrated, and flowers from her garden had adorned the altar. I'd learned about the flowers by eavesdropping. She'd managed to work it into a discussion of who'd brought what to the feast. Of course, there'd not been the slightest hint of boasting, but I knew that providing the flowers was a real coup in the world of church ladies.

With the initial gossip exhausted, the others headed to the undercroft. My mother lingered for a moment to admire the flowers and soak in the morning. So we were the last people to be greeted by Father Griesmaier on our way out.

"Ah, Mrs. Riley, I see you managed to find that lost lamb of yours who seems to wander off on Sundays." He smiled slyly while pressing my mother's hands between his.

"Yes, Father. He's not as regular as the Lord would want, but he's as fine a son as a mother could hope for," she replied diplomatically.

"Indeed," the priest continued, as if I were invisible, "he's a good man. And as for you, I hope you saw that today's rosary is 'The Joyful Mysteries'—a favorite of yours, I believe."

"I did see that, Father. Mrs. Flannigan and I will be praying the rosary this afternoon. Riley is taking Tommy to the park. Right, Tommy?" she asked, turning to my brother. He'd managed to sit quietly, probably fidgeting less than I did. Now that he was liberated from the pew, the kid nodded excitedly. Father Griesmaier gave him a vigorous hair-rubbing, which added to its usual state of disorder despite my mother's best efforts. At least his shirt was tucked in, which was saying quite a bit for him. In fact, he seemed more able to care for himself these days.

"I'll see you at the saints' feast," the priest added as my mother headed out, Tommy following with his excited, lurching gait. "And Riley, can I speak with you for a minute," he continued as I did my best to slip out.

"Sure, Father, what is it?" The priest waited until my mother and brother were out of earshot. Then he looked around to be sure we were alone. People were milling outside, enjoying the sunlight—perhaps the last they'd see for a while—but they were clearly engaged in their own lively conversations.

"This week, it seems we are twice blessed."

"Meaning?"

He smiled. "The parish treasurer told me that St. Teresa's received an extremely large, anonymous donation."

"Really?" I asked with my best impression of innocence. "How much, may I ask?"

"The gift was $150,000, and the donor's attorney said his client instructed that the money was to support Tommy's Fund. That will put the program on solid footing for a very long time." So the life insurance company had finally settled with Laurie Odum and she'd upheld her end of the deal.

"That's certainly good news, Father."

"Indeed it is, my son. And might you be able to shed some light on the circumstances of this donation?"

"Why would I know anything?" I shrugged.

"Because I'm a fine judge of character. I'm a man of the cloth, but the cloth isn't pulled over my eyes. As a priest, you get to know about people—sometimes a great deal more than they imagine." He lowered his chin and peeked over the top of his glasses, waiting for my reply.

"Well, Father, it sounds like maybe we should just chalk it up to another one of those joyful mysteries that my mother will be praying about, eh?"

He chuckled quietly and shook his head. "Maybe so. But I suspect that the Lord is not the only one around here working in mysterious ways."

Seeing a chance to change the subject, I asked, "You said the church was twice blessed. What else happened?"

"Riley! Surely you listened to the Notre Dame-Navy game and heard how Dave Waymer broke up the fourth-down pass in the end zone in the last minute. It was a pigskin miracle, if ever there was one."

He put his arm around my shoulders and guided me out the door and to the undercroft, the whole time talking about whether Rick Slager could take the Fighting Irish to a national championship. Father Griesmaier had pinned his hopes on Joe Montana. But a shoulder injury had sidelined him, which was too bad because he was a Sicilian kid from the coal-mining hills of Pennsylvania—just the heritage for a tough quarterback. And this led the pudgy priest to a digression about the virtues of Joe Theismann (an *Austrian* boy, the priest emphasized) who'd taken Notre Dame to the Cotton Bowl in 1970. Becoming a bit uncomfortable with his effusive ethnic pride, he hastened to note that Theismann had taken over from Terry Hanratty, a proper *Irish* lad who had led the Notre Dame to the national championship in 1966 (giving me a hearty pat on the back, as if I had something to do with it).

It was like the who-begat-whom stuff in the Bible, except with quarterbacks in South Bend, Indiana. I suspect his jovial recounting of the lineage would've gone on much longer had we not reached the undercroft, where piles of kielbasas, pierogi, and pasta, along with tureens of borsch and goulash, and a decadent tray of syrupy baklava, lay waiting on long tables.

Pleasantly stuffed, Tommy and I slipped out of the feast. I considered a change of clothes, but where we were headed wasn't likely to be muddy—and it would even be sort of special to walk the Japanese Tea Gardens in our Sunday duds.

I parked near the de Young Museum and we walked down to the gardens. The sun was still out but a breeze had kicked up, making me glad I'd brought along Tommy's hat. He liked his dark blue knit cap because he'd seen fishermen on the wharf wearing them and he loved stories of seafaring adventure. Just past the entrance, Tommy stopped to admire a bonsai tree on display alongside the tea house.

"Is that a tree?" he asked.

"Sure is, pal. It's called a bonsai tree."

"I think it's better than a real tree," he said, reaching out to touch it. I started to grab for his arm, but an old Japanese fellow who I took to be the caretaker smiled and said softly, "That okay. He innocent like child. He not hurt it."

The man was right. Tommy touched the evergreen branch with great tenderness and then ran his finger along the trunk. "It's so small," he marveled. "Will it grow up?" The old man explained that it was really a very old tree. His great-grandfather had kept it carefully trimmed, and then his grandfather, and then his father, and now he was the tree's guardian.

"Like Riley is for me. Like I'm older but people think I'm a kid." Tommy seemed delighted with the comparison.

"Yes," the old man said. "You like Moyogi bonsai. Strong, upright person," he said, straightening his back and thumping his chest, "who shows his own character." Tommy was obviously delighted. "And you," he said, nodding slowly to me, "bonsai master. You allow him to stay small inside. Much patience." He smiled approvingly.

We thanked him and wandered through the paths. The garden's walls and lush growth blocked the wind. And between the warmth of the sun and a full stomach, Tommy was growing tired. He was dragging his right leg more than usual along the gravel path, so I suggested that we rest on one of the wooden benches beside the koi pond. After a few minutes, Tommy's eyes closed and his head dropped onto his chest.

I looked out across the garden, the beautifully manicured hedges, the finely sculpted shrubs, the elegantly placed paths, and the thoughtfully chosen monuments. The Japanese gardeners and I both understood that we can improve on nature. They pruned trees and shrubs. I removed rats and cockroaches.

In California, growing stuff is easy. But to be beautiful, plants need a gardener who's willing to trim branches and pull weeds. Just like cities need exterminators.

— End —

ABOUT THE AUTHOR

 Jeffrey Lockwood is a most unusual fellow. He grew up in New Mexico and spent youthful afternoons enchanted by feeding grasshoppers to black widows in his backyard. This might account for both his scientific and literary affinities.

He earned a doctorate in entomology from Louisiana State University and worked for fifteen years as an insect ecologist at the University of Wyoming. He became a world-renowned assassin, developing a method for efficiently killing billions of insects (mostly pests but there's always the innocent bystander during a hit). This contact with death drew him into questions of justice, violence, and evil.

His career metamorphosed into an appointment in the department of philosophy and the program in creative writing at UW. Unable to escape his childhood, he's written several award-winning books about the devastation of the West by locust swarms, the use of insects to wage biological warfare, and the terror humans experience when six-legged creatures invade their lives.

Pondering the dark side of humanity led him to the realm of the murder mystery. These days, he explores how the anti-hero of crime noir sheds existentialist light on the human condition: In the end, there are no excuses— we are ultimately responsible for our actions.

FIND JEFFREY AT:

WEBSITE: JeffreyLockwoodAuthor.com

Goodreads, Facebook

EMAIL: Lockwood@uwyo.edu

Dear Readers,
If you enjoyed this book enough to review it for Goodreads, B&N, or Amazon.com, I'd appreciate it!

Thanks, Jeffrey

Find more great reads at
Pen-L.com